DARKLY

DARKLY

A NOVEL

MARISHA PESSL

DELACORTE PRESS

Text copyright © 2024 by Marisha Pessl
Jacket art and design by Casey Moses
Frame art and texture used under license from Shutterstock.com
Interior art credits see pages 403–404

All rights reserved. Published in the United States by Delacorte Press, an imprint of Random House Children's Books, a division of Penguin Random House LLC, New York.

Delacorte Press is a registered trademark and the colophon is a trademark of Penguin Random House LLC.

Visit us on the Web! GetUnderlined.com

Educators and librarians, for a variety of teaching tools, visit us at RHTeachersLibrarians.com

Library of Congress Cataloging-in-Publication Data is available upon request.
ISBN 978-0-593-70655-8 (trade) — ISBN 978-0-593-70656-5 (lib. bdg.) — ISBN 978-0-593-70657-2 (ebook) — ISBN 978-0-593-90264-6 (international ed.)

The text of this book is set in 11-point Adobe Garamond Pro.

Editor: Beverly Horowitz
Cover Designer: Casey Moses
Interior Designer: Megan Shortt
Production Editor: Colleen Fellingham
Managing Editor: Tamar Schwartz
Production Manager: Tim Terhune

Printed in the United States of America
10 9 8 7 6 5 4 3 2 1
First Edition

FOR WINTER, AVALON, AND RAINE

DARKLY

T he website is stark and black, like the Darkly Rasputin box, with the blood-red Victorian letters of Hecate.

The site crashed again this morning, due to heavy traffic. It's been down all day.

And I've been in a state of panic, certain I'm too late, that in true Arcadia Gannon fashion, I've squandered what little crumbs of luck were tossed my way. But now I see, as I move through the crowded school bus and throw myself into the last seat, the site is live again.

Yet my relief quickly slips from excitement to worry. Because this means I have less than six hours to catapult myself out of early retirement and seize my destiny.

THE
(Louisiana Veda (Foundation

seeks 7 high school students
to take part in an inaugural
summer internship program.

Earn £2,000/week
Responsibilities include:
Office organization
Community outreach
Data entry

To apply, please answer the following:
What would you kill for?
All applications must be submitted by 15 March at
03.00 a.m. GMT.*

***Only direlings need apply.**

I hunch low in my seat, careful to hide the screen of my phone from the kids around me—no need to give them free arsenic to sprinkle in my tea. I pull on my headphones and crank the volume to Ella Fitzgerald's "Blue Skies."

Yes, I'm the only junior who still takes the bus—no wheels of my own, no boyfriend or bestie to give me a ride. This has forced me to punt the smidgen of respect that should rightfully be mine, having survived nearly three years of the hellscape known as Eminence High School. I used to have friends here, but one moved to San Francisco and became cool. The other moved to South Florida, akin to being launched into outer space.

I am the girl who runs an antique shop. And like some odd bird species sequestered for decades on a musty island, I have evolved to be at home among the old-fashioned and passé. My best friends in the world are Basil Stepanov and Agatha Sweeney, both over seventy-five, with cataracts. My ideal wardrobe consists of cloche hats and box-pleated skirts. If I had it my way, the world would go back to communicating by telegram and candlestick telephones. Two years ago, at Holiday Assembly, I tripped on the risers in front of the whole school, and as I fell, I blurted without thinking, "Jeepers!" I also know too much about Humphrey Bogart and the Great Depression for it to be remotely healthy.

I spent years trying to hide my antique nature, to pretend my natural tendency was not toward Parcheesi, needlepoint pillows that read BEE NICE OR BUZZ OFF, and high-neck silk blouses in rose, lavender, and powder blue.

But it was a whole lot of effort and stress. And it didn't even work. Everyone still called me Nana. Now, I hide from exactly no one that I use the word *muss* in ordinary conversation.

As the bus bounces out of the lot, I scroll to the bottom of the internship page—and wish I hadn't.

429,222

No, it's not the number of page views or likes. It's the number of kids who have applied.

To seize my destiny, I'm competing with over four hundred thousand teen geniuses.

I know for a fact they're geniuses, having wasted an inordinate number of hours *not* expertly crafting my own application—as I should have been doing, night and day. Instead, I've been freaking out over the competition, trawling social media for the thousands of hashtags that have popped up like poisonous dandelions in every corner of the internet ever since the internship was announced a month ago:

#louisianarises

#louisianaforever

#louisianalivesagain

Everyone and their brilliant cousin is applying, *literally*—from the sixteen-year-old star of the Warsaw Philharmonic to a thirteen-year-old from New Jersey who sold her first AI app to Google for seven figures; from Steven Spielberg's favorite godson to the tenor who performed "Somewhere Over the Rainbow" at the White House two weeks ago and made the president cry. Not to mention the girl who invented a sock that will never get a hole in the toe.

If that isn't enough to make me feel unworthy, the different countries of the applicants scroll relentlessly along the bottom, a simultaneously gratuitous and haunting information feed.

France . . .

China . . .

United States . . .

Brunei . . .

Republic of Belarus . . .

I'm pretty sure what all of this means is that I, Dia Gannon, aka Nana, of Eminence, Missouri, with a GPA of 2.7 on a good day and nothing to recommend me except an embarrassing knowledge of 1930s put-downs, have a better chance of getting admitted to Harvard, Stanford, and Yale as lightning strikes me while winning the Powerball lottery as the #1 USTA Junior Tennis Seed than I do of winning this internship.

Of course, the situation is so "Emperor's New Clothes" on steroids with a healthy dash of pigs flying that when I'm not fretting about my competition, I am disturbed.

Because something is very wrong here.

Everyone is so excited to hear her name again—Louisiana Veda—groundbreaker, feminist idol, OG boss woman, ingenious inventor. This past month, there have been a zillion articles in every major newspaper written about her and her defunct company, Darkly, frothy pieces breathlessly recounting her accomplishments: her first masterpiece board game, Ophelia; her mysterious island factory; her love affairs. Oh, how much of a disruptive genius she was, a visionary, how underrated, iconic, misunderstood.

And how tragic, given the way her life ended.

Yes, it's suddenly very trendy to love Louisiana Veda, forgetting how for so long she was ridiculed, a cautionary tale, a woman who drew too far outside the lines and got destroyed for it.

And in all the hysteria and hullabaloo, no one has bothered to notice how unlike Louisiana Veda this internship actually is.

The woman has been dead for thirty-nine years. I've read all the profiles written before her death and after. I know about the lawsuits, the scandals, the hate-filled editorials, the names they called her—joke, delusional, fraud, crazy, witch—the "No comments." I know how she willed her own legend into being with the grit of a war general staging a near-hopeless offensive and a confidence that was provocative, threatening, and unheard of in a woman.

She was an orphan, after all, who never knew her parents—and never cared to.

"Right now, I might be related to Queen Elizabeth," she announced with deadpan certainty in some ladies' magazine, to a confused reporter who didn't know what to do with her. "Just as the electron, according to Heisenberg's uncertainty principle, has no known location and speed, so do I live on the outskirts of the impossible and the mythical. My parents could be werewolves. That unknown makes me an inescapable force of nature."

And every few years, there are the breathless announcements from Christie's and Sotheby's auction houses, touting that the original prototypes of each game, the ones she crafted by hand, are monumental works of art, filled with secrets, hidden mysteries, and a dark, bewitching beauty—surprising everyone by commanding prices in the tens of millions, year after year.

"It is a testament to the endurance of Louisiana, how she continues to fascinate as an artist and a human, how relentlessly she holds our attention, even in death," the Director of Something or Other is always officially stating.

And never in any of this has there been any mention of a foundation.

Suspicious, too, is the announcement itself. I've been studying it for weeks, and I can categorically state: there is no concealed map, clue, invisible illustration, riddle, play, illusion, or trapdoor to be found.

If you know anything about Louisiana Veda, this makes zero sense.

Louisiana Veda created layers of deception at the openings of her games. She loved beginnings. And she took her time with them, taking players—innocent bystanders, she called them—by the hand, gently leading them through the creaking iron gate, down the path, and into her game, the sprawling forest she grew by hand. Every tree, stone, blackbird, shadow, and viper is there for a reason. Nothing is random, sloppy, or accidental in a Darkly.

A Darkly is a black fire lily, equal parts magic and danger.

It is the secret club at the end of the alley you can reach only by following faint footsteps in a locked graveyard yesterday. They are terrifying, shifting worlds of strangers and allies, ghosts and fiends, rolling hillsides cloaked in fog, out of which anything can step.

The gaming manual for Hecate is 74 pages.

The gaming manual for The Red Hounds of Garsington is 99 pages.

The gaming manual for 18 Lost Icelandic Sailors is a monster 211 pages.

So how could the real Louisiana Veda—even dead—be behind such a meager premise as "What would you kill for?" And the job duties so drearily listed: office organization, community outreach, data entry. How could her foundation understand so little about her?

Then there is the fine print: *Only direlings need apply.*

It's an obvious reference to her eleventh game, Rasputin, the controversial conspiracy game of hypnosis. A direling is a master of manipulation, someone who spins a web of lies and kills without mercy—the winner of the game.

After public outcry in 1980, with parents contending the game promoted deceit in their children and endangered their well-being, by encouraging them to sneak out of the house in the night to play the game in backyards, playgrounds, and basements, Rasputin was pulled from shelves. Louisiana apologized, saying she regretted the game. Darkly recalled all eight hundred thousand copies.

So why would her foundation support the use of such an inflammatory term as *direling*?

"Dia Gannon! Are you snoozing again on my bus?"

I look up, jolted at the sight of the bus driver, Mr. Jasper, scowling at me in the rearview mirror. The entire busload of kids has turned to stare at me.

I realize we have pulled over at my stop, Dinglebrook Shopping Center. I grab my backpack and take off down the aisle, a few kids snickering as I pass. At least today—probably because they notice I'm unusually on edge—they don't whisper, *I smell cookies and old carpet* or *Nana, the hair looks a little blue today.*

Outside, I turn to apologize to Mr. Jasper. He might be rude, but he *is* over sixty-five and a member of AARP, which means I can't help but relate to him. But he's in a bad mood, probably due to another arthritis flare-up, and only slams the door in my face.

As the bus teeters down the highway with an exhausted groan, I shrug on my backpack and start across the parking lot.

My family's store, Prologue Antiques, is sandwiched between an out-of-business Carpetmania and the eternally popular Wok & Roll Hall of Flame.

The shop actually looks busy today, which means there is exactly one car out front that doesn't belong to an employee.

I had planned to work on my Louisiana Veda application at the shop.

Prologue Antiques is the best place to hide and dream, a deserted secret garden where it's always nightfall, even at noon in July. This is thanks to the dim green warehouse lighting, the labyrinthine aisles clogged with shadows and towering stacks of Victorian hatboxes, the stained-glass lamps, church pews, and display cases stuffed with grand estate jewelry resembling giant rainforest beetles playing dead. There are ads for five-cent sodas no one has ever heard of—Fine Cola and Duchess Pop—faded Gibson Girls in corsets, staring dolefully out from swings. Tarnished silver, Wild West tintypes, diner jukeboxes, Southern belle crinolines, pianofortes, high-relief cameo brooches, Victorian chatelaines—I love them all. Even though I'm always trying to sell them, when I do, I'm sad. It's like losing a family member.

Unfortunately, as I slip inside Prologue today, a full-blown Battle of Old Baldy is going down.

"Gigi Gannon promised she would be here to handle delivery. Where is she?"

My mom's two full-time employees, Agatha and Basil—both predating most objects for sale in here—stand speechless before a gray-haired customer in tweed waving his cane in their faces.

"You're not prepared to accept new inventory? I've just driven seventy miles! What kind of operation is this?"

"It's actually . . . ," whispers Agatha.

"By Jove, it's Dia!" shouts Basil, his face brightening. "Dia, may I introduce Mr. Asquith. He is delivering pieces your mother bought last night at his estate sale in Kansas City."

"Of course. So nice to meet you," I say hastily, heaving my backpack behind the counter. "Where's my mom?"

"Gigi popped out," says Basil. "Any idea where she went, Agatha?"

Agatha blinks, a shaking hand fumbling with the beaded chain on her glasses. "I believe it was . . ."

Agatha has not finished a sentence in eight years. She is Irish and was my late grandmother's best friend. For years, she was her right-hand woman in the shop. Now, after a head injury from a car crash, Agatha has no idea where anything is, and never will again. But given the fact that she's eighty and is the kindest human on the planet—and as much a part of the history of Prologue as the Ming dynasty vase containing mysterious ashes and the 1960s Milan glazed chocolate doughnut coffee table that we will never sell—she doesn't have to.

"She probably took one of the B-B-Barnabys to the vet," says Basil. He is stuttering, which means he is fatigued and stressed, maybe even experiencing flashbacks from his time serving in the 21st Infantry Regiment in Korea. "Have you m-m-met the Barnabys?"

Mr. Asquith clearly has not met the store cats, and looks like he'd rather have a pacemaker implanted.

"Don't worry, Mr. Asquith," I sing, grabbing the clipboard. "I handle all deliveries, and I've been expecting you. Remind me what pieces we're receiving?"

"A few odds and ends belonging to my late wife, Dolores."

As he says this, a massive moving truck pulls up outside. THE DUKE OF MARLBOROUGH'S WHITE GLOVE TRANSPORT. LUXURY SHIPPING FOR PRICELESS TREASURES!

My heart sinks. My mom's appetite for antiques is fifty times larger than our budget.

"A few odds and ends" turns out to be: eight Swiss grandfather clocks, a billboard from the 1985 Cannes Film Festival, a road sign—GRAND CANYON NATIONAL PARK, 6 MILES—and a sculpture of the late Mrs. Asquith, who apparently resembled an eight-foot bronze Sasquatch with the weight of a dying white dwarf.

Two hours later, I'm still helping the movers unload and making sure Agatha and Basil remain in the stockroom, where it's quiet and cool, so they won't have heightened blood pressure from the commotion, while also trying to locate my missing mom and distracting Mr. Asquith with the Steinway on which Cole Porter supposedly composed "C'est Magnifique," to avoid writing him a check.

My family's shop, Prologue Antiques, gets its name from Shakespeare: "What's past is prologue." It was started by my grandmother, who collected a lifetime of forgotten things. When she died, years before I was born, my mother, Gigi, took over the store in the automatic way one bears a family name. I love my mother, but she'd do better with a profession that doesn't involve real estate budgets, mortgages, inventory, the precise documentation of provenance, or a detailed five-year plan—like being a dog walker.

When Gigi Gannon does breeze in, with wet hair and flip-flops, I know way too much about the late Dolores's extensive breeding operation for purebred Chinese shar-peis.

"Mr. Asquith! Hello again! Cocktail cabinets arrive in one piece?"

"Don't you mean grandfather clocks?"

"Oh, right."

Beaming, my mom hugs the man as if he's her long-lost uncle. Gigi Gannon is not beautiful. Her gray-streaked hair is too frizzy and wild, her midnight-blue eyeliner drawn too haphazardly over her eyelids. But her warmth is contagious—and mesmerizing. Such high-flying spirits cause many strangers, including Mr. Asquith, to short-circuit in puzzlement as they face the sudden northeastern gale that is my mother, trying to determine where it's coming from, if a dangerous storm is approaching.

And there is, of course. My mother is a squall—though relatively harmless, she has been known to turn more than a few umbrellas inside out and suddenly kill the power.

"I was quite miffed, frankly," says Mr. Asquith, "how you were nowhere—"

"You've met my daughter, Arcadia? She runs the whole operation."

"Who? Oh. Well, she was relatively helpf—"

"Dia, please pay Mr. Asquith so he can go home? It's a long drive back to Columbus."

"Columbus? Why would I be driving to Ohio?"

After a surprised nod at the grandfather clocks crowding the front entrance like prom kings awaiting dates that will never show, Gigi is already off, racing down the aisle.

I head after her. "Mom, where are you going?"

"Sluder invited me to his hotel opening in Farmington. He did the trees."

"How much do we owe Mr. Asquith?"

She's hurrying past Art and Lighting into Vintage. "Thirty grand? What do you think about gumdrop topiary for the entrance? Sluder can do it in five minutes with a chain saw."

"It's too dark out front. Mr. Asquith says you agreed to seventy."

"Maybe it is seventy."

She yanks off her T-shirt, rooting through Depression-era housedresses.

"Mom, please stop buying things. We have to move some of these big-ticket items before we add to inventory, or we won't make rent."

"Did you clean out that storage room by the boiler? I remember some rainy-day treasures down there." Gigi is pulling on a black vintage 1950s Chanel sheath, holding up her hair so I can zip the back. "Can you close tonight? Sluder wants to take me out for sushi."

"Sure. Who's Sluder again?"

She fishes out the black Liza Minnelli faux pearls from the costume jewelry display, which I know for a fact give her neck hives, yanks loose a tan leather Halston clutch, causing beaded purses to avalanche across the carpet, and she's off again.

"The landscape architect." She is walking backward, winking at me as I pick up the bags. "Love you, babe. Did you know there are over forty types of pine?"

DERRINGER STREET CHAMBERS
20 GROSVENOR SQUARE
LONDON

Louisiana Veda
Darnamoor Manor
3 Starne-upon-Sea
Thornwood, England

2 February 1985

My darling Lou,

I hope this letter finds you well. I hope as you read this you stand in
your vast gardens--the one you never allowed me into--under a blue
sky, and a fleet of bluebirds chase the clouds. I hope you are filled
with a sense of divine triumph. Because this lightness in this minute,
your belief in the supremacy of your future and what you have built,
the joy you feel upon opening this letter, anticipating my words of love
-- it will be your last.

This is your termination. Your face is a rotten peach, your eyes, holes
of glue, your body, a charred carcass from which the flesh will drip,
your brain, a bolted cellar flooded with the foulest waters, your words,
ashes that will collapse to silence in the breeze and leave no trace.

The pain you have caused me in your cathedral of lies, the deluded
attempt to "do right" (as Gattie tells me you call it), the acts of evil
that fooled us all, the despair you have cooked up and fed me upon
which I must now gorge until the end of my days, it has carried me into
the dark.

There is only one thing that gives me momentary respite, one thought
that allows me to lift my head from the mud and breathe before I sink
back down to the boiling depths of Hell.

And that is: I will descend on you like a locust, like a maggot, like the
Devil collecting the withered soul eternally due him.

I am coming for you, my love.

And I will destroy you.

Wood

3

An hour later, I've paid Mr. Asquith and ushered him out, flipped the CLOSED sign, and switched off the lights in the front window displays. I've sent Basil and Agatha home early so Basil can soak his corns in Epsom salts while watching *Mister Ed,* and Agatha can make her Thursday-night walking club.

It's just me left with the Barnabys—the five lunatic black cats that haunt the store. They are half poltergeist, and they dart, skid, and leap suddenly off ledges all day, making people jump and drop precious things.

I load the Louisiana Veda Foundation website and create my account, input my name and age, birthday and address. I try not to look at the counter, because applications are streaming in by the second in the run-up to the deadline.

607,918

Germany . . .
England . . .

Japan . . .

Singapore . . .

What would you kill for?

I close my eyes and start to write. I have no plan. But after a few minutes, it feels like the door in my heart has been crudely sawed open. Words gurgle out, ugly and gelatinous. Tales of my mom and her boyfriends, with their beaded bracelets and Sanskrit chest tattoos, their guitar EPs released on SoundCloud, called "Don't Leave"—which makes you want to do that immediately. Agatha's silent acts of kindness and Basil's war wounds. How I am lonely and lost, literally collecting dust balls, because after a day in the shop I often find them clinging to my shoelaces and hair. I am stuck inside this shop that I love. But wouldn't I kill to get out of here? Out of the dust and rust, to be somewhere else, someone else?

When I come up for air and read through it, I realize I sound like a whiny young Unabomber crossed with an ornery Mr. Allnut from *The African Queen*.

I'm about to delete it all and start over when one of the Barnabys, with a shrill yowl, launches off the Biedermeier armoire and lands on the desk, right in front of me.

I push her off. Thankfully, she missed the keyboard. But she leaps back up and prowls under the desk light, mewing.

I try to scratch under her chin to calm her, but she is upset and jumpy, tail twitching. Then she flees into the shadows, vanishing down the aisle.

That's when I hear it.

Someone is here, in the back of the store.

In Funereal Oddities? No. It's Fine Dining.

I listen, motionless, hoping I'm imagining it.

On the most cheerful of nights, Prologue Antiques is as murky and mysterious as a massive fish tank no one has cleaned for a year. Now, the darkness seems to conspire against me, hiding something.

I wonder if I forgot to lock the back door in the stockroom, after I took out the trash.

No. I never forget.

I can hear the ticks of the grandfather clocks, like nervous, drumming fingertips. The air vents wheeze in the ceiling. Outside, a rush of cars coast through the intersection, a honk.

There it is again.

Footsteps.

It must be Basil. A few times this year, he's returned to the shop unannounced after closing, searching for his harmonica, or his 1887 Morgan silver dollars, or muttering that he needs to disengage Uncle Bob, the howitzer cannon his troop operated in Korea. The last time it happened, my mom, hearing someone rooting around Estate Jewelry, assumed it was a burglar and crept into Armory, loading an 1873 Winchester and taking aim. When Basil came out with his hands up, he was so distressed he fainted—and not because she nearly blew his head off, but because Armory is his domain. All of the rifles and pistols in his collection are old geezers like him, slow and meandering, bullets flying everywhere except where they're pointed. He was devastated that she'd almost gotten hurt.

"Basil?" I call out, though it's doubtful he'd hear me. He refuses to update his hearing aids, wearing a pair from the 1990s with dead batteries, so they're actually hearing *thwarts*.

But it doesn't sound like Basil. His movements are soft, slow. This sounds like someone heavy, deliberately searching for something. Maybe a burglar saw the CLOSED sign, lights off, and assumed the shop was empty? Maybe my mom was blabbing again as she waited for her oat latte at the Grind, telling everyone in line: *I own Prologue. We have a fortune's worth of antiques, paintings. Jewelry too. Seriously, we're the Louvre, right in the middle of Missouri, and I'm not even kidding.*

He's in the stockroom now. How did he get in there?

I inch past a set of fireplace tools, and though the poker is missing, there is a pair of iron tongs. I grab them and move closer, stopping outside the door.

I feel something, a draft, followed by a faint thud.

I yank open the door and switch on the light, expecting to see a masked intruder caught with a bag of loot, seconds before he slams me in the head with the Carrara marble bust of Benjamin Franklin missing his left ear—

Only the empty stockroom stares back.

The light is bright. All of the pieces crowding the shelves, waiting to be cleaned, mended, glued, labeled—they look untouched. Nothing is tipped over, missing, or out of place.

I step inside, moving down the aisle to the back door. It *is* unlocked.

I wrench it open and stare out at the empty parking lot.

There's just a dumpster, broken pavement. Beyond that, the mangy woods are filled with inky darkness.

I strain to hear footsteps hurrying away, a car slinking off. But there is only the generic pulse of Chinese drums pumping out of Wok & Roll and the clatter of plates in the kitchen.

I close the door, locking it.

"Hello? Anyone here?"

Someone is calling from the front of the store now.

Still wielding the fireplace tongs, I sprint out, back toward the entrance. I have every intention of using them on whoever is behind this prank.

"Hello?"

I know that voice.

I'm so horrified I stop dead.

"Anyone here?"

I manage to dart behind the display of pocket watches and peer over it, praying I'm wrong. But I'm not.

And I want to evaporate.

It's Choke Newington.

Choke of the Gladstone-Hill Golf and Tennis Club Newingtons. He looks like an accidental superhero. His real name is Herbert, and he makes people laugh, including the most calcified teachers at Eminence High. He lives on a giant estate, with a house so far away from the road it's more myth than reality. His parents are high-powered lawyers who jet to Abu Dhabi and London, and they only live in Eminence because they were childhood sweethearts here. Choke drives a blue 1998 BMW convertible with a tattered copy of *Lonesome Dove* on the back seat underneath an embarrassing pile of dirty lacrosse shorts, and he smells like windbreakers on a sailboat.

I would absolutely hate him, of course—if I didn't love him. We were best friends in preschool through third grade. I remember playing cops and robbers with Choke in the mud kitchen, and how sweet he was, always sharing his exotic lunches with me—Brie and baguettes, spicy tuna rolls with wasabi peas. He even came over for a playdate twice, which meant we roamed the forgotten aisles of

Prologue unsupervised for hours, pretending we were scuba-diving through shipwrecks at the bottom of the Pacific, chased by a supernatural octopus, which was actually Agatha and Basil meandering down the aisles, wondering how to use the pricing guns. Then, one summer, after camp in Maine, Choke returned to school with gleaming blond hair and a tan. The other boys called him *bro*. He played football during recess. And while he was never mean to me, he was gone. Like a bird when it finally notices the cage door was always open and how beautiful the world is out there.

This would all be fine, securely tucked away inside the past in the chapter called "Funny Connections Made in Childhood," except I cannot look directly at Choke, thanks to a catastrophe four months ago.

It was a Friday after school and we ran into each other in the stairwell. There was an explosion of papers, and his head hit my chin. I tripped. He fell. I helped him to his feet, saying, "Sorry, Choke." We stared at each other for what felt like five minutes, and I stepped toward him, sort of hypnotized, sensing he was about to kiss me. "Oh," he blurted in surprise. "You want me to . . ." I was mortified, and I started to flee. And I would have—all the way to Miami—but he grabbed my arm, pulled me into him, and he kissed me.

That started the crazy.

We didn't stop. Not when Ms. Peabody wandered downstairs, muttering to herself about cheese sandwiches. Not when Coach Ed and Assistant Coach Philomena lugged four massive net bags of inflated rubber balls to the first floor. We only ducked into the alcove by the fire extinguisher. What did it mean? Had Choke gotten ahold of every diary I've had since fifth grade, and seen his name splattered gruesomely across every page? Then Headmaster Rune entered, arguing on the phone with his wife about why she spent three hundred dollars on a table centerpiece to impress relatives they hadn't seen in fourteen years. I pried loose from Choke's arms and ran away.

When we returned from the weekend, I was certain the earth had stopped turning.

Instead, our kiss was a bad trend. It was the pageboy haircut, zoot suits, plaid tights, hair snoods, and dickeys—an exciting new invention everyone was certain would revolutionize the world. Instead, it became a joke.

Choke never said a word to me about the kiss. He never even looked at me again. Now, every time I see him, I pretend to have amnesia.

"Oh, hey, Dia," he says now. "I didn't know you work here."

"This is my family's shop."

"Right. I remember."

"Was that you digging around in the stockroom?"

He looks confused. "What? I just came in." He indicates the front entrance. "I know the sign says Closed, but the hours say ten to eight and it's seven-forty-one."

He looks fresh, wearing white tennis things. I'm greasy, with sweat stains under my arms and frizzy hair. I also notice that not far from Choke's feet, one of the Barnabys is mistaking a pile of Moroccan rugs for a litter box.

"Is there something specific you're looking for?"

Choke's eyes drift up to the green Murano glass tube chandelier hanging over his head like a giant poison squid.

"I heard this place has cool antique jewelry. I'm looking for a ring. Or, like, bracelet? For my girlfriend, Hailee. Oh, you know Hailee."

Of course I know Hailee. Everyone knows the world's most beautiful human. Choke started dating Hailee right after our kiss. Which means unlike *my* kiss, her kiss was the invention of blue jeans.

"Sure, we have an unusual selection of bracelets, rings, and necklaces. My favorites are nineteenth-century cameos from New York City debutantes and rose-gold bangles from haunted estates in the French Quarter of New Orleans. I'll pull a few choice pieces. Do you have a particular price range?"

Choke is listening to exactly none of this. He has noticed the computer screen.

"You're applying to the Louisiana Veda thing," he says, running a hand through his hair. "I sent mine in the first week. Not sure why. I don't know anything about Darkly games. And I scare easily. Do you?"

"Scare easily?"

"Know anything about Darklys."

"A little."

"Ever played one?"

"Yes."

"Which game?"

"Disappearing Act."

He frowns. "Is that the one where you're trapped in a mansion during a snowstorm with no electricity and you have to, like, fumble around the grounds to rescue your family from a murderous fiend, who may or may not be you, losing your mind?"

"No, that's Headcase. Disappearing Act is the one where you're the park ranger searching the forest all night for the missing boy who vanished from his mom's RV."

"Oh yeah. I heard that one's terrifying."

"It is."

"Why, exactly?"

"The gaming manual stipulates the game must be played at night. Outside. There's a small black Darkly radio that plays the soundtrack, and the music crackles with the past, creating this feeling of a separate realm. Like, anything is possible. But the story the game tells—a twisted mystery unfolding with cards, dice, and envelopes, equal parts chance and skill—it stays with you forever. It makes you question the world you live in and the people you love. You feel a bond with the other players. You'll never forget them. Then there are rumors about the lucky few who win."

"They're cursed, right?"

"Or chosen. No one knows which. We owned an original, actually."

I feel an immediate spasm of embarrassment in my stomach. I sound like I'm trying too hard to impress him. Also like one of those Darkly geeks. Glooms, they're called—the megafans, mostly young women hiding out in the murky corners of the internet raging about how the murderous machine of macho-driven capitalism destroyed Louisiana Veda, how if it weren't for their brutal agenda, her name would be up there with Walt Disney's.

But Choke is smiling as he leans over the counter, his blue eyes bright. I can smell peppermint on his breath.

"Hold on. *You* owned an original Darkly? When?"

"We used to have this annual junk toss, where people all over Missouri toss their junk in this giant purple dumpster we put in front of the store for a month."

"Oh yeah. I remember news crews interviewing your mom about that."

I feel my cheeks flush. The thought of Choke watching Gigi's infamous local news clips—where she performed stunts like climbing into the dumpster and pulling out ugly paintings and candlesticks—renders me mute.

But then he's tilting his head, waiting for me to go on.

"When I was ten, someone tossed in this giant garbage bag. It was filled with old baby clothes. But in with the bibs and blankets, we find a Darkly. Disappearing Act. The game was a hit when it was released in 1973. Sold out at a hundred and fifty thousand copies. But this wasn't just the game. It was one of Louisiana's prototypes. One of the three she made by hand."

"Damn."

"It's like finding a Basquiat in your basement, right? We tried to find the idiot who tossed it out, because you are ridiculous if you picked up an original Darkly and shoved it in with a bunch of old pajamas. I wanted to put out an ad to find the owner. My mom refused. We fought about what to do. In the end, she convinced me the best thing to do was to play it. That's what they're meant for. Not to be put behind glass or displayed on the wall. So that summer, we rented an RV and took a road trip to the Grand Canyon, playing the Darkly every night. We camped out under the stars, brought strangers together. It was the best summer of my life."

Choke smiles and crosses his arms. "Why is that?"

I can only stare.

"Go, Dia!" my mom shouts.

Meeting her excited gaze across the game board, I reach out and flick the arrow on the black spinner. It whirls—and stops on the question mark.

"Clue," someone announces.

I try to steady my nerves as I draw the top card from the black deck. My mom flips the red-sand timer and places it on the picnic table.

I turn over the card. It's a watercolor sketch of words crudely carved into a tree trunk.

"'Quercus dame greets the hawk, sunset burning nine o'clock, find the woman where she lies, severed pinky, footsteps die.'"

"More gibberish."

"This is giving me the creeps."

"Shh," my mom says. "Dia will solve this. You just watch."

"Thirty seconds."

The words evoke images. I close my eyes, watching them drift through my memory of the Darkly map carved and painted onto the board: eight campsites, four lookouts, thirteen trails, nine strangers camping in the park, one river. What happened to the little boy?

"When Dia was four, I'd ask her where I put my car keys. She always knew."

"Fifteen seconds."

"I call her my x-ray girl. She sees what no one else can."

"Ten seconds."

"They should send her into space. She'd find intelligent life."

"Can anyone actually win this thing, or is this just to scare us out of our minds?"

Quercus. The genus of an oak tree.

Dame, a woman.

Suddenly, the idea hits me. I grab the Disappearing Act backpack and dig through the strange objects inside: picture frame with a disfigured face, rosary beads, broken Timex watch. No, no. I pull out the plastic tree, the kind from a toy railroad set, two spindly branches raised upward—to greet the hawk? I grab the flashlight and the switchblade, fit the base of the tree into the small hole at the center of the board, turn on the flashlight, position it exactly at nine o'clock—setting in the west, a sunset. I point the beam at the tree.

Find the woman where she lies.

Sure enough, the shadow tossed onto the gameboard resembles a woman with her arms raised overhead, fingers splayed.

Severed pinky, footsteps die.

I open the switchblade and cut into the game board, exactly where the pinky would be on the shadow's right hand. The wood is soft. It gives way easily.

"What is she doing?"

"Destroying your masterpiece—"

"Two million bucks down the toilet."

"Shhh," my mom says.

"Three seconds."

I remove the cut-out piece.

"Two—"

Someone screams.

"There's something inside!"

I pull out the object: a tiny carved wood sneaker, painted blood-red.

A moment of shock. Then they are all on their feet—cheering, hugging me as if I'm a hero, as if this is real, not just a game.

"Told you," my mom laughs.

"What?" I blurt. I am aware that Choke just asked me a question.

"What happened to the kid in Disappearing Act? I mean, who took him? You eventually won, right?"

I shake my head. "No, actually. In Utah, my mom met her third fiancé. Darryl was more inclined to battle-of-the-band nights at dive bars than playing a game, even a Darkly. And anyway, if I had won, I couldn't tell you. There's an unspoken pact among Darkly winners never to reveal what happens."

Choke frowns, a curious glance at the surrounding shelves. "So where is it?"

"We sold it to keep the shop."

He looks upset. He opens his mouth to say something, probably to ask what kind of mom lets the windfall of an original Darkly slip through her fingers. But then his phone is ringing.

"Hi, Mom. Oh, can you give me one minute, I'm—four pounds, Italian butcher. Okay. Actually, I stopped first at—" He eyes me, cringing in apology as he checks his watch. "I'll head over now."

Choke hangs up, shuffling to the door. "Sorry, Dia, I got to run. There's a terrible crisis—guests are arriving for the party and there's not enough Wagyu beef. I'll come back some other time, okay?"

The door dings closed.

I stand there, frozen. I have a foolish, humiliated feeling, as if I took off all my clothes with very little prompting in an elevator with Choke while he remained dressed. And now he just exited, whistling, into the lobby.

As I lurch out from behind the counter to lock the door, I catch sight of Choke in his BMW, window unrolled, lazy smile. The light turns green, and he's gone, speeding away to tennis and Hailee and Wagyu beef hors d'oeuvres.

And I am left behind with mothballs and dust and hat trees.

I feel a boiling, mad resolve. I will win this internship. I will find out about this foundation. I will tell whoever these people are who Louisiana Veda was and what she means to her fans so they never produce such a lukewarm invitation with her name on it ever again.

I will get out of this shop—out of this life.

That's when I notice the computer.

I stare at it stupidly, wondering if I'm hallucinating, if I hit my head—like Agatha did during her car accident, when she woke up thinking it was 1980.

One of the Barnabys is sitting on the keyboard, staring at me.
I race over, pushing her off.

No, no—

I hit REFRESH, BACK, REFRESH. I try to reregister, clear the cache. But the same message comes back every time, like my own reflection I can never outrun.

"Noooooo," I scream.

The shop seems to flinch, afraid, and go still around me.

**Thank you for submitting your application
to the Louisiana Veda Foundation.
We will be in touch shortly.**

Two months later, we are all working late at Prologue, stickering furniture for our Summer 50% Off Sale.

"Holy pretzel," mutters Basil.

Agatha gasps. "That is so . . ."

"Looks like an official funeral notice from Western Union."

My mother pops her head out from behind a lampshade. "Oh, yes. That came yesterday for Dia."

I'm barely paying attention, too busy lugging a massive totem pole from 1950s Camp Windswept in the Adirondacks from the back of the shop to the front. As the only employee with a functioning back—my mom, since Sluder stopped calling, has had a pinched nerve—I've been hauling heavy things all day, rearranging the shop so it looks "fresh," even though in Prologue that's an oxymoron.

"Dia, come here and open this. Looks like Dracula is desperate to get ahold of you."

"If I were you, I . . ."

I set down the totem pole and move to the front counter, where

Agatha, Basil, and Gigi are scrutinizing a heavy black envelope under the light.

Miss Arcadia Gannon, it reads in lurid red letters.

When I read the return address, my heart stops.

I rip it open, pulling out the heavy black card.

Congratulations, Arcadia Gannon!
You have been chosen for the
Louisiana Veda Foundation's
summer internship program.
Please report 3 June 06.00 a.m. sharp sharp
to the St. Louis International Airport,
where you will fly to
Darkly Headquarters.
London, England.

I am so stunned I cannot move.

It can't be real. Someone is playing a trick on me.

"What is it?"

"Dia?"

Agatha's blue eyes blink worriedly behind her glasses. "She isn't so . . ."

"Absolutely, I agree," says Basil with a grave nod. "It's as if Dia just read, 'On behalf of the United States Army, I regret to inform you that your father was killed in action.' That's how they did it. Switching out the words as needed, to 'taken prisoner by enemy forces,' 'presumed dead.'"

Gigi grabs the card, squinting at it as I race to the computer and load the website.

Thank you to everyone who applied for
the Louisiana Veda summer internship program.
Below please find this year's winners.
We ask that you grant them space and privacy.

Poe Valois III of Paris, France, age 17
Franz-Luc Hoffbinhauer of Berlin, Germany, age 17
Cooper Min of Washington, DC, USA, age 17
Torin Kelly of Dublin, Ireland, age 17
Everleigh Aradóttir of Reykjavík, Iceland, age 17
Mouse Bonetti of Lagos, Nigeria, age 17
Arcadia Gannon of Eminence, Missouri, USA, age 17

LOUISIANA VEDA

INVITES YOU
TO

DARKLY'S

15-YEAR ANNIVERSARY PARTY

WITH

SCARES, SCARS,

AND

A SURPRISE UNVEILING OF DARKLY'S
MOST TERRIFYING GAME YET

15 JUNE 1985
8 O'CLOCK SHARP

BUSES WILL TRANSPORT GUESTS TO DARKLY PIER
NO CAMERAS
BLINDFOLDS REQUIRED

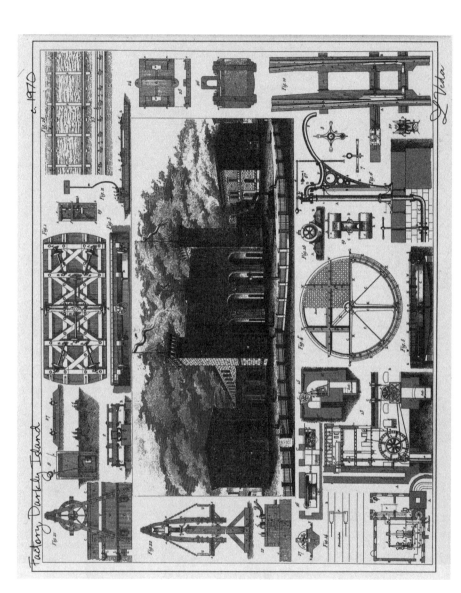

Factory, Darkly Island

c. 1970

L. Veder

6

"ondon? For the summer?" my mom shouts. "Leaving in two weeks? Why not join a colony on Mars and get emancipated, while you're at it?"

We are setting the table for dinner. Gigi is so distraught she has set out eight glasses, four soup bowls, and five salad forks, even though it's just the two of us eating takeout from Wok & Roll.

"How did this internship even happen? Someone contacted you?"

"No. I applied. Same as thousands of other kids."

"How do you know it's not a scam, so they can extort money from us?"

"No one is extorting anything, Mom."

"You remember Disappearing Act. Don't you see? Someone is coming out of the woodwork now, saying it's theirs and we owe them a fortune."

"This has nothing to do with that, Mom."

But Gigi slings herself into a seat at the table, staring at nothing in front of her, face red. I know her panic has little to do with me leaving and everything to do with Sluder not answering her texts.

She's scared to be alone again, and the Darkly internship happens to be the shiny new object within reach, to seize and try to smash against the wall.

"What will you do all day? Isn't this Louisiana person dead?"

"There's a foundation. I'll be learning about contemporary art auctions, and board-game creation, and manufacturing."

That's a lie. I've heard nothing about what I'll be doing. Thankfully, Gigi's too swept up in her own distress to notice how suspicious this sounds.

"We can't afford it."

"Everything is paid for. And I get a weekly stipend."

"I'll have to hire two new people for the shop."

"Basil already posted an ad in assisted living. He's interviewing two people this week."

Gigi doesn't seem to hear me, gnawing her fingernails. "No. I'm sorry, Dia. I need you at the shop this summer. We have to clean out that storage room by the boiler, and there are a million things to deal with, and—"

"No, Mom."

The anger, when it comes, feels like a great swing of an ax on a long-dead tree.

"Because I'm up all night paying *your* bills, fixing *your* accounting errors and loan applications, and paying taxes, trying to make sure we don't lose everything and end up on the street, I bomb every test at school and fall asleep daily on the bus. So you are very much mistaken, Mom. *I am going!*"

Gigi stares at me like I just shot a gun an inch from her forehead. She starts to cry.

"London's just so far," she says.

The Veda Seven, the internet calls us.

In the aftermath of the announcement, with our names made public, there is a flurry of online speculation as to who we are and why we won.

Are they ingenious prodigies? Brilliant teen sensations? How did these random mystery kids no one has ever heard of beat out six hundred thousand others?

Was there some kind of Darkly lottery? Random names pulled from a hat? Are these kids nepo babies on steroids—the progeny of the most powerful secret families on the planet?

"Pourquoi ces gens?" a French influencer sneers on TikTok, cutting to crude stick-figure cartoons of each of us with seven dancing question marks for faces.

I read and watch every post across dozens of languages and hundreds of feeds, filled with embarrassment and disbelief, as if I'm floating above myself in some parallel universe. Because the Arcadia Gannon they are hashing over—like she's the odious self-centered starlet of a popular TV drama—has nothing to do with me.

One of the rumors, which starts to gain momentum days after the announcement, is that none of us are real, that we've been created out of thin air to inflate the price of the Darkly games. This is because all seven of us are *unvisibles,* as someone on X calls it, kids who have chosen—for their mental health, privacy, or some other personal reason (which, in my case, is because I have an enormous antique store to run)—to maintain a strict zero-internet presence.

Of course, I'm already aware of this, having tried and failed to find a crumb of personal information on the kids I'll be working with all summer—kids with names so opaque it's like Louisiana Veda invented them herself.

Poe. Franz-Luc. Cooper. Torin. Mouse. Everleigh.

They are invisible vaults that do not unlock with any type of search. Even looking up their last names and cities leads to no obvious information about their families, just pages of generic returns and obscure genealogy records of people alive a hundred years ago.

Only Valois turns up anything specific—Poe-François Valois is a Zurich-based financier who is chairman and CEO of various international real estate companies.

In the absence of anything credible, I invent glittering personalities, faces, wardrobes, and mammoth IQs for each of these kids, which only fills me with more dread.

How could I have won along with them?

If I'd secretly prayed my newfound celebrity would trickle down to a more positive experience at Eminence High, I'm disappointed. My win is the equivalent of a rain leak in the gym roof.

I catch people staring at me, whispering, but in the bugged-out, bewildered vein of *Why her? I mean, Nana, of all kids? Seriously? Do meritocracies even exist anymore?*

"The Louisiana Veda Foundation is clearly an outreach program for those in their End of Days," a few kids joke on the bus.

Once, across the courtyard after school, I meet eyes with Choke Newington. He stares at me with an expression that isn't usually there. He looks serious, even a little angry. Is he also outraged that I won, aggrieved by the unfairness of it all?

But then he's swept into the riptide of his friends and Hailee—gone.

Not that I have time to worry about any of this.

I have eighty-nine pages of fine-print forms to fill out. Parental agreements, legal releases, medical evaluations, including thirty-two pages of something called a Loaded Psych Eval 3—all of which must be signed by a parent or legal guardian.

A man by the name of Nile Raiden, senior barrister at Derringer Street Chambers—"preeminent practitioners of global law," according to the London firm's taciturn website—sends me an icy email stating that "failure to complete all attached forms by the assigned deadline will result in immediate release from the internship. Forgery, deception, and diminished transparency will also be grounds for dissolution. Should you find any of the foregoing unsuitable, please notify me, and the offer of internship will be bestowed upon a runner-up."

Nile Raiden's photo reveals a thin, unsmiling bookmark of a man, with cropped russet hair, a sharp stare, and an otherwise unremarkable face. It's his résumé that is ornate and sprawling.

Experience as a barrister for over twenty years. A broad range of complex criminal cases, intellectual property law, inheritance, fraud, defamation. Year of silk: 2006. Year of call: 2001. His father, Wood Raiden, is one of the firm's founders.

It's all very intellectual and highbrow—a world away from me and Eminence. I sense there is no room for error here.

And so I am calculated.

I fill out all the forms myself. I make an appointment with my pediatrician to complete the medical documents. Thankfully, she's either too overworked or has seen too much lately to question the brazenly disturbing questions, including "Have you ever felt the need to notify authorities about the patient's potential for violence? If so, please describe."

I keep the completed documents stowed in the lockbox under my bed, waiting for the moment when my mom is at her most distracted.

Because Gigi Gannon can abruptly pay attention. She can, out of the blue, put on her Groucho Marx glasses and study something with unwavering concentration for *hours*—rental contracts, antiques restoration history, the inlaid wood pattern of intertwined rosebushes on a Louis XIV table—finding the minute mistake that escaped everyone else's notice.

Then she will dig in, bringing a dramatic end to the proceedings, standing her ground like Moses announcing an incendiary eleventh commandment.

Though she's dropped the subject, remaining mute at any mention of my absence from the shop this summer, I can tell she's still stewing. She'd love to find a valid reason for me not to go.

And there are reasons. The contracts are exhaustive and

one-sided, granting total rights to the Louisiana Veda Foundation in the event of anything at all happening in the known and unknown universes. Ever.

All phones, laptops, tablets, and recording equipment must be relinquished upon arrival. *These personal items will be returned upon completion of the internship. Communication with personal family members and friends may be achieved at Derringer Street's discretion by email at a designated computer center.*

And yet, even considering that, one clause in particular stands out.

In section Q, page 37 of the "Professional Employment Agreement," concealed after a paragraph about property damage, it reads: *And unto all parties herein, I, Arcadia Gannon, hereby release the Foundation from liability in the event of my death, decapitation, and/or dismemberment.*

I do some research, learning that this language is actually pretty common for people employed at large manufacturing plants operating heavy machinery, like paper pulp digesters and vacuum drum washers.

Is this just a blanket bit of legalese the lawyers threw in for good measure, in case of a fatal accident? Or does it mean we are going to work in the Darkly factory?

It's an electrifying thought—too outlandish to seriously consider.

The factory has given rise to almost as many legends as Louisiana Veda herself. In 1970, after the success of her first game, Ophelia, with her newly minted fortune, Louisiana bought a secret island somewhere off the coast of England.

There, she built her factory.

She was so careful to hide the location that supposedly she bought five phony factories across England to use as decoys.

In the aftermath of her death in 1985, a handful of former employees went public, anonymously damning Darkly with tales of enslavement, Louisiana the insane dragon lady who tortured workers with her crushing demands and lethal temper. Crying and screaming and other strange sounds echoed all night across the sprawling fortress, which was characterized as a kind of labyrinthine prison.

Supposedly, there was the Test Floor, where numbered strangers were bused in to road-test the new games. They were forbidden to leave, not for months, forced to wear blindfolds and live in locked cells, playing new games for weeks at a time, enduring hours of interrogation. No one was allowed to utter the name Louisiana Veda. And when the mastermind in question deigned to visit—there are tales of a tall and silent figure watching from the doorway, wearing a black hooded cloak, her face always obscured—no one was allowed to say a word to her, or even glance in her direction. There one minute, gone the next, she was never spotted twice—*like a poltergeist, like a madwoman the executives wheel in and out of her locked tower for lurid effect, an embarrassment.*

There was also the Origin Floor, an area where Louisiana and a handful of trusted creatives toiled day and night to conceive each monumental new game.

The accusers went away as swiftly as they appeared. I never really believed the stories.

But they were another expansive stone addition to the mysterious wall that is Darkly—too high to see over, no known beginning or end.

There are rumors today that the factory has been left to rot. Monstrous vines twist through the roof. Hallways are spangled with mold. Entire wings supposedly burned down in a fire, Louisiana's original sketches and drafts, her grand plans for future Darkly games, all destroyed.

Now and then, some daredevil kid will video her attempt to track down the location, scaling fences and trespassing through some random old laboratory. *This must be it,* the girl whispers, shivering into the camera. *This is where she built her empire. I can feel her energy.*

But it's all bogus.

It's only when I have one day left to turn in the documents that my mom returns home from another first date. She wanders into the kitchen, opening a fresh bottle of merlot, lipstick on her chin. That's when I fish the signature pages out from under the bed.

"All he talked about was reupholstering his chesterfield sofa. I mean, how does anyone think that's good conversation for a first date?"

"That's awful. You forgot to sign these, Mom."

She takes the pen and scribbles her signature. "He didn't ask me one question. Not one. I could have been a wall sitting there. What are these again?"

"Tax forms." I flip to the next page. "This was the pediatrician?"

"Michael? No, he's a serial entrepreneur, which appears to mean 'unemployed.'" She signs the next page and the next.

"You're going to meet someone wonderful this summer. I can feel it." I gather the papers and slip out.

"Maybe the universe is trying to tell me, 'Love yourself first,' you know?"

"Definitely. Good night, Mom."

"Love you, babe."

9

"What may I bring you for dinner this evening?"

I turn from the airplane window to see the first-class attendant smiling down at me. I study the elegant menu clutched in my hand.

NORMANDY LAMB CHOPS WITH MINT YOGURT SAUCE
SIDE OF ROAST BOEUF WITH CAMPAGNA POTATOES
AND HENS OF THE WOODS
POULET ANGLAISE WITH CELERIAC COMPOTE

"I'll take the chicken, please."

"And to drink?"

"Water. Thank you."

She jots this down and moves to the passenger behind me. I return my attention to the billowing pink clouds out the window, twisting my shoulders into an uncomfortable angle to make sure my face is hidden from the other passengers in row 1.

I am a ball of nerves. I feel more fragile and awkward with every mile I am whisked from home.

I never should have left my mom. I never should have left Prologue or the Barnabys, Basil and Agatha, or Missouri.

Because, with the exception of Missouri, they won't be able to survive without me. It was clear when I said goodbye this morning. Agatha was whispering to herself, unable to find her glasses, even though they were hanging around her neck on the beaded chain. My mom was tying a price tag of $19.99 on a French garniture set worth $5,000. Basil was stuttering when he asked if I might have time to pick up a Venti coconut latte at Starbucks for him before I left, even though I had just handed him that very beverage. The Barnabys were jumping around like mad, scratching the furniture and leaping onto chandeliers. My mom noted this was a sign all five were about to have kittens, which caused her to wonder how the tomcat got in—the disturbing fact that Prologue Antiques is about to be taken over by a fiefdom of jumpy, black shadow-cats utterly lost on her.

Making matters worse, something else on this plane makes it clear I have no business being here, and upon landing, I should book a flight home and join witness protection.

Because there is another one of us on the airplane.

The boy in 1F.

I first noticed him standing in a bookstore in Terminal 8, when I was trying to find the gate for my connecting flight. He was flipping through an aggressively thick paperback and was so gorgeous that I actually backtracked to make sure he was real, and also to see the title.

Anna Karenina.

An hour later, he was boarding my plane.

He saunters in, tall with moody black hair in his eyes, gray sweats, a cigarette-alley slouch. He sets down two massive leather duffels, one in the aisle so no one can pass, one in the seat beside him that belongs to a bald businessman, who for some reason is intimidated and waits in silent irritation. I notice the side of both bags is emblazoned with a gold Victorian royal PV3, which instantly sets off an alarm bell due to the fact that I have committed the names of the other interns so intrinsically into my brain it's hard-wired to pick up on anything, however minute, that could evoke one of them.

It must be Poe Valois III of Paris, France, age seventeen.

But that's not even the crazy thing—the boy is carrying a black leather briefcase, and it is *handcuffed to his left wrist.*

Like some kind of gangster.

Whatever priceless thing is inside, it's been orchestrated with the airline ahead of time. Because as soon as the flight crew see this boy, they're on high alert, crowding around him and nodding like he's a sultan. The boy pulls a necklace from his shirt, revealing a collection of tiny strangely shaped black keys. Using one in the form of a circle to unlock the cuff, which falls open in an accordion way I've never seen before, he hands the briefcase to the pilot. With a grave nod, as if it contains the boy's own beating heart, the man whispers, "Thank you for your trust, sir," before vanishing with it into the cockpit.

And then—as if nothing at all extraordinary just happened— the boy sits with a yawn, pulls out a laptop covered with cool stick-ers, and starts to compose a classical symphony using some kind of elaborate composition program.

He writes musical notes across nineteen bars, wearing the same absorbed scowl I once saw on a silver-print portrait of

Beethoven—not looking up for an hour. The reason I know it's a symphony is, at one point, he fusses with the buttons on his headphones and they lose the Bluetooth connection, and the most beautiful, brooding orchestral music I have ever heard blasts out of his computer into first class.

A few people look up in surprise, and he kills the sound.

"Sorry for the disturbance, ladies and gentlemen," he announces with a sheepish grin.

He has a lilting French accent. So it *is* Poe Valois III of Paris, France.

Never in my life could I have imagined a boy to make Choke Newington look dreary. But here, impossibly, is such a boy. His hands look like they regularly sculpt life-sized human figures out of wet clay. His eyes are dark yet warm. I find myself thinking it must be the light in first class that makes him so perfect, and upon disembarking in five hours to the harsh fluorescents of an airport, he will devolve into a moderately handsome teenager in keeping with the rest of humanity.

Except why is he on this flight out of New York City? If he lives in Paris, wouldn't he simply take a train through the Channel Tunnel, or a quick flight from Charles de Gaulle, or use his family's private helicopter? Because he looks like he regularly enjoys a helicopter. Possibly one of those stadium-sized yachts drifting around the Mediterranean, too.

Everyone smiles and goes back to sleeping or watching a movie. Not me. I can't take my eyes off him, wondering how I'll survive a summer working in close proximity to him.

He eats dinner, picking at the Normandy lamb chops.

After that, he uses the bathroom.

After that, he motions to the flight attendant with a shockingly tiny gesture that could only have been learned after spending his childhood in an echoing château—nothing else could explain the expectation that, mais oui, everyone is attuned to his movements at all times. Instantly, the copilot emerges with the mysterious briefcase.

Poe turns on the overhead light, opens the case in his lap, using another one of those odd keys around his neck, and he removes a Darkly game.

I am astonished. It's an original. Removing an original Darkly in flight, even if it *is* first class, is like unrolling Andy Warhol's *Shot Sage Blue Marilyn* in a back booth at McDonald's.

The businessman seated next to him does a double take.

"Is that an—"

"Absolutely," says Poe with a mischievous smile. "Want to play?"

The businessman chuckles. "Which one is it?"

"Eighteen Lost Icelandic Sailors. 1978. Recover the drowned bodies of the missing sailors, take over their ghost ship, discover why they perished, unearth their hidden diaries that contain their hideous secrets about what went down on their voyage, send their bodies home to grieving families for a Christian burial, all the while trying not to drown, go mad, or be devoured by a twenty-seven-foot sea monster."

The businessman leans in, studying the ornate wooden board. I've seen photographs before, but they did not do it justice. It's a maritime ocean map emblazoned with the legendary Darkly scroll, carved with detailed circles and nonsensical words, drawings, diagrams, and odd crisscrossing longitudes.

"And that's—"

"Louisiana Veda's original prototype. One of two copies in the world."

"I had a client who bought one," the businessman notes. "The Death of Alice Something—"

"The Demise of Alice Hayes. One of the ghost games."

"Ghost what?"

"After Louisiana's death, they discovered fifteen original games she had created. Never released or mass-produced. They go for the highest prices. Conquistador. Fringe Theory. The Donwaldt Island Mystery. The games released during her lifetime are called the vitals."

The businessman is rapt. "My client spent a fortune buying the thing. Another on tutors, psychologists, mathematicians to help crack it. He was hell-bent on winning. Poor man died in a car accident without making it even two squares down the board. His wife went nuts. Swore it was the game that killed him. She made sure it left the family. Donated it to MoMA with the provision that it could not be displayed until fifty years after his death." He frowns. "But is it really wise? Taking that out here? Isn't it worth, like—"

"Four million pounds. Yes. Do you know what they say about Darklys?"

"Not really."

"They own you. Not the other way around. Like bloodhounds, they're loyal to the death. Surprisingly impervious to abandonment. They bond with their first owner and will do anything to be played, again and again. But not won. Never do they wish to be won. People claim if you have a Darkly in the house, put it in the back of your closet under a boatload of junk, forget about it. Within days it'll be out on a table under a light, waiting. No one will remember putting it there."

"But it's all nonsense."

Poe smiles. "Want to find out?"

The man laughs, an uneasy frown—*Who is this kid?*—and returns his attention to his spreadsheets.

Though as he types, I notice, he cannot stop looking back at the game.

DARKLY

From the desk of Louisiana Veda

Mr. Wood Raiden
25 Eaton Place
Belgravia, London

6 February 1985

Dear Wood:

After the hikes across the lonely mountains, after all we've seen and done, the love we shared, the fortune you and your army of leeches have gorged upon--fruits of the kingdom I built--you should know better than to threaten a law of nature. So, consider this:

First, the rain will come. Then, the roof will cave. Then, you drown.

L

There's still time to back out, go home before you make a fool of yourself, my mind chatters as I wheel my bag through Heathrow Airport.

In the chaos of customs, I lose sight of Poe Valois III. But as I step out into the cool, gray morning, the crowd jostling me as they make their way to the taxi line, I notice a gray-haired man in a black suit standing a distance away with a sign.

GANNON, it reads.

Poe stands beside him, talking intensely on the phone, duffels at his feet, the briefcase shackled again to his wrist. His looks have not diminished in the frank light of morning. In fact, he looks even more windswept and cool. As I approach, it takes everything in my power to pretend not to notice him. But that's like pretending not to be struck by lightning.

"Gannon?" asks the man bluntly. He has a thick British accent and the harried demeanor of someone chastised for running late.

"That's me."

With a curt nod, he takes the handle of my suitcase, pulling it toward a gleaming black London taxi by the curb.

"What about the others?" Poe asks, pocketing his phone with a frown.

The man heaves my suitcase into the trunk. "I've only got Gannon and Valois."

"You were on my flight."

I feign blasé curiosity as I turn to him. This makes him smirk, which means he was well aware of me gawking at him for seven hours, like some runny-nosed kid at a zoo unable to pull herself away from the leopard exhibit.

He holds out his free hand. "I'm Poe."

"Dia."

"Are you also in the dark about this internship?"

"Definitely."

"I wonder if the other interns weren't fools like us and refused to sign those draconian contracts, so it'll be just the two of us all summer."

This prospect renders me mute as we climb into the taxi. Working alongside Poe and only Poe for the entire summer would be the equivalent of being a pebble of moon rock in orbit around Alpha Centauri.

I start to worry about the taxi ride. How will I maintain an hour's worth of conversation?

But Poe makes himself at home in the back seat, in a waft of cologne that smells like a forgotten closet in Versailles. He props his long, muscular legs up on the pull-down seat opposite, dons a beanbag neck pillow, headphones, aviator sunglasses, and with a monster yawn and a tap on his phone—I lean in, curious to see what kind of music mythic boys listen to; it's M83's "Couleurs"—he appears to settle in for a nap.

I am left trying to ignore his sprawling presence. It's like trying to forget a lion dozing beside me. I feel the simultaneous need to play dead, run for my life, and make detailed scientific observations. For example, his fingertips are smudged black and red-brown. Is it oil paint from the masterpiece mural he has been painting since he was seven? Dirt from a recent archaeological dig in Greece? On the inside of his left wrist is a tattoo. It's a long cylinder with a double helix of lacelike DNA twisted around it. Along the side are letters and roman numerals.

TPS.XXIV.III.XXIV

TPS. It must be the initials of the girl he loves. Theodosia Palmer Salvatore? Tabitha "Peaches" von Strickenbaum? She must be a raven-haired classical pianist who looks like Ava Gardner.

And 24/3/24. The date of the fateful twilight when they first kissed?

As the taxi veers onto the highway, I force my attention from Poe to the window, watching the squat brown houses and small European cars grow fewer and fewer, until after an hour of driving we are bouncing down a deserted country road.

"How much longer until we reach London?" I ask.

The driver looks uneasy as he meets my gaze in the mirror.

"Not London, miss. Thornwood."

Thornwood?

That's wrong. The email from Nile Raiden clearly stated we would be residing in Central London, within walking distance to foundation headquarters.

And yet after another half hour and a stop for gas—petrol—we are bouncing down a dirt road. Wizened trees reach overhead, blotting out the sky. Poe has not stirred, his head tipped back in the seat, mouth open, occasionally shuddering like a screen door not closed all the way.

Every time I consider nudging him awake, asking if he's heard of Thornwood, I lose my nerve and continue to stare out the window, at once mesmerized and worried by this motley overgrown forest with its half-dead trees and scabbing bark.

We stop in front of a crude steel gate. It looks like something outside a military compound. The driver unrolls the window and types a six-digit code into a rusted panel. With a blood-curdling wail, the gate pulls open.

We drive on, lurching in the ruts and mud. The forest grows dense. Black brambles and ferns and bulbous gray rocks soak up the morning, replacing it with looming nightfall.

We speed around a bend. Abruptly the road veers downhill. I grab the door handle so as not to be flung on top of Poe as we swing out into a rocky shoreline and jerk to a halt.

Yards away, a narrow pier juts out into choppy, silvered water. A distance beyond that is a white van and a sagging gray boathouse, where five people are filing out and making their precarious way down the boardwalk over the rocks, awkwardly hauling suitcases.

The other interns.

They're heading for an old boat moored at the end. A green flag whips wildly at the stern. I can make out the legendary white Darkly scroll. Though I'm too far away to read it, I know the notorious tagline is scrawled underneath, the cryptic phrase endlessly debated.

Wander where the witch lies.

Who exactly is the witch? Louisiana? Is she a force of good or evil? What kind of lie is it? Is she lying on the ground, sleeping, dying, or telling malevolent tales?

Whatever it means, the general consensus from Darkly fans is that it's an empowering call to arms, a salvation, and a battle cry.

Though I spent the past few weeks dreaming and worrying, agonizing over what I would be doing all summer, with whom and why, now I understand I have no idea what is going to happen. Perhaps this internship isn't so unlike Louisiana Veda, after all.

Poe, roused from sleep, pulls off his sunglasses.

"What's happening?" he whispers, squinting out the window.

"We're going to the Darkly factory," I say as I climb out.

24 December 1930

DEADLY FIRE KILLS FAMILY

A family of five, including three young ch
dren, were burned to death early Sund
evening when a fire swept a dwelling at 1
Hollywick Street, Sedgeford. After a
investigation Chief Fire Marshal Lewis J.
Willard declared that fireplace embers wer
improperly disposed of hours before inside
the house. He does not suspect foul play.

11

Poe and I make our way down the dock, hauling our bags against the onslaught of wind.

I notice our taxi is already pulling away, vanishing down the road. Something about the hasty exit seems deceptive, and I stop to stare after it, shivering at the sight of the empty beach. The opposite shoreline isn't visible, cloaked by dense fog.

I assume someone from the foundation will be here to welcome us. But as Poe and I step alongside the boat—the *Elvira,* it's called, and it looks bruised and barnacled, like it just surfaced from the bottom of the sea—I see there is no one else here, only the interns.

They sit in sulky silence on the benches along the bow, clutching their belongings, scowling every time the boat jerks or a spew of salt water flies. And I can't help but stare. Because the whole world has been wondering about them, and *I* have been wondering about them, but nothing comes close to the vibrant reality.

They look like characters torn from five different novels.

There's a grim girl, at least six feet tall, with chin-length peroxide-blond hair and bangs that hang in her forehead like the thick bristles of a broom. She wears a kelly-green fifties chiffon dress that is way too big, and she sits staring out at the fog with hunched shoulders, arms and legs crossed, which gives her the air of a tightly knotted rope. Her mud-caked combat boots are propped on a blue backpack.

Beside her sits a girl with an Elvis swirl of black hair on top of her head, the ends dyed neon blue. She's Asian, with a focused, no-fools-will-be-tolerated frown. Even though the boat rocks and bounces, she reads a thick hardback in her lap while absent-mindedly flipping the charm on her necklace, which appears to be in the form of a single gold eye.

Then there is an overdressed boy wearing an expensive-looking suit, gold watch, two giant Louis Vuitton bags beached at his feet. He is Black and is tying with expert speed a red silk tie around his neck in a Double Windsor knot.

Next to him is a redheaded girl with black glasses and uncombed hair in a messy bun, which appears to be an unsuccessful attempt to hide how scarily beautiful her face is. She is dressed in oversized gray sweats and, having removed her sneaker and sock, is inspecting her big toe's mangled nail, which looks like it's about to fall off.

Finally, there is a heavy blond boy with flushed cheeks, wearing a neck brace. His T-shirt reads UNBEKANNTES FLUGOBJEKT, and he's the only one who seems remotely friendly, smiling at us.

"Can't wait any longer, have to come back later for the skivers."

An ancient woman, with a face as wrinkled as a ball of furiously discarded paper, peers out from a door in the hull. She spies Poe and me, scowling.

"Expecting an Order from Saint Michael, are you? Go on, take a seat. Got to get a ramp on the mornin' to miss this storm, or I swear on the soul of Saint Thistle, this is the final hour of daylight you burrs'll ever see."

Her British accent is like a mouthful of pine cones. I can hardly sift through what she said before she vanishes back into the hull, door slamming.

Poe, with a mild grin, throws on his duffels and climbs aboard—his briefcase drawing a few curious stares. I step after him, taking a seat beside the redhead.

My only thought is that they all just had a heated argument. Nothing else could explain how sullen and mad they look, how intent they are on ignoring each other.

Poe looks amused. "Thanks for the hero's welcome. I'm Poe."

"Dia," I say.

"Mouse," says the Black kid, eyeing us with a distracted smile.

"I'm Franz-Luc," says Unbekanntes Flugobjekt in a thick German accent. "But you can call me Franz if that is easier."

"Cooper," says the Asian girl, barely glancing up from her book.

"I'm Everleigh," says the blond girl in the green dress.

"Torin," says the redhead, shoving her foot back into her sneaker.

It's then that Everleigh—Everleigh Aradóttir of Reykjavík, Iceland—pulls her gaze from the water. Her face is splotchy, and her crystalline-green eyes are red from crying.

"You shouldn't have come here," she whispers.

"Oh, God, not again," says Torin, rolling her eyes.

"Seriously," says Cooper. "You need to chill."

The girl ignores them. "We should have gotten word to you to send help."

"You should try some deep breathing for relaxation," says Franz.

Poe stares at her. "What's the matter?"

"She's been freaking out since we got here," mutters Cooper.

"When did you get here?" I ask.

Cooper shrugs. "Late last night. First she tried to call a taxi. Then she tried running away. She ran all night in the forest, screaming there was no way out. She found the fence but couldn't get over the barbed wire. Slashed her whole arm."

I notice the painful-looking scratches, which explains why she's holding her arms tightly crossed.

"They're keeping us captive here. Against our will."

"That's not true," says Cooper. "The captain *told* you. The foundation people are waiting for us on the island to give us orientation. After that, they'll take you to the airport. So stop whining about it."

"I don't want to go to an island. I want to go home. I'm not even supposed to be here."

The kid named Mouse is ignoring all of this, staring with confident ease out at the water, as if the rest of us are strangers having an embarrassing tantrum in a doctor's waiting room, people who have nothing to do with him.

But the sight of this girl having a panic attack and the others surveying her with cold irritation, it makes me lean over and put a reassuring hand on her shoulder.

"Don't worry," I whisper. "I'll help you leave if that's what you want."

She jerks away from me, glaring. "You don't know anything."

Suddenly, the door to the hull opens again, and everyone jumps as the old woman scrambles out. This must be the "captain" Cooper was referring to, I can only guess. Wiping her filthy hands on her grease-streaked overalls, she moves to the helm.

"How long is this boat ride?" Franz asks.

The captain pretends not to hear him, flipping switches, squinting dead ahead.

Franz continues to smile. "I have a history of extreme sea-sickness. Any advice on how not to throw up? Staring at the horizon doesn't work for me, and neither do the acupressure wristbands."

This admission appears to be akin to announcing a hatred of the sea, because the captain turns and surveys Franz with marked disgust before darting along the sides of the boat, untying the ropes. Ornery tufts of silver hair jut out from her old striped fishing cap. She looks cracked and sun-dried, like a once-pristine doll forgotten on a beach for twenty years.

Moments later, we are motoring out into the bay. Everleigh has descended into a shaken trance, staring ahead as if she expects at any second, something—a sea monster—to emerge from the fog.

That's when I notice the book Cooper is reading.

The Unfiltered, Unflinching, Illegal, Utterly Dangerous Darkly Gaming Manual, Version 4.0 by 4 Anonymous Champions.

I peer closer, my eyes straining to make out the tiny words on the page.

I am unable to lawfully detail anything of what I found when the prize was at last placed in my arms, when I summoned the strength to unlatch the heavy black lid and stare inside. But let's just say it was a kingdom revealing the stunning breadth and scale of Louisiana's genius and vision. It was a secret invitation to the labyrinth, a confession, and a dream. A death, too, because she never did live to see any of these things come to fruition. But oh, my, what if one day—

Suddenly, Cooper slams the book closed and, with a hostile glare at me, shoves it into her backpack.

I grasp the boat railing for dear life, my hair whipping my face, freezing waves drenching me.

My right leg is asleep from stepping hard on my suitcase to prevent it from flying off the boat every time the *Elvira* is blasted by a whitecap. I keep my eyes locked on the captain, partly for reassurance, partly out of curiosity. The way she works the controls, never needing to actually glance down at the needles or gauges, staring at the waves without the slightest hint of worry—though once I swear she actually reprimands them; "Blaggards!" she shouts—suggests the old woman has taken this journey a thousand times before.

Where did she come from? Did she know Louisiana? Our presence appears to be a horrible nuisance, because she doesn't look at us, not once. She seems eager to deposit us, wherever we're headed, as quickly as possible and be rid of us.

As the minutes tick by and the sea and mist show no sign of relenting, it starts to feel as if we're spinning in a doomed airplane inside a cloud, no up and no end. I start to panic, not unlike

Everleigh, who seemed so hysterical and fragile before but now appears to have a valid point. She stares grimly ahead, her torso frozen twenty degrees forward, making her look like the battered wood mermaid nailed to the bow of a pirate ship.

However arrogant and annoyed the other interns were before—all of that has been stripped away by the sea, leaving them sodden and shivering. They look out with dazed incredulity, probably wondering, like me, how the glamorous public reality of winning the illustrious Louisiana Veda Foundation internship turns out to be *this*.

Just as I start to imagine the headlines (LOUISIANA VEDA INTERNS VANISH INTO WATERY GRAVE) and the ensuing #justiceforthevedaseven, and how my mom will mourn me (*How can I keep Prologue afloat now?*) and Choke Newington hearing about my death (Choke, to whom I will be as vague in his memory as the cashier who handed him his Starbucks through the drive-thru window last week)—only then does something appear out of the fog ahead.

It's an enormous dark shadow. That's how it looks at first.

No, it's a cliff—a black mountain rising out of the sea.

The ocean rages against the rocks along the shoreline, plumes of seething waves exploding. And rising atop the island, the fog thinning around it as if in deference, turning its dark face toward us, as if sensing intruders—

The Darkly factory.

It is a sprawling expanse of intricately layered gray stones. The facade is massive—four archways like four open mouths. Two monumental towers like devil's horns pierce the sky, dark-green Darkly flags atop the spikes.

The captain, a pleased smile as if spotting an old friend, braces herself against a fresh blast of wind. She cranks the wheel, and the boat veers inland with a yowl. I can see that beyond the cliffs spangled with silver grass, there are other structures on the island. But nothing I can make out really through the fog, only a jutting roof, a steeple.

We barrel toward an old dock, which resembles a long fish bone picked over and tossed along the shore. There is a faded billboard, some of the panels missing.

WELCOME TO DARKLY. WANDER WHERE THE WITCH LIES.

Three men in tan trench coats are waiting for us, I see, hats pulled low against the wind. As we jet closer, the shortest one steps forward, waving.

"Welcome!"

It is a surprisingly cheerful voice. The man is middle-aged, with thinning copper hair and a corporate folding-chair stiffness— a welcome sight in this wild place. I recognize him immediately as the attorney who sent all the emails—Nile Raiden. His smile has an official tightness, the kind normally seen in marble lobbies behind concierge desks.

The captain maneuvers alongside the pier, and the two other men with muted stares help us disembark.

"Good morning to you all!" shouts Raiden. "How was the journey in? Uneventful? We must proceed swiftly. We have a very tight schedule. If you could each just deposit your phones, recording devices, cameras, everything, er, *here*— Where did—? Oh . . ." Flustered, he points out the filthy plastic barrel behind him, which looks like it normally houses fish guts. "Do not fret. Your luggage is heading around to the other side of the island. The ascent there is not as steep. Less of a chance your pajamas end up floating around the North Sea." He chuckles thinly.

Turning, I see now the two men with the captain are motoring swiftly away with our belongings, heading around the jutting rocks of the cove.

"Aren't we're staying in Central London?" asks Cooper.

But Raiden is already off, striding down the dock with a grand wave of his arm, as if he's a real estate agent escorting potential buyers through a new house.

"This is Torment Point! Named by Louisiana herself. When she was first brought to the island, it was this spot that sold her. She knew she would build the most incredible world here, on this dark and howling island. Now we really must get a move on. Time is not on our side, I'm afraid!"

Maybe it's the fact we're confused and freezing, maybe it's the man's flighty exuberance, but none of us move. We only watch him go.

I didn't notice it before—it was concealed by the gray grasses fringing the rocks—but a precarious set of black wood steps zigzag up the cliff face. They look like they're clinging there due to static. Raiden is starting up them.

Poe, hugging the briefcase to his chest, considers the scene in thoughtful surprise. Franz is busy peeling off his foam neck brace, wringing out the seawater. Cooper is looking tearfully back the way we came, as if praying that out of that grayed nothingness a rescue boat will appear. Torin looks like a scared little girl. Everleigh stares after Raiden with deadpan gravity.

Only Mouse is unfazed. Even though he looks like he just drowned, his blue suit completely soaked, he tosses his phone in the barrel and takes off down the pier.

"You don't have extreme reservations?" Franz calls after him.

"My curiosity has beaten my fear," Mouse shouts over his shoulder.

Raiden has stopped on a landing midway up on the stairs, waving.

"Let's go, please! All of your questions will be answered during the presentation!"

For the first time, I hear biting impatience in his voice, like a concealed switchblade in his hand suddenly catching the light. Then it's gone.

"There is a great deal to cover! Not a second to waste, I'm afraid!"

We ascend the steps in shivering silence, slammed by the wind, gray clouds roiling overhead.

I am last, because I keep stopping to stare below, transfixed by how high the cliffs are and the ocean's ashen complexion, how it sizzles and boils, fighting the rocks.

At last, I've reached the top. I step out onto a wood platform, the railing splintered, half of it missing, so there is nothing stopping anyone from plummeting straight off the side.

Never have I seen a place so strange.

It is a vast, windswept expanse. Narrow stone pathways crisscross in every direction through a sea of tall grass. Fringing the periphery, tucked in knotted groves of exotic trees and shadows, are a handful of squat stone cottages. There are other things here, too, sculptures and wrought-iron gates too far away to make out. At the very center of the field in front of me is some kind of gazebo, tangled with black vines.

Beyond that, atop a sloping hill, sits the factory.

This is a different view than the one from the ocean—the side entrance. There are no windows, only two annexes of gray stone, a single door at the center painted Darkly green. The entire structure is surrounded by a crude chain-link fence.

I realize this island must be laid out like a board game. Of course Louisiana would design her island to be like one of her games.

"If you could please make your way inside the auditorium!" shouts Raiden.

The other interns are filing down the path toward a slumped wood barn, where Raiden holds open the door. He seems to be staring at me.

"We have a great deal to cover!"

By the time I catch up, hurrying through the dark entrance strewn with gravel and dead leaves, I find the others in an empty theater with bare wood walls, raw beams overhead. They are removing their jackets and soggy shoes, grabbing gray flannel blankets from a pile on the floor, and making their way to the back, where there is a meager display of cheese, crackers, and grapes, some of which, I notice, are moldy.

Raiden stands on the stage, a bare projection screen on the wall behind him.

"Help yourself to tea, snacks, whatever you need—but we really must get started."

I grab a handful of crackers and pour myself a tea. It's black, and so hot it scalds my hand through the cheap paper cup. I move down the aisle, taking a seat in one of the folding chairs.

"Welcome. I would like to thank you on behalf of Derringer Street Chambers, the foundation, and Louisiana. She would be grateful for the efforts you took to arrive here."

He sniffs, clasping his hands. It's then that I see how unsure the man is, how nervous, like a teacher who has been training for years, now in front of real students for the first time.

"I gather you are expecting a grand kickoff meeting, balloons, and a banquet. But given the nature of what is at stake, I'm afraid we've no time for a circus." He clears his throat and, for a second, seems to lose his train of thought. "My name is Nile Raiden. I am a senior barrister at Derringer Street, a firm that has long represented the Veda estate."

He turns, clicking a remote. A photo appears on the screen of a smiling boy with blond hair and freckles.

"Meet George Grenfell. Fifteen years old. He has gone missing. One night, he was tucked into his bed. The next morning, he had vanished. We need you to find him."

With a grim nod, Raiden stares out at us, watching this odd statement sink in.

"Whoever finds him—or finds out what happened to him— you will each receive one million pounds and exclusive ownership of an original Darkly of your choosing. This may be any one of the twenty-eight board games, including all licensing and gaming rights. Rasputin. Headcase. Abigail Cox. Seventy-Five Years to Life. This arrangement is part of the trust Louisiana set aside for the recovery of her stolen game. Given the immense value of the prize, you can fathom how grave a situation we consider this, how critical it is that the matter is resolved in an expeditious fashion with no one else getting hurt."

No one speaks. Poe shifts in his seat. The words burn through my mind.

Stolen game?

"Nearly forty years ago, Darkly's fifteen-year anniversary party was held here on this island. The first and the last time outsiders were ever allowed in. At some point that evening, a priceless piece of intellectual property was stolen from the factory's Imagination and Expansion floor, Tomb 605. The lone copy of the twenty-ninth Darkly game. Valkyrie."

I stare in surprise. There are twenty-eight Darkly games. Thirteen released to the general public, the vitals. Fifteen discovered after Louisiana's death, the ghost games.

Never have I heard of a twenty-ninth.

Raiden strides across the stage with an absorbed frown. "The game was a pet project of Louisiana's. It was meant to be Darkly's crown jewel. But after a series of prototypes and testing, something went wrong. The game was pulled from production. Why? We don't know. All records have been lost. Test copies were destroyed, save Louisiana's original creation and the gaming manual. These two items were stolen from the vault—the tombs, as they're called.

"It was a perfect theft. Louisiana hired detective agencies, police, the best investigators in the world. Every living soul within a hundred miles of the island that night was questioned and monitored in the ensuing years. To no avail. The game vanished into thin air. In Louisiana's will, mere weeks before her death, she made a provision that her legal team should never stop searching for Valkyrie until it is found, scouring the remotest, darkest corners of the world, so it could be recovered, the perpetrators brought to justice, the game destroyed."

Raiden pauses to stare grimly out at us. "And that is what we have done. For decades, there was no trace of the game. Many of us assumed Valkyrie was stolen to be a trophy, a crown of power to show off in private, alongside the Fabergé egg and the Rembrandt. Or was the game mislaid, the thief long dead? We wondered if it sat stowed in secret somewhere, forgotten in a basement. Accidentally discarded in a landfill, piled under the dirty diapers and defunct electronics? Unfortunately, we were wrong."

He sighs. "The game is here. Six months ago, we heard of four teenage players. Now, there are four hundred. It happens at night. In secret. Where? We don't know. The people behind it are cunning. We believe the rollout has been decades in the making. The perpetrators know we search for it. So far, they have made no mistakes."

He shakes his head in apparent bafflement as he paces the stage. "Louisiana left us no manual. All we know about Valkyrie is that it spans three nights, three chances to win, and it was designed for teenage players." He waves a hand. "All winners of the game are visited by an ethereal Valkyrie, a death spirit. She will transport them off the battlefield, away to Valhalla—paradise—never to return. Apart from this myth of the Valkyrie, and of course, the famous Wagner opera"—he pauses to clear his throat—"we know little else."

"Excuse me, Mr. Raiden?" interjects Franz, raising his hand. "Can you be more specific when you say winners are transported 'off the battlefield, away to Valhalla'?"

"Smuggled? Murdered? Assisted suicide? We have no idea. We had hoped the challenge of Valkyrie would preclude these disappearances from ever occurring, that it would end up to be a hollow ruse. Then, tragically, four months ago, Valkyrie had its first winner. George Grenfell."

He turns to study the boy on the screen. "There will be others. Unless the game is found, the criminals behind its contraband release exposed and prosecuted. We are working closely with Metropolitan Police. But Valkyrie has so far proved to be confoundingly elusive. How did the boy first hear of the game? How was he recruited? Where do they all play?"

Raiden shrugs, wringing his hands. "As representatives of the Veda estate, obviously we wish to protect children, first and foremost. But we also seek to preserve the integrity of the Darkly legacy. We wish to spare the Louisiana Veda brand any further indignity."

"You mean you want the value of her games to continue to skyrocket," says Mouse.

"Ja, that is correct," says Franz. "Louisiana Veda is enjoying a resurgence. If she is canceled for this terrible thing she created, even if it *was* stolen, there will be no more posthumous glory for her. And no more lucrative job for you, Mr. Raiden."

If the man is offended by these accusations, he gives no indication. He actually seems amused. "You will have full access to the Darkly grounds, including, with special permission, the factory. You will reside right here on the island for the duration of the internship—"

"Excuse me?"

"*This* freezing shithole?"

"What?"

"You're joking."

Raiden holds up his hands. "*For your own protection.* Here, you will be safe. You can work in peace. Louisiana Veda was an artist. Decades ahead of her time. Alive, she was fawned over and exalted. She was also naive and preyed upon. As a result, even today her list of enemies is long. There are a great many people who still wish to hurt her, and now, because of your association with Darkly, the same goes for you."

Raiden barely pauses to let this sinister declaration sink in— *we are in danger?*—before he claps suddenly, an official smile.

"What else? Details of George Grenfell and the night he vanished may be found in Cabin One. You will reside in Cabins Eight and Nine. Food will be stocked weekly in the canteen. You can communicate with your old lives at the business center at Derringer Street. Darkly Island is tucked into the North Sea six miles off the coast of England. The town of Thornwood is closest, accessible by boat. The captain will transport you to and from the pier. She resides in the lighthouse on the far western shore. Call her any hour, should you require assistance. Pick up a new mobile from the boxes in the back. You will be given a van for transportation. Every Wednesday, starting tomorrow morning, at least one of you will travel to my offices in London to brief me on your progress. On behalf of Derringer Street and the Louisiana Veda Foundation, we thank you for your service."

He bows. And then—I can't quite believe it—a glance at his watch, a sniff, as if he just paid the check at a restaurant where the food wasn't as good as he'd hoped, Nile Raiden is leaving.

Everyone stares, bewildered, as he jogs down the stage steps. Then they lurch to their feet.

"Hold up, Mr. Raiden—"

"This is bullshit!"

"So we're monkeys in a Darkly laboratory?"

"I will be hereby heading home, danke."

Nile Raiden stops at the doors.

And when he turns to face us, that's when I realize his blustery corporate confusion, the bumbling worry, is an act. Our outraged reaction now—our protests and complaints—this is the moment he has been waiting for.

"Dear me. I forgot to mention it, didn't I? Yes, by all means, *leave* if you don't have the stomach for it, if it's all too much to bear. You can all fly home tonight and be done with me, Darkly, and Louisiana."

He tilts his head. "Of course, none of you have a legal leg to stand on. I personally wrote your contracts. You gave it all away—your voice and history, your memories of what happens here. Stay, leave—it makes no difference. Anything you overhear, unearth, if it delights or horrifies, you must remain silent about it for the rest of your lives. Failure to do so will damn you. And I'm not talking about a court of law. Derringer Street has a global reach."

He clasps his hands as he watches these ominous words sink in. "But before you book your flights home to your thrice-divorced mom on Percocet, the billionaire magnate father who can't remember your middle name, your Art of Perfecting the Smile certification course, the moth-eaten junk shop, the trek to O'Malley's at three a.m. to pry your drunken father singing 'The Fields of Athenry' off the back booth by the dartboard"—he sighs theatrically—"do consider what you are giving up. The good you might do for George Grenfell. For yourselves. This internship, however odd or dangerous, is your winning lottery ticket. A boon that I'm certain will never happen for any of you ever again. So, until tomorrow?"

With a knowing smile, he slips out. The door thuds closed.

Everyone is too stunned to move.

Then Torin gasps, tears in her eyes. "I'm getting on that boat. Right now."

Franz nods. "Me too."

"I *told* you all something was off," says Everleigh. "But would you listen? No. Too blinded by the star power of Alabama Vida, or whoever the hell this woman is—*was*—"

"We'll go to the newspapers," says Poe. "Blow the lid on this internship. We already have public interest. Everyone will be dying to know what this is all about. A scam. And anyway, no nondisclosure agreement stands if there is a physical threat or safety issue."

"That man is pretty confident he has his bases covered," says

Cooper. "I mean, he outright threatened us. He even implied that Derringer Street owns the newspapers. And our lives. And futures. Didn't you hear him? 'Derringer Street has a global reach'?"

"Those contracts we all signed," says Franz. "Anyone actually read them?"

"That was all hot-air intimidation," says Mouse. "The man has nothing on us."

"Yeah," says Torin. "I mean, they can't do this. We have, like, basic human rights and freedoms—"

I can still hear them arguing as I grab a phone from the box and slip out.

Nile Raiden is far ahead, moving swiftly down the path, shrugging on his trench coat. He's on the phone—probably updating one of his Derringer Street partners on orientation.

It's not promising. They appear to be utterly useless.

He spots me, but glances away with bored indifference before vanishing down the steps.

I hurry after him, curious to see where he's headed. I step up onto the landing, and—after a tense exchange with the captain and the two other men—he boards the *Elvira*. Then they're taking off into the fog, heading back toward the mainland, I can only guess.

I start down the stone path, following it through the overgrown hillside, where it cuts harrowingly close to the edge of the cliff. It leads me straight to a slumped gray-shingled cottage.

CABIN 1 reads the weathered sign by the door.

14

There's nothing much here, only a long wood table and chairs, desk lamps, and a folder.

I pick it up. It's exactly as Raiden said: a few papers about the case and a photo of George.

Chipping Norton Constabulary. Subject, George Grenfell, returned home by train from his boarding school, the Bromsbury School, on the evening of Friday, February 2nd—

I shrug off my backpack and pull over a chair to continue reading.

Then the creak of the door makes me turn.

Everleigh shuffles in. With a solemn stare, she takes a seat across from me, pulling off her coat without a word.

I assume it's only she who decided to stay. But the door swings open, and Poe, Mouse, Torin, Franz, and Cooper all file in—reluctantly, like this is some kind of mandatory high school detention. They take a seat around the table, no explanation, not even the barest smile. All of us are adjusting to the strange new reality—this Darkly game into which we have been collectively thrown. Seven pawns assembling on the opening square.

I know why they changed their minds, of course.

It's the same reason I decided to stay. The Dia Gannon who exists off this island, the lonely and awkward Nana reeking of mothballs, I don't want to be her anymore. And as much as I dislike Nile Raiden, however manipulative he and his firm may or may not be, I believe he was telling the truth when he said this is a winning lottery ticket, one I will never have again.

"My mom is the 'thrice-divorced mom on Percocet,'" announces Franz quietly.

This elicits a few sad chuckles.

"And my dad is the billionaire magnate," says Poe. "I just visited him in New York. His second assistant penciled me in for fifteen minutes, between breakfast with top investors and ringing the opening bell of the stock exchange. My mother—a woman of uncertain origin and repute—was a cabaret dancer at Folies Bergère he spent twelve minutes with eighteen years ago. So you can imagine how much he lives for seeing me each year."

Everyone takes in this frank confession with startled silence.

I had not thought anything could make Poe more beautiful. But now, knowing his family life is scandalous, filled with irate proclamations, slammed doors, lawsuits? It turns his profile, as he scowls out the window, into the most glorious and obscure musical rest.

"Well, I would be leaving this creepy horror movie right now and going home," blurts Torin. "Except I hate it there. My mom's in Ibiza on a honeymoon with her new husband. My dad is at a bar getting bombed. And he does get stuck in the back booth by the darts, except I usually collect him at one, not three. If I wait until three he will have another six pints and get sick all over the bathroom floor. Which I'll have to clean up. Then I'll have to buy a new bath mat."

"Derringer Street has been spying on us," says Cooper.

"Vetting us in the privacy of our own lives," adds Mouse with a shiver.

Suddenly, I recall the night I was filling out the application, how I swear I heard someone rooting around the shop. I never did get to the bottom of what it was.

Then I have an idea.

"Everleigh," I say, "what did you mean when you said you're not supposed to be here?"

She shoots me a sullen look. "My stepsister filled out the application. She's the Darkly fan. Not me. There must have been an autofill mistake. Because my name randomly got mixed up in something I know nothing about." She sniffs, wiping her eyes.

I turn to Poe. "What would you kill for?"

He runs his hand through his hair, shrugging. "I have no idea. I was under the gun preparing for Chavannes. So I had one of my tutors fill it out. Because while I am a Darkly fan and vigorous connoisseur, I couldn't waste even a minute on such an inane question. Because we are all beasts at heart. We kill for what gives us the most pleasure. Obviously."

"Obviously," says Mouse.

"Excuse me," says Franz. "Forgive my ignorance, but what is Chavannes?"

"Chavannes-de-Bogis. Switzerland. Where the annual fourteen-hour test to enter Potestas is held."

Poe holds up the tattoo on his wrist, waiting for some sort of grand recognition to dawn—except it doesn't.

"You know. The Potestas Society? Highest one percent of IQs in Mensa."

"What do the roman numerals mean?" asks Cooper, frowning at the tattoo.

"The day I passed."

He smiles, clearly used to this astonished reaction. "Yes. I see the modern world in patterns and symphonic movements arising for a few choice seconds out of quantum chaos. I know human beings to be blinkered, organic masses who follow predictable pathways of behavior, like mice in a lab. The only real mysteries for me exist beyond the speed of light. But that doesn't mean you should be intimidated. No way. I'm just a normal guy."

No one reacts, waiting for him to laugh and say he's only joking.

I sensed Poe was brilliant, of course. But now, in addition to his looks—which have not diminished but, like some crazy reverse desert mirage, have only grown more vivid with more time and closer inspection—he has an intelligence that is massive and rare? What does it mean to be that smart? It must be like having a small astrophysicist always wandering beside him.

"Okay, Einstein," says Mouse. "You're a genius. Tell us who stole Valkyrie and where George is so we can win the prize money and get out of here."

"To do that, I'd need a time machine, made out of a not-yet-invented material, using a not-yet-invented fusion, traveling at never-recorded speeds. And I'd be wearing a not-yet-invented space suit so my flesh doesn't melt. But if I were to guess? It was someone who loathed Louisiana. This person was close to her, knew her secrets, how Louisiana didn't want the game released. Planned to blackmail her with it. Only shortly after the theft, Louisiana died. So the plan was defunct. Hence, the game sat dormant for so long. Now there is a new plan in motion."

I consider Poe in stunned awe all over again. *Someone who loathed Louisiana?* He made those connections *that* fast while we're all still getting our minds around a twenty-ninth Darkly game?

This makes Poe clear his throat and sigh politely, like the statesman of a rich and exotic country at the UN waiting for someone to figure out how to translate.

Franz whistles. "Ja. Well, I also did not have a lot of time. But my reasons were not so impressive. I was attending Mystical Ancient Day, the international paleocontact summit in Oslo. I got bitterly drunk alone in my hotel room, and I submitted a single idiotic sentence. That I would kill to know the truth behind the helicopter hieroglyph carving from the Temple of Seti the First. I didn't think I'd win in ten million epochs."

"You wrote one sentence. *One sentence?*" Mouse scoffs. "My application was a work of art. Forty thousand artfully chosen words, a treatise on how I would kill to make the world a better place, which would require me being president of the United States, a budget of ten billion, and over two hundred invisible assassinations and targeted acts of global blackmail. I cited Plato, Bob Dylan, Descartes, Nietzsche, Stalin, to name just a few, and I worked on the essay every day for three months, a political science professor at Harvard editing my work. I was polishing until three minutes before the midnight deadline. I was one hundred percent certain I would win."

"What about you?" I ask Torin.

"I wrote that I would kill to find my birth parents. I'm

adopted. But my biological mom used an alias. I've never been able to find her."

"Well, I didn't even submit a single word," notes Cooper.

"Excuse me?" says Mouse, making an outraged face.

"I mean, yeah, I *registered*. But I had to attend an Embalming and Cremation Success seminar in Boca. On the drive home, our car broke down. My dad and I had to hike for six hours on the side of a highway through the entire state of Georgia to find a gas station. I missed the deadline."

She nods at our confused stares. "We own a bankrupt funeral home. I help out because my parents can't afford an employee. Raiden was talking about me when he mentioned the Art of Perfecting the Smile course. I'm studying mortuary science online to get my certification as an FD. Funeral director. It's super important for families to see a peaceful countenance on loved ones if there's an open casket. And, no, putting makeup on a corpse is not weird for me."

Her face flushes, her fingers nervously flipping the gold eye charm on her necklace.

"What does that symbol mean?" I ask.

"Morticians' Kids Alliance. We Zoom once a month." She shrugs. "I don't have a lot of friends."

"Me neither," says Franz.

With a sad smile, he slowly un-Velcros his neck brace and places it on the table, staring at it.

"Ja, so, I have zero spine, neck, or posture issues? I started wearing this in public because it makes people smile when they look at me. Sometimes they even offer assistance. I prefer that to them not seeing me at all. I have the kind of face people see through."

His words come and go with an intoxicating simplicity. For a minute no one says a word.

Something about the emptiness of this cabin, the assembled strangers, the gray nothingness in the windows making it feel as if we are suspended in the sky—there is freedom here. Somehow it's so easy to talk, to confess everything and anything to these total strangers.

"I think I know why we were chosen," I say.

Everyone, still digesting the admission from Franz, turns to me.

"They needed a certain type of kid to make it into Valkyrie. Kids who are curious and intelligent, but with zero family oversight. Loners."

"You mean, if something bad happens to us," says Everleigh slowly, "if some Valkyrie comes in the night to take us away to Valhalla—kidnapping us, saving us from our lives, or whatever—they know our parents will be too preoccupied or disorganized or drunk to find out what really happened to us."

I nod. "Something like that."

An uneasy silence descends.

"There's a fantastical leap in your hypothesis, Arcadia," says Poe, crossing his arms. "Supposing we *are* each bright and scrappy latchkey kids with a perfect amount of drive, grit, and baggage, who scored high on some secret Derringer Street algorithm. Fine. But out of six hundred thousand kids, *we* have the best chances at cracking Valkyrie?"

His skeptical gaze moves to Franz, the neck brace, around to the others, and stops on me—the suggestion being that while he is willing to accept he scored high on some secret behavior chart, he doubts the rest of us should be included.

I shrug. "We must fit some kind of profile. That's why they chose us. I mean, my cat submitted my application."

I wait for one of them to laugh, to tell me not only is their mom their best friend, but she's a woman of high moral standing. How their dad would swoop in like a superhero to avenge their death. Even my own head is chattering: *It's not true. No, Gigi, Agatha, and Basil would move mountains to save you from harm.*

But then picturing them as they doubtlessly are right now, bumbling around Prologue looking for a permanent marker, without the slightest inkling of where I actually am, how easy it was to fool them, imagining how my mom receiving any phone call from smooth-talking Raiden would probably start flirting, wondering if he's married, mentally opening a London Prologue II on some tree-lined cobblestone mews before she even hangs up—I know I'm right.

The others appear to be drawing the same conclusion. They all have the same mad look, like kids who have finally climbed the ladder and taken a peek inside the attic they were always deathly afraid of—realizing with a sort of giddy lightness that there was never a ghost hiding up there, only piles of junk.

"Now what?" asks Everleigh.

I open the folder and remove the photo of George Grenfell.

"We find him."

9 JULY 1985   © WOOD RAIDEN

LOUISIANA VEDA, PIONEER AND INVENTOR, FOUND DEAD

Louisiana Veda, founder and creator of the popular Darkly empire of mysterious games, was found dead yesterday from apparent suicide. She was 36.

Police responded at 11:20 p.m. to an anonymous phone call reporting a body discovered in the Thames River, close to Tower Bridge, according to Inspector Thomas Stone.

The mogul infamously started her gaming company, Darkly, out of a vacant classroom when she was a homeless art student in London. Her first game, Ophelia, a mind-bending locked-safe labyrinth of wit and murder, which the *Globe and Mail* called "more of a dark lake in which one wishes to drown than a board game," sold one million copies in its first six months and spawned clubs, books, secret societies, and a renaissance of the board game as a coveted art form. Prime Minister Margaret Thatcher went on to chide the House of Commons and the British public for "calling in sick and causing England to grind to a halt in order to stay home and play Prodigal," Darkly's third blockbuster.

Darkly Eve became a cultural phenomenon, whereupon for over a decade on December 24 at midnight, a new game was released to great fanfare, with shelves clearing in seconds and public fighting, which at times turned violent, driving prices of the controversial new releases into the stratosphere.

More recently, Darkly has been plagued by a spate of wrongful death lawsuits, following the release of games critics have called too sinister and dangerous, including 1980's banned Rasputin.

Apart from a single *Tatler* profile at the outset of her meteoric rise and a few scant TV spots, Veda shunned formal interviews—opting for staged photo ops with doppelgängers and elaborate trickery, which increasingly drew fire from fans. Veda rebuffed astronomical bids for her company's sale from Mattel, Hasbro, and Milton Bradley. Proclaiming herself a "legendary spinster," she never married and is survived by no known relatives.

Darkly representatives could not b reached for comment.

15

"**T**ake the next exit," says Torin beside me, frowning at the directions.

"The town is called St. Hapsburg," says Poe, leaning forward an inch from my shoulder.

I try to ignore his close proximity while steering the dented white unmarked van—which reeks of mildew and screams *This vehicle is suspicious!*—down a busy highway called the M11. Cars careen past on all sides, more than a few honking because I'm finding it hard to remember to keep on the wrong side of the road while not barreling into the guardrail.

I had hoped my decision to leave the island this afternoon to visit George Grenfell's house—where he disappeared—would give us a new sense of purpose and camaraderie. But it has not thawed the unsettling mood.

Not that I blame anyone. I can feel how flimsy this is, how strange.

One awkward school photo, plus three pages of piecemeal

information, hastily typed, was all there was to read in the Derringer Street file on George Grenfell.

He is fifteen, an only child. There was nothing to read about his hobbies, habits, family, or friends—only that he had been home for winter holiday from the Bromsbury School, a boarding school in the village of Hawling, when he vanished sometime in the night.

Nothing in his room was amiss—no broken window, no evidence of a struggle. He left everything behind—phone, wallet, laptop, clothes, even his sneakers.

The only evidence that George's disappearance was tied to Valkyrie was that days later, performing the umpteenth sweep of George's dorm room at school, an investigator found a menu for Chinese takeout pinned to a bulletin board.

Flying Swallow Chinese Palace. Classic Dim Sum.

Met Police were aware of the theft of Valkyrie—and had been ever since the game was first stolen in 1985. Last fall, when Derringer Street began to hear whispers of the game's emergence, the Art and Antiquities Unit ordered all officers to be on the lookout for flyers.

One of the little things known about Valkyrie was that one of the main gaming elements, traditionally in the form of dice, playing cards, tokens, or a spinner, was the public posting of homemade flyers, the kind found on a million street corners: ads for guitar lessons and lost cats stapled to telephone poles, takeout menus and pizza coupons tucked into doorways.

The officer, having read the memo about Valkyrie, called the number to Flying Swallow Chinese Palace on a whim. He was greeted with the recording of a woman whispering, "Hello, George. Will you play Valkyrie with me tonight?"

After the recording played once, the line was defunct. A trace of the number revealed it was linked to a prepaid phone in the Czech Republic.

That was everything. There was nothing else to read.

This lack of information had plunged the seven of us all over again into sullen silence. Poe took off to inspect the island. "I'll check for booby traps," he'd announced cryptically over his shoulder. Mouse and Franz were hungry, so they went to find the canteen— a sagging green cottage with a musty kitchen stocked with boxes of Special K, cans of cucumber seltzer, a fridge filled with wilted fruits and vegetables. Torin, Cooper, and Everleigh left to find our bunks, Cabins 8 and 9.

By the time I caught up, finding the twin gray cottages at opposite ends of a black pond choking with weeds—the girls had already claimed the top three bunks by the windows, leaving me with a choice of claustrophobic bottom bunks. I chose the one under Cooper. The mattress and pillow seemed the least musty. I pulled my suitcase beside my bed and unpacked the few things I'd brought into a single drawer, noticing how the walls were so warped I could see between the beams straight to the outside.

The feeling was creeping in that if I didn't get moving, do something, I, too, would plunge into doubt, succumb to the feeling that I should go back where I belong—with the cobwebs in the vintage tea set aisle of Prologue.

That was when I announced the idea to go to the mainland. There was only one place to start—where George Grenfell disappeared.

My idea was met with zero enthusiasm. Torin and Cooper only stared at me, then muttered that it was already pretty late. So I took off on my own, finding the captain mooring the *Elvira* to the dock, having just returned from dropping off Raiden and his goons.

"I'd like to go to the mainland, please."

The captain looked irate, clearly on the verge of telling me off before jerking upright with a gasp, eyes bulging.

"Bloody hell, it's a whole gang of ye?"

I turned to see in surprise the other interns making their way down the steps after me.

"You'll be botherin' me day and night, won't ye, go here and there? Now I'm a chauffeur service, fancy that. Well, one trip a day, no more, you hear? And the return by three. Or the sea'll make a feast outta ye."

Now I am driving everyone down a gloomy country road, past empty green pastures and broken stone walls.

"The house should be coming up on the right," says Torin, pointing.

I slow, making the turn—and immediately slam the brakes.

A massive wrought-iron gate bars the way, an elegant *G* emblazoned in the middle.

Beyond it stretches a driveway, straight and meticulous. And at the end, so far in the distance it looks like a painting, stands the house. Actually, more like *fortress*. It's the kind of place that has its own echo and postal code, and can be seen from outer space.

"This can't be right," Torin says.

"Sure it's not *Prince* George?" says Mouse from the back seat.

"Fourteen Deer Park, St. Hapsburg," says Poe. "That's the address written in the file."

"You'd think Raiden would find it relevant to mention George disappeared from Buckingham Palace," says Franz. "He's probably not even kidnapped, but trapped in a dumbwaiter in the fourth ballroom."

"The house has its own Wikipedia page," says Cooper, squinting at her phone. " 'Manderson Gate is a Grade Two–listed country manor. The estate was first constructed by the Duke of Beaufort in 1685 with over one hundred rooms, six hundred park acres, and twenty-three separate structures, including a hunting lodge. The seat is currently owned by Roger Studdart Grenfell, long-standing member of the House of Lords. During World War Two, the estate served as a psychiatric hospital for the British Army.' "

"Amputations, shell shocks, shanty surgeries, and morphine," says Poe with a nod.

"We cannot go in there unannounced," says Torin.

"I bet George's disappearance has nothing to do with Louisiana Veda," says Mouse. "He was kidnapped because someone is trying to extort money from the family."

"May I help you?" a posh male voice croaks on the intercom.

I roll down the window, suddenly unsure. Our pretense for dropping by today was concocted on the ride here, when we believed George was an ordinary boy who vanished from an ordinary house—not a palace ripped from *Nicholas and Alexandra*.

"Hello? Anyone there?"

"Go on, you can do it," whispers Poe teasingly, his dark eyes boring into mine. I have the disturbing thought that he's so brilliant, he knows exactly what I'm going to say before I do.

"Hi," I blurt. "So sorry to bother you. We're friends of George's from the Bromsbury School. We hoped to pay our respects to the family."

There's a crackle of static. "George's mates from Broms, you say?"

"Mates from Broms?" whispers Franz with a worried cringe.

"Yes, sir," I manage.

"Sir? Should she be saying 'sir'?"

"Shhh," says Cooper.

"One moment."

For minutes, nothing happens.

I am sure we're going to be coolly ordered to get lost, and the seven of us will have to come up with a new plan.

But then there is an electronic beep, and—much to my surprise—the iron gates float open before us.

16

Manderson Gate is even more forbidding up close—towering limestone columns dappled with orange stains that look like they hail from the 1500s. The facade of fifty dark windows dully stares us down. The serene perfection of the landscaping is surreal—geometric green lawns, sculptures of goddesses, gumdrop trees, walls of forest in all directions as far as the eye can see.

A tall man in a gray suit and earpiece—he appears to be an actual live butler—waits for us in the massive doorway.

I slip out of the van, hurrying after the others across the gravel. I notice Everleigh, with her shoulders hunched, can't stop shivering, and Cooper is scowling up at the mansion like its very existence is a personal insult. Thankfully, Poe appears to be in his element. He jogs up the stone steps with an easy shrug.

"We apologize for the unannounced arrival. But we happened to be nearby, and of course we've all been worried sick about George."

"The Grenfells very much appreciate the visit. Right this way, please."

With a wave, the butler escorts us into a marble entrance hall—not telling us to use the servants' entrance or to remove our shoes, to my surprise, not even with the slightest look askance at our crusty hair from the boat ride. He whisks us across the black-and-white tiles, past marble busts, a twisted staircase. There are eighteenth-century portraits of men in red foxhunting jackets, women in tiaras and pale satin gowns. We file down a dim hallway, past a dining room, a glass conservatory stuffed with exotic plants. He leads us into a sitting room.

All I can think is how much Basil, Agatha, and Gigi would be awed by this place, how funny it is that we make our living saving and selling the stale little crumbs cast off from estates like Manderson Gate. But here it sits in its majestic splendor, the entire six-tiered cake.

"Do make yourselves comfortable. Mrs. Grenfell will be right with you." The butler ducks out.

I take a seat on the couch to keep myself from getting too nervous. Unfortunately, I see that the others are completely breaking character, because George's privileged schoolmates from Broms would probably *not* be wandering around with wide eyes and freaked-out gasps of "Oh. My. God. *Seriously?*"

Poe pulls a tattered leather book off the shelf. "First-edition *Great Expectations*. Not bad. Oh, never mind." He sighs with feigned disgust. "It's not even *signed* by Dickens. What a load of camel dung."

Everyone giggles; then, hearing a sniff, we fall silent, turning to see a petite blond woman watching us from the doorway.

She knots closed a voluminous terry-cloth robe over a black one-piece bathing suit, a royal *G*—like the one on the gate—embroidered at the shoulder. Her hair is wet at the temples. She seems to have been summoned from swimming laps in the pool.

"Thank goodness you've come," she says.

None of us move. This is not the greeting we expected.

"Sorry. I'm Penelope, George's mum." She smiles warmly, clasping her hands as she hurries toward us. "I've been waiting for you for weeks. I asked the school to send along the names of some of George's friends, so I could reach out. When they said they didn't have that information, I was irate. I marched in there, and—" She swallows, shaking her head. "I mean, George had *friends*. We know that he did. Yes, he's shy. But wherever he goes, he's loved. And the police need to know who these kids are, so they can ask questions and find out what this is all about—"

She falls silent, a hand over her mouth, seemingly embarrassed by the outburst.

"I'm sorry. It's been a difficult time. At least you're here now."

She takes a stiff seat opposite me. Poe, Cooper, and the others crowd around, exchanging covert looks—probably as surprised as I am by Mrs. Grenfell. She's so thin and delicate, with her perfectly manicured hands and champagne hair in a meticulous twist. She has the air of a fragile origami crane that could be destroyed by a few drops of water.

"So you all attend Broms? You're the same year as my George?"

"Yes," says Poe smoothly. "Most of us are on the foreign-exchange program. George was tasked with being our ambassador. He was brilliant. Really made us feel at home."

"We also bonded over the school newspaper," blurts Cooper.

"And the mutual feeling of being der Außenseiter," says Franz. "The outsider and misfit."

I am sure Mrs. Grenfell is finding all of this overblown and suspicious. But then, she seems grateful to hear any detail about her son, however random.

"I didn't know he wrote for the newspaper. Only his photography. Geometry. And violin. He loved being on the cross-country team. That was a new sport. And of course there was his band."

She says it with peculiar emphasis, eyeing our faces closely.

"Forgive me," says Poe with a frown. "What band do you mean?"

She shrugs. "Last winter, every time Roger and I called the halls to talk to George, the boys who answered said he was out practicing his band. Do you know anything about it?"

We exchange looks, shaking our heads.

"You told the police?" asks Cooper.

"Of course. They confirmed George played in the chamber music orchestra. But that's not a band. I tried to find out more. But no one has any idea. Was it code for something else? Everyone wishes I would stop asking."

She takes another frustrated breath, tilting her head. "Was my son involved in something illegal? You can tell me. Please. I promise not to say a word to your parents. Or anyone."

We eye each other uncomfortably again.

"Sorry," says Torin. "We don't know anything like that."

"Ja, we probably know even less than you do about what happened," says Franz.

At this, Mrs. Grenfell seems to deflate. It's obvious she knows nothing about Valkyrie or Louisiana Veda's connection to her missing son. Keeping her in the dark must be at the insistence of Derringer Street. They are surely spooked and on high alert, especially given the powerful standing of the Grenfell family. Still, I find it cruel that she knows nothing.

"What is the status of the investigation?" asks Franz. "The school refuses to tell us."

The question—stated in Franz's flat German accent—sounds strange. But again, Mrs. Grenfell seems too distraught to notice.

"They treat me and Roger the same way," she says. "We call every week, demanding answers. They have nothing new to say. Neither do the police. My son vanished into thin air. Yes, I dismantled their kidnapping command center. But a bunch of detectives sitting around my house day and night, eating pastries and making a mess, waiting for a ransom call that never comes? We did that for weeks, and it scared them off—I'm sure of it. All day I sit here waiting, wondering how long this will go on. Did he run away? Was he afraid of someone? Did he not want to be George Grenfell any longer?"

Her voice breaks as she wipes the tears from her eyes. "You're all coming, aren't you, to the candlelight vigil for George this Saturday? We're walking the streets. Shining flashlights into every shadow of that school. Because the truth of where he went is there. I'm sure of it."

"We'll be there," says Poe.

"Mrs. Grenfell," I say gently, sitting forward, "I wonder if we can take a quick look at George's room? I'm sure the police went through it. But maybe there's something—I don't know—that we will recognize as important that the police somehow missed."

She sits up in surprise. "Of course. Come."

She's already on her feet, reknotting her robe, a hopeful smile—which makes me feel guilty for lying to her as she escorts us up a staircase, past the crystal chandelier as big as a Volkswagen. She races down one landing, then another, beckoning us to keep up, as if George were kidnapped only a few minutes ago and there's not a second to waste. An anxious hand fumbling with the wet hair at the back of her neck, she glides past floral bedrooms, bouquets of fresh lavender, and medieval tapestries, into a remote wing that is clearly George's: hunter-green walls and vintage posters of David Bowie.

Mrs. Grenfell opens a door to a dark bedroom, ushering us inside. It feels—and smells—like the reptile exhibit of a failing zoo. George's violin case sits like a small black casket on a carved chest by a music stand.

"So this is George's secret lair," says Poe with a knowing nod.

"He loved spending time holed up in here practicing his music." Mrs. Grenfell moves to the window, throwing open the heavy curtains, revealing a princely view—perfect green lawn, strict gray drive, the wrought-iron gate at the far end. "Take a look. Spend as much time as you need. Call me if you find anything."

We eye each other in astonishment. Were we really just invited to snoop unchecked around George Grenfell's room?

No one says a word until we hear Mrs. Grenfell's sandals retreating downstairs.

"Okay, soldiers," whispers Poe with a grin, flipping open the latches on the violin case. "Let's find out the name of George's mysterious band."

I search George's closet. Torin roots through the bureau. Poe tackles the desk, bed, under the mattress. Everleigh checks under the carpet and all furniture, and behind the framed posters of art and music festivals hanging on the walls: Venice Biennale, Miami Music. Mouse inspects the framed photos on the bedside—mostly George posing with his mom and dad—even opening the backs of the frames, in case there are hidden notes inside.

George's father, Roger Grenfell—illustrious member of the House of Lords—is much older than his wife. In all photos, he resembles an unwieldy old marble bust that can never quite find the ideal placement in a room.

George looks like his mother—delicate and spoiled, but also a little sensitive and interesting, with sunken, sleepless eyes and an anxious mouth. All of the trinkets he's collected, displayed on window ledges and mirrors and piled in junk drawers—bar napkins and caviar menus from Gstaad, drink stirrers, key chains, stickers, a tarnished silver saltshaker engraved with the words *Why not?*—suggest the exact life that Manderson Gate resoundingly proclaims the second you turn down the drive: *This is a swimming-pool, hidden-door life of parties and weekend boat rides, and if you're wondering what it all means, you're not meant to be here.*

All I can think of is the sad way Mrs. Grenfell talked about George's *friends.* By the look of this room, he didn't have any.

But he liked math—trigonometry and geometry. Mouse finds desk drawers stuffed with protractors and compasses, sheets of graph and tracing paper, where George drew fastidious triangles, conch shell spirals, rectangles missing one side. On one cluster of pages a single 4 was repeated at least fifty times, each line assigned different numbers.

"He has a thing for four," mutters Poe, inspecting the drawings. "Like Einstein and one-thirty-seven."

On a bulletin board there are photos on display. They were obviously taken by George—stark black-and-white forests of pine, zebra shadows of tree trunks in the snow. They are drab, not very good, but they all evoke a feeling of bored waiting, like George was always expecting something to emerge from those trees. That makes me like them. Because I understand it, the endless staring at quiet, unmoving things.

Cooper searches George's camera collection—two Leicas and a Canon. Poe inspects the violin case, violin, bow, packets of extra strings, the chest filled with sheet music, Beethoven and Bach and Liszt. Mouse has the idea that maybe George took a photo of Valkyrie, the secret setting where they play the game—or even this band.

But no—the digital camera only has twelve pictures of cows grazing in a pasture. The film cameras are empty.

Franz goes through the sheets on George's bed, pillow, pillow-cases, the old toys stacked along the shelves.

After almost an hour of searching, we have found nothing.

"So here sat George," says Poe, taking a seat at his desk. "If he was only here a single day and made it through three nights of Valkyrie, he played at school. When he came home for the break, he must have known he had won. He was expecting the Valkyrie. He said nothing to his parents. So he wasn't afraid."

I step to the window. "You can see the gate from here. Maybe he saw a car in the middle of the night and there was some kind of signal that it was time."

"He went willingly," says Mouse. "A struggle would have woken the whole house."

"Really?" says Torin. "He was so brainwashed that he just strolled out of his life? I mean, I can understand hating living here, Little Lord Fauntleroy trapped in the castle. But wouldn't he have been scared? Wouldn't he have left some message or clue behind for his mom, or the police, in case Valhalla isn't all it's cracked up to be?"

"He knew in his heart he was going somewhere wonderful," whispers Everleigh.

She steps beside me, staring out the window, a far-off expression on her face.

"Okay, well, I have an idea," says Mouse.

He is studying the forest-green wool scarf hooked on the back of the door. There is a gold patch at the bottom with a crest.

THE BROMSBURY SCHOOL, it reads. NON DUCOR DUCO.

"'I am not led. I lead,'" says Poe.

Penelope Grenfell is upset at the news we didn't find anything—and to see us go. She waves at us fitfully from the front steps as we drive away.

"Come back anytime. And I'll see you at the candlelight vigil!"

Within minutes, we are winding down country roads, heading toward the Bromsbury School. Mouse figured out it was only thirty minutes away.

"George probably went home every weekend," says Franz. "It's so close."

"Yeah," says Cooper. "He needed his staff to do his laundry."

"That's unfair," says Torin. "I mean, yes, you're right. He is incredibly spoiled. But I like George. I don't know why, but I do."

"I like him, too," says Franz. "I believe he wanted to change his life. That must have been why he played Valkyrie."

Mouse's idea is to break into the school somehow, find a way to follow George's footsteps. If we learn his schedule, we can wander the same paths, classrooms, and hallways that he did, so we can look for some sign of Valkyrie.

Not that we'd be able to recognize it. Would it be a random flyer advertising horseback riding lessons or a used piano for sale? Did someone at school tip George off to the game, tell him what to look for?

We are hashing it over, when swinging the white van up to the entrance, again we are confronted by an iron gate. This one is even taller and more severe than the one at Manderson Gate.

"Another barrier to keep out the ugly, unloved, and unlucky," says Cooper.

"Us, in other words," says Franz.

"Speak for yourself," says Poe.

On the opposite side, across a deserted cobblestone courtyard, sits a hulking Gothic building with turrets and towers, windows of stained glass. But these whimsical details look downcast and glum, given that the limestones are stained black like mascara after a century-long sob.

"They definitely use 'cane' as a verb in there," says Poe.

"We could pose as prospective students," says Torin. "Get a tour of campus?"

"They'd see right through it," I say.

"Ja, no student goes in there willingly," says Franz.

A man and woman emerge along a side path from the woods, heading toward the building entrance. They notice our van and stop, frowning. I shift into reverse, swing out onto the road, and we take off again.

"So they're still on edge after what happened to George," notes Poe.

We cruise along the fence, passing another gated entrance, where, sure enough, two uniformed police guards stand outside an entry booth. The extensive Bromsbury grounds are visible beyond the bars. I slow, noticing that a bell has rung, marking the end of the school day. Students are spilling down the paths, everyone in uniform—dark-green blazers and gray slacks.

We reach the end of the school property and coast along the main street of Hawling. From the thatched cottages lining the road, it looks like nothing much has changed here in three hundred years—a café, a bookstore called Fine Print, a pub, and a church.

"Dia, pull over," Poe orders, pointing at a vacant parking space behind a Bromsbury School bus. "We'll split up. It's Darkly game theory. The sea serpent in Eighteen Lost Icelandic Sailors exploding into fourteen small serpents is six hundred times more lethal than one vicious large. Torin, you go with Franz and Cooper. Mouse with Everleigh. I'll go with Dia. We will commence an outrageous offensive. End of the day, no more classes, everyone's off to play rugby and cricket. We'll look like students. Teachers will be too tired to notice they've never seen us before. Try to get in any way you can, dorm windows, service entrances, air shafts. Take photos of all flyers. Maybe George was a loner. But somebody in that school knows about him. And somebody knows about Valkyrie."

Everyone is struck by his sudden intensity. I sense from the excited gleam in his eyes that the spiked iron fence around the Bromsbury School is just another maze for him to solve in record time, a living labyrinth that he hopes might present a moderate challenge.

I park the van, and though Poe and the others immediately file out, I hesitate, a little nervous. Because not only did Poe arrange to be with me—and only me—he left his hand on my shoulder three seconds too long, and I'm pretty sure it had nothing to do with finding a good parking place.

I'm about to climb out when I realize Everleigh is still in the back. She seems to be quietly crying again.

"Are you okay?" I ask.

But she only glares, head down, and ducks out.

It's decided that Torin, Cooper, and Franz will head along the east side of the fence. Mouse and Everleigh will hike north around the corner, away from the guards, where the grounds are mostly wooded.

As for Poe and me—without a word, he motions for me to follow as he slips around to the back of the school bus.

I move beside him, wondering what he's planning. Before I even know what he's doing, his hands grip my waist and he lifts me right into the empty bus, pushing me forward and scrambling in after me. Then we are both crouched on the floor in front of the last seat, Poe's knee touching my thigh as he peers down the deserted aisle.

"What are we doing?" I whisper.

"Hitchhiking." He leans over me to check out the window, so I catch a glimpse of his bare torso as his white T-shirt brushes my knee.

"What if this bus stays parked here all day?"

"We'll get to know each other, I suppose."

He sits back, staring at me, his muscular arms hooked around his knees. All handsome teenage boys in close proximity always reveal something gross: bad breath, teeth unbrushed, sleep in their eyes. Even Choke Newington once had dried soap behind his left ear for an entire November. But Poe is gorgeous everywhere I look.

So I focus on the bus aisle, checking over the seats, trying to maintain an expression of bored curiosity, even though it's like a cheap motel blind that keeps rolling up.

"Why were you named Utopia?"

Startled, I venture a glance back at him. He's surveying me with such intensity, it's like one of those blue alien lights shining down in a backyard, seconds before someone half-asleep in pajamas gets abducted.

"It's a family name," I say.

"No, it's not." He frowns. "Arcadia. The Greek vision of paradise. Unattainable beauty in nature. What, the word kept appearing to your mom when she was pregnant with you? First, in a women's magazine at the doctor's. Then, on a bumper sticker in traffic. But it was you who in—third grade?—ashamed at the prospect of being so boldly named 'Paradise,' downgraded to Dia. 'Day.' Ordinary and without shortage. That was a mistake."

"No, actually. That's not it."

Except, much to my horror, that *is* it—though instead of the doctor's office, it was a faded postcard of Eakins's *Arcadia* that fluttered to my mom's feet in Prologue's Rare Books. And I changed my name in *second* grade.

He tilts his head. "Quiet free-spirit Subaru, Chantilly lace and mourning artifacts, Saturday nights at the secondhand shop? Etta James and shopping carts, *Out of the Past.* No boyfriend. A desire to do something monumental, no clue what yet."

I can feel my face burning. I have to say something smart back—anything to stop this human haiku x-ray riff of scarily accurate information. How did he know Basil's favorite film noir? And while my mom drives a Toyota, it has an intense free-spirit vibe, thanks to the dream catcher on the rearview mirror.

"You've been unable to take your eyes off me since the airplane. Is it me you're after or my Darkly?"

"Excuse me. No. I am not after you."

"My Darkly, then. It'll cost you a fortune. I'm cheaper. And not as scary."

The devilish smile and the laser stare—he's teasing me.

I knew Poe was confident. How couldn't he be, with an intelligence like that and a sad family like that, all of it giving him a wounded glory in my head? But this is a different level of arrogance. His brain is some kind of supercomputer that spits out by the nanosecond automatic stunning conclusions about the world and the people in it. Which means it's time for me to move away from him before he unlocks me and sees that I believe, against my will, that he is perfect.

"People are not cheap two-dimensional paper dolls," I manage, "who can be cut out on a dotted line in three seconds."

"Paper dolls are three dimensions. I don't believe in lies, Dia. Or in wasting time."

"Human decency is a waste of time?"

"If two people like each other, they can't be kept apart any more than a set of double asteroids orbiting each other can shift their dynamical center of mass."

"Are you trying to put me to sleep?"

"Quite the opposite. I'm waking you up."

"That is so— I hardly need you of all people to wake—"

Suddenly, he jerks forward, pressing his finger to my lips.

I am delirious, certain he's going to kiss me.

Then I realize someone has just boarded the bus.

Within seconds, we are on the move, a shadow passing over the seats. We bounce down a driveway, a honk, a hard right. Poe crashes into me as we swerve downhill. I elbow him off, which makes him smirk.

The bus coughs to a halt. The doors open, and the driver climbs out.

We wait. Then, Poe is on his feet, opening the back, jumping out. He holds out his hand to help me, but I ignore it.

We are alone, behind some kind of auditorium in a lot filled with empty school buses.

Poe beckons me after him as he takes off running into the trees, down a steep slope to an open lawn where a few students are making their way along the paths.

Musty gold light, towering stone buildings, the insect tangle of old bicycles by a flagpole—the campus has an otherworldly feel. The kids all look as dated as I do, with their spectacles and low ponytails, boxy green blazers and untucked blouses, running like they're all late for church.

Poe is a distance ahead. He stops to make sure I'm still following before darting into an athletic building.

I clear the distance and yank open the door, stepping into a tidal wave of students. Everyone is rushing, pushing and pulling on sweatshirts, lacing up sneakers. It's so crowded I don't notice Poe until he's right behind me, whispering in my ear.

"Go into the girls' locker room and put on a uniform. Now. While it's still crowded."

"I don't take orders from you," I say.

"It'll help you be part of the wallpaper."

I turn, catching his wink before he's gone in the crowd.

As much as I now dislike Poe Valois III, I have to admit his idea is pretty good.

Entering the locker room, I find it not only packed, but right beside the door are two laundry bins filled with athletic uniforms. Gray shirt, dark-green shorts, white athletic socks with three green stripes on the ankle—I grab a set and slip to a back corner, undressing and pulling on the uniform. I expect someone to shout *Excuse me, who are you?*

But no one looks at me twice.

I retie my sneakers, shove my clothes in an empty locker, and move to the crowded bathroom mirror.

"Anyone know where the cross-country team meets?" I ask.

The girl beside me, dabbing on lip gloss, raises her eyebrows, probably due to my glaring American accent. She nods at a girl with black hair. "Sophie? Cross-country?"

"We start in Corning Field."

"Do the boys meet there, too?" I ask.

"No, they're down at Petersburg."

I smile my thanks and duck out, before someone asks *Who was that?*

The crowd has thinned. I can see Poe waiting for me in the front lobby, but I speed-walk down the hallway in the opposite direction, passing displays of faded black-and-white photos of 1940s cricket teams and dusty trophies. I pass an old man with a mop.

"Where do I find Petersburg Field?"

He points to the doors just ahead. "Straight and down the hill, miss."

"Thank you."

I hurry outside, down a set of deserted steps. Any moment now, I expect to see Poe, or a teacher scowling at me: *Hey, you're not supposed to be here.* But Poe's words urge me on: *an outrageous offensive.* I've decided not only to lose him, and never be alone with him again for the rest of my life, of course. But also, the thought of arriving back at the van triumphant, with a windfall of information on George Grenfell—wrangled from my own efforts and not his conceited mega-brain—fills me with silent delight.

Sure enough, as I reach the bottom of the stairs, I see a track and field below. A group of boys are stretching and chatting with a man who holds a clipboard. As I move down the next flight, the boys take off running, heading straight into the woods.

I start after them, cutting quickly across the grass into the trees, so the coach doesn't see me.

They're fast, sprinting uphill. I veer onto the narrow path behind them, though it takes all of my energy to keep them in sight, their gray shirts streaking far ahead.

Thankfully, after a minute, I see one boy lagging behind. I round the bend. Then, turning to make sure there's no one behind me, I push myself to catch up. He is slight, with freckles, and looks about thirteen.

"Hi," I say.

Gasping for air, he glances over at me with a confused frown.

"What do you know about the disappearance of George Grenfell?"

It's like I threw ice water in his face—at first, he is shocked. Then he scowls, leaping over a log and picking up his pace.

I race to keep up. "Sorry, but George ran cross-country. You knew him."

"Are you trying to get me binned?"

"They want to pretend George was never here. But he *was* here."

"You must be daft. Didn't you hear Anderson? We're not to discuss the matter. We're to leave it with the police. Any gossip among students will get you sent to the chancellor."

"But do you know where he went? Did he confide in you?"

The boy, bug-eyed, abruptly cuts away from me like I'm some sort of contagious fiend, heading into the trees—except he trips on a branch, flailing, and hits the ground with a yelp.

I stop in surprise, panting, and move to help him. But he shoves off my hand and stumbles to his feet.

"You want to play."

Chills inch down my back. I realize he means Valkyrie.

"Yes. I do."

"It's under the kiss." Wheezing, a hand slapped to his chest, he points somewhere behind me.

I turn. The forest is dense there, sloping down into what looks to be a ravine.

"What's the kiss?" I ask.

But he's sprinting off.

"Wait!"

He tears up the hill without a look back at me. Gone.

21

*I*t's under the kiss.

For a moment, I do nothing but stand there, listening to his retreating footsteps.

The forest seems to huddle around me, tentative and afraid. It's already letting go of what little daylight there was, sinking into glum shadows of late afternoon.

Suddenly, I feel how alone I am.

Is that boy playing a trick on me? Did he want to get rid of me, so he directed me clear in the opposite direction, sending me off to search for nothing in the forest?

I should have waited for Poe. I should be trespassing with a buddy, even if that buddy *is* an arrogant savant.

There was something on the boy's face I didn't like—something smug.

Clearly, he had played Valkyrie.

Do they all play Valkyrie at this strange school?

I glance over my shoulder. Nothing here but a bird scuttling through the branches.

I start down the hill, heading in the direction the boy pointed. There are dense rhododendrons, so I can't see what's at the bottom. But then it's so steep that I'm slipping, and before I can grab a branch to brace myself, I'm sliding down the incline, falling onto muddy ground.

I stumble to my feet. It's an expanse of trees knotted with brambles. I push through them. Sure enough, there is something here.

An overgrown railroad track.

I move along it, and within a few yards I see that it cuts into a sloping hill. There's a tunnel—a giant pipe, big enough to walk through. The opening looks like a dark, yawning mouth.

It's a serene, ordinary day, I remind myself as I walk toward it. *I'll take a quick look and get out of here. I'll bring the others. I am safe on a school campus with lots of security.*

There's no one here.

There is some kind of flat expanse on top of the tunnel, where it looks like students hang out, probably sneaking out of the dorms after curfew to hook up, share a cigarette. I can see a few rusted cans and a plaid blanket.

The kiss?

I stop a few feet from the tunnel entrance. It's not long. I can see the round hole of light at the opposite end. But the middle grips at darkness that is absolute.

I take out my phone, hit the flashlight, and take a step.

When I see what's hanging on the walls, it takes all of my courage not to turn and run.

Because here it is. I'm positive. Valkyrie.

There are flyers taped everywhere, too many to count—covering every inch of the tunnel, new taped on top of old on top of white on top of yellow. Black. Green. Pink. Red.

Lost Dog. Name is Bane. Does not like people. Approach slowly.

HOT male models needed, must be 18, big money

Bring justice to Tina Lynn! On Saturday, December 1, 1996, Tina Lynn Mason at 22:49 left to buy cat food at Sainsbury's . . .

I see something else ahead. Sitting in the shadows in the middle is a church pew.

DJ Club Midnight Girls Night

Pit bull puppies for sale

Work from home—never leave your couch.

Looking for love in a snowstorm? Call this number and stay warm.

There's a smell of metal and rot. I know it's only my fear, but with every step it feels like the walls are tightening around me, the light at the end stretching out of reach. The writing on the papers is all different—handwritten, typed. And the phone numbers are different, though they all start with 0800.

Vespa for sale, ice cream pink, $800

Essay Writing: the solution to all your problems

Fairy tale story time at the library, 10 am Thursdays

My eye catches something else. Far overhead, a familiar face stares out. I raise my light and step closer.

When I see who it is, my mind starts to scream.

No. It can't be real.

I reach up, trying to grab it. Suddenly, there is a grunt, a crash behind me. A shadow leaps up the wall. Before I can turn, someone shoves me hard, and I'm slammed against the wall.

I scramble to my feet and take off running. There's another crash, footsteps. I turn, catching a fleeting glimpse of my assailant sprinting out the opposite end—green Bromsbury blazer, shaggy brown hair. I stumble out into the sunlight.

A hand grips my shoulder. I whip around, screaming.

"Dia?"

It's only Cooper. Franz and Torin are jogging down the hill right behind her.

"Oh my God—Dia?"

"What happened?"

I can only stare, my mind trying to sort through the disjointed chain of events.

I was attacked. Shoved by a Bromsbury student hiding behind the church pew. But before that, taped up inside the tunnel, I saw . . .

A pale-blue missing-persons flyer with a crude photo. Black-and-white.

Have you seen me?

It was my own face staring out.

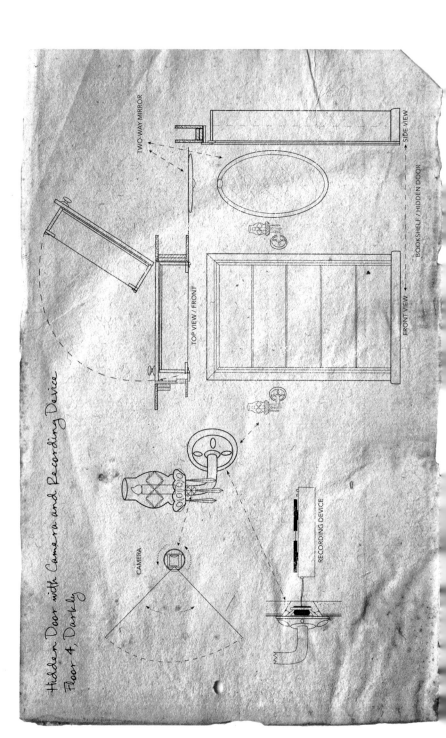

Hidden Door with Camera and Recording Device
Floor 4, Darkly

TWO-WAY MIRROR

TOP VIEW / FRONT

FRONT VIEW

BOOKSHELF / HIDDEN DOOR

SIDE VIEW

CAMERA

RECORDING DEVICE

"Three hours late?" shouts the captain.

She holds up her lantern, eyeing us crossly as we file onto the boat. "You thought I was tellin' tall tales when I said back at three? After that, the sea is a vengeful sister, happy to escort you to your downtrodden end." She widens her eyes in surprise. "Why, you seven look like you brushed shoulders with Death herself."

"Can you get us to the island safely tonight or not?" snaps Poe.

"I will try, sir. No sea ever proved too fraught for the captain." She grins. "Course, you'll have to ride in 'er belly—if you don't know each other well yet, you will by the time we arrive or meet your death, not sure which it'll be first."

With a smirk, she opens the door to the hull. We file into the claustrophobic space without a word, taking a seat on the dirty cushions, a flickering gold bulb the only light.

Within minutes, engine howling, we are lurching across the bay.

It feels unwise to start back to Darkly Island at this hour, but

I'm too shaken and tired to come up with a different plan. We all are.

Because it wasn't just *my* face we found in the tunnel. An inspection revealed all seven of us were there.

Torin is *Cheap ballroom dancing lessons.*

Cooper is *Mini car for sale.*

Poe is *Private chess tutor.*

Franz is *Spend the summer at the German Institute!*

Everleigh is *Cheap roof and gutter repairs.*

Mouse is *Private detective for hire, anonymous.*

The papers were creased and stained with rainwater, as if they had been there for months.

The question of who did this, how they got hold of our photos—these were our class pictures from school—not to mention who shoved me inside the pipe, it was so unnerving that we fought most of the drive back to the pier. When we weren't arguing about what to do or what it meant, we stared in unsettled silence at the pages where our own faded faces smiled out.

Was it a threat from whoever was behind Valkyrie? They could have easily pulled our names off the internship website, or tracked down our pictures from an old yearbook or pulled them off a school portrait photographer's website. Was it a signal to telegraph that they knew what Derringer Street had tasked us to do—that our endeavor was defunct before it had begun?

Or was it a summons to play the game?

Poe, when we caught up with him back at the van—his amused stare replaced by surprise when Franz handed him his flyer—dialed the number immediately.

It was answered by a nonsensical recording followed by a click.

Was someone live picking up, listening, or was the recording cutting out?

"It's Poe," he said. "I'm ready to play Valkyrie."

The line went dead.

All of us—even Everleigh—ended up calling the number on the flyer. We, too, were met with strange voices and incomprehensible recordings we tried to decode on different internet translators to no avail. Poe claimed it was no actual language, but garbled nonsense.

The others left messages. I chose not to.

It wasn't just our faces we found. There were four other kids—two boys, two girls.

Who are they? Students at the Bromsbury School? Are they already playing Valkyrie, or was this their invitation waiting to be noticed?

We ended up taking down our own flyers but leaving the others untouched. Now I worry that was a mistake.

Is this how it begins, how players get hooked? How many secret spots in how many schools are suddenly wallpapered with these flyers? Do innocent kids steal into some secret place to meet up with friends, drink from a stolen flask of whiskey, only to be confronted, by surreal surprise, with their own grinning picture? And a phone number that tantalizingly suggests the answer to it all is a simple call away. Is this mystery a gift, a boon—or the start of a doomed fate unraveling?

I think back to everything I know about Louisiana Veda, but I can't figure it out. Valkyrie was supposedly her masterpiece, but one she decided to destroy, only for it to be stolen—by one of her enemies, most likely.

Darkly games are not evil. Yet they contain evil. They teem with murderers, captors, goblins, tormentors—many of whom appear at first glance to be trustworthy or benign. The goal of the player, the pawn, is always to root out the evil, unbury it and bring it into the light, no matter how impossible the task or how chilling it is to see.

The end goal, the win, is always truth, freedom, strength—and even love.

And yet the reality of playing a Darkly didn't always lead to that. There were so many angry parents, lawsuits and boycotts and withering condemnation, especially toward the end. And though I always found the complaints unfair—Louisiana promised a perfect game, never to make the world perfect—I remember a few years ago reading a post by an anonymous winner of Forest Past. She confessed that the dark truth of the game played with her head to such an extent that after she won, she lost her job, her boyfriend, her friends, and all of her money. She left home and confessed she was now living on the street, trying to find her way. She dreamed of going back to the game, to be who she was when she was playing.

It was an eerie story. It vanished hours after it was posted.

But whatever the result of playing and winning—the goal of all Darkly games is for darkness to be vanquished by light, evil by good, lies by truth, no matter how harrowing the path. This is how it is in Disappearing Act, Hecate, Seas of Torrent, Beatrice Portinari.

Everything I've ever read about Darklys confirms this.

And so it must be for Valkyrie.

But then, who knows how the rules may have shifted in the years after the theft, how the game itself has been changed or manipulated to suit some other malignant purpose?

The wind on the sea is howling. Every few seconds, the *Elvira* slams a wave, slinging me against Poe, who deliberately chose to sit wedged beside me. His elbow and thigh knock constantly into mine, but he hasn't really even looked at me, too absorbed in his flyer.

If he's drawing dazzling conclusions about them, mentally tracing where the papers were printed, analyzing word choices, colors, and subject matter to compile a vivid portrait of the culprit, he is keeping these truths to himself.

He's been unusually silent, I notice, ever since we showed him the tunnel.

"There's only one thing to do," says Mouse with a frown. "We take these to Nile Raiden tomorrow. Total transparency. See what he has to say."

"Tomorrow I'll be gone," says Everleigh. "I'm getting out of here."

By now, we are used to the proclamations of her imminent exit. But the funny thing about Everleigh: she keeps saying she's leaving, but she doesn't actually go.

The boat rocks to a halt along the dock. We struggle off, up the steps along the cliff. The island is cloaked in darkness. I'm the first to reach the top.

That's when I see, far ahead on the hillside, that all the lights to the Darkly factory have been switched on—from the ground floor to the roof, including both towers. The whole building is electrified, suggesting people are actually at work in there.

"Louisiana's mad ghost haunts the factory," says Cooper. "Awesome."

"The lights are probably just on a timer or something," mutters Mouse.

"A timer still working after forty years?" says Torin.

Everleigh is looking on in mute horror, a hand clutching her throat.

I'm too exhausted to worry too much. I move around her,

heading after the others. But just as I'm about to enter the cabin, I can't help but stop and turn back.

The factory appears to have followed me like the moon. It's still there, the walls lost in the overcast night, so it's only a constellation of tiny gold windows suspended in the sky.

Minutes later, I am climbing into bed. I pull the thin gray blanket over my shoulders, closing my eyes, and feel instantly as if I'm still on the boat, Poe's shoulder brushing mine. I wonder about home—Gigi, Agatha, and Basil, the question of how they're coping without me—but my worry cuts to black as I fall asleep.

"Mr. Raiden is expecting you," says the receptionist with a curt smile.

She looks bewildered as she takes note of the stench of seaweed drifting around us, the ocean and island mud and brine, thanks to the crack-of-dawn boat ride with the captain. She slips to her feet, beckoning the seven of us to follow her out of the reception area through a set of hulking mahogany doors.

Derringer Street Chambers is housed in an elegant town house at the corner of Grosvenor Square in the Mayfair district of London. Though the trek to get here took forever, as soon as we were cruising in the white van down the elegant boulevards, past Piccadilly Circus and the Ritz, I couldn't help but feel glee at the sight of the crowds hurrying along the sidewalks in overcoats.

Agatha used to visit. Long before her accident, when I was little, she told me stories about London—about high tea at the Dorchester and Christmas lights on Oxford Street, how strangers were so polite they blurted "Sorry" for no reason and never left home without their black brolly, which in my mind turned London into a city teeming with characters from *Mary Poppins*. I find myself wishing I could call Prologue and get her on the phone.

You'll never believe where I am.

Now, as we file after the receptionist down the hallway, I steal glimpses through doorways at cavernous double-height libraries and dim offices where unsmiling barristers type on computers.

"Take a seat. Mr. Raiden will be with you shortly."

She indicates a solemn gray conference room. The others file in, and I'm about to follow when, glancing down the hall, I catch sight of something very strange.

Blue oxford shirt, striped red tie, a sweeping cloud of gold hair—no, it can't be.

And yet that profile—I've stared at it an embarrassing number of hours, so many I can draw it by memory in the margins of any blank page.

As soon as I spot him, he's gone. I hurry after him, around a corner, down the hall, past a plant, then I stop, because he's three feet away, his back to me, chatting with someone in a doorway.

I must have a ghostly look on my face, because the woman inside frowns at me.

"Yes? Can I help you?"

The boy turns.

It's Choke Newington.

He is so startled to see me he jumps, splashing the coffee he is holding down his pants.

"Dia?"

He jerks the mug away with a wince, and the coffee splashes again, this time on the carpet. He rocks back, knocking into a foxhunting painting on the wall, the gold frame going crooked. He tries to right it with his elbow, but it drops abruptly to the floor.

"Thank you, Lexi, for your insight," he says. "I will definitely check out *Donoghue v. Stevenson.*"

He ducks a few feet down the hall—away from the confused stare of Lexi—sets the mug on the carpet by his feet. Then he is blotting his pants with a napkin.

"What are you doing here?" he asks quietly.

"I won the Louisiana Veda internship. This firm represents her estate. What are you doing here?"

"I'm working here for the summer."

He clears his throat and finally looks at me. It's obvious from his pained expression he'd prefer to be looking at one of those London LOOK RIGHT sidewalk signs painted on the ground. I can barely blurt, "Well, see you," before fleeing around the corner.

"*Wait!* Dia!"

He races after me, grabbing my arm. I stumble on the foxhunting painting now in the middle of the hall, and he almost spills the coffee again.

He runs his hand through his hair with a sigh. "Sorry, I wasn't expecting to see— Yeah, I got in yesterday, so there's jet lag. And a hangover." He winces, lowering his voice. "Except it's more of a hang*current*. When exactly do these things go away? Anyone know? Some of the first-years took me out to experience pub culture, and the drinking age is eighteen, which is awful. Can I have your number?"

I manage to find the Post-it where I've written down my new phone number. He takes a picture of it. Then I am free to escape down the hallway.

Choke is in London. *Choke is in London?* It's a horrific punting of the laws of the natural world. Like ghost orchids and penguins and sea turtles, Choke is not meant to exist, much less thrive, outside his natural, highly specialized habitat of Eminence, Missouri.

I'm so lightheaded from the weird coincidence that it takes me a minute to find the conference room again. By the time I slip inside, Nile Raiden is seated at the head of the table, inspecting the flyers.

He looks tired—surprisingly so. His eyes are red-rimmed, his sleeves rolled up, tie slightly askew, as if at nine in the morning he has already been slogging at work for half a day. He picks up Everleigh's *Cheap roof and gutter repairs.*

"You say you found these in a remote part of woods at the Bromsbury School?"

"Yes," says Mouse.

"And all of the numbers lead to nonsensical recordings?"

"It's an AI-generated language, with inputs from Chinese, Japanese, Korean, maybe some Turkish," says Poe.

"Dia was the one to discover the tunnel," says Torin. "When she wandered in, she disturbed someone—another Bromsbury student, we think. He shoved her before he fled."

"Boy or girl?" asks Raiden, turning to me.

"Boy, I think. I didn't see much."

"And so far, none of you have heard anything else? There's been no contact?"

"No."

"Nothing yet."

Raiden sniffs, returning his attention to the flyers. "After George's disappearance, police performed a vigorous search of school grounds. They combed the woods again and again. They certainly would have found this. That means it must be fairly new."

"Maybe it went up when you announced our names on the foundation website," says Poe. "It was a pretty public announcement. Destined to draw attention."

"Doesn't this mean our mission is dead now?" says Torin, crossing her arms. "I mean, clearly these people know about us and our search for George. We can't very well play Valkyrie now and expect to find out who's behind it. Our cover is blown."

"Not necessarily," says Raiden with a thoughtful frown.

He is abruptly on his feet, collecting the pages. "This is very good work. I'll get these to our investigations department. In the meantime, nothing has changed. You will proceed as discussed. And you will notify me at once if you hear anything about the start of Valkyrie?"

He eyes us with a questioning look. We nod.

"Wonderful. I'll see you next week."

He seems satisfied—and eager to end the meeting. As he moves briskly to the door, I swear I see a pleased smile on his face. What does it mean? That in spite of the unpromising start, we are actually inching toward the elusive opening of Valkyrie?

If he is concerned for our well-being or worried about anything, he shows no sign of it.

I scramble to my feet. "One last thing, Mr. Raiden?"

He stops at the door.

"We would like to request a tour of the factory. Today."

I didn't tell the others what I had planned to ask. Now they're staring at me in surprise.

"We need to understand the island and the layout of the factory if we're going to figure out who stole the game that night."

I see a flash of irritation on his face. But then he nods.

"Of course, Dia. Let me see if I can dig up those old keys."

3946090076

Bella
1976

"The first thing to understand is that this factory is condemned!" shouts Nile Raiden over the wind.

He moves to the door in the rusted fence, chained with three padlocks. Frowning, he flips through at least thirty keys that look like they open a two-hundred-year-old gate, trying them in the locks.

"Wander away from the main structure—five floors and a basement—venture out onto the factory roof, balconies, towers, trespass into the manufacturing plant or the shipping docks? You will get injured. You may die. Do not be adventurous. Do not be rash. Do not use the elevators. They aren't functional. They will kill you. The central stairs are sound. Some rooms, offices, various laboratories on the sixth floor, are roped off. For good reason. There were a series of electrical fires making the walls unstable. If you see tape barring the way reading 'Do not cross'? *Do not cross.*"

Raiden drops the chains to the ground and swings open the door, the wind blasting his tie into his face. We mutely file through, heading up the steep hill on a winding path.

That Raiden should so offhandedly be directing us toward a derelict building feels a little surreal. But then, it speaks to his confidence in the legal papers we all signed. He betrays not the slightest concern as he strides nimbly ahead of us up the stone steps.

"You'll find the factory directory in the lobby. Darkly's fifteen-year anniversary party, the night of the theft, was June the fifteenth, 1985. There was a presentation of Darkly's latest game, Contraband, followed by dinner and dancing. The guest list included movie stars, authors, musicians, a few close confidants, a chef, and a server. Valkyrie was stolen from the fourth floor, Imagination and Expansion. Tomb 605. Feel free to take a look."

Raiden reaches the top step. I'm right behind him, passing between the two stone egrets, seven feet tall at least, spangled with moss. One is missing a leg, the other an eye. They're from Tea Ceremony, the sixteenth Darkly game, witnesses to the murder of the emperor, if I remember correctly. Raiden strides across the barren patio, the flagstones broken, and stops at the hulking iron doors. He fumbles to find the correct key for this tangled set of chains.

"What do we do if we get hurt in there?" asks Everleigh.

"Follow my instructions and you won't."

Raiden unlocks one last padlock and sets about trying to wrench open the doors, pushing with gritted teeth. Finally, one gasps open, revealing an expanse of sooty darkness.

He steps back, wiping his face. "Stick together inside. Barring anything unforeseen, I will plan to see you next week for the update. Good luck."

"You're not escorting us inside?" asks Cooper.

But Raiden is already starting for the steps. "Unfortunately, I am needed back at the office. Better if you're on your own. Fresh eyes."

Suddenly, he stops, turning back. "But I warn you. While combing the submerged shipwreck has its pleasures, it is also a distraction. There is a ticking clock. Not just for George. But for others. This factory, while fascinating, sits squarely in the past. It's already been combed, searched, and itemized. And it's out there"—he points at the gray sea behind him—"where the villains wait."

He continues down the steps, leaving us staring after him.

"That was weird," says Torin.

"He is the definition of 'eichhornlich,'" says Franz. "Of, or pertaining to, a squirrel."

"He practically tripped over himself to get away," says Cooper. "Like he's scared to set foot inside."

"Because it's haunted," says Everleigh.

"He's just an underling following orders," says Poe.

"Yes, but whose orders?" asks Franz. "Louisiana's?"

If Poe has an answer to this, he keeps it to himself. He moves across the patio to the door, a quick duck of his head—as if to make sure there is actually a floor—and he vanishes inside. I take a deep breath to steady my nerves and move after him.

It's a dark lobby. I can make out an elaborate black mosaic *D* under my feet, some of the tiles missing. The cold, stale air carries a mysterious caramel sweetness.

Something is suspended high overhead. It startles me. Because it looks like a real woman in a black dress hanging upside down by her ankle. I take a step, trying to understand. I see it's actually a chandelier in the form of Ophelia, from Louisiana's first game.

The objective is to escape out of the twisted tower where she has been locked away by her family. When she's caught, when the pawn loses, she is hung upside down and incinerated over a fire, ending the game. This Ophelia is made out of plaster and bronze, faded crinolines and ruffles, wires and pantaloons, her hair a kind of synthetic black straw, arms outstretched. She is festooned with what looks like a thousand wax candles. There are no features on her face, or they are lost in the darkness.

Ahead is a marble reception desk in front of the Darkly banner. WANDER WHERE THE WITCH LIES, once painted with great flourish and pride, now peeling and splotched with moisture. Far to my left, an iron staircase twists down through the ceiling. Beyond that are the elevators, four empty doorways.

To my right is a long display case, small items crowding the shelves. Poe stands inspecting it.

I step beside him. Inside, there are hundreds of objects— talismans, lucky charms, figurines, embroidery. They are artifacts from each of the games, I realize. These are the things hunted and craved, yearned for and warred over, usually represented by a card or a game piece made of silver, metal, or wood. But here are the real objects, life-sized.

Some I recognize. Others I don't.

A real taxidermy raven from Seas of Torrent. The dried nosegay from Prodigal. The seismic brain-wave printout from Headcase. The rubber mask of Rasputin from Rasputin. The ceramic poison cup, encrusted with what looks like real blood, from Hecate. The secret saint's diary from Ophelia, embossed with the charred cross.

A child's worn red sneaker—I realize it's the one I uncovered in Disappearing Act. Beside that are a pair of child's glasses. A watch. A dirty, balled-up sock. A pocketknife. These are the precious things from the game I never had a chance to find.

"Oh my God."

"Seriously? That is *so* creepy—"

The other interns are filing in, gasping as they notice the chandelier.

"Is it Louisiana mummified?" asks Franz.

"Ophelia from Ophelia," shouts Poe over his shoulder. Then, turning back to the display case, he shakes head, whispering something in what sounds like Latin.

"What?" I ask.

"Such folly. Such human error. Why are these things being left here to rot? It'd be more lucrative to open a Darkly museum. Feed the insatiable appetite for Louisiana. Or sell them at auction? 'Louisiana Veda: The Private Collection.' For all of Derringer Street's obsessive legal precision, their actual preservation of the Darkly world leaves something to be desired."

"You mean, they're actually working against her."

"Deliberate subterfuge or laziness, I can't yet tell." He seems about to add something, then frowns, absorbed in a drawing on the bottom shelf—a detailed medical diagram of a cross section of a serpent, as if the beast was given an actual autopsy, probably from 18 Lost Icelandic Sailors.

"Check this out," whispers Cooper behind me. "Here is the mailbox and the red-wax letters from Served Cold Since 1962."

"The one about the anonymous mail-order-revenge company?" asks Franz, moving beside her. "I always wished that one was real. I have a host of people back at home I would like to sign up for a lethal comeuppance."

"What is all this stuff?" whispers Torin.

"The objects that inspired Louisiana to create the games," says Poe. "The keys. The ciphers. Access to these? We could win all twenty-eight."

"All twenty-nine," corrects Everleigh.

As the other interns crowd the display case, I slip back to the center of the lobby. The only daylight drips in through tiny portholes dotting the left wall. The glass on most is smashed, and tangled vines grow through, including an actual tree, the trunk bending across the floor.

The cryptic intensity of Nile Raiden, the question of the stolen Valkyrie, poor lost George Grenfell, our faces on those flyers—somehow all of that is irrelevant now.

Because it hits me. I am standing at the doorstep of one of the most sought-after mysteries in the world, a place most people don't even believe is real—something hashed over and whispered about, sought and scorned by millions, from die-hard Louisiana fans to the haters.

This is the heart of the old dead world that is Darkly. This is the hidden headquarters, the workshop of one of the most provocative inventors who ever lived—a woman worshipped, then ridiculed, then discounted, long dead.

Here I can get to the bottom of it all. Buried here somewhere, left to rot, is the truth of who she was.

And nothing—not Raiden's cryptic warnings, not the other interns, not even my own fear, which seems to be growing exponentially the longer I stand here—will stop me from inspecting every inch of this place.

I notice something—a map—hanging across the lobby between the elevator banks.

I step over and see with a shiver it's the directory Raiden mentioned.

Basement—Incubator and Orphanage

Floor 1—Exhibition Pavilion

Floor 2—Covenants

Floor 3—Emergency and Vanquish

Floor 4—Imagination and Expansion

Floor 5—Big Bang

Floor 6—Testing Laboratory

Towers—Royal Court

To reach Darkly Manufacturing and Export Bay use Southshore Tunnel

I creep to the edge of one of the open elevator banks and venture a look. The actual elevator is suspended high overhead like a giant wasp nest tangled with cables. Below, some two stories down, in the basement, vines are growing out of piles of junk, folding chairs, doctor's tables, a blackboard with a ghostly chalk diagram still visible.

"We should split up," I say to the others as I start for the stairs. "It'll be dark in two hours. We shouldn't be wandering this place at night. Cooper and Franz, you cover the top three floors with me, including the towers. Poe and Torin, you take three and four. That covers Imagination and Expansion, where Valkyrie was stolen. Mouse and Everleigh, check out the basement, floors one and two. We'll meet back here in an hour."

"Raiden said the towers are off-limits," says Poe.

"It says 'Royal Court.' Louisiana's office is probably up there. We have to take a look."

As I start up the clanging old steps, I can feel him watching me. He seems to find it amusing, how I'm deliberately trying to avoid him. Or, does he see how I'm a die-hard Louisiana fan who hopes to find something to vindicate her, to prove she was everything she claimed to be? But he says nothing else, and a minute later when I glance back over the railing, Poe is gone and it's Franz and Cooper stomping after me.

I wait for them to catch up on the second floor, Covenants. Here, there are red walls, a wizened 2 painted on a black door, and beside that, a small frame. At first, I think it's directions to the fire exit, but it's a sketch of a man's face.

"Covenants?" asks Cooper. "What do you think it means?"

"Contracts?" I whisper. Peering through the porthole window, I can make out a narrow unlit hallway strewn with papers.

"Next time, I'm taking my chances on the killer elevators," gasps Franz, behind us.

We start up the next flight. I can hear the others ascending below. We pass the third floor, Emergency and Vanquish. The fourth, Imagination and Expansion.

"This is where Valkyrie was stolen, ja?" asks Franz.

We pause to stare through the broken window—nothing noticeably different about this hall except the walls are painted green—then we continue to the fifth, Big Bang.

"I wouldn't be surprised if we find nothing in the towers," says Cooper.

"Why do you say that?" asks Franz.

"Because Louisiana wasn't a real person."

"Oh, I get it. You're one of those kooks who thinks the moon landing was staged."

Cooper pauses to look over the iron railing—a vertiginous fifty-foot drop to the lobby that I'm avoiding because it makes me dizzy—then continues up the steps.

"It's the book I'm reading," she says. "Four anonymous champions talk about the experience of winning a Darkly. Four different people playing four different games. Ophelia. The Red Hounds of Garsington. Lost Suitcase. And Beatrice Portinari. They don't know each other. But they all talked about how, the day they won, they sent in the little winner's letter with their contact information and photographic proof of the win to the PO box in Scotland. Weeks later they were contacted by executives of Darkly. They were promised an afternoon with Louisiana, garden tea in her private home, a tour of her factory. They were told they had been accepted for a lifetime into the Darkly family. There was all this preparation to meet her—the queen, you know—signing nondisclosures, a blindfolded car ride from London." Cooper shakes her head. "The day it's supposed to happen—this is four different years—no one shows. No phone call. No explanation. A total ghosting. All four are convinced that Louisiana is a seductive fiction created by a team. A glamorous enigma to sell a product. The brilliant genius woman inventor who fights to become the greatest game maker in the world, then she is so lonely and lost she kills herself?" Cooper rolls her eyes. "It's way too dramatic to be real."

"Except that's a pretty common story throughout history," says Franz simply. "Unless you think Jimi Hendrix and Van Gogh and Janis Joplin were all actors too?"

Cooper only shrugs.

"What about Louisiana's *Time* magazine cover?" presses Franz. "The TV appearances?"

"That was a hired model who memorized a script."

"And where is this model now?"

"Probably dead. Or living by a different name in Switzerland."

Franz is frowning. "But if they had actors posing as Louisiana, why not send the actor to have tea with the winners at some fake estate, then? Ghosting them was a far more dangerous choice. One that would give rise to stories that can't be controlled. If your theory is correct, Cooper, it would be more likely that they followed through on the ruse. The story we have been left with in the aftermath of Darkly's rise and fall suggests someone unstable and shy and eccentric calling the shots. Someone exactly like Louisiana Veda."

"Guess we'll never know," Cooper mutters sullenly.

I have remained purposefully quiet during this maddening conversation. Because it's a popular Darkly conspiracy theory— one that infuriates me and all the other glooms—that Louisiana is not real, but a manufactured persona concocted by an ingenious marketing committee. The suggestion is that no woman without money or connections could do what she did. Of course, it's ludicrous. Louisiana was seen by too many people in the early days of Darkly, including her own fans, for her to be a fake. There are interviews with professors at the art school in London where she lived in the stairwells. They found her there, working all night. They knew her.

I'm about to point out as much—that not everything outstanding and rare is malarkey and too good to be true, that to believe she never existed is yet another cruel attempt to erase her—when I stop, suddenly uneasy.

Franz notices, turning. "What is it, Dia?"

I peer over the railing, staring into the blackened, empty expanse so far below it seems to cut a mile into the earth.

The other interns—they were here, seconds ago. Now, there's no sign of them.

"Where is everyone?"

Franz and Cooper pause, listening.

"They moved out onto the different floors?"

"We'd still hear them," says Cooper.

They both appear to find this as weird as I do, but we're almost at the top, so we keep climbing.

We stumble out onto the sixth floor. Testing Laboratory. Pale-blue walls. There is a painted 6 and another small framed sketch, this one of a test tube filled with a black boiling liquid. The corridor door here has been removed. Beyond it stretches a shadowed hallway identical to the others.

"Yeah, we are not going up there," whispers Franz.

He is inspecting the staircase curving up into a brick tower, the bottom roped off.

I step beside him. It's a precarious ascent. Move under the rope, traverse a narrow landing—one side totally caved in, rotten wood beams and the floor ten feet below—to rickety spiral steps with no railing. At the top, high overhead, I can make out a small black door.

"I'll take a look," I say, ducking under the rope.

"Dia, I really don't think it's safe," says Franz.

"My best friend, Basil, is a Korean War vet. He told me if you walk through any bombed-out building, keep to the treads closest to the wall—they'll hold your weight—"

No sooner do I say this than a beam snaps, and I scream as my leg falls through. I manage to leap onto the next step, hugging the wall as wood and bolts shower the floor.

"Oh my God," says Cooper, a hand over her mouth. "You almost died."

"I would urge you to turn back, except you can't now," says Franz.

"There's got to be another set of stairs on the opposite side," I say. "I'll meet you in the Testing Laboratory."

I smile with more reassurance than I feel and start up again.

When I'm about halfway, I look down and realize I'm alone. Franz and Cooper must have decided to explore the Testing Laboratory.

But it's too quiet. Wouldn't I hear them? Voices? The only sounds are my own footsteps as I climb higher, trying to keep my balance.

Within minutes, I've reached the black door. It opens with a shrill wail.

And instantly, as I step up into the small room, I am astonished, because this, I know, is where Louisiana Veda worked.

A throne on top of the world.

There's nothing left but a stark wood desk, not even a chair. But there are windows revealing a 360-degree view of the ocean—gray and swirling—and an electric sky with an orange sun sliding through the clouds.

The entire island is visible from here: Torment Point, the small black lighthouse where the captain must live, the meager cottages where we sleep, the auditorium, lake, strange black sculptures, pathways crisscrossing the island, the back of the factory, shipping docks.

I step to the desk, the floor sagging dangerously under my feet as I pull open a drawer.

Papers, notebooks of ideas, Louisiana's sketches. If they were ever here—and they must have been—they are long gone. There's nothing left but an empty bookshelf, an old-fashioned brass telescope on a stand, and, pushed against the shattered window behind me, a giant ceramic gray pot. The plant long dead, only dry dirt is left.

I crouch beside it, sliding it an inch from the wall, in hopes of finding a scrap or trinket. That's when I see something in the floor.

A trapdoor. The plant was purposefully concealing it. There is even a little bronze latch and a handle. I heave the pot aside and twist the latch. It opens with a wheeze.

I am staring down a dark chute with a metal ladder, ghostly blue light below.

It's possible that I'm too shocked to think clearly, but I don't hesitate. I scramble onto the ladder, feeling for the rungs under my feet, and climb down. When I reach the bottom, it takes a moment for my eyes to adjust to the strange blue vision in front of me and behind. I'm inside a corridor so narrow it's like a vein in a throat. There appears to be a black carpet running along the floor, and even on the walls, which erases all sound, so when I take a step it's like I didn't move at all. That's when I realize, turning, I'm staring into a round porthole next to a sign that reads TESTING LABORATORY 16.

It's a small, white-tiled room, with a small table and chair. It looks like a doctor's examination room.

I fumble my way to the next porthole, a few feet away.

TESTING LABORATORY 14.

It's identical, but with green tiles. I slip to the next.

TESTING LABORATORY 12.

These tiles are pink.

I realize that I'm staring at Franz and Cooper. They are on the other side of the porthole less than a foot away, inspecting the room.

"Hey," I shout.

They don't react.

"It's me, Dia. I'm inside the walls!"

They don't even look in my direction. The glass is soundproof, I realize, and on the other side there is some kind of two-way mirror. Or maybe not even that.

"Everleigh?" says Franz.

His voice echoes through an old speaker somewhere here with me in the watery blue darkness. It sounds like he's right beside me.

"Her fear is totally bogus," says Cooper as she opens a cabinet.

"I agree. All that simpering. *Riiiight.* She's the one hell-bent on winning."

"Oh, yeah. I watched her last night when she thought we were asleep. Shrewd as a CIA spy. She was scribbling like crazy in a little black notebook, nary a tear nor whimper. She locked the notebook inside her suitcase. I'll try to steal it tonight."

"Poe. You buy his whole Einstein business?"

"I guess. One thing odd I noticed? He didn't actually turn in his cell in Raiden's bin. He flung it, *while* it was ringing, by the way, into the ocean and watched it explode on the rocks."

Franz nods. "I like that, actually. Pure poetical nihilism. What about Dia?"

"She's the black hole. Can't tell a thing. You?"

Franz shrugs. "The whole old-fashioned grandmother's-pearls vibe must be fake. We still on for tonight?"

"Oh, yes." Cooper smiles eagerly and slips through the door, Franz slinging his arm around her shoulder, which makes her laugh.

They know each other, I realize. *They're old friends.*

I fumble along the wall to eavesdrop on them in the next room, Testing Laboratory 10.

But it's empty. I try the other way.

Testing Laboratory 14. They're not there either.

Where did they go? A room on the other side of the hallway? How do I get there?

My heart pounding, their words ringing in my ears, I race in the opposite direction, certain this will take me to the other side. But when I reach the end, I'm facing another corridor that looks different from where I started.

Somehow, I've gotten turned around. Another ladder cuts down through the floor.

To Floor 5?

Crouching, I can see that it continues on, to 4. And 3.

This is how Louisiana ran her factory? Spying on her employees? It's unsettling, creepy, and absolutely paranoid. But Louisiana must have had good reason. Something must have made her think this invisible observation was necessary—a liar, a leak, a turncoat in her midst, a so-called friend intent on destroying her?

The question of what these secret corridors mean, the conversation I just overheard between Franz and Cooper, tangle around in my head as I climb down the next ladder, stumbling out into another icy-blue hallway. This light burns from little blue bulbs high in the ceiling. The longer I'm drenched in it, the more I feel as if I don't have a physical body at all, as if I'm floating. I feel a powerful urge to get out of here, into fresh air and gravity and sunlight.

That's when I hear the screaming.

26

Who is it? Boy or girl? I can't tell.

But it doesn't stop, and seems to echo through speakers all around me. I can't tell which direction the sound is coming from, so I just start walking, passing more dark portholes into more rooms. They are black wood studios, with drafting tables and easels and bulletin boards, giant goosenecked lamps. There are signs. *Explosion 2. Explosion 6. Explosion 10.*

The longer I run, the more I feel like someone is tiptoeing after me, as if this ragged breathing, the only thing I can actually hear, is not my own.

I have to get out of here. Which way is the way out?

I start down the next ladder. Floor 4, Imagination and Expansion. Tomb 101. 107. Tomb 605—where Valkyrie was stolen— must be somewhere here. And yet the screaming is louder now. It makes me run on and on, my mind urging, *Get out of here—*

I've reached the end of the hallway. Blinking into the liquid darkness, I can see what appears to be the seam of a door. I push against it and stumble out into a constricted spiral stairwell, different from the one we climbed up before. It twists into darkness below.

I start down, gripping the railing all the way to the bottom. I lurch through another door and find myself staring down a tunnel stretching a surreal distance ahead, long as an airport runway. There's a track for some type of trolley running along the wall.

The screaming is still going. Someone is being attacked.

It's coming from the double doors far ahead. I rush toward them, past a giant rusted sign.

TO DARKLY MANUFACTURING AND EXPORT BAY

WARNING: AUTHORIZED PERSONNEL ONLY

I push open a door and burst into a vast warehouse. It's cold, but there's sunlight. Daylight streams in from the broken skylights at least forty feet above. Stacked wooden crates, metal containers stamped DARKLY and SEAS OF TORRENT and HEADCASE, storage shelves rising five stories on either side. Catwalks and conveyor belts crisscross overhead. Green metal machines with mechanical arms and ancient computer screens sit hunched and morose in the shadows like a giant's forgotten collection of robots.

There is a loud humming. One of the machines is running.

The screaming has stopped. I freeze, listening. The silence is worse than the scream.

"Oh, God—"

"Is he dead?"

I race toward the voices, streaking down another aisle, and stumble out the end. Mouse, Torin, and Everleigh are bent over Poe. He's lying on the ground, shirt off, jeans torn, his chest streaked with blood.

Torin gasps as I race over to them. "Oh my— Seriously, Dia?"

"You scared us. I thought you—"

"We need to call an ambulance."

"No." Poe sits up, wincing. "I'm fine."

Torin is pressing his T-shirt, soaked in blood, into what appears to be a wound on his left side. He looks shaken.

"What happened?" I ask.

"We were attacked," he says.

Torin nods, trying to catch her breath. "Mouse wanted to understand how the games left the island. So he and Everleigh went to check out the shipping bays. And Poe and I"—she turns, pointing at the catwalk overhead—"we noticed one of the machines was on. It was roaring and clanging, really odd, so we walked out along there to see what it was. Someone crept up behind us and shoved us both off."

Poe is squinting up at the catwalk as if he expects the assailant to still be there.

"I managed to grab the railing and leap into that cart." Torin points at a wheeled canvas bin. "But Poe fell onto the conveyor belt, and he went into the machine."

"The thing was eating me alive," says Poe. "Engraving 'Made in England' on my left side. I held on. Almost lost a foot to a rotor. Mouse managed to pull me out before I was turned into the thirtieth Darkly."

Everleigh is flipping handles and pressing buttons, trying to turn off the machine. Finally, the rollers slow, and the loud hum peters off into silence.

"What did the person look like?" I ask.

"Black clothes, head to toe," says Poe. "Some kind of mask."

"It was the Rasputin mask," says Torin, a hand over her mouth. "I saw it as I hung on, as he ran off. Those black eyes and the beard. I recognized it from the display in the lobby."

"Where were you, Dia?" asks Mouse.

His voice is so offhand, so quiet, I don't pick up on the faint accusation at first. He is staring at me closely. All of them are.

I realize they are actually wondering if I had something to do with this—even Poe.

"I heard screaming on the fifth floor," I say. "I came immediately."

I sound like I'm lying. And I am, of course. The truth is, I was inside the walls spying when I heard the scream. It would be so easy to say it. *I found a trapdoor in Louisiana's office.*

But I don't. And thankfully, no one is even looking at me. They're staring at Everleigh.

She pulls her phone from her jacket pocket. It's ringing shrilly.

Suddenly, another phone goes off. Poe's.

Then Torin's.

Mouse's.

And mine. UNKNOWN reads the number.

"Hello?" I answer.

"Dia Gannon? Is that you?"

I am so astonished, I cannot move.

Her low, childlike voice with the hopscotch British accent is a combination of crystal ball and campfire, hints of wisdom and impending secrets that sound as if they are floating in a green glass bottle sent here from the past. It's a voice that makes you sit forward, desperate not to miss a word.

I watched her lone interview with Johnny Carson on *The Tonight Show* a hundred times, and the last one she ever gave on *Des O'Connor* after Hecate was released, when people were starting to understand that these games and their creator were something extraordinary.

"I've been waiting to talk to you, Dia," says Louisiana. "Will you play Valkyrie with me tonight?"

May
1953

Mouse directs the clattering van down the dark road. I sit
alone in the back.

I am terrified. Not that I can talk to anyone about it.

No, I will not say a word. If Louisiana's factory and secret blue
portholes inside the walls revealed anything, it's that I've been far
too trusting since I arrived here.

I don't know any of these kids. Not really.

"Will you play Valkyrie with me tonight?" Louisiana whispered
in my ear. "Meet me at the Inn in St. Carthen Borne. Ten p.m.
Don't be late."

All of us heard a similar recording—Louisiana's voice, eerily
friendly, as if she were a favorite distant relative. The only differ-
ences were the locations and times.

St. Carthen Borne is a small village eight miles north of Thornwood. The Inn is a pub that has been closed for a year. The other
interns were told a bridge, a church, a parking lot by a river, a hiking
trail, a vacant house for sale, a graveyard. All locations are within a

twenty-five-mile radius. Poe was the only one ordered to London—the lot behind Goodwin's Court. 2 a.m.

"Obviously, the perpetrators of Valkyrie have created an AI version of Louisiana's voice," says Cooper.

"You think there will be a lethal school bus picking us up, one by one?" asks Franz.

We barely have time to change our clothes, call the captain, and board the boat.

Yet the uncomfortable mood isn't just due to the invitation to play Valkyrie. The disorienting events in the factory have left us all unsettled, and like me, the other interns are keeping their thoughts to themselves.

The attack on Torin and Poe—they are both still shaken. The Rasputin mask was not missing from the display in the factory lobby, as I pointed out to Torin as we left, which made her doubt what she saw.

"Maybe it wasn't Rasputin," she whispers tearfully. "Maybe it wasn't even a mask. I can't remember now."

Poe's wound is much worse than he lets on. He sits in the row in front of me in the van, and when I watch him change the bandage, I am horrified at the sight of bloody, torn flesh, what looks like actual letters burned above his hip. We have all told him he needs to go to the hospital, advice he blows off with obvious irritation.

"No vital organs were compromised," he snaps. "Except my pride."

He's not going anywhere, not with the start of Valkyrie hours away. He stares morosely out the window, saying nothing. And though our eyes meet once—I feel a flutter of electricity shoot through me, along with the guilty thought that if he had been with me, he wouldn't have gotten hurt—he only looks away with an annoyed frown.

I suspect he's trying to forget the attack, mentally preparing to play Valkyrie. He wants to win.

Then there was the reappearance of Franz and Cooper at the factory. There was no sign of them anywhere, not until we were outside, helping Poe down the factory steps. Abruptly, they were right behind us, shouting that they'd been invited to play Valkyrie.

"Louisiana called us up—"

"She summoned us like she was right here beside us—"

"Yes, we know," mutters Mouse.

But their reaction to news of the attack on Torin and Poe was bizarre. Maybe it was because of what I'd witnessed, eavesdropping on them inside the walls, but they weren't as surprised as they should have been. Wasn't there something a little flippant and cold about how they asked only a few questions, asking if Poe was really okay, then darting past him where he was struggling through the chain-link fence, so eager to board the boat, get to their assigned location, to play the game?

I can't stop wondering about what I overheard. How do they know each other? What was their plan for *tonight,* as Franz whispered? They had been hashing over all of us. To decide who could be trusted, who was the competition? Or was there some other reason?

Though I no longer trust them, what they mentioned about Everleigh does ring true, now that I take the time to watch her.

She was supposed to have left this morning. But here she is, riding in the passenger seat beside Mouse. She is not crying. She sits stiff and silent, staring straight ahead. She isn't afraid. No, when she reaches out to change the radio station, turning up the volume, there is a poised smile on her face. She is actually excited.

Not that I even have time to worry about Everleigh—or any of them.

In less than one hour, I will face the first round of a new Darkly game. I try to think back to the summer I played Disappearing Act—what I did, how I managed to get past the first round. But those nights seem so far away now, a page ripped from some other girl's history, someone who is careful and thoughtful and strong, someone no longer me.

"Dia, this is you," says Mouse, eyeing me in the rearview mirror.

I realize we have stopped at a vacant intersection. THE INN reads the sign on a shuttered cottage. I climb over the seat and slide open the door, scrambling outside.

It's quiet here. Dark. No streetlights. Nothing around but woods beyond a stone wall and the night sky. The six of them consider me without a word. I can't tell if it's because they now find me as suspicious as I find them or they're genuinely afraid for me.

"Cooper?" I blurt.

She leans forward, a questioning frown.

"That book you're reading. What do the four winners say you need to do to win?"

She sighs, not bothering to hide her exasperation. "Anticipate six moves ahead, let go of the railing, jump when you can't, don't let the crowd's eyes pierce you, the game board is all around you in the past, present, and future, and avoid the witch."

"Avoid the witch? What does that mean?"

She glares. "I actually haven't read that far. Sorry."

I slide the door closed and head to the picnic table. By the time I take a seat, the van is gone.

28

The night is bright with moonlight. Yet it feels drained of all life—as if everyone has fled due to some dire warning I never heard, and I'm the only one left. I'm too nervous to sit, so I walk around the Inn, peering into the dirty windows at the stacks of boxes and overturned furniture. I wonder if the people behind Valkyrie are watching me from somewhere, if this is some final test before they decide to let me play or not.

Abruptly, my phone starts to ring, the UNKNOWN on the screen causing my heart to stop.

"Dia?"

I'm so panicked I can't immediately place the voice.

"It's Choke."

Choke? He keeps talking, but I don't hear it, because I notice, far down the road in the shadows, a gleaming black van.

How long has it been waiting there, watching me?

". . . wondering if you're free to grab dinner with me and some friends in Covent Garden . . ."

The van is slinking toward me.

No driver is visible. The windows are black. I want to turn and run, not just back to Darkly Pier but all the way home to Eminence.

"You still there? Dia?"

"I have to call you back."

I hang up as the van pulls to a halt feet away. Seconds tick by, a screaming paralysis turning me inside out. Then the door slides open.

My hands are bound behind my back. I'm tied to some kind of chair.

A Darkly game is warred and won in the mind before the box is even ripped from the plastic. Louisiana Veda said that somewhere.

Except now I don't want to win. I want to live.

Wander where the witch lies.

I need to say it. Why don't I just say it?

The blackout hours leading up to this moment have bulldozed my memory and common sense. There was the ride in the van, the thin, eyeless figure, head to toe in black nylon, fitting the blindfold over my eyes, the small brick room where I was kept, the table with the old photocopied pages, the crude typing.

Valkyrie Terms & Conditions, Arcadia Gannon, Valkyrie Player Number 407.

What did I read about all of the different Darkly games? What do they signify again—the cards, the dice, the gifts pulled from the velvet drawstring bags? Ophelia and Prodigal and Lost Suitcase.

What were the words of advice from Cooper? I can't focus on any of it now, all of it fitful and torn up in my head.

A light flashes on. It burns like an eclipsed sun through the blindfold. I can feel people around me, rapid breathing, anxious footsteps.

"Name?"

It's an old woman. She sounds like a witch presiding over a sadistic school for girls.

"Dia Gannon."

"Player number?"

"Four hundred and seven."

"Do you understand and agree to the terms and conditions of Valkyrie?" This is an old man on the other side of the room. He sounds like an eighty-year-old judge speaking from his courtroom pulpit, where he gleefully sends innocents to the gallows.

My mind is stuttering, *No, no, I just want to go home and watch* The Caine Mutiny *with Basil and Agatha and my mom, who is probably about to marry her third husband, who she met yesterday when he wandered into Prologue mistaking it for a hardware store.*

"Yes," I say.

"Exit phrase?"

This is a soft-spoken man who sounds like he plucks the wings off live butterflies for fun.

"Wander where the witch lies."

"Uttering this phrase at any time will result in your irrevocable elimination from all Darkly games. Please confirm your agreement."

"I confirm."

"Begin."

Just as I realize someone has cut the zip ties on my wrist, the blindfold is whisked away.

I blink in the burning light. I can see now that they pulled clothing over my head. I am wearing a boxy canvas tunic that looks like something patients wore in a Victorian madhouse. It is stained and smells like detergent.

In front of me sits a circular poker table with brilliant green felt. Laid out on top is a Darkly.

Valkyrie, it reads, inside the legendary windswept scroll.

Everyone talks about it, the instant grasp of a Darkly on your attention, its insinuation into your brain forever, even against your will.

The board is plain pale wood, an elaborate maze, hand-carved and painted by Louisiana herself, watercolors in blues and grays, black ink. It's a basement cellar. No, a prison cell. Strange cinder-block walls crisscross at odd angles, interrupted by colored rect-angles, black circles, and tiny squares.

There is no obvious start, no clear pathway for the player. No gangplank or sidewalk or grid.

But there are labels on the different-colored shapes, tiny carved scribbles that I have to lean forward to read, like the lettering in Seas of Torrent, but even more deranged.

SPACE ROCKET. DEAD KING. BEAST BED. RADIO TO MARS.

The board is a disorienting web, no evident symmetry or safe zone.

What is the objective? Where do I need to go?

In front of the board stands a single wood piece, the elegant, doomed black pawn.

That must be me.

To the right of the board sits a gray velvet drawstring bag, heavy with . . . tokens? No, figurines, given the sharp outlines pok-ing out of the fabric.

There is a giant ebony hourglass, a foot tall at least, the sand inside glittering gold.

To the left of that sits an ornate wood spinner. A brass winding key and a long brass needle. The wheel is intricately carved with three concentric circles.

The smallest at the center is painted black. The other two have delineated sections, each with an illustration.

MARIA TALLCHIEF: the bottom half of a ballerina wearing a tutu, standing in first position.

LOCKS AND MAZES: a screaming mouth, with a labyrinth drawn on the tongue.

SECRET SOCIETY: massive double doors festooned with scrolls and gargoyles.

DETECTIVE: a single bulging eye, peering through a magnifying glass.

SLAUGHTERHOUSE: the silhouette of a vulture in a tree.

I am dying to inspect them all, but I can feel the crowd growing impatient.

I reach out, grasping the key, and crank it as hard as I can. The three circles whirl in opposite directions, creating a dizzying illusion.

It's a face, floating toward me.

Click. Click. Click.

The outer circle slows and stops. So does the middle circle.

I'm so startled by the abrupt stillness I can hardly focus on the sections the needle now slices.

WHISPERS BEYOND THE GRAVE: four sets of hands resting on a card table, two of which are monster claws.

In the middle circle, DARK: a four-paned window, scribbled black. I can make out fiendish eyes floating there.

And, of course, the center black circle. The end of the needle is trapped there.

Two hooded figures—faces hidden—step toward me into the light, grabbing the gray velvet bag, holding it open for me.

I reach inside, rooting through dozens of tiny metal objects, each one different and unexpectedly heavy. I come across something small and smooth, and pull it out.

A bird.

"She will find the dove in the dark whispers beyond the grave," an old woman shouts.

One of the hooded figures picks up my pawn and sets it on the board. It's in the upper right corner, no square, nothing there but one of the walls. Then with a theatrical twirl of their black-gloved fingers, the figure seizes the hourglass, quickly flips it. Gold sand begins to rain into a perfect pyramid at the bottom.

How much time do I have?

A mallet raps, twice.

"Valkyrie 407 hereby underway."

The crowd begins to hiss, a sound that seems to ooze from the floor.

What are they waiting for me to do? What is the next move? Are there other players? Who am I playing against? There are no cards here, no dice, no Darkly radio. But the wheel makes this a game of chance.

Find the dove in the dark whispers beyond the grave.

I remind myself that I don't have to understand. I don't have to win or even decode the game board of Valkyrie.

I need only to find out who is behind this and where George Grenfell went, if he's still alive.

I'm playing my own game.

The two robed figures grab the edges of the poker table, whisking it back into the shadows, the game floating away, revealing a gaping dark hole in the floor.

There's nothing to see inside it, no bottom, a void.

The other kids who made it here before me—this must be where their fear eats them alive. They must shout, without thinking, *Wander where the witch lies. This was a mistake. Please take me home. I promise not to tell—*

And they go home. Don't they go home?

I'm about to say it, the words on the tip of my tongue, when my chair pitches forward. All I can do is scream as I plummet through the hole.

Did I lose already? What did I do wrong?

I crash into something.

A canvas cart. I am on the move, clattering across rough concrete through a cavern of darkness, heading for what looks like an open doorway far ahead—dim light, a gray brick wall.

I am speeding faster and faster. Just as I remember Cooper's words—*six moves ahead, let go of the railing, the game board is all around*—I blast through, the cart tipping, and I am dumped onto a wood floor.

I scramble to my feet. I'm in the middle of a long, empty hallway—brick walls, eerie pale light. The thump of bolts behind me makes me turn. The steel door I just crashed through is now sealed shut.

I can hear something coming.

A crowd appears at the very end of the hallway, thundering toward me.

It's a mob.

Though my inclination is to run, I stand frozen, trying to understand what it is I'm seeing.

The men wear tuxedos and top hats. The women wear black and cream and wine-colored dresses made out of taffeta, with hoop skirts and crinolines. Wire spectacles and white gloves, ringlets and ribbons—we once had a mannequin wearing a dress like these in Prologue, until Gigi declared it too creepy. She swore the fabric breathed on its own, making *shhh* noises for no reason. I try to remember what I researched and wrote on the price tag: *Summer Day Visiting Dress, 1840?*

One of the men, as he sprints toward me, actually checks a pocket watch hanging from his waistcoat on a gold chain, another thing we sell back at Prologue.

What is going on? The people are rushing toward me. Yet they don't see me. No. They are panting and sweating, running from something behind them.

Within seconds, the mob is all around me. They don't speak or give me the slightest notice. Yet they're afraid. I let them sweep me along, the elbowing and shoving getting worse as we lurch around a corner, flooding into an alcove. Just as I start to worry that I'm going to be trampled, we spill into a lobby.

It's a theater, the carpet red and gold, the walls gilded. Painted angels adorn the open doors ahead, where the crowd, handing their tickets to an usher, streams into a dim auditorium.

I notice the sign propped on a wooden easel.

THE WINCHESTER HISTORICAL SOCIETY PRESENTS
AN EVENING WITH THE FOX SISTERS
A CONVERSATION WITH THE DEAD
APRIL 12, 1850, 7 P.M.
WARNING: THE SICKLY, PEEVISH, AND FAINT NEED NOT
ENTER, FOR THEIR OWN SAFETY

The Fox sisters? 1850?

This must be Whispers Beyond the Grave. Valkyrie has a game board, but it's played in the real world. It's a real-world simulation.

Real people, real costumes, real fear.

But what do I know about 1850, other than the fact that it predated the Civil War? I wish that I listened more to Basil because he would know something about it. What would he tell me? *For starters, a dollar then is worth forty smackers today.*

"Ladies and gentlemen!" The tall, red-haired usher looks angry as he tears the tickets. "If you could kindly take your seats, the performance is about to begin. There will be no late arrivals. Ticket, miss? Your ticket!"

I can only gape in stunned confusion. He scowls, beads of sweat sliding down his temple.

"Only ticketed patrons can enter. No exceptions."

The crowd shoves me aside. Yet, fumbling in the pockets of the tunic, I feel something.

A single red ticket. ADMIT ONE.

I step back into line, thrusting the ticket at the usher. Though I know he and these people aren't real, only a staged play, and he is an actor—his face betrays not the slightest trace of this fact. He looks past me with weary agitation, as if he's done this job a hundred times before.

"Tickets! Please have your tickets ready! The performance is minutes away!"

The crowd is pushing past me. Who are these people?

There's no time to stop and wonder. I stumble into the auditorium. It's small but lavish, with rows of red velveteen seats and a painted mural on the domed ceiling. Stage lights and catwalks are suspended overhead, and mounted atop the proscenium of the stage is a giant digital clock with blue numbers—a jarring interruption to the antique dream of the scene.

The timer is counting down from what looks to be fifteen minutes.

14 minutes, 3 seconds.

The red curtain is open, revealing a stark setup onstage.

A small square card table, four chairs. A black curtain hangs along the back wall.

Seats are filling quickly. I push my way down the side aisle as far to the front as I can, sitting beside a woman in a gray dress and a man in a tuxedo. Both of them smell musty—like Prologue. Neither one speaks. They are both wringing their hands, breathing hard— craning their necks, worried glances back at the doors, as if they're expecting something to appear.

Police?

They don't seem to know each other. I gather no one speaks English, which makes me wonder if they've been brought here and threatened, if that accounts for the terrified looks on their faces.

I'm tempted to whisper something to test my theory, but I'm afraid of being tossed from Valkyrie, the game over before I make my first move. I sit back in my seat, trying to calm down, my mother's boast crashing through my head.

I call her my x-ray girl. She sees what no one else can.

Except the opposite is true now. I'm succumbing to panic, too scared to notice anything but the crowd and the blue clock, its numbers spinning irrevocably toward zero.

13 minutes, 8 seconds.

Find the dove in the dark whispers beyond the grave.

I look around the theater, no sign of any bird. Doves—what do I even know about doves? They're a sign of peace and a staple of magic tricks. I remember a meandering war story about a pigeon told by Basil. *All pigeons are doves,* he said. *Remarkably smart and easy to train.* A gun sergeant in his battalion kept a pigeon as a pet in his bunker by the Kŭm River. He fed it peanuts and sent it out in the morning to visit other battalions, where it would tap out dancehall songs in Morse code to improve morale. *I can't give you anything but love, baby. That's the only thing I've plenty of, baby.*

I sit forward, willing myself to take note of details—Louisiana always buried a powerful key at the start of every Darkly, something that will unlock the end. One tiny clue and the entire mystery is eviscerated, hanging open like a gutted fish.

There is a large wood table in the middle of the center aisle—some kind of sound system set up there, with a black rotary telephone and a seat for the director. An old red London phone booth stands in the very back, between the doors.

That's when I notice a boy glaring at me from the aisle. He wears the same boxy canvas tunic over street clothes. He looks about fifteen, with shaggy blond hair, and he brazenly sizes me up before making his way to an empty seat three rows behind.

He is another kid invited to play Valkyrie tonight. My competition.

He's not the only one. I spot two other kids wearing the same tunic, a Black girl way in the back, arms crossed, a nervous expression, and a tall dark-haired boy with braces, who looks petrified. There's another in the very front row, too, a blond girl. She deliberately rises, stepping to the edge of the stage to inspect it—

It's Everleigh.

She is carefully surveying the card table, the chairs—then she's looking up at the ceiling, the clock, the painted dome, the crisscrossing catwalks.

Any other intern, I'd be relieved. But from her measured stare, I can see that Franz and Cooper were correct. This girl is anything but scared.

And she knows much about Valkyrie than she ever let on.

No sooner do I think this than she turns and looks at me. She saw me minutes ago, because there is no surprise on her face. And though she bites her lip with a little cringe—an unconvincing attempt to summon her old persona of terrified little girl—I stare coldly back.

You're not fooling anyone.

Suddenly, the theater plunges into darkness. The crowd screams.

Everleigh scrambles to take her seat as a bright spotlight clangs on. A hunched woman is slowly wheeling an old clattering library cart across the stage.

T he woman wears a dark-green dress, black hair in a severe bun. The cart she is pushing is heavy, the shelves cluttered with books, candles, colored glass bottles filled with different trinkets and charms. They are apothecary bottles, the kind found in old doctor's cases. My mom sometimes tries to convince customers they are a "must-have for organizing your pantry!" Except they're old and impractical, with moldy little crumbling corks and weird odors.

The leap of the woman's shadow behind her, the whisper of her dress and slippers, the crowd mesmerized as they watch her progress across the stage, the eerie blue numbers spinning overhead—*10 minutes, 15 seconds*—all of it is so intense I almost leap out of my seat.

I need to do something—make a first move. But how? With what?

"Tonight, you will witness the ghostly malignant," the woman announces in a low, rasping voice. "My name is Leah Fox. It is my pleasure to bring you a conversation tonight between my sisters and the dead. They are rarities, my dear sisters—half specter, half child, born between the living and decayed. With each presentation, they inch closer to the latter, I'm afraid. It takes a terrible toll to face the departed. To withstand their vile urges and rage."

She pauses to raise a theatrical arm in the air, like an orchestra conductor, moments before the start of the symphony.

"They will be congregating here, the apparitions, and one will fight to the surface, demanding to be heard. For your own safety, you must remain in your seats until the chime of the bell, the signal that my sisters have successfully escorted the damned back to their graves."

With a sly smile, she hastily crosses herself. "Please join me in a round of applause for my sisters, Miss Kate, age thirteen, and Miss Margaretta, sixteen. And may God have mercy on us all!"

There are only a handful of uncertain claps as two dark-haired girls—one in a midnight-navy dress, the other in withered-cherry red—shuffle out from the shadows. They are much older than the woman said, probably in their thirties, with thick pancake makeup and tired expressions. But they hold hands and bow, their unsmiling faces so identical they might have been twins, if not for one being taller. They move beside the card table and face each other.

"Who will be our lucky volunteers tonight? Who longs to touch what cannot be seen?"

Everleigh eagerly raises her hand. So does the blond boy and—I look behind me—all the other kids playing Valkyrie, even the scared kid with the braces.

9 minutes, 5 seconds.

"You." Leah Fox points at Everleigh, who hops to her feet.

"You and you, and . . . one more brave soul?"

The blond boy and the Black girl skip up the steps after Everleigh. I raise my hand, but I'm too late. Leah Fox is pointing at someone in the back.

"You."

It's Poe.

With a jolt of shock, I watch him jog down the aisle and take a seat at the table.

Then the spotlight goes out, plunging the auditorium into darkness once again.

"Silence!" bellows Leah Fox as the crowd starts to whimper. "I now ask the four volunteers to close your eyes and clasp hands. Do it now."

There is the rasp of a match. Leah Fox removes a red wax candle from her cart, lighting the wick. Poe, Everleigh, and the other players have joined hands, closing their eyes. With methodical steps, Leah Fox circles the card table behind her sisters, candlelight tripping over their faces, hollowing their eyes and pulling down their mouths.

"Sisters, begin your descent."

And then my skin starts to crawl, because Margaretta and Kate are tipping back their heads, fingers gripping some kind of invisible pole between them in such perfect unison they look like a single marionette tied together. They sing a song in low voices.

"Mr. Splitfoot, come and play.

Save your doom for another day.

Nightie baby, one, two, five,

Suck on our souls and eat us alive."

8 minutes, 15 seconds.

Mr. Splitfoot. I've actually heard the name before. It was Agatha who told me about it, before her accident. It was from a fairy tale, what British children in olden days called the devil. She had a longtime employer so superstitious that she invoked the name whenever bad things happened out of the blue. Agatha could never figure out how much the woman was joking or serious. She sang the rhyme, though the words were different.

Mr. Splitfoot try, he may / he won't behave no, not today.

"Mr. Splitfoot?"

There is a resounding wooden knock. The crowd cries out.

The knock has no obvious origin. It sounds live, not from a speaker—as if one of the people onstage just struck the floor with a stick.

Except none of them moved.

"Mr. Splitfoot, have you brought us a friend?"

Crack.

"What is the name? Alphabet letters. Count them out now! A is one. Z twenty-six! Go now! Quickly!"

Crack crack crack.

As Mr. Splitfoot raps out letters, the sound thumping and echoing, the crowd shifting in alarm, I notice the black curtains at the wings of the stage. They are moving, as if there are people behind the scenes. Techs, stagehands? The curtain in the back is also moving, rippling as a figure strides across. If I can covertly climb back there—making it to one of the small flights of stairs on either side of the stage—I might see the people running this game.

5 minutes, 11 seconds.

It's dark enough in the audience to move undetected. At least, that's my hope. I slip to my feet, ducking low as I scramble past legs and feet and crinolines. People flinch, but otherwise they barely notice me, too enthralled by what's happening on the stage.

"Timsbury!" bellows Leah Fox. "Is that correct?"

Crack.

"Mr. Splitfoot, come and play.

Save your work for—"

"Who does he wish to converse with? Volunteer one, two, three, or four?"

Crack.

I stumble into the aisle and see, in surprise, that at the far back of the auditorium a dense crowd stands mesmerized, the light from the clock painting their faces deathly blue. There are too many people clogging the back aisles to get around to the side. The fastest way is to continue down the next row. I step past the outstretched legs, tripping on someone's cane, an old man gasping.

Crack crack crack crack.

"I'm sorry? Some fool is disturbing the descent! You there! Stop!"

I freeze.

Leah Fox, shading her eyes, is staring right at me.

So is the entire auditorium—all faces turned to me in alarm. I try not to react, my eyes flicking to the aisles. I'm trapped. Nowhere to go. All I have is the marked feeling that this auditorium and everything in it is a bomb about to explode—

4 minutes, 3 seconds.

The volunteers still grip hands, eyes closed—but Poe is shaking his head, mouthing something. *Dia, stop. No, don't do it. Sit down. You don't understand—*

Crack.

"Ah. You wish to feast on her foolish soul, Mr. Splitfoot?"

Leah Fox is immobile. Everyone looks confused, turning, awaiting something. The two Fox sisters are slowly raising their arms.

Crack.

With a triumphant smile, Leah Fox points right at me.

"Go ahead and eat!"

She blows out the candle.

Darkness crashes down like the ceiling caving in. The screams of the crowd seem to burst from the walls. People are diving out of their seats, pushing me down as they try to flee. I am shoved to the ground, the crowd kicking me as they race past.

I roll into a ball, bracing myself against a seat. If I can stay like this, stay alive, the timer will run out and this will be over. Or, I can say the exit phrase. Why don't I say it?

I can feel a break in the stampede. I struggle to my feet, blinking at the dark figures pushing past. I manage to slide out the end into the side aisle, though immediately I'm shoved backward again by a flood of more people, my head knocking the wall.

Find the dove in the dark whispers beyond the grave.

Suddenly, hands grip my waist. I am being lifted out of the crowd, slung over someone's shoulder. I kick, trying to free myself, then I'm abruptly set down into a cold, dark space.

"Paradise. Are you hurt?"

Poe's face floats before me. He is running his hands over my shoulders and back and head.

"This is no Darkly. This is hell. No logic, skill, or design. Only an inaccessible mosh pit of animal fight or flight. Three minutes left. Stay here, Paradise—do not move. I'm coming back."

Before I can answer, he is gone.

I'm alone in the darkness, screams echoing from every direction.

I realize I'm backstage, the curtains now closed. The card table is a few feet away, the chairs tipped over. Everleigh is gone, though on the floor lies the ghostly tunic of one of the players.

Someone used the safe words.

Leah Fox—there is no sign of her. But her two sisters have not moved. I can make out their floating, pale faces only a few feet away, arms still held in that odd position, eyes closed.

They are still singing. Their words snake through the shouting.

"Mr. Splitfoot, come and play.

Save your doom for another day—"

Crack. Crack.

The sound of Mr. Splitfoot, it's coming from under one of their skirts. I crouch, crawling alongside Margaretta, feeling for the hem, hoping she can't sense me because of the crinoline—

Someone slams me from behind. I cry out as I fly forward, hitting the ground on my stomach, air kicked from my lungs. I roll upright. Margaretta and her sister have fled into the wings. It was another player who ran into me—the scared boy with the braces. He rolls on the floor, holding his shoulder in pain.

Something about him is familiar. As he scrambles to his feet, I catch sight of his white socks, three dark stripes on the ankle. He moves to collect the items now strewn around the stage, which appeared to have exploded out of the cardboard box he was carrying.

"Not what he said!" the boy whimpers. "Not what he said!"

He freezes, petrified by something emerging from the curtains. It's Leah Fox, little more than a black specter as she wheels the squeaking cart toward him.

"No. Please, no!"

Instead of running—because he could run away, leap through the curtains—the boy crawls toward her. He madly ransacks the bottles and books on the cart, glasses crashing, spinning across the floor. "Which one is it? Which one? Tell me! Make it stop! Oh—!"

Leah Fox is bending over him, slow, deliberate. What is she doing?

"Wander where the witch lies!"

It happens so quickly. One second, the boy is there, a fluttering of shadows and dark shapes, the next, he's gone. I am staring at his white tunic tossed to the floor.

I step over to the cardboard box, now abandoned in the middle of the stage. There are things in there. A mitten. A tin teacup. I take a step, my foot kicking something else, sending it spinning across the floor. It's a small birdcage.

Something is alive inside, a fluttering white cloud. I step closer. It's a dove.

I lean down, opening the door. Then I feel someone grab me, a hand on my shirt, wrenching me back.

I turn, coming face to face with Leah Fox. She's in a kind of trance, eyes rolled back, her lips moving fast, hissing under her breath: "Suck down her soul, eat her alive." She pulls me roughly after her, a strong smell of cigarettes and saccharine perfume.

I shove her off, fleeing into the stage curtains, groping my way through pitch darkness, feeling along the wall. A props table, power cords, a life-sized human skeleton. I've reached the back curtain, a plastic plant pushed into the corner. I move behind it, crouching. I can hear the library cart squealing toward me.

The timer must be seconds from running out. I could say the exit words.

Wander where the—

I feel something on the floor under my hand. A trapdoor—like the one in the Darkly factory.

I fumble along the edges, certain I'm hallucinating. But sure enough, there's a hatch here—and even a latch. I wait, holding my breath, watching the cart wheels, the black cloud of the skirt floating past me. I yank the handle. The door opens—and I am staring all over again at a metal ladder extending down a constricted brick hole.

I clamber onto the rungs, sweep the door closed over my head.

The difference between the hysteria out there and the quiet here is so abrupt, it feels as if time has cut out. I blink into the murky green light below.

You are Arcadia Gannon. You are still alive. This is only the stolen twenty-ninth Darkly come to life. And there is an end to this.

I start to climb down.

I jump off the ladder at the bottom. I'm alone in an alcove—dim fluorescent light, cracked orange tiles, a green door.

Beside me is a clothing rack stuffed with dresses, tuxedo coats, petticoats. Two sagging boxes sit on the floor, piled with scuffed slippers and leather shoes.

I hear voices, footsteps. I wheel around, cramming myself between the wall and the costume rack just as the door opens. The hard pulse of techno fills the room. Two men shuffle inside, the door slamming.

I hunch lower, holding my breath.

Within seconds, they're rooting through the costumes, inches away, roughly pulling things out—a top hat, a cane. Then they start up the ladder. One looks ruddy, with a pronounced chin. The other is fat, with a beard. As the door opens in the ceiling, I swear I hear one of them mutter, "Time for a fucking raise, man." Then there's screaming, crashing, a thump—and everything is muffled again.

Are those employees of Valkyrie? Extras like in a movie? My

heart pounding, I slip out from behind the costume rack and tiptoe to the door. Carefully I crack it.

I peer out into a deserted corridor—mottled yellow tiles, flickering fluorescents.

Sticking my head out, I see a piece of ripped notebook paper is taped to the door. *Whispers Beyond the Grave,* someone scribbled in black marker.

I dart out and take off down the hallway, passing another door, another paper.

Detective, someone wrote.

I pass the next.

Unexplained Phenomena.

These are the categories from the Valkyrie spinner. These doors must lead into the different scenes where kids are playing Valkyrie.

I stop at the next—*Locks and Mazes*—and try the handle.

"—except John has no clue how to do it. He's dead weight. He thinks I'll clean up after him—"

"—but what happened, Shirley—"

"Poor thing was nearly devoured—"

I retreat, racing away from the laughter.

What is going on? No, no—I don't need to understand any of this, I remind myself. I only need to find a clue to take back to Raiden. A name. A face. A location.

I pause, looking back. The corridor seems to stretch a mile in both directions. What will I say if I'm caught? Does the escape phrase even work down here?

Surely, the timer in Whispers Beyond the Grave has run out by now, the first round of Valkyrie finished, winners declared, lights on, everyone thanked for their participation, the Fox sisters giggling, *Wasn't that crazy? We really scared you there, didn't we?*

No, the first round of Valkyrie won't end like that.

I should have waited for Poe. I wish Poe was racing beside me, making some brilliant calculation from the pounding techno music and the faint smell of pot on the players who climbed into Whispers Beyond the Grave, pinpointing where this warehouse must be, who these people are, an escape route: *Seventy-three miles south of Birmingham, these people are part of a criminal cabal of prominent German game makers, I can tell from the shape of the light sockets this building was constructed in 1926, which means there's a fire escape exactly here—*

Footsteps ring out behind me. I speed-walk toward the corner ahead, a casual glance over my shoulder.

A masked man, head to toe in black, is shoving a blindfolded player in a tunic out of one of the doors. He stops, staring right at me.

I veer around the corner and break into a sprint. I reach another door. *Loot* reads the paper.

I lurch inside. It's a large storage closet, dim, the strong smell of a pet store. There are rows of bins and cages, shelves, each one labeled. *Fortune Teller.* That one holds at least a hundred versions of a single tarot card, the Hanged Man. *Red Wolf.* That is an animal cage, but empty. But there's a dirty pillow, bowls of dog food and water.

I hurry down the next aisle. Where to hide? Then I stop.

I am staring into a cage filled with at least a hundred live white doves. They peck at birdseed and flutter onto swings. Two lie dead on the ground.

I open the latch, fingers shaking, Basil's whisper in my head. *They're remarkably smart and easy to train.* I grab a handful of birdseed and sweep the nearest dove into my palm. It barely flutters as I spill the seed into my tunic pocket and urge the bird inside.

I hear the door opening. I dart to the end of the row.

I wait, holding my breath as I watch a dark figure streak down the other side of the aisle. He's looking for me. He knows I'm here. I backtrack, passing bins filled with the same dolls, another with test tubes, teddy bears, bowler hats, compasses, black umbrellas, piles of *Life* magazine—all the same copy, I notice, a blond woman in a bathing suit. I reach the door and slip back into the corridor, taking off running, footsteps cracking behind me.

I yank open the first door I reach—*Obsolete.* It's a small alcove, like the one I climbed down into before, a clothing rack—this one stuffed with gray house-painting suits—a ladder. I race to it, climbing up, and heave open the door, crawling out into a cold corridor.

This is not a theater like in Whispers. It's an alley, raw brick, stone floor.

I check on the bird. Still warm. Still alive.

I fumble along the wall, feeling the rungs of another ladder, this one leading up to the ceiling. I start to climb. At the top, I step out onto a catwalk. It cuts along the beamed roof of a warehouse, like the Darkly factory. It's dark and silent below. Yet I can hear, somewhere nearby, the yowling horror of what must be Whispers Beyond the Grave.

Far ahead, at the end of the walkway, I see something. The blue light of the timer.

I take off for it. I can just make out the blue numbers.

0 minutes, 12 seconds.

11.

10.

I sprint toward it, the narrow pathway shuddering under my feet. When I am over the theater, I stop in dazed disbelief. Some twenty feet below is the opposite side of the painted dome. A twisted pathway is crudely painted there in glow-in-the-dark green paint.

4.

3.

I wheel around, searching for some kind of way down, but then, I trip, losing my balance. I scream as I plummet with a shout, reaching out, managing to grab something. A lighting cord.

I'm going to die.

I crash onto the dome. It's made of cheap cardboard, and it tears right under me. But the cord holds and I'm swinging sideways across the theater toward the stage. I collide with one of the Fox sisters, who screams as I fall on top of the card table. It collapses as a delicate two-note chime sounds.

I feel the dove flutter out of my pocket as I sit upright in the bright light and sudden silence, wondering if I'm dead.

1 March 1961

Mrs. Eve Humphrey
Lead Investigator, Her Majesty's Child Protective Services
14 Quakers Alley
Colchester, Essex
United Kingdom

Dear Mrs. Humphrey:

It has come to my attention that after the great search efforts and
headway we collectively made this year to track down and remove the
unattended foundling from the library, nothing permanent has been
done, and the girl has been returned to her mother.

The reason I know this is that I have strong evidence the child has
returned (see the attached photos). This farce cannot go on. I will
contact your superior and demand an explanation as to why, after
almost a year now of sounding the alarm, we still have a child
living in our library.

Your prompt response to this matter is required.

Sincerely,

Penny Malden

Penny Malden
Head Librarian
Bury St. Elmswood Public Lib

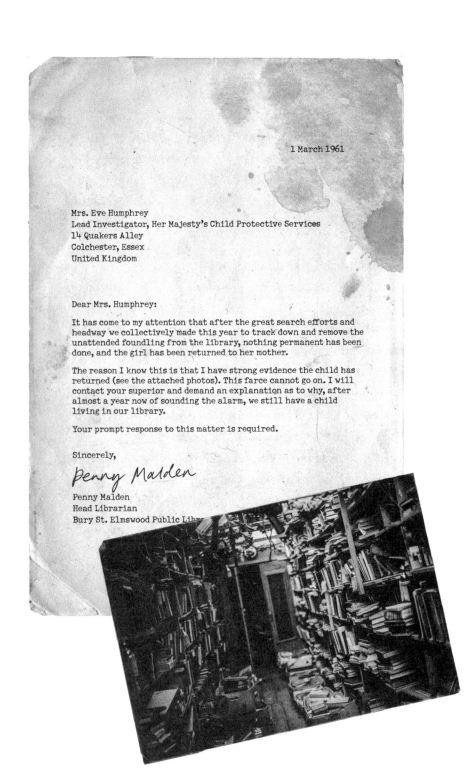

33

When the captain sees me stumbling down the pier, she seems to understand that something significant has happened to me. Though she scowls, she disappears into the hull and emerges with a flannel blanket, which she throws at me, and a cup of sloshing black tea, shoving it into my hands.

"She appears at the final hour," she says. "To keep us in doubt. The last child. Peace be to Saint Mary."

"The others are back?"

"Took them, one by one, this morning. Might as well drive a hackney carriage with all the mad back-and-forth." She squints at my forehead. "You don't need to go to hospital?"

I shake my head. I've already seen the bruises on my arms, the gash by my eyebrow, having wandered into a Pret A Manger bathroom in a town somewhere. My arms and legs are sore, and I have a haunted look that did not dissipate even after splashing water on my face.

"I'm fine. What time is it?"

"Six o'clock in the evening. The flea in the pirate's beard."

Apparently satisfied with this odd pronouncement, she draws up the anchor.

The sun is gone, the sky chalk white. For the first time since I've arrived here, there is no fog. The sea is rough, but I can make out the overgrown shoreline of this tattered patch of England, lined with a threadbare ribbon of sand. Small white cottages dot the hillside, and far ahead on the horizon floats the dark green of Darkly Island.

I'm grateful for the daylight and the company, even if it is the captain. Her wizened gruffness eases the memory of playing Valkyrie, turning the experience from a monster—which felt, up until only a few minutes ago, still very much alive—into a nightmare, an ordeal, but never real.

The conclusion of the game is still a blur. I don't know if I passed the first round. I also have no idea what happened to Poe or Everleigh. What I am positive about is that the boy who crashed into me with the cardboard box was from the Bromsbury School. I recognized those striped athletic socks. I also think he might have been the same person who shoved me in the tunnel.

But what happened at the end?

All I saw in those fleeting seconds as I struggled to my feet was the surreal sight of the mob, no longer hysterical but blank and exhausted. A bag was shoved over my head. I was pushed into a speeding wheelchair, veering down one corridor and another. I was placed in a van by a masked figure, then dumped, along with my dead phone, beside the picnic bench outside of the Inn. The intersection in the fading afternoon was as deserted as when I first saw it.

I hiked back to Darkly Pier along the road, asking anyone I passed for directions to Thornwood, refusing a ride from the one woman who stopped in a blue car. Her face, however friendly, looked eerily familiar. I wondered if I saw her inside the mad crowd, which led to the next unnerving thought: *Is the game still happening?*

Did Poe find what he was looking for? How did the other interns make out?

I had climbed outside the game—into the basement corridors and catwalks and storage rooms, all of it presided over by those tall, insect-like figures in black, the silent manipulators, the puppeteers. And what I saw before crashing through the domed theater—the painted pathway in the ceiling—it had to be an extension of the Valkyrie game board.

I am dying to tell Poe about it, to tell all of them. Whatever my suspicions before about Cooper and Franz, and even Everleigh, I want to put that aside, now that we are all marked by the disorienting ordeal of the first round of Valkyrie.

I drain the tea, noticing that there is no sign of the captain. The motor is idling, and the *Elvira,* bucking in the waves, is drifting harrowingly close to the rocks along the shoreline. I slip to my feet and find the old woman at the bow, scowling in consternation at a dock. It's been badly damaged by a storm, planks ripped, mooring beams gone. At the very end, a broken lantern hangs upside down, dangling from electrical wires.

The captain is leaning far, far out of the boat in an attempt to recover the lamp when the blast of a wave sends the boat reeling sideways. I am thrown backward into the benches as the captain, with a sharp cry, is tossed clear over the side. I scramble to my feet, racing to help her, but she's already back aboard with a nimble leap. And then both of us are staring in dazed astonishment as the dock, pummeled by a fresh wave, tears completely loose as if it's nothing more than a stale slice of bread, the beams crumbling and vanishing in the waves.

"They hope you drown in the sea!" the captain bellows, raising a fist to the sky. "I won't let that happen! You hear me, Madam?"

She is extremely distraught. She sniffs, wiping her face.

"Madam?" I ask. "Do you mean Louisiana?"

She glares at me. "You think this is the king's bloody jubilee? You'll take a seat and mind your bloody business before you're tossed to the rocks like an empty can of Vimto fizzy. Because when you're chucked in there"—she juts her thumb over her shoulder—"no one will be divin' in to save you!"

She returns to the wheel, the *Elvira* veering away from shore, motor yowling. I step after her.

"You knew her."

Maybe it's my exhaustion after Valkyrie, but I feel I have nothing to lose. I had been hoping to find the right time to ask her this, away from the others, when her sour grumpiness had eased just a little. If there was ever any clue that the captain was here back in the days Louisiana was alive, it's her face, as weathered as an old Wellington boot, her ease with this patch of sea, like a blind woman who knows every inch of her house.

"What was she like?"

The captain wrenches the wheel, cranking the motor higher, and the boat is flying fast toward the island, tripping over the waves.

"Every morning. Four o'clock. She'd be waiting for me there. On that dock."

She shouts this so suddenly, her eyes fixed ahead, I am stunned.

"Louisiana lived there?"

I turn back, craning my neck to make out something else on the hillside with the demolished dock—the faintest splinter of roof, the top of a chimney.

But there's only dark forest, quickly retreating.

"In her black suit and houndstooth coat, a scarf in pink, green, and yellow like a laugh at her throat, I'd ferry her to her work at her factory. Every night, stroke of midnight, I'd bring her home. Never a change. Always alone. Fifteen years. That's how she did it. While the rest of the world was still dreaming, she had already worked a day. That was Madam."

The captain cranks the levers, the boat now flying with such velocity I have to grip the railing. My mind screams a hundred questions.

You worked with Louisiana for fifteen years? What was she like, underneath the glamour and the rumors and the mystery and the myth? Who was she really?

Yet I'm afraid to speak or even breathe, for fear of sending the old woman back into her ornery silence.

"Oh, yes, the stories are true," she says. "Her beauty burned the eyes. It was quite impossible. And her mind—a machine from the future, relentless and powered by pure magic and the divine. But what nobody knows about is her heart. It was bigger than the stars. No one knew that. She didn't want anyone to know. She knew they'd kill for it."

She shakes her head, lost for a second inside some private memory. Then she eyes me with a mischievous smile.

"Madam rescued me when I was just sixteen. I had run away from home and was living behind a pub. One day, I opened my eyes and she was there. 'What do you say I give you a chance? Tell me what you wish to be.' 'A captain,' I replied. I had happened upon a Popeye comic book. It was the only thing I had to keep me company. Well, one week later, I was manning the *Elvira*. I never stopped. Not even after she died. She kept me on the island. Made sure I had a home. Set it up in her will, much to their chagrin. They can't get rid of me. When Madam makes a promise, it's forged in forever."

She is referring to Derringer Street, I realize.

Removing a handkerchief, she blows her nose. "You should have seen the men tripping over themselves to touch her hand." She chortles, stuffing the rag back into her pocket. "But she never brought one home here to her secret sanctuary—too cunning for that. No, she never disclosed her secrets to any man. Never brought strangers to her factory. They'd only try to take it. Take *her*. It drove them bonkers. 'This is mine, Captain.' That was the rule. Her kingdom stayed hers. She was not to be domesticated, taken from the wild, trapped in the exhibits at the zoos, where all the other girls in love perform tricks for peanuts and popcorn."

"But the night of the Darkly anniversary party? Louisiana brought strangers here that night." I'm so swept up in her words I shout it without thinking—and regret it instantly. It's a risk to be so direct with the captain.

But then I see from the far-off look in her eyes she is sort of like Basil, and a lot of elderly, when asked about the past—first loves, heartbreaks, chance encounters, wars. It's like dessert. They start with just one bite, then an hour later they've eaten an entire éclair, a tray of napoleons, a whole key lime pie.

"Raiden told you about her stolen game, did he?" The captain eyes me with grim curiosity.

"Yes."

"I was there. I was Madam's eyes and ears, shuttling guests to and from the island. I knew it would end in catastrophe. Months before, I warned her, 'Madam, do not do this.' No. Twenty-six guests, a chef, and a server from the shelter. Delivering a boatload of serpents to Eden. Everyone was a suspect, even Gattie, though she was long gone by then. For years, they interviewed everyone. Monitored us. Probably still do. Rightfully so. But it was a beautiful night. Nobody saw a thing."

She sniffs. I sense she means to add something.

"Nothing was strange?" I ask. "No one vanished for a time?"

"I always thought the game was stolen by goblins. So perfectly gone it was."

The *Elvira* lurches. I see that we have arrived at the island, the boat swinging to a neat halt alongside the pier.

I don't move, not wanting the spell to break, to keep peppering the captain with questions: Who were these twenty-six guests? Who did Louisiana think stole her game? She must have known something—or had suspicions.

The captain hops onto the dock, busy with tying the ropes. I step after her.

"Gattie," I say. "Who is that? I've never heard the name before."

The captain nods, a sad smile. "The most loyal of all. Her shadow. The secretary. Except she wasn't in the end. Even she left. Broke Madam's heart. They all left. I was the one who stayed. The only one."

She boards the boat, and without a glance back at me, probably sensing she said too much, she is gone again into the hull.

34

The captain's words are still ringing in my head—*I was the one who stayed*—when I come upon the others, holed up in the canteen.

I stumble through the doorway, relieved to be reunited with them at last after traipsing around the island—finding no sign of them in the cottages, or on any of the winding paths—but then for one uneasy moment, I feel as if I'm crashing a party.

They are sitting on the counters in sweats, wild-haired and barefoot, eating Special K out of the box, talking in low voices so intensely it's a few seconds before they notice me.

"Dia!" shouts Torin.

"Gott sei Dank," says Franz.

"We were so worried."

They crowd around me. Franz hands me a box of Special K, patting me on the head. I notice he and Cooper have strange lacerations on their hands, and Torin's left arm is covered with odd scribblings in orange marker.

"I told you not to move," Poe says, staring down at me with faint accusation.

"I don't always do what I'm told."

"I went back for you."

He seems hurt or disappointed—I can't tell which—and I don't know what to say, or how to begin to explain what happened. Then Mouse is grabbing my arm, pulling me over to a green chalkboard. A rectangle with shapes and lines is drawn in white chalk. I recognize it as the Valkyrie game board. Underneath it is a version of the spinner, where they have written different categories. *Detective. The Greys. Unexplained Phenomena.*

"We're recounting what happened to each of us and rebuilding the board," Mouse explains. "Recollections, spoken lines, set pieces. We're putting it all down. From that, we hope to have a clear picture of Valkyrie."

"That way, if we ever play again, we do not get smashed like Ungeziefer on a windshield," says Franz.

"Who made it to the next round?" I ask.

Cooper shrugs. "We don't know."

"None of us know a thing," says Mouse. "What about you?"

I shake my head and scramble onto the counter beside Torin. Poe tosses me a can of cucumber seltzer from the fridge.

That's when I notice Everleigh. She is the only one who didn't react to my arrival—no greeting, not even a smile. She sits alone on the opposite side of the kitchen, bruises on the inside of her left arm, staring at all of us as she shoves handfuls of Special K into her mouth.

"Okay, let's get Dia up to speed," says Mouse. "Who's going first?"

35

Valkyrie began for them the same way it did for me.

Van ride. Blindfold. Wheelchair.

The chorus of voices in the warehouse—most of them were old, we all agree, over sixty, at least. The spotlight. The wooden game board on the card table, carved with shapes and words. The dizzying spin of the three wheels. The mystery clanging pieces in the gray velvet bag. The black hourglass with the gold sand.

Torin spun *Detective, Slaughterhouse* and pulled a mitten figurine from the bag.

She was trapped in an old haunted house, as she called it, doors bolted, panes painted black. Three creaking floors with an attic and a basement, a croaking record player, plants, musty portraits of unknown people. A neon-blue clock in the kitchen counted down fifteen minutes.

"I started to go down to the basement. It was pitch-black. No lights. The sound of scratching. Then a bulb flickers on. There's a hunchback old woman down there in a black dress hauling a sack. She started toward me. I screamed the exit phrase and they took me away."

Mouse spun *The Greys, Bad Dream* and chose a tiny doll.

He was also locked in a house, this one cavernous, having dinner at a dining room table with a family of seven, whose faces he could not see, concealed as they were in voluminous black hooded cloaks. This family appeared to be the Greys from the spinner—a mother, father, and five adult children, all girls. They neither acknowledged Mouse at the table, nor said a word in answer to his questions, only ate a putrid porridge. When Mouse got up to inspect the house, proceeding up a flight of stairs and down a hall lined with armor, they started to chase him, chanting nonsensical words and making strange clicking noises. One carried an ax. Another, head to toe in black, carried a basket filled with glass syringes. Mouse found the experience so horrifying that he could not remember the exit phrase, and hid sobbing behind a tapestry, certain he was going to die, until the clock ran out, the lights came on, and the Greys vanished.

"I am positive I did not make it."

Franz spun *Locks and Mazes, Ghost Dog* and pulled a raven from the bag.

He was shoved into a grain silo containing odd pieces of furniture and a massive dead tree, which stretched high overhead. He could see and hear something alive by the ceiling, black and fluttering—a raven. Within seconds, a howling white dog was pushed through the door as well as a woman wearing black goggles on her face and a backpack. She strolled in circles around the tree as the dog snapped and lunged at Franz. He scrambled to climb, up and up to avoid both of them. Yet, the tree limbs were so thin and spindly, they snapped under his weight, sending him constantly falling back below.

"It was like climbing eggshells," he whispers.

It went on and did not stop. He had plummeted to the ground, the dog biting his ankle, the woman bending over him—he holds up his pant leg to show me, and I stare in shock at the red marks of an actual animal bite—when he screamed, "Wander where the witch lies." The game ended immediately. The woman left. Two figures in black hauled the dog away—then Franz. A bag over his head, he was shoved into the wheelchair, then into the van.

Cooper spun *Maria Tallchief, Bird Hunter* and took a test tube from the bag.

She was dumped outside in a dense forest where someone—what she believed to be the bird hunter—was shooting at her. Gunshots echoed all around, bullets ripping through tree trunks feet away from her head. And though she was convinced it wasn't real—it could *not* be real—she saw bullet holes in the tree trunks as she ran for her life. She caught a glimpse of a figure in green camouflage, eyes obliterated by goggles, advancing behind her, rifle in his arms. She arrived at a lake and was fleeing toward a shack perched on the shoreline when a screaming old woman shot out of the door, pointing a rifle at her. Cooper tripped on a hidden piece of twine, a booby trap, and fell into a pit. When she heard the woman's footsteps getting closer, fresh ammo loading, Cooper was so shaken she screamed, "Wander where the witch lies." Everything fell silent. She waited for what felt like hours. Then two figures in masks arrived to haul her out with a rope.

"All my reading and plotting and planning," says Cooper quietly. "All out the window. I never saw any test tube. Or anything about a professional ballet dancer. Only a red London telephone booth standing in the middle of the forest. Totally surreal."

Poe spun *Whispers Beyond the Grave, Deadeye Man* and pulled out a sailor.

Unlike the others, he was not afraid. He was intent on solving the game.

"Perhaps I'm naive, but I trusted, no matter what, those masked figures in charge would not let me die. A high teenage body count would surely defeat their purpose of world domination."

He was with me in the theater, of course. The only difference was the added menace of the "deadeye man," a hulking man, at least six foot five, wearing circular black lenses.

"I'd look over my shoulder, and there he'd be, this beast of a man following me like an insidious hex."

What did he want? What was he trying to do? Poe never figured it out. He managed to elude him by hiding, and after leaving me on the stage, he combed the screaming crowd for some sign of the sailor.

He had all but given up, a minute left, when he noticed a man having escaped the mob by scaling a heating pipe—like a sailor climbing a ship's mast. Poe headed for him. He pulled off one of the man's shoes and saw tattoos of a rooster and a pig on his ankle—"common sailing symbols," he said, "the superstition being that they will prevent the sailor from drowning"—when I came crashing through the ceiling and the chime sounded, ending the game.

And finally, Everleigh—she spun *Whispers, Dark* and chose an umbrella.

She has the least to say, only that she noticed a black umbrella on Leah Fox's library cart. Trying to grab it, she knocked over the jars and bottles, one smashing, spilling black liquid across the floor.

"It smelled so foul," she says, wrinkling her nose. "Definitely some black-magic potion."

As they each tell their stories, I hang on their every word. The nightmare of their individual experiences aside, it's what they pulled from the velvet bag that strikes me most. These were the objects they were all tasked to find—and I saw many of them in the closet where I found the live doves.

Loot.

"Dia, it's your turn," says Poe.

I tell them. When I reach the part where I hid behind the plant, found the trapdoor, climbed down into the basement, and then fled from the masked figure up into the ceiling, they are incredulous.

"*You* made it beyond the boundaries of the Darkly," says Poe. I catch a hint of annoyance in his voice.

"I think so."

"And on this catwalk, you saw a portion of the Valkyrie game board painted on the ceiling?" asks Mouse.

"A pathway. It made me remember what Cooper told me. From her book. 'The game board is all around you.'"

They look stunned, maybe a little jealous, too.

"That is impressive," says Franz.

Cooper scowls, crossing her arms. "Except wait a minute—how did you know to feel in the dark for an escape hatch in the floor? I mean, that's pretty random."

"I found the same thing in Louisiana's office. At the Darkly factory."

I confess how I wandered inside the walls, found the portholes and speakers for eavesdropping. Of course, I leave out the part where I spied on her and Franz, though I'm aware of them eyeing each other, doubtlessly wondering if I overheard their private conversation.

I can tell from the silence that follows they're not only surprised by this, but they're noting that I said nothing before. But how can I tell them the truth? *Sorry I didn't say anything. But I didn't trust any of you. And I still don't.*

"The kid who ran into you," says Mouse. "You're sure it was the same boy from the tunnel at Bromsbury?"

"I think so."

"We can get our hands on a school yearbook, identify him from a photo. Maybe he knew George."

For a moment, no one speaks, thinking it over. Then Torin takes a nervous breath. "There is one more weird thing that happened," she says. She exchanges an uneasy look with Franz.

"Ja, I was back to the island first," he says. "When I walked into the cabin, it was obvious someone had been snooping through our things. Our bags had been moved. Clothing. Photos. I keep a needlepoint pillow of the sarcophagus lid of Pascal the Great under my pillow to contact other life-forms in my subconscious as I sleep? I found it outside in the bushes."

"Same thing in our cabin," says Torin. "Someone went through our stuff."

"Was anything stolen?" I ask.

"Our toothbrushes were all moved to different sinks," says Cooper. "Which is super gross. We need new toothbrushes."

"Someone went through my makeup," says Torin. "My mascara was taken."

"I can't find my comb," says Mouse.

"I wrote a snail mail letter to my father," says Poe. "Stamped. Ready to mail. It's missing from my briefcase. Yet the most valuable asset on the island, Eighteen Lost Icelandic Sailors, remains handcuffed to the foot of my bunk bed, untouched."

"That means the motivation was lurid curiosity," says Mouse.

"Or the acquisition of a series of mementos, a terrifying prelude before the serial killer strikes," says Franz.

"It's got to be the captain," says Cooper.

"No way," says Mouse, frowning. "I mean, she's nuts. *Obviously.* She'd have to be, living here. But she doesn't seem interested in us enough to go through the trouble of rooting around our things."

"She wouldn't have had much time to do it," says Torin. "Going back and forth all day in the boat picking us up."

"Someone else is here on the island," says Franz. "Hiding."

Everyone turns, waiting for him to explain.

He shrugs. "It's nothing I've seen. Just the feeling we're being watched. I felt it even before what happened to Poe."

"I feel it, too."

Everleigh blurts this suddenly in a tense voice. "My hair dye was stolen. I have a box in my luggage. It's empty. The applicator, comb, bleach, even the latex gloves. Everything was taken."

This outburst reminds me all over again how odd she is. During this hour of talking, she is the only one who has remained mostly quiet. Now, whatever conclusion she has drawn about her stolen hair dye, though her face flushes with embarrassment, she chooses not to say another word.

It's late.

We are all so drained, even Franz's unsettling suspicion—that a stranger is here, spying on us, playing tricks, someone rash and unhinged who, spotting an opportunity, decided to push Poe and Torin off the catwalk at the factory—is met only with mute unease. I suggest that we hike the island in the morning, figure out where every path leads. It could tell us how the thief got the game off the island without detection and also reveal signs of anyone else hiding here.

We head outside. As I follow the others down the wood planks to the fork where our cottage sits on one side of the pond, the boys' on the other, I am aware of Poe pausing, watching me go with a thoughtful smile. Though I want to talk to him—say thank you for pulling me out of that mob—I am exhausted, my whole body sore, so I slip inside the cabin without a word.

My clothes have been rifled through in the drawers, but nothing is missing. Only my toiletry bag and my dirty laundry—T-shirts and jeans—have been moved. The only memento I brought from home—a framed photo of me, Gigi, Agatha, and Basil in front of Prologue some hot summer afternoon years ago—was knocked off the bedside table, probably by accident. I find it wedged behind the bunk by the radiator.

It's strange. But I'm too tired to think much about it. We change into our pajamas and climb into bed.

I don't know what it is that wakes me.

A dream? The lost feeling of home? Some vestige of the adrenaline from playing Valkyrie? Or is it something malignant rattling around in my head, the feeling that something is not right?

My heart slamming my ribs, I sit up, listening—for footsteps, the sound of ragged breathing, the sign that someone else is here.

All I can hear is the moan of the wind and Torin muttering in her sleep. My phone, I see, is fully charged now, and not only do I see that it's 2:19 a.m., but Choke Newington texted me right after I hung up on him.

Call me please

The idea that I hung up on, then literally *forgot* Choke Newington is a surreal reality that I never could have imagined.

But then I sort of forget even that. Because I understand what is unnerving me.

The portrait of Louisiana painted by Raiden at orientation—when he spoke of how she was preyed upon—is so very different from the focused and controlled powerhouse that the captain described.

Never a change. Always alone. Fifteen years. Her kingdom stayed hers.

It's as if they are talking about two different people.

The shock of learning that Louisiana's private home is secretly holed up on the mainland with the demolished dock, so close—I don't know what it means. But it had to have been deliberate—Raiden failing to mention this. And who was the captain talking about when she shouted at the sky, *They hope you drown in the sea?*

I have to go back there—if not for any other reason than to better understand Louisiana. And I need to go not tomorrow in the light of day, when the captain and Raiden and who knows who else will doubtlessly try to stop me—but now.

Before anyone catches wind that I even know about it.

I feel a dark excitement as I silently climb out of bed and dress, yanking on my sneakers, grabbing my phone. I don't have much in the way of a plan—only a vague story Basil once told, about a successful midnight raid on the Nakdong River after stealing the enemy's assault boat. I hope I've seen the captain cranking levers and hauling up the anchor enough times to generally understand how to drive.

I'm pulling open the screen door when I hear a creak behind me.

"Dia? What are you doing?"

I stop, turning. Everleigh has climbed out of bed.

I'm tempted to lie. But I'm too tired to come up with anything plausible, so I tell her the truth.

"I'll come with you." She scrambles down the ladder, pulling on her jeans and grabbing a sweatshirt. "I can drive the boat."

I have the sudden worry that I might not be safe alone with her—the way she behaved during Valkyrie and afterward, all of those deep stares and the pointed silence. But then Torin and Cooper are sitting up, yawning, rubbing their eyes.

"What's going on?"

Before I can stop her, Everleigh is explaining and they're getting dressed, too.

Within minutes, the four of us are filing outside. As we slip past the cottage where the boys sleep, Cooper stops.

A light is on inside. Someone appears to be awake.

"Maybe we should wake them so they can join us," she says.

Everleigh shakes her head. "Too cumbersome. We don't need them."

"Girl power," says Torin, giggling.

"We'll be in and out fast," I say. "We can tell them all about it in the morning."

But Cooper is unconvinced, staring at the cottage. Maybe she's scared to be without her secret ally, Franz. Or is she still spooked from Valkyrie? Because she hasn't quite been herself since the game. No more arrogance or scathing attitude or even the slightest eye roll.

But then she hurries to catch up with me and says nothing more about it.

Miss Bella Downling
c/o Deathly Mystery Shop
193 Hopkins Street
London, England

21 December 2001

Miss Downling:

It has recently come to our attention that you are making unauthorized usage of the copyrighted Darkly® games Forest Past and The Red Hounds of Garsington, as well as extensive usage of Darkly® signage, logo, badges, insignia, and merchandise in your newly opened mystery shop, Deathly, located at 193 Hopkins Street.

Your game entitled The White Wolves of Yesterday is essentially identical to the aforementioned Works and clearly uses the Works as its basis. You neither asked for, nor received, permission to use the Works. The use of these Works infringes upon the rights of the Louisiana Veda estate under Laws 1.321–8.932 of the UK Commonwealth Trademark Office.

We demand that you immediately cease the use, advertisement, and distribution of The White Wolves of Yesterday and remove all signage, stickers, and merchandise illegally using the Works and Darkly® logo.

Further:

We hear of certain "insider" tales you have been sharing with customers, boasting of a deal to publish an "anonymous coffee table book" about Louisiana Veda and Darkly® with On the Downlow Publishers. We are compelled to remind you of the provisions set forth in the Agreement you signed with us dated 9 August 2000. Failure to adhere to all obligations set forth in said Agreement will result in its immediate breach and the termination of benefits to you, including, but not limited to, your generous annual stipend.

If we do not receive a response from you by 2 January 2002, assuring us that you are in full support and compliance of all requirements set forth in this letter, Derringer Street will be forced to take all necessary actions to rectify this troubling matter.

Sincerely,

Nile Raiden

Nile Raiden
Senior Counsel

A full moon drenches the ocean with silver light as we motor the *Elvira* toward the mainland. Everleigh's skill behind the wheel is impressive. Without a word, she unmoored the boat and maneuvered it out into the bay with the lights off, engine purring. When we are a safe distance from the island—no sign of the captain—she cranks the motor, sending us flying across whitecaps.

"You didn't think to tell us you served as an admiral in the naval service?" shouts Torin.

Everleigh shrugs. "I grew up on a boat. My family fishes herring for a living."

Minutes later, as we are motoring along the shoreline, solemn and smudged black with overgrown trees, I climb out onto the bow to look for the demolished dock. Cooper slips after me.

"What's gotten into Everleigh?" she whispers. "Forty-eight hours ago, she was whimpering that she had to go home. Now, she's like a Green Beret."

She's been lying to all of us, I think. *Just like you and Franz.*

I shrug. "She's not afraid anymore."

Cooper shivers, smiling. "That makes one of us."

Suddenly, I spot the remnants of the dock in the underbrush.

"Right there," I shout.

Everleigh tries to moor the *Elvira* onto what is left of the landing—there is one remaining post—but it doesn't hold. The tide is coming in, and the waves break violently, sending giant swells under us. Everleigh manages to negotiate the boat into an inlet buffered by trees, where the wind is quiet. She moves as close as she can to the shore and drops the anchor. Then she's in the hull, emerging with life vests, tossing each of us one.

"We're going to have to swim from here."

I jump first. The water is icy, the current vicious. I manage to kick my way to the narrow strip of beach, the sand black and rocky. The three others are right behind me. Shivering, we make our way through tangled brambles and find a path by the dock. Teeth chattering, a mutual look of unease, we start up the hill.

It's steep. We move single-file, stumbling in sodden sneakers, ropes of thorns clawing our legs. We stop at the top of a set of stairs, confronted by a crude chain-link fence—similar to the one around the Darkly factory.

Far beyond it, across an overgrown field, sits a red brick Victorian house.

"Look up the word 'haunted' in the dictionary, it shows this," whispers Torin.

She has a point. There are turrets and spikes, and what looks to be gargoyles crouched at the corners of the roof. The windows are black, the shingles caved in and crumbling. The house looks terrifying—leaden and empty and unhappy. Yet, all I can think is that in Louisiana's heyday it must have been draped in sun and music and mystery. Louisiana Veda would have crafted a beautiful world here—*her secret sanctuary,* as the captain put it.

"No wonder Raiden keeps everyone away," says Cooper, beside me. "He doesn't want people to be possessed by demons."

"You think that man would care if we're possessed by demons?" asks Torin.

"If it means we can't play Valkyrie and he'd have to deal with the inconvenience of finding new gullible idiots to do his bidding? Yeah."

I start to climb the fence. "You three check out the grounds. We'll meet up here in an hour."

"Wait, you're actually going in?" says Torin.

I swing my legs over the top of the fence and jump down into the grass. It reaches my waist.

"To me it's just another antique shop."

As I head for the house, trying to keep to the buried path, Torin and Cooper take off along the fence, vanishing somewhere in the woods. But Everleigh has decided to follow me.

"I'm not afraid of old things either," she says with an odd giggle as she catches up.

I see now that the gargoyles along the roof are birds. They are made of stone, all different sizes, some perched with open beaks, calling a silent warning cry, others crouched as if hiding. They're ravens, I assume. Ravens appear in many Darklys, usually as the harbingers of gutting news. But then I see that they have long, scaled dragon tails wrapped around their clawed feet. They're probably some mythical bird that turns up in one of the more obscure ghost games.

We move up the steps to the sagging porch, the shadows clogged here like mist. There's a black swing beached in dead leaves. I try the front door, expecting it to be locked.

But it drifts open with a creak.

We stare into the entrance hall. It looks like one of those sunken ships preserved for a hundred years in dark, icy waters, because the house is stuffed with things, all of it eerily frozen in place. A chandelier draped in cobwebs. A tarnished gilt mirror speckled with rot. Hats crowd a hat rack—bowler hat, straw hat, fedora—all covered in dust. A pair of black leather gloves rests on a side table, as if Louisiana left them there minutes ago, before she was called to the telephone.

"Wow," whispers Everleigh as she steps inside. "It's like she's alive in here."

I manage to nod, noting with a shiver that this contradicts what she claimed before, that her stepsister was the Louisiana fan, not her. Because the look on her face is pure Darkly gloom as she moves to the gloves, bending toward them in awe, then scrutinizing a porcelain bowl filled with loose pound notes and a set of small keys. Then she moves to inspect a wood mantel clock.

"Time stopped in here at 9:07," she whispers.

I step inside and the massive door closes behind me with a belch, as if it just delighted in swallowing us whole.

38

We don't mean to split up.

But we're both overcome with a scared excitement—as if we've stumbled upon a forgotten Darkly amusement park. Everleigh, under a kind of breathless spell, starts up the mahogany staircase that looks like it was built for Louisiana Veda to make a grand entrance in a ball gown. She vanishes somewhere on the next landing.

I stare, transfixed, at the hall in front of me. It's a portrait gallery, cloaked in darkness. I head for it, inspecting in bewildered awe the damask walls covered in paintings. There are jesters and generals, empty landscapes of solemn winter snow. I wonder who the people are, if Louisiana knew them. Or are they total strangers, this expensive artwork some underling picked up at a gallery? The sort of thing you put on your walls to try and convince yourself that you're someone, you're something—that maybe you weren't before, but you are now.

I pass a blue sitting room, furniture draped in ghostly white sheets, a dining room, a music room with a piano and a gold harp.

Stepping inside, I note that while there are no photographs, a giant portrait of Louisiana commands the far wall. She wears hunting boots and a red jacket, riding a rearing black horse. Her gaze is so dark and powerful, so strangely bright, I feel as if she's caught me red-handed and she is wondering why I'm sneaking around her house.

I slip into the next room. It's a double-height wood-paneled library with rolling ladders and a trellised walkway. A reading table sits in the center, a giant black globe of Earth beside it. There's nothing on the table except a large platter covered with an antique glass dome. It's a cloche—French for "bell." They were popular during the Victorian era to display everything from dried roses to fossils to tea cakes.

Inside this one is a stack of books. There are nine—all library books, I see from the stickers on the spines. They're old, the titles nothing I've ever heard of, though the tattered fabric covers—one features a small black bowler hat, another a red knight holding a blue sword—remind me of the dry, windswept tales we sell back in Rare Books at Prologue.

A Biography of Viscountess Aberhorne and Her Bygone Friends.
The Forgotten Family Trees of Great Britain.
The Ghosts of Queen Victoria.

I bend down to see if there's a drawer—maybe some locked secret compartment where Louisiana stored letters or a diary? I check the end tables beside the couch, a writing desk by the window.

There's nothing here.

I'm about to duck out when, running my hand along the books, I notice they also have library stickers. I take a step back, squinting at the shelves above.

Everything in here is a library book.

I pull one off the shelf. *19th-Century Explorer Maps of Foreign Lands.* I flip to the back. There is an old-fashioned library pocket, due-date slip taped there, a faded red stamp.

January 12, 1976

Property of the Bury St. Elmswood Public Library

I put the book back and grab another, and another.

Every book is from the Bury St. Elmswood Public Library.

I move up the spiral stairs, passing through cobwebs, thick dust icing the shelves. The same is true for every book up here.

That's when I hear footsteps. Someone is in the portrait gallery.

"Dia?"

It's Everleigh.

"Up here."

She races in, out of breath. "I found her bedroom. The curtains are open. The windows shattered. The wind is insane up there. But I swear I just heard someone outside screaming. I thought it was you, so I came . . ."

I move to the railing, listening. Then I take off down the stairs.

"Let's check outside."

"Hello?" someone calls out. "Anyone?"

We find Torin by the front door, the ashen look on her face making us both stop dead.

"Someone is here," she whispers.

W e race after Torin outside, through the grass and brambles, around the side of the house to the back, where there is a crumbling stone patio, a loggia of rotten wood, overgrown labyrinths of plants and weeds. Torin is so distraught, all we can get out of her as she runs is "She's trapped."

"You mean Cooper?" asks Everleigh. "Where is she?"

"The graveyard. She went in to see Louisiana—"

I don't understand what she means until, racing around a hedge, we stumble out onto a pebbled path leading up a hillside. At the top sits a stone mausoleum. Torin tears up the hill, heading straight for it, and as Everleigh and I race to catch up, I see beyond the steps there is an iron door, a heavy lock on the handle.

Cooper is banging and whimpering on the other side.

"Oh, God, get me out—there's something in here—oh, God—"

"Cooper, it's Dia."

"Get me out! I don't want to— Wander where the witch lies. Wander where the witch—"

Everleigh, Torin, and I exchange shaken looks.

"She thinks this is part of Valkyrie?" whispers Everleigh.

Torin is crying. "I don't know what happened. I was down on the patio when I heard screaming."

"Wander where the witch lies. Wander where the— Someone's in here—leave me alone!"

I press my ear to the door. Cooper is fumbling around inside, hysterical.

If something else is in there with her, an animal or person, I can't hear it.

I inspect the lock. It's old, similar to the ones that Raiden unlocked at the Darkly factory. There's a keyhole, but without the proper key it will require a heavy-duty bolt cutter.

"No! Nooo—"

"Cooper, it's Dia. Don't worry. We're going to get you out of there."

"*You* did this! I saw you! You stay away from me! Keep her away—"

I take off down the hill. As I veer onto the path, Cooper's shouting and pounding echoing through the night, I venture a look back and see Torin and Everleigh staring after me.

You did this. Cooper thinks I'm responsible?

I tear around the hedge, through a tangle of plants, tripping on the uneven stones, my hands and legs shaking so badly I have to stop to catch my breath. Which way am I going? I have no idea if there's a toolshed here, much less a hacksaw or wrench. Now, I feel how isolated I am, how the inky shadows have an animal stillness beyond the trees. The wind hisses in every direction. The ocean roars out of sight. The house rises over me with implacable darkness, its secrets buried alive in the black windows.

I don't know what is happening or what it means.

Only that if Torin or Everleigh did not lock Cooper in that tomb, then someone else did.

W e try everything to get her out—an ax, iron rod, fire poker, even the keys in the bowl by the front door.

Nothing works.

The bolts on the tomb have oxidized, so there is no dismantling the handle. The lock doesn't budge, not even after Torin and I beat it with a hammer. How it was so swiftly and cruelly attached to the door—someone playing a trick on Cooper—fills me with such deep dread that I can only think one thing: we have to get her out.

We sit outside the door. After a while, she does seem to calm down. But her silence is troubling. I'm afraid that something happened, that she was attacked by something in there with her. I also worry she thinks I had something to do with this.

"Cooper?" I ask. "How are you doing?"

It takes her a few seconds to answer. "I'm awesome. I just love to be sealed in pitch darkness inside an oxygen-less marble closet with a dead legend."

"You don't have your phone?" asks Torin.

"I dropped it somewhere."

"Tomorrow we'll have to get a bulldozer," says Everleigh.

"Can you tell us exactly what happened?" asks Torin.

"I opened the door to take a look inside," says Cooper. "There was a crack, footsteps. I swore I heard someone shout 'Dia!' before I was shoved and the door slammed behind me. I heard the lock click, a giggle. Then it was so dark, all I was aware of was my own screaming."

"It wasn't me," I blurt—though instantly, from the nervous looks on Torin and Everleigh's faces, I realize by announcing it wasn't me, it definitely seems like me.

I decide to return inside the house to search for something else to break down the door. Everleigh wants to join, but Torin is too scared to stay alone with Cooper. And though I'm afraid, too—each footstep on the old wood floors sends chills up my spine—after a time my fear hardens into numb resolve.

Soon I've searched every room in the house, the guest rooms and parlors, the game room—where I suspect someone deliberately removed all Darklys, the shelves now empty. The house is so filled with shadows and beautiful things I feel like I'm scuba-diving alone through a reef at the bottom of the ocean. There is so much to look at, so many details and shocks—like the huge portrait of a nude Louisiana peering out from her walk-in closet. Her clothes still hang on the rack, untouched, identical satin blouses with ties at the neck in black, white, and pale blue. The drawers are still filled with hundreds of perfectly folded silk scarves, the shelves lined with identical black boots with the sturdy one-inch heel, the soles worn.

There are six portraits of Louisiana. But I find no personal letters and not one photograph. I remember reading in old magazine profiles and gossip columns how she had been spotted out to dinner in New York and Paris with prominent businessmen, senators, British lords, their names generic and their faces unsmiling—they resembled the men on money.

But where are they here? The captain appears to be correct. They were never allowed in, not even their memories. Unless Raiden and Derringer Street Chambers confiscated all of Louisiana's personal effects, locking them away somewhere, leaving only things that tell nothing of her story—just the sofas, chandeliers, and silver trays engraved with the elaborate *D*. Maybe they are waiting for the prices of her original games to rise even higher before announcing a grand estate sale or an exclusive museum, as Poe suggested.

I search for a trapdoor. If one had been built into the Darkly factory and the Valkyrie warehouse, there might be one somewhere here, too, right? I even wonder if the perpetrator who locked Cooper in the tomb is hiding, unseen, in the walls, staring out at me, right now. I look for some sign of a hatch under the carpets, planters, chairs. I find nothing. With every passing minute, the house's heaviness seems to grow, and I find myself eager to get out of here, away from its drifting solemn darkness. I am desperate for light and air.

When the night is draining away, daylight clipping the edges of the sky, all of us take turns again with the ax and the hammer, but we are no closer to freeing Cooper. Everleigh goes down to check on the *Elvira*. When she returns, she looks shaken.

"I don't know if the hold was loose, or someone pulled up the anchor, or it was the strength of the tide, but our boat is beached."

"What does that mean?" asks Torin.

"We're trapped here. We'll have to phone the boys and get the captain."

I go down to the beach to investigate. Sure enough, the *Elvira* is now lying sideways between the rocks and sand like a child's forgotten toy boat. Had someone gone down there to mess with us, thwart our ability to leave?

Everleigh calls Franz, alerting him to what happened. Within minutes, he calls back to tell us the captain—and Raiden—are on their way.

"Raiden?" whispers Torin worriedly. "They had to tell Raiden? He's going to kill us."

"Or send us home," says Everleigh. For the first time, she seems legitimately upset by the prospect.

I also dread the idea of facing Raiden. I don't know what he's capable of, but even more troubling than his wrath is the idea of being dismissed, having to leave before I've found George, or learned anything substantial about Valkyrie or Louisiana. The implication in his emails was that we were totally replaceable. *Should you find any of the foregoing unsuitable, please notify me, and the offer of internship will be bestowed upon a runner-up.*

We have no choice but to wait. We take a seat on the tomb steps.

"At least I have light now," Cooper mutters behind the door. "I found my phone."

"What do you see in there?" asks Everleigh.

"Louisiana Veda, I guess?"

She pads to the other side of the tomb. "Okay. There's a marble sarcophagus with a gigantic lid, the Darkly scroll etched on the top. I get strong *Citizen Kane* vibes. The woman saw herself up there with Cleopatra, clearly. She dreamed not big, but gargantuan. Let's see. 'Louisiana Veda, November seventeenth, 1948, to July eighth, 1985.' Major cobwebs. Leaves. Dead spiders. What was here with me was a mouse or chipmunk maybe, which thankfully has taken a hint and left. But there are, like, other slots here where other family members are supposed to be buried, all of which are sadly blank. Oh, wait—"

We can hear her rooting around inside.

"Kitten."

"What?" says Everleigh.

"There's someone buried in here with her. All it says is 'Kitten. April second, 1981, to December twenty-fifth, 1984.'"

"Pet cat?" whispers Everleigh, wide-eyed.

"Louisiana does strike me as the ultimate crazy cat lady," says Torin.

"Well, she died at three years old," says Cooper. "Whatever she was."

It's almost noon when Nile Raiden and the captain finally appear, hauling a leaden toolbox.

I can see Raiden is livid. He gives orders in a muted voice, deliberately ignoring us. He has clearly reprimanded the captain for telling me about the house, probably even threatened to toss her off the island, because she moves with teary subservience behind him. He pulls on welding gloves and headgear, then, producing a serious-looking saw, orders Cooper away from the door as he severs the lock.

It takes a moment for Cooper to stumble out, shading her eyes in the light. She drops to her knees and starts to cry.

"Trespass like this again and you're out," says Raiden. "The only reason the four of you are still here, not wedged in a middle seat homebound for your tedious destiny, is that I hear you managed a foothold in Valkyrie." He squints at us with faint skepticism, then spins on his heel, striding down the path. "One more chance. That's all."

"Someone was here," I shout after him. "A stranger did this to

Cooper. Poe was attacked by a stranger at the factory. Who is living here?"

He stops, turning back, his face red. I can see he wishes to tell me off, but he hesitates, probably because he can't decide which lie to spin.

"Why didn't you tell us about her house?" I ask.

"This property is not your business," he snaps.

"We need to understand Louisiana so we understand her enemies. That will reveal who stole the game and why they are trying to destroy her."

"I set the parameters, Arcadia. They were not random. They were not for fun. They were to keep you from harm. You will stick to them if you wish to continue with this internship. And survive the summer."

I'm startled by the menace in his words as he starts down the path.

"Let's go," he yells over his shoulder. *"Now!"*

Raiden and the captain deliver the four of us to Darkly Pier on the mainland without a word before taking off again in the skiff—probably to work on towing the *Elvira* off the beach. Or does Raiden want to inspect the house, make sure we didn't steal anything? Or is it to make sure my theory—that there is a prowler or squatter or madman on the property—isn't true?

As soon as we make our way down the dock, Poe, Franz, and Mouse step out of the boathouse.

"And here arrive the infamous housebreakers," says Franz with a cheerful wave.

Poe stares at me. "I went to find you, Paradise. In your bunk. You were gone."

He came to find me? "Why?" I blurt.

He smirks. "I wanted to talk."

I'm about to ask *about what?* But then, the idea of being woken up and taken out of my bed by Poe and whispering with him in the middle of the night is so dangerous, maybe it's better I don't know. If I could make out with Choke Newington in a high school stairwell that smells like glue sticks, so smitten in his arms I would have been unaware of the world ending—there's no telling what I am capable of alone with Poe Valois III in darkness with the sound of the ocean crashing around me.

We are all starving. Franz and Mouse suggest we go get a bite to eat. So we pile into the van and drive to town. Thornwood is only a few minutes away, a gang of plump old shops huddled under oak trees. We clamber into a pub called the Blind Bull, squeezing into a single booth, and order cheeseburgers and milkshakes.

"You should have heard Raiden cursing out the captain on the boat ride." Mouse whistles, grinning. "I thought his head was going to pop off he was so furious."

"If he didn't tell us about Louisiana's mansion," I say, "what else isn't he telling us?"

"What was her house like?" asks Franz.

"Pretty awful, actually," says Torin through a mouthful of fries. "It was all ego and empty echo. I think she had like six giant portraits of herself to keep her company."

"She's buried with her cat," says Everleigh.

"We don't *know* Kitten is a cat," says Torin.

"Yeah, might be a capuchin monkey," says Franz.

"Or her murderous alternate personality like Norman Bates's mom?"

Poe frowns. "So this fifth party who was present, locking you in the tomb. You never actually saw this person?"

Cooper shakes her head. "It happened too fast."

"The house creaks. The wind howls," says Everleigh. "A million times, I turned around, feeling someone there, a figure watching me from the window or the hill. Some vengeful spirit from all the horror movies I've ever seen. But I saw nothing."

The sky has darkened. Rain starts to pummel the windows. We tell the boys the rest of the story, careful to keep our voices down. I feel relieved, but almost as quickly feel like a rope is knotting around my throat when Cooper, a wooden glance in my direction, mentions that she heard someone shout my name before she was locked in the tomb.

"I wasn't there," I say. *"Obviously."*

"Obviously," says Mouse.

"I was in the house. In the library. Everleigh will vouch for me."

Everleigh nods, but not with the enthusiasm I was hoping for.

"Do enlighten us, Mr. Da Vinci," Mouse says to Poe. "Everything is a predictable pattern? So, what's the pattern here? Who did that to Cooper?"

It appears from Poe's pleased nod that he has been waiting to be asked exactly this. Now, he brazenly considers me, eyebrow arched. I can feel my face flush.

"Ninety-three percent chance it's a former Darkly employee," he says. "Male. Sixties. Someone invisible on the periphery— maintenance or housekeeping. A little senile and nostalgic, haunted by the old times. He wanders the mansion and the island undetected by the captain and Raiden, resents the intrusion of outsiders. It's the same person who shoved us off the catwalk and rooted through our luggage. He's mostly harmless. But worth talking to, I suspect, to hear what he's observed in the years since Louisiana's death. And what he witnessed while she was alive."

I can't help but smile at Poe in relief. *Thank you.*

Mouse—seemingly irritated I'm not the culprit—drains his milkshake. "And the remaining seven percent?"

"It's Louisiana," announces Poe. "Alive."

He nods at our startled looks. "It's the Shakespearean Holy Trinity Church paradox. The only way to prove with absolute certainty it was Louisiana who died back in 1985 would be to remove her body from the mausoleum and perform a DNA test. Derringer Street would never allow that—consecrated grave, soul resting in peace, *aeternum vale,* and so on. Let's not tamper with such a lucrative myth currently printing money. So we will never truly know who is buried in her grave. But that's the beauty of the past, right? All of the must and murk and shadows are the raw wet clay out of which we can fashion the greatest of myths."

He's staring at me now as if he can see me as a lonely kid wandering the corridors of Prologue. In fact, his gaze is so intense I find myself grabbing my milkshake and taking a long sip even though it's empty.

"What I want to know is," says Franz quietly, "what did Dia find in the library?"

"It was pretty strange, actually," I say. "All of the books are from a public library in a town called Bury St. Elmswood. They still had the return slips and cards in the back."

"I love those old library cards," says Torin.

"That's weird," says Mouse.

He shows us the newspaper article he just pulled up on his phone.

LOCAL LIBRARY TORCHED.

The old woman has narrow, dark eyes, made large by the thick lenses of her glasses, and bright-orange dyed hair. When she peers out at the seven of us, standing on her front porch, she seems on the verge of slamming the door.

Then Poe steps forward, and it's like a moth shown a porch light.

"Hello. We're looking for Penny Malden. The former librarian at the public library at Bury St. Elmswood?"

She blinks in surprise. "I'm Penny."

"We are local students writing a coffee table book about the best public libraries in England. Your name came up on a shortlist of wonderful librarians. We were hoping, if it's not too inconvenient, to interview you for our book."

She looks startled. "Oh?"

"Does the name Louisiana Veda mean anything to you?"

"That odd woman who made all those toys years ago?"

"Board games," says Franz.

"May we come in and chat?" asks Poe.

She stares at us, as if she isn't sure we're real or figments of her imagination. But then—resigned to either possibility—she opens the door for us, turning and wandering down a dim hallway, leaning heavily on a cane.

Penny May Malden, librarian, had been interviewed by a reporter for the local newspaper, dated 1976: LOCAL LIBRARY TORCHED. We found out from a UK people search she was still alive, age eighty-nine, and still living in Bury St. Elmswood at 4 Sea Gleam Way.

With no transportation back to the island possible, no word from the captain or Raiden, we decided to pile into the van and take the two-hour drive north to the seaside village of Bury St. Elmswood in Norfolk. We wanted to see if we could answer the question of why Louisiana would have had those books.

"She could have afforded to have all first editions," Everleigh noted. "So why choose to have such a grand library for those old books that smell like dirty socks?"

Bury St. Elmswood is poor. The town is laid out like a microscope's slide of bacteria—every house a flattened, colorless square. There is little green. Half of the buildings are boarded up—pizzeria, arcade, motel. We pass a town square, where a few people appear to have washed up like debris on a beach. Penny Malden's cottage is one of many dotting a straight road leading with grim certainty to a patch of gray sand by the North Sea.

We move into a dark sitting room piled with shopping bags, a line of exotic potted plants and trees by the sliding glass doors. We find Penny watering some with a tin can, and when she turns, she gapes at us, startled, as if in the seconds between front door and living room she has forgotten who we are.

"Thanks for speaking with us, Miss Malden," I say, holding out my arm for her. She scowls but, after a moment, takes it, allowing me to slowly usher her toward what I know is her favorite chair, because it's directly in front of the TV, with the carpet threadbare where her feet rest—just like Basil's.

"You have a beautiful home," I say. "Your plants are incredible. You've got a green thumb."

"I've got a hernia and gout," she says.

"Can we help you with anything? Fix something?"

"Eh? Oh, er—the shelf in my bathroom."

"I'll take care of it. Anything else? Are you hungry?"

"Can of Pepsi. And a box of my amaretto crisps?"

I nod, slipping into the kitchen, as the others, following my lead with gentle movements and a lot of deference, take a seat around her.

"So, what, Paradise," says Poe, stepping after me. "You're an elderly whisperer?"

"Basically."

He frowns, opening a cabinet. "Where would she keep those armadillo hips?"

I toss him the box of King Charles' Coronation Amaretto Crisps from the twenty-four-box value pack on the counter. Then I tiptoe out and down the hall, past piles of shopping bags stuffed with coupons. I find the bathroom in the back. The shelf in the medicine cabinet has indeed crashed to the floor. It looks like it happened three years ago. I pull it out from behind the toilet and pick up all of the medication bottles, the toothpaste, a few crusty green bottles of perfume. L'Air de Flâneur Paris.

Old bottles of lotions and perfumes and powders are crowded everywhere, even the back of the toilet, as if they've sprouted like mushrooms on a dank forest floor. I tidy up a little—fixing the bath mat, refolding the towels, wiping away the dust balls behind the door.

When I return to the others, Penny Malden seems at ease, even content, as she sips her Pepsi, an open tray of cookies on her lap.

"What can you tell us about the fire in the library?" asks Poe, on the stool beside her.

She stares at him, so startled that for a moment I'm sure she's going to order us out of the house.

"Oh, yes, the fire," she whispers, pressing a hand to her heart. "Awful. We were the lifeblood of this town. We were the hope. Everyone laughs at us now. Reporters from London show up with cameras to tell us we were voted, every year, ugliest village in England. And we're sinking into the salt marshes. It was because my library burned. We were a beacon. I took great care to make it enchanted. Human Anatomy. South America. Angel wing begonias and African violets. A real jungle for the children to run around. They came from miles for story hour. We had a glass listening booth. Records of every opera."

She shakes her head, her trembling old hands fitfully pulling a cookie from the box. "We hoped to rebuild. But the councilmen refused the permits. Too much moisture—wouldn't pass inspection. 'The salt marshes,' they were always beefing. 'We're all destined for the salt marshes.' What a load of twaddle."

"Did they ever find out who started this fire?" asks Poe.

She nods as she crams a cookie into her mouth. "We all knew who was behind it. Told them so. But they didn't lift a finger."

"Why not?" asks Mouse.

"She was a cockroach. Crawled into the beds of half the men in town. There wasn't one copper who didn't know her, if you know what I mean. The happily married, she went after those first. She posted her filth on *my* bulletin boards, so it was always right under my nose. 'Call this number for haircuts.' 'Need help cleaning the gutters on your roof?'" She gasps in disgust. "And when she did her nasty business, day and night, she'd drop off her devil child at *my* library. To spite me. Left her there for days."

She shudders, her wizened hands fumbling as they wrench more cookies from the plastic. And though the seven of us exchange uneasy looks—*devil child?*—we can tell from Poe's subtle shake of his head he's urging us all not to startle her with more questions. *Let her speak.*

"We didn't know it was happening, at first. Only saw her messes in the morning. Books would move as if they had legs. *Night Climbers of Oxford* would walk to South America, *Charlotte's Web* into Murder Mystery. Took me hours to clean up. She'd fiddle with my skeleton in Human Anatomy. Steal from Lost and Found. So I went there at night to watch. Slept there. Thought there was a ghost. Books went missing. Always the same blood-soaked nine. I tried to hide them, but she stole them back. Once the power went out from a bad storm, and the electrician found the girl living in my ceiling like a rat. We called Child Protective Services. And she would go with them for a spell. But as soon as she was returned to the mother, it happened again. Over and over, year after year, that foul woman left her child in my library. Murderous little thing. She tried to kill me more than once. Locked me in the listening booth. And she did kill me in the end. Took away my retirement. Gone from the birds-of-paradise."

Her voice trails off, her face frozen, lost in some sour memory.

All of us stare, waiting for her to go on, swept into the chilling, fragmented story she just told, about the little girl abandoned in her library.

Abruptly, she sits up, pushing her glasses up the bridge of her nose. "Here to check the cable on my telly, are you? Haven't been able to get Sky Anytime or Create and Craft. Something wrong with my satellite. You've got to get to the roof to check it. You can get there by the stairs, just there."

She points vaguely over her shoulder. "Now, the mother lives like a queen," she mutters through a mouthful of crumbs. "Rubbing our noses in it. Must have had naughty pictures of somebody in ladies' knickers in Parliament. Because she's got the life of Riley now. Refuses to move away, even when no one wants a thing to do with her. We all see her Wednesdays at Sheffield's, and we walk past, wrinkling our noses from the stench."

She pauses to gulp the Pepsi, wipe her mouth on her sleeve.

"I'm sorry, Penny," I say, leaning forward with a gentle smile. "Who, exactly, are you talking about?"

44

The bright-blue house sits facing the beach at the end of the road.

It's larger than the other cottages, with meandering glass additions and an unsightly cable satellite on the roof. But exactly like the others, it stares out, blank and unmoved, at the North Sea, with its water the color of dirty laundry, the dull breeze, scattered birds. But there are circus sculptures in the yard: a giant gilded clock that looks like it's meant for a train station, a pewter bear on a unicycle, balancing a ball on its nose. But even these whimsical details have the feeling of refuge, where something ends up after a long and difficult life.

We knock, no sound within but a TV's canned laughter.

Abruptly, a woman pulls open the door. She is old but with voluminous blond hair, which appears to be a wig, gold hoop earrings. She wears a turquoise tracksuit with roses embroidered down one leg.

"We're looking for Dove Gavenaught," says Poe.

"Yes? I'm Dove." She tilts her head, hand on her hip, her gold bracelets rattling like a flock of loud birds.

"Sorry to bother you. We are local history students performing research on unsolved arson cases in England. We hoped to ask you a few questions about the public library."

"Not that blasted business again." She frowns, shaking her head. "*She* put you up to this, did she? Penny the pisser? I've said it once and I'll say it again. I had nothing to do with it. I was in Brighton. Got me plain as day on CCTV in a bowling alley drinking white Russians until after three in the morning. I even sent a copy to that blasted woman so she would stop this slander—"

"Yes, we believe you," says Poe. "But would you mind if we come in and ask you a few questions? We promise not to take up too much time."

"Stay all day if you'd like. Got no plans except watching *Hollyoaks,* and a walk with Diana. Don't mind Di there—but don't look at her direct in the eye either, if you want to keep your noses. Where'd you say you were from?"

We follow her into a brown glass solarium, overhead fans spinning an uneasy hum. A German shepherd—Diana—raises her head from the couch to stare at us. Dove grabs an open can of beer off the coffee table and pads into a kitchenette. There are at least twenty newspaper articles magnetized to the fridge. I step closer to read the headlines.

DIET FOR REVERSE AGING.

WOMAN LIVES TO 106.

"Suffolk," says Poe.

"Clearly, you had nothing to do with the fire," says Mouse. "Any idea who did?"

"I do." She sighs. "Anyone who would set out to burn such a beautiful library would have to be a twisted soul. There's only one twisted soul in town."

"Who?"

"The librarian. Penny. Odd thing, though, I heard from the fire marshal, and he told me this in confidence, all the books were removed beforehand. That's the funny rumor of it all. Not one was left. Not one burned page. Doesn't make much sense, does it?"

"Did you frequent the library?" asks Poe.

She takes a long drink of beer. "Sure."

"And you took your daughter there sometimes?"

She doesn't like the question. She jerks to her feet and thrusts a long, pink manicured fingernail at Poe, bracelets rattling. The dog lifts her head.

"If you mean that business with Penny and Eve, the wench from Child Protection, I did nothing wrong. They were wrong to take her from me. What would they have me do? Leave her with some crusty psycho in day care? Alone in a trailer, hoping no one came in? Why not use what no one set foot in. It sat empty, that library. And my May loved it."

She nods, making some indignant point to herself, before taking another swig.

"Do you have a picture of May?" asks Everleigh.

"What mother wouldn't have a picture of her daughter? I got a whole room."

She beckons us to follow, opening the door into a child's bedroom a few feet down the hall. The walls are purple. There are stuffed animals and a lavender lace canopy bed. All around the room—covering every surface—are framed photos of a little girl. She has short black hair and a sharp gaze.

Without a doubt—it is Louisiana Veda.

It's her face, her eyebrows and chin. Even as a baby, it's obvious—even dressed up by her mother like a rare collector's edition Madame Alexander doll in frilly red velvet dresses with gold bows and knee socks.

I can see from the stunned looks on the other interns' faces, they also recognize her.

"And where is May today?" asks Poe, clearing his throat.

"I've no goddamn idea." Dove scowls, as if it were a ridiculous question.

"When was the last time you saw her?" asks Franz.

"It was sixty-two years ago in June." She shakes her head, tears in her eyes. "She was behind it."

"Who?" asks Poe.

"The librarian. Penny. Meanest witch you ever met. Doused in her vinegar perfume, she would hunt May. All night. Evil pumps through her heart, not blood. They say she was in with the South Parade Gang. And she had the nerve to condemn me? I earned a living best I could. I'm not proud. There were lots of Alfreds. But it was all for May. The job in Hamburg was a windfall. Three days was a long time, but the money would set us up for a year. I taught her how to survive until I could come back for her. How to raid the garbage of Rialto Roma for the spaghetti. She got scared? I made her read those books, let those stories keep her safe in the dark. She had her favorites. She'd hide in the glass booth and put on a record. And she did it. They never harmed her. My May was clever like that.

"The day I collected her, we were so happy. I bought her the fanciest bike in Colchester. Stars on the handlebars. A red seat. I never taught May to ride a bike. So we go to the parking lot of Pet Supplies, and we practice. And she falls and falls. But she keeps getting up. No matter how scraped her knees get, how bloody her elbows. One afternoon, I give her a little push, she wobbles, and—oh boy, she's got it. She rides fast, round and round in a circle, laughing her head off. And I'm crying and shouting for joy, 'You did it! You did it, my girl!' But she's not stopping. No, something is wrong. The laughing stops as she rides straight out of the lot. I run after her, shouting, 'May, that's too far now. May, come back!' But she doesn't, does she. No, my girl doesn't even turn back. She just pedals faster and faster, until she turns down the end of the road."

Dove Gavenaught is crying. She falls silent, swallowing, wiping the tears from her eyes.

"I searched the streets for months for her. I called the police. She had no money. Nowhere to go. Who stole her? Who made the arrangement with her to leave me so that she could sail away, so proud? Detectives searched every house for her, every backyard in the whole of England. They put out notices. They're still out there. But no one saw my May ever again. Gone. Like a raindrop in the sea."

I can't move. I can't speak. None of us can.

What Dove Gavenaught does not know is so impossible and enormous we can only stare.

How could she not know—how could no one here know—that the *whole world* saw her daughter again, that she grew up to be a legend?

I wouldn't have believed it possible. But then, I had wandered the streets of this tattered town, seen the boarded-up windows and glum stares of the houses. If there was ever a place left behind by the rest of the world, cut off and dislodged like some bit of trash caught in the branches of a roaring river, it would be Bury St. Elmswood.

"After she was gone," Dove continues in a quiet voice, "I didn't see a point to living. And I lived that way, I'm afraid to admit. A life with no care for tomorrow is an ugly life. Only thing that kept me alive was, I needed to be here when she did come home. Because she would. I was her mother, after all. A girl never leaves her mother. Not really. But then our glorious heavenly father, he saw my suffering and heard my prayers. He took pity on me. He thought, 'Poor Dove, waiting for her child. She deserves something for her heartache.' So I won the lottery."

She smiles at the surprised looks on our faces.

"Oh, yes, I sure did. Like in a movie, I won. Fifteen million pounds, untaxed. I didn't even know I was buying a ticket. That's the joke. Turns out every time I bought two cartons of Sir Filbert's menthols at Brooklands, that was registering me for Britain's Royal Lottery every week. Funny thing is, it was May always badgerin' me, telling me to quit. 'It isn't good for you, Mum.' Turns out it sure *was* good. Only thing in the world she was ever wrong about. Come. I'll show you."

The seven of us exchange skeptical looks—*Britain's Royal Lottery?*—then we follow Dove as she proudly beckons us into the hall to a framed letter on the wall by the kitchen.

Britain's Royal Lottery. July 5, 1981. Congratulations, Dove Lucretia Gavenaught! You have won our Ultimate Jackpot X—15 million pounds—distributed to you in monthly installments for the rest of your life!

"This letter is how you knew you had won?" asks Poe.

"Well, sure. And they showed up in person at my flat to make sure I got the letter."

"*Who* showed up?" asks Mouse sharply.

"The people from Britain's lottery division. They had balloons, said I was the luckiest woman in England. Never would I have to worry again about rent, or how to pay for a pint."

"Do you remember the names of these people?" asks Everleigh.

"Mr. Peter Smith. I still talk to him. Argue, mostly. Because it's a very short leash, this lottery. Last year, I hoped to buy the Three Bluejays. A pub. Before that, the arcade and a laundromat. Always, a flat no. 'That's not the terms of the lottery.' Well, the terms of the lottery are stricter than His Majesty's Prison Wakefield."

"How do you get in touch with Peter Smith?" I ask.

"Got it right here, his private office phone number, though I don't see what business it is of yours." She points at a blue Post-it on the refrigerator.

Mouse is already looking it up.

"It's Derringer Street Chambers," he whispers.

"There's no such thing as Britain's Royal Lottery," says Franz under his breath. "It was Louisiana."

"What's that you're whispering?" shouts Dove with an indignant frown. "You're in my house, you can say it to my face."

And for the first time since we've met her, Dove Gavenaught looks at us as if it's just occurring to her that we might not be who we said we were.

We say goodbye to Dove—even though we are dying to stay and fire a million questions at her.

What was your daughter like? Who was her father? Did she display early signs of genius? Did she love mysteries and riddles and games? Was she quiet or amiable? Morose or shy?

But we are eager to hash over the discovery of Louisiana's childhood in private. So, after Poe darts into the bedroom to take a few pictures, with tacit nods—Mouse covertly pointing at the door—we file out, leaving Diana growling and Dove staring after us in bewildered confusion before she closes the door.

The setting sun spills tired light across the sky, softening the faces of the stark brick houses.

"We should have told her," says Torin as we head down the path.

"No," says Poe. "That kind of truth? It'd have to be delivered in bite-sized pieces over the course of a year so she develops a tolerance. Otherwise, it'd be such a jolt to her system it'd kill her."

Franz nods. "Ja. 'Hello. Your daughter was actually a genius who created a new art form, rose to the apex of global popularity, fell from grace, was derided and ridiculed, and she killed herself. Now, billionaires snap up her works like free doughnuts, and she's not even around to enjoy the resurgence of her glory. Her empire is controlled by a bunch of sinister legal pencil-necks. So, yeah, she was dead, alive, and dead again. For real this time. Sorry.'"

"And your dead daughter is also your Royal Lottery," adds Mouse.

Franz frowns thoughtfully. "You think playing the generic part of Mr. Peter Smith is handed down like an internship from goon to goon at Derringer Street?"

"It must be Raiden who handles her," says Cooper.

Poe shrugs. "Louisiana arranged with Derringer to make sure her mother is taken care of, but kept in line, so she doesn't squander her fortune on tracksuits and racehorses and pubs."

"What did she call her clients again?" asks Torin.

"Alfreds," whispers Mouse.

"And I was complaining about my mom's Percocet," says Franz.

"I still think we should have said something," says Torin.

"It isn't our truth to tell," I say. "If Louisiana wanted her mother to know, she would have told her."

"To think she left it all behind one day," says Everleigh. "Finally, with the bike, she had the means to get out, so she just rode away from her entire nightmare childhood, heading toward something new. That took an incredible amount of courage."

"But how did she do it?" asks Cooper. "No one to help her? No money? She slept on the street and somehow survived?"

"It probably wasn't as spontaneous as her mother thought," says Poe. "Even as a child, Louisiana had a flair for theatrics— the grandest of exits and the shock of an entrance years later as a mysterious, impoverished art student with a fascinating board game for the world to play."

Everleigh shivers. "We'll never know what she did."

"No wonder Louisiana, all those years later, came back here as a powerful woman and torched the library," says Franz. "Being abandoned there as a child for weeks on end? And crazy, angry Penny trying to hunt her down, thinking she's a devil child? And another woman at Child Protection hauling her away all the time? I mean, don't get me wrong. I love a library. In the day. When it's open. But at night? As a child alone in all of those dark rows, smelly pages, stories?"

"No wonder she became Louisiana Veda," says Cooper.

"But why would she want those books in her own house?" asks Torin.

"She loved them," I say. "I can't tell you how many times people cleaning out their attics or basements or garages—even young people—drop off boxes at our shop. And a few weeks later they're back, really upset, asking if we have sold that little red leather music box that plays 'Auld Lang Syne,' or the baby doll in the black velvet dress with the scribbles on the cheek." I shrug. "These old things, they don't look like much, but they bookmark our lives. They have a silent permanence that people and places do not. Something to carry with us. Always. They were there when no one else was, looking on without judgment when all of these wonderful and terrible things happened to us. And still, they are there. They survive. And somehow, they remember. The worry is, if they're gone, we are gone, too."

We have been wandering out into the sand toward the ocean. Now, I realize the others have stopped. I turn back, surprised to see as I shade my eyes that everyone is staring at me in alarm.

"What is it?"

I've been so absorbed in Louisiana's story, I haven't noticed my phone ringing.

I pull it out.

UNKNOWN.

The others scramble to take out their phones, too, holding them up like grenades that might explode.

For a moment, I am aware of nothing but the shrill ring— cutting into the feeble whimpers of the North Sea and a seagull crying somewhere overhead.

Then Poe's phone starts to ring.

And Mouse's.

And Everleigh's.

"Hello?" I answer.

Valerie—
I must tell you AGAIN the
absolute importance of keeping to
the schedule my Gattie sends you
each Sunday. How else can I see
her advancement in the pool???
We have paid Paul for the
summer and he has informed us
you only show up half the time. I
must remind you Gattie and I
chose you because we are a team,
built on TRUST.

You must STICK TO THE SCHEDULE.

Bella's education, creativity, and happiness are crucial to this—great research and care have been given to this matter and we need you to do your part. Otherwise we will make alternative arrangements.

Contact Gattie with any concerns.

Lou

I t's the same beginning.

Same ride in the van. Same warehouse with the darkness and the canvas tunic shoved over my head, the bright light hot against the blindfold. This time it's tied a little loose, and it falls slightly down my nose. I can see the forms of people drifting around me like eels, getting ready, passing papers back and forth. It has the quiet formality of a courtroom before a trial, everyone with a role to play—bailiff, security officer, judge, and jury.

I'm more afraid than before. Because this time, I know what to expect: fifteen minutes of a hell I cannot begin to conceive.

"Player number," shouts the old man.

"Four hundred and seven."

"Exit phrase?"

"Wander where the witch lies."

"You may begin."

My wrists fall free. The blindfold is pulled from my face. And there it is again on the green poker table, which seems to float in the liquid darkness in front of me. Valkyrie.

The wood spinner. Gray velvet bag. The hourglass with the gold sand.

I lean closer, my eyes smarting in the blinding light as I stare at the board. It looks older, more detailed than I noticed before, with shadows and ink textures—more like a map. I notice the wood along the bottom edge is mottled and cracked from water damage.

My pawn has advanced a short distance along the top, about an inch toward the center.

I scan the writing on the colored shapes: SPACE ROCKET. BEAST BED. RADIO TO MARS. DEAD KING. TIMBUKTU. CLOUDS. LOOT.

Loot?

It's written in a small brown rectangle, centered along the bottom of the board.

That was the word on the storage closet where I found the dove and all of those other items, what I and the others pulled from the gray velvet bag.

I turn my gaze to the spinner. First, there is the outer circle: UNEXPLAINED PHENOMENA. WHISPERS BEYOND THE GRAVE. DEATH-BED CONFESSIONS. SECRET SOCIETY. OBSOLETE. MARIA TALLCHIEF. THE GREYS. LOCKS AND MAZES. DETECTIVE.

These are the doors of the rooms I passed—settings for each session of Valkyrie.

And the middle circle—my eyes scan the Gothic writing: GHOST DOG. FIRE. DARK. BIRD HUNTER. DEADEYE MAN. BAD DREAM. SLAUGHTERHOUSE. WINDOW. EVE.

These must be the obstacles, the elements of villainy or terror added to the scene.

And the black circle at the center—I had wondered before if I had missed seeing something. But it's painted the blackest of blacks, no words and no pictures.

"Failure to take a turn in the next ten seconds will result in your termination from Valkyrie," a woman shouts.

I grab the winding key and crank it hard, the circles clicking and whirling.

The same face appears out of the movement, surveying me, before fading as the circles slow and abruptly stop.

DEATHBED CONFESSIONS, it reads on the outer circle. And on the inner, DEADEYE MAN—what Poe had spun. *This beast of a man following me like an insidious hex.*

Two hooded figures are approaching, holding open the gray velvet bag.

The bag of loot.

I shove my hand in, riffling through the countless pieces, coming across something buried at the very bottom, small and flat, a pin on the back.

I pull it out. It's a heavy brooch, with intertwined silver roses framing a black-and-white photo of an unsmiling young woman in a straw hat. It's a Victorian mourning brooch, probably dating back to the 1830s. We had a few pass through Prologue, so at least I understand what it is—a photo of a dead woman. Victorians loved to photograph the dead, especially those who died young, propping them up and opening their eyes, posing around them as if they were alive. They then wore the pictures in remembrance, thinking there was nothing remotely strange about doing so.

"Find Lucinda's lock in the deadeye man's deathbed confession," a woman shouts.

The mallet raps twice. A black-gloved hand flips the hourglass, the gold sand raining down as two figures grab the table, the game vanishing into the shadows, exposing the dark hole.

"Valkyrie 407, round two hereby under way."

Find Lucinda's lock? Who is Lucinda? The woman in the picture?
I stare at the photo of the woman, trying to remember if I saw this brooch somewhere in the aisles of the storage room marked *Loot.* I didn't see it. But it must be there. Everything else I and the other interns drew from the velvet bag was there.

Suddenly, I'm tipped forward in the wheelchair, plummeting through the hole. I slam the canvas cart below and take off across a dark room. I'm being wheeled fast, by a man with heavy boots. A door in front of me opens, and I'm tossed out onto the floor of a dim hallway all over again.

I scramble to my feet, staring down the empty corridor.

Both directions are identical. It must be the same corridor as before—in the same warehouse.

This time, I will not be bumbling and hysterical. I only need to climb beyond the boundaries of Valkyrie. This is what we all decided as Mouse drove us in the van to the different drop-offs told to us by Louisiana in a crystalline voice that seemed so alive. Mouse, Torin, and Franz did not make it past the first round. They are heading back to the island to wait.

I realize I can hear faint music, a woman singing along to an organ.

"Draw me nearer, nearer, blessed Lord,
To Thy precious, bleeding side . . ."

I wheel around and start running toward it.

48

I reach a simple black door at the end of the corridor, music trilling within. I push it open.

It's a musty, dark room, packed with people. The morose hymn is being sung somewhere in the back.

It looks like a large parlor in an old Victorian mansion, a little like Louisiana's, but more formal with wine-colored wallpaper, flickering oil lamps on the mantel and bookshelves. The women wear dark dresses, and the men waistcoats, many of them with beards. The way they're huddled in anxious groups, whispering, crying, the feeble light cutting up their faces—the scene is so sinister I stand in the doorway, transfixed.

Then I notice the digital clock over the fireplace.

14 minutes, 12 seconds.

I step inside. Immediately, the door starts to creak closed behind me. I catch a fleeting glimpse of a black-masked figure poised on the other side as the lock clicks.

I fight my way deeper into the throng, pushing past a sniveling woman wiping her nose on a handkerchief, another tearfully reading from a pocket Bible, their faces barely surfacing from the darkness. I trip on the slippered feet of a group of older women huddled on a sofa, whispering, crossing themselves in a language I don't understand. Polish? Turkish?

Lucinda's lock. Is one of these women Lucinda? I stare at the tiny brooch in my hand, the woman's face submerged in shadows. And what kind of lock is it? A locket on a necklace, a lock on a suitcase or purse? A lock of hair?

Except it doesn't matter, I remind myself. I don't need to win this round. I need only to find the trapdoor to climb beyond the borders of the game, get back downstairs, backstage, where the people running this operation congregate. I bend down, trying to make out the floor in the forest of legs, bustled skirts, walking canes.

It's heavy carpet, no obvious break for a door.

I take off, shoving my way toward the closest corner, where a gray-haired woman wearing a large hat sits playing a parlor pump organ. She sings softly, a scarf tied in a bow at her throat, a black bracelet of braided rope, fingers heavy with gold rings. Her hat, I notice, has a real stuffed blackbird perched on the brim.

"Let my soul look up with steadfast hope
And my will be lost in Thine . . ."

She doesn't notice me as I duck behind her stool, pulling up the corner of the carpet, groping the wood floors. No door. No planter as a marker either. I continue crawling along the periphery, feeling along the wall. How do the players get in and out of here? I pass a life-sized framed print of a skeleton on the wall and a whimpering woman who rises, vacating a chair. I scramble up onto the seat to look out across the room.

There are at least sixty or seventy people here. The ceiling is low. There's a rectangular table in the middle, where people are bent over what looks to be a guest book, scribbling condolences? Opposite me, beside a closed black door, a gold bell cord hangs along the wall, the kind used to summon servants. Abruptly, the door opens and a sweating bald man sticks his head out.

"I'm next—"

"Please, I must see him—"

"I beg you—"

"Stop this!" the man bellows. "You must wait your turn!"

"But he's not long for this world—"

"I must see him before it's too late!"

"He has asked to see Dodgson. Has Dodgson arrived?"

"I'm Dodgson!" a girl shouts.

I see from the tunic it's another player of Valkyrie. The girl has black hair and braces, and she rudely elbows her way through the people to reach the door. She says something else and slips under the man's arm. I catch a fleeting sight of candlelight in the room, elongated shadows, a window heavy with curtains, before the door slams, locks hissing into place.

11 minutes, 46 seconds.

Now what? I scan the crowd, the tearful faces in the shadows. No potted plant, no obvious trapdoor to crawl out of here.

That's when I notice, far across the room, a woman in mourning attire.

Black dress, gloves, shawl, and hat. A black chiffon weeping veil erases her face.

And the second I notice her, as if my gaze were a tap on her shoulder, slowly she turns to look at *me*.

She grabs the handles of a cart, laden with colored bottles, trinkets, and books—exactly like the one Leah Fox pushed. The crowd yelps, lurching out of her way as she slowly turns it in my direction.

She's coming for me.

I jump off the chair, ducking low as I push through the legs and skirts, petticoats and walking canes. A woman drops a burning candle with a sharp cry. Another shrieks as she douses the flames with a shawl.

Who is that woman? What does she mean to Valkyrie? What did Cooper tell me?

Avoid the witch.

7 minutes, 10 seconds.

I have reached the door. It's going to open again, I know, and when it does, I'll be ready. I wedge myself into a ball, hiding behind a chair.

Within seconds, the woman in the veil is approaching, the jars on her cart clinking and rattling like a collection of bones. She shoves her way through the people, searching for me. What does she want? The glass jars are filled, exactly like before, with strange liquids, herbs, and powders. *Definitely some black-magic potion,* Everleigh said. There is a stack of faded books, some sort of shriveled rodent preserved in formaldehyde, a collection of tiny green bottles.

As she pushes past, I reach out, on my stomach, and grab one.

L'AIR DE FLÂNEUR PARIS reads the faded type.

For a moment, I can only sit very still, the words trembling before my eyes.

Where did I see them before?

It was in Penny Malden's bathroom. *Doused in her vinegar perfume.*

Suddenly, it hits me. All sound cuts out, and I cannot breathe.

Because I understand Valkyrie.

And when she did her nasty business, day and night, she'd drop off her devil child at my *library.*

She would hunt May. All night.

I taught her how to survive until I could come back for her.

It all fits. It was why Louisiana created Valkyrie, why it had to be locked away forever, why she would be destroyed if it ever came to light.

Valkyrie is the story of Louisiana's childhood. The game board, with its crisscrossing rows and sections, is a map of the library at Bury St. Elmswood.

Human anatomy. South America. Angel wing begonias and African violets.

And the objective? The player must survive three nights of hell without ever being found by the librarian—*meanest witch you ever met.*

There is so much more to comprehend—the circles on the spinner, the loot in the bag, the different-colored squares labeled DEAD KING and RADIO TO MARS.

But there's no time. *5 minutes, 29 seconds.*

It's too late to get behind the scenes. My only chance now is to do what was set forth for me to do, so I can make it to the final round.

Find Lucinda's lock in the deadeye man's deathbed confession.

The door opens beside me. I jump to my feet as the crowd surges, shouting.

"Routledge?" shouts the bald man. "Has Routledge arrived? If you are here, say something!"

"I'm here," I shout.

49

"I'm Routledge!" I yell.

Before the man can stop me, I duck past him. And because he has stepped outside to push people back with his cane, I slam the door behind him and slide the iron rod into place, locking him out.

"Hey!"

It's a bedroom, dark as the depths of a putrid pond. The only light is a lone oil lantern burning on a table, the flame turned to a teardrop illuminating a four-poster canopy bed, laden with curtains, where a massive man—the same deadeye man Poe described—lies tangled in sheets, black lenses on his eyes.

Three people sit in chairs around the bed. There is a priest, a gray-haired woman in a dirty mustard-colored dress, eyes closed as she fumbles with a rosary, feverishly whispering a prayer. Beside her is a man with red hair, also praying. I recognize him immediately as the usher who collected tickets back at the theater with the Fox sisters. A doctor with sideburns leans over the dying man, busying himself with a table crowded with bottles and bowls, syringes and knives. Some kind of tube is attached to the deadeye man's forearm, feeding a white liquid into his arm.

And though I move closer to them, staring at their hands, faces, watches, and rings, I see nothing that strikes me as any kind of lock.

Standing at the foot of the bed is the other Valkyrie player, the girl who entered before. She turns to me, glaring as I approach the bed, brazenly leaning over the dying man. He is pale, his perspiring skin gaunt and almost translucent. His lips are chapped, his breath heavy and slow, lungs rattling. *How do they make this scene feel so real?*

"I'm here," I say, my voice lodging in my throat. "Routledge is here."

"At last, you've come." He turns to face me, the black lenses he wears carving his eyes into holes. "You must listen to my every word."

"Yes."

"I loved her. Her passing ruined me. You must bring it to me before I die. Or I'll kill you, Routledge." He coughs. "Not tonight. One day when you least expect it, Routledge. I'll come back from beyond and I'll kill you. You'll never be rid of me. Unless you find her. Right now."

The man reaches out and grabs my wrist, twisting it with such force that I cry out. The others don't react. But the other Valkyrie player steps forward, eavesdropping, as if in his words she's searching for her own clue.

I manage to wrench away, but stumble right into the lap of the gray-haired woman, who raises her head with a gasp. I'm sure she's going to yell at me. But instead, she whispers something so quietly I have to lean forward to hear it.

"Help me. I need help."

The look on her face sends me lurching backward into the shadows along the wall.

The timer must almost be finished. There's no way out of here.

Lucinda's lock?

That's when I have an idea.

I race to the door, slide the bolts, and fling it open. The furious bald man who has been pounding relentlessly to get in gapes in surprise.

"He will see everyone now!" I shout. "But you must hurry before it's too late."

I dart out of the way, pressing my back to the wall as the crowd, in a stampede, swarms the deathbed. I can hear the deadeye man shouting, "Stand back! No! Leave me in peace!" as I force my way back into the parlor.

I'm aware of someone holding on to the back of my tunic. It's the other Valkyrie player, the girl. She seems to think I have the answers to get her out of this.

And maybe I do.

1 minute, 8 seconds.

Where is she—the woman in the veil?

I wheel around, eyeing the few people huddling in nervous clusters, the singer still crooning at her organ.

But the woman in the veil—she stands facing the far corner. Sure enough, as if sensing my stare, she begins to turn the cart around, heading toward me.

My heart is hammering. Because it's there in my memory, the odd thing the boy did—the boy from the Bromsbury School. Rather than running away, even though he was shaking with terror, he ran toward her, trawling through that cart.

Which one is it? he'd shouted. What was he so desperate to find? What did he want?

"Are you nuts?" The other Valkyrie player grabs my arm, pulling me back. "If she captures you and whispers the death phrase, you'll never make it."

"Make it where?"

"*You* know."

"I don't, actually—"

"To Valhalla, with the Valkyrie. You'll be set for life—"

"What does that mean?"

I catch only a glimpse of a knowing, crooked smile on the girl's face as the woman in the black veil reaches out, seizing both of us by the throat. The girl shrieks. I wrench loose, ramming the cart hard as I can into her skirt, an explosion of bottles as she falls backward, books tumbling across the carpet. Trinkets, dried flowers, splattered red liquid.

That's when I notice the cover of a book staring up at me.

It's black. A red knight with a blue sword on the cover.

I flip to the title page. *A Biography of Viscountess Aberhorne and Her Bygone Friends: A Conversation with the Dead, Decayed, and Forgotten.*

My head is light. I grab another.

The Forgotten Family Trees of Great Britain. I turn the pages, staring down at an elaborate family tree. *The Lewishons. The Smiths. The Greys.*

I grab another, this one yellow, ballet shoes on the cover. *The Greatest Ballet Dancers of the 20th Century.* I turn to the contents, scanning the names. *Chapter 4: Maria Tallchief.*

Astonished, I grab a thin orange book, a black bowler hat on the front.

Secrets of the World's Most Dangerous Cabals, Conspiracies, and Conjures.

Chapter 1: The Bilderberg Group. Chapter 2: Lincoln's Ghost Train. Chapter 3: Ghostlore. Chapter 4: The Leopard Society.

These are the books I found displayed under the glass dome in Louisiana's library.

They are also the nine categories on the outer Valkyrie spinner.

Suddenly, I remember Dove's words. *She got scared? I made her read those books, let those stories keep her safe in the dark. She had her favorites.*

And what did Penny tell us, still seething even though so much time had passed?

Always the same blood-soaked nine. I tried to hide them, but she stole them back.

I shout as a hand grips the back of my neck. The woman in the veil is twisting my collar, choking me.

"You . . . will . . . never . . ."

I shove her off, rolling away. Where is the book for this scene? Deathbed confessions?

I spot a small blue book under the table. I dive for it.

The Ghosts of Queen Victoria: Death and the Macabre in Victorian England.

There are photos of Victorians strolling, horses and carriages, parks and daguerreotypes, hats festooned with feathers, family portraits with the dead, a pair of black braided rope earrings . . . I stare at the caption, forcing my eyes to focus. *Victorians were fond of mourning jewelry, showcasing the locks of deceased loved ones in everyday hats, belts, rings, and bracelets. The elastic, lightweight texture of hair made it a sought-after material for jewelers. They would braid the hair in intricate patterns and harden the shape with glue.*

Lucinda's lock of *hair*.

I saw it—

I leap to my feet, and instantly I'm jerked backward, slammed to the carpet. The woman in the veil is bending over me, pinning me to the ground, her boot twisting into my ribs.

"You . . . will . . . never . . . leave . . . me. . . ."

18 seconds.

I reach out, fumbling along the cart, grabbing the first jar of liquid I can reach, throwing it at her. The shriveled rodent and the acid it's submerged in hit her in the face. She screams, and, shoving her off, I lurch to the singer at the organ—

8 seconds.

I grab her hand, wrenching the black rope bracelet from her wrist. I race back into the deathbed room.

5 seconds.

I fight my way toward the deadeye man, but I can't make it. It's too crowded.

3 seconds.

I step back and lob the bracelet over their heads. It falls, hitting the man on his chest, and, miraculously, he jerks up and catches it in his hand as the chime sounds.

The room goes quiet. The lights come on.

All I can think as the bag is shoved over my head, hands forcing me roughly into a wheelchair, all I can hear, is Dove Gavenaught's hoarse voice whispering fitfully in my head.

They never harmed her. My May was clever like that.

Poe and the other interns sit around the table, staring at me. We are holed up in Cabin 1. The wind outside in the gray afternoon rattles the latches on the old windows and the shingles on the roof, as if in anxious answer to what I just told them, what I discovered about Valkyrie during the second night of the game.

No one seems to know what to say. Their eyes move from my face to the chalkboard, where I drew my best recollection of the Valkyrie game board—the map of the library in Bury St. Elmswood, the three-circled spinner, the different sections and rows of books, the colored shapes and the words I remember.

Loot. Dead King. Radio to Mars. Beast Bed. Space Rocket. Clouds. Timbuktu.

Finally, Poe laughs. "Well done, Dia. I believe you cracked the code."

"We have to get back to Louisiana's house as soon as possible," I say. "Those nine books in the library are the nine settings of

Valkyrie. Deathbed Confessions, The Greys, and so on. Every player has fifteen minutes to find the book on the cart in order to understand where they are and find the solution. We have a cheat sheet for the last round of Valkyrie if we get our hands on those books."

"Hold on," says Cooper. "So Louisiana made Valkyrie about herself?"

"It's her secret autobiography. We'll never know her true intentions. Was it meant to be a simple board game, and after the theft it fell into the wrong hands? And now, the thieves have made a real-world nightmare from her initial plans? Or did she always design it to be this horrifying ordeal to survive?" I shrug. "What we do know is that the game is the terror of her childhood. She was dropped off, alone, as a child at the library, ordered by her mother to hide from the librarian. Penny hunted her in order to haul her away to Child Protection."

"Eve was the woman's name," says Poe. "Dove mentioned it."

"Isn't Eve one of the categories on the middle spinner?" asks Everleigh.

"Yes, I remember I saw it," says Franz.

I add the name Eve to the chalkboard. "So if this outer circle represents the nine books that were Louisiana's salvation, the vibrant, terrifying reality in which she hid as a little girl to keep safe, then this next circle, with Eve and Dark and Deadeye Man and Window, is . . . ?"

"The immediate threat to her survival," says Mouse.

Poe nods, his eyes bright as he grabs the chalk from me, scribbling in the remaining categories. "There's also Bird Hunter. Bad Dream. And Fire."

"Slaughterhouse," adds Torin.

"The middle circle is everything she was afraid of," I say.

"They're not literal. I doubt it was a real slaughterhouse. These were the things alive and terrifying in her child's imagination."

"What about the black circle at the center?" asks Cooper.

Everyone falls silent, considering it. Then it hits me.

"There has been one constant threat in every round of Valkyrie," I say.

"The fiend with the death cart," whispers Franz.

"The librarian," I say. "She's the black circle. Penny Malden was always there, every night, wheeling that creepy library cart around. In Louisiana's imagination, there were foul and evils things on that cart, what is actually there now—rodents and guts, poisons and bad perfume."

"Dove Gavenaught called Penny a witch," says Everleigh. "She probably called her that in front of Louisiana. So that's what she was in her mind. A witch hunting her in the library all night."

Everleigh nibbles her fingernail. "Wonder if this witch has something to do with the Darkly tagline."

" 'Wander where the witch lies,' " says Torin.

All of us thoughtfully consider it, staring at the chalkboard as Poe writes *Witch* inside the inner circle of the spinner.

"Oh my lord." Franz gulps. "I just thought of something."

We turn to him, waiting for him to go on.

"Remember how Penny said Dove advertised her services? By secret coded ads for dog sitting and gutter cleaning. Remind you of anything?"

"The summons to play Valkyrie," says Torin.

"Penny said it was posted on her community bulletin board. So that section of the library has been re-created as the literal opening to Valkyrie. 'Estate Jewelry' and 'Italian Motorbike for Sale.' "

"If everything about Valkyrie is tied to this nightmare from

Louisiana's childhood," I say, "so, too, is the idea of the Valkyrie, the ethereal goddess coming and taking away the brave and the slain to paradise."

"I've got it." Poe suddenly stops pacing. "The end of the game, the big win? I think it's to reach the listening booth. It's where Louisiana must have put on headphones and a record of Wagner's 'Ride of the Valkyries.' Remember how proud Penny was, talking about the glass listening booth and the opera records? She also said May locked her in there once."

I nod. "That's right. And Dove said when her little girl was scared, she'd go in there and put on a record."

"It was probably 'Ride of the Valkyries.' Had to have been."

Poe pulls out his phone, and within seconds the bright, wailing strings of the orchestra overtake the cabin, bringing to mind a fleet of soaring army airplanes zigzagging across the sky.

And it does make sense, that a child listening to this could imagine herself invincible.

"The question now is," says Everleigh, "does the perpetrator behind Valkyrie know the game is about Louisiana? What's the connection to the theft, and why has the game appeared now? What do they want?"

I tell them about the other player with me, what she said. "It's like she knew what was at the end of the win. And she was dying to get there."

"What have the kids been promised? Some kind of perfection? Being set for life?"

Mouse shrugs. "I tried to get some of the extras to talk—how they came to be there, who's in charge. They ran from me like I was some kind of contagion."

"They've been threatened," says Mouse. "Imprisonment. Something happening to their families."

"Next time you have to get behind the scenes," says Franz. "Climb into the corridors and out the window. If you find the location of that warehouse and the grounds, we can return with the police."

"If there *is* a next time," says Mouse. "I'm pretty sure I didn't win."

"I don't think I did," says Everleigh.

"Nor I," says Poe.

They turn to me with questioning looks.

Out of all of them, I'm the only one who believes that I won, though now I wonder.

Poe spun *Detective*, *Fire* and drew a clawed bat, folded as if asleep, from the bag. He found himself in an antique six-car train stopped on the tracks in a dense forest—that sounded identical to the one Cooper had run through in the first round. A real fire broke out in the front car, causing a stampede. The mob shattered the windows, scattering into the woods. Poe held back to search for a trapdoor, some way to get behind the scenes. Finding nothing, he had no choice but to follow the crowd. He was sprinting through the forest, passing a red London telephone booth—the same one Cooper described—when a deafening chime sounded and the masked figures hauled him away.

Mouse spun *Locks and Mazes* and *Dark*, drawing a small painting of a geometric face from the bag. *Modigliani*, the figures called it. He was shoved into an echoing room of darkness where a group of people stood at easels pretending to paint the giant tree in front of them, which rose to the ceiling—no light except the dim blue numbers of the timer. He panicked, at first, then remembered what Franz had described about the same scene, the tree with the spindly branches inside the silo. He figured the location had to be the same. Rather than climbing, he searched for a trapdoor. He swore he actually found something there, a seam in the concrete. That was when a hand gripped his shoulder and he realized he had been caught by the witch.

Everleigh spun *Secret Society* and *Eve* and pulled out a tiny stepladder. She said she was pushed through a door into what appeared to be the initiation rite of a secret society known as Ram's Head. Nine people clothed in robes, holding torches, were detailing in an unknown language—made-up, she was sure—a rite of passage in which she seemed to be the central victim, given the way they were staring at her. She was so afraid she leapt to her feet, trying to flee. But she was caught, strapped to a stretcher, causing her to scream "Wander where the witch lies," whereupon the lights came on.

After Everleigh finishes her story, we fall into thoughtful silence.

Solving this first piece of Valkyrie is not the triumph I expected. I was so excited to make it back to the island, to tell the others what I understood. Now, all I can think about is how lonely and afraid Louisiana must have been—day and night, hiding in the dark stacks with no one there to comfort her. Nothing except the nine library books, *the same blood-soaked nine,* and a harrowing opera on a record.

I never considered myself lucky, having Gigi as my mother. But whatever her failings, she always came home at the end of the day. She might have been tipsy and ranting about Marvin's Italian family restaurant or Heath's construction business or Herbert's new folk song and how it was going to make him famous. But she always had dinner on the table, opened my bedroom door to check on me in the dark, tucked the blanket under my chin, a kiss on my forehead, a whisper that she loved me before she tiptoed away.

I realize with a start that my phone is ringing. Everyone watches me, rapt.

I pull it out, my heart stopping at the sight of UNKNOWN. I answer pressing SPEAKER, because I want all of them to hear it, whatever is coming next.

"Hello?"

"Dia?"

"Choke?"

He sighs. "Thank goodness. You *are* alive. Is everything okay?"

"Yes," I manage. "I'm fine."

"Cool. So, I'm counting on you meeting me for dinner tonight."

The other interns are listening with confused surprise. I hit MUTE.

"He's a friend from home."

"Well, you aren't free tonight," Poe snaps. "We are due in two hours at George Grenfell's candlelight vigil."

I nod and hit UNMUTE. "I'd love to, Choke. But it'd have to be later. Nine o'clock?"

By the time Choke tells me where to meet him and I hang up, Poe has already barged out of the cabin, door slamming. I watch him from the window, stalking down the cliffside path.

I have to admit it's a strange new reality—that the glorious Poe Valois III's dark mood is because he's jealous of my date with Choke Newington.

Of course, it's not really a date. I know there must be some underlying reason Choke is so desperate to get ahold of me.

CONFIDENTIAL

(1982)

COMPLETE/PROBLEM?	Paid	Date
Status X		18/1
X Oliver von Hildew	1000	
Morgan Downting	500	4/3
Maximilian Valentine	2500	26/3
St. Edmond's Chil~~en's Home	11000	11/4
X Lady Clare Vale~		6/5
X Harry von Hilde~		
Morgan Downti~		
X Maximilian Vale~		

Gattie —   3/1/83

Please see that
Wood receives this at
Derringer ASAP

xo

$\mathcal{L}$

51

"I wish to thank the students and faculty of the Bromsbury School for the outpouring of support," Penelope Grenfell says with a tearful smile into the microphone. "I know how deeply he cares for this community, how much you share in our grief. Tonight, we celebrate George, in the hope that it will bring him home."

Standing atop the church steps behind the podium, Penelope Grenfell does not appear to have coped well since the last time we saw her. Her eyes are bloodshot, and her champagne hair has a dent in the back, as if she forgot to comb it this morning. George's father, Roger Grenfell, stands awkwardly behind his wife and looks like he'd rather be duck hunting.

Beside me, Franz wrinkles his nose. "I *think* she means 'I know nobody knows the first thing about my little Liebling Georgie. And you're all obviously here because it's mandatory, like taking Latin.'"

I can't help but smile as I resume my surveillance of the crowd. Franz and I are stationed by the churchyard entrance. Poe and Torin are somewhere on the opposite side of the lawn. Mouse, Everleigh, and Cooper are in the rear.

All of Bromsbury School appears to be here—some three hundred boys and girls in uniform. I've been searching for the brown-haired boy who shoved me, but so far, there's been no sign of him. The older kids pass out white candles. Someone else hands me a flyer.

Bring George home! Call the anonymous tip line. No questions asked.

A choir director leads a group of kids in a harmonized rendition of "Let It Be." Then the chancellor praises George's compassion and heart, telling a story about how he played his violin at a soup kitchen without telling anyone. A prefect appears, talking sheepishly about how George hated the outdoors and went to "legendary lengths" to avoid the three-day wilderness camping trip required for graduation. As a first-year, he rubbed himself with poison ivy. As a second-year, he feigned a sprained ankle.

"Come home, George," the boy says. "But you still have to go camping in order to graduate!"

The speeches all sound strained and awkward. I feel sorry for George, wherever he is.

The unspoken questions of who exactly George Grenfell is, where he went—and most sinister of all, if he's even still alive—hang in the air like inky shadows clogging the periphery of a summer day. The assumption seems to be, at least among students, that he walked out of his life by his own free will and needs to be convinced to return home, which seems odd, considering what he was involved in, and the length of time that he's been gone. But then, like Mrs. Grenfell, maybe most students don't have a clue about Valkyrie.

Or do they? How many of them have gone down to the kiss and seen their own face staring out?

The walk around campus is set to begin. Someone in the front starts to play "Blackbird" on a trumpet as students file out of the gate. Mrs. Grenfell hurries to the microphone again, holding up the tip-line flyer.

"Remember, no observation or worry is too small, so do not hesitate to call, please—"

"It's like they're all in on it," whispers Franz as we follow the crowd.

"What do you mean?"

"It's like they all know where George is. Because they're not concerned. They're not worried there's some deranged kidnapper on the loose. They must all know about Valkyrie. They're brilliant liars."

I'm tempted to blurt, *You're a brilliant liar, too. How long have you and Cooper been friends?*

But I chicken out. I need more time to piece it together, to understand the connection before I confront them.

We make our way down Main Street, passing the café and the bookstore. I see the old white Bromsbury School bus is parked in the same spot as it was before, the driver probably enjoying a pint at the Golden Lock, the pub. Turning to stare at its stucco-and-wood facade, I notice a face in the window.

I recognize the boy instantly.

I race into the yard. He is wiping down a booth, pausing to glance curiously out at the procession before setting out the silverware.

Franz steps beside me. "What's wrong?"

"That boy in the window."

Seeing us staring, he freezes—then ducks out of sight.

"That's the boy from the tunnel."

We sprint inside. There's no sign of the boy. But he was in such haste to flee he left a crate of glasses in the booth.

"The busboy!" I shout at the hostess. "Which way did he go?"

"Felix? Down there."

Franz and I take off down the hall, barging into the kitchen. It's hot and crowded with cooks. I veer around the tables, noticing the screen door hanging open. I race through it into an alley.

Sure enough, Felix is scaling a wall far at the end, jumping down on the opposite side.

I run after him, starting up the wall.

"I'll go around the other way and cut him off!" Franz shouts somewhere behind me.

I leap down into the alley and jog along the chain-link fence. The boy vanished somewhere here. The fence lines a few backyards, rose gardens, a handful of cottages. At one, a woman is sitting at a table with an umbrella, smoking a cigarette.

"Did you see a boy run through here?" I shout.

She points and I head in that direction, the fence stopping behind a house that looks abandoned, windows boarded up, a beat-up Triumph in the yard. I notice some of the tall grass by the back seat has been bent—and it looks recent. I climb the fence, as quietly as I can, and creep alongside the car, then yank open the door.

Felix leaps out—but I'm ready for him. I close the door on his leg, not too hard, but he trips, hitting the ground.

"Stop running from me, Felix. I just want to talk about George."

He rolls upright, scowling. "Who are you?"

"I'm his friend. I'm trying to find him."

"George doesn't have any friends. Except me." He rubs his shin.

"Is that why he started playing Valkyrie? To get friends?"

He makes a face. "It was nothing like that."

"What was it like, then?"

I can see that he wants to run again. His gaze flits somewhere behind me, back to the fence. But then I take a step toward him and he seems to understand there's nowhere else for him to go.

He shrugs. "It started as an investigation," he notes quietly. "George overheard two first-year girls whispering about it. They sneak out after curfew, go to a tunnel by a railroad track. If you call the right number scribbled in graffiti, the ad like 'Keep Warm in a Snowstorm,' within weeks, your face appears on a flyer. It can turn up anywhere—telephone pole, window of a Thai restaurant. You see yourself. If you have the guts to call the number? It begins."

"Valkyrie."

He shoots me an apprehensive look. "George told me half the school does it. They're obsessed. It's a rite of passage. A dare. Can you survive a nightmare of pure hell and live to tell the tale? The cool kids were doing it. They were climbing out of halls, two, three in the morning to play. George planned to report it. But he needed evidence.

So he found the number. 'Keep Warm in a Snowstorm.' Played the first round. It was after the second that everything changed."

"Why?"

"He figured out how to win. He said there was a method to it all, a design that unlocks the whole thing. I tried to do it based on what he told me, only to get captured by that beast woman. She will lock you in a closet, George told me, unless you whisper the safe words."

He means the librarian. The witch. But I'm struck by something else he said.

"George uncovered a design? Did he tell you what it was?"

He shakes his head. "He wasn't sure. But he had noticed certain items are present in every setting. First, you have to find the book on the cart that will tell you where you are. The books hold the key to the scene, I guess. Then, you find this 'lost and found,' he called it. The different objects in this box are the things the current players all pulled out of the gray bag. They are there to help you. Like a secret weapon. After that, he wasn't sure. But he must have figured it out, right, because he won."

"How do you know he won?"

"After he played the third night, he vanished. We have this band. Gobsmacked. He used to meet with me to rehearse. But he didn't show. I learned later he left school. Ran away. Which is why Broms is very tired of talking about George Grenfell. George was gone twenty-four hours before they even noticed he was missing. He went home that night to pack. He was leaving the country. He told me he was going to Chile."

"How do you know he didn't make it?"

He pulls out his phone, showing me a text message.

valkyrie is here

I'm more than an hour late to meet Choke.

By the time I leave Felix and track down the other interns, then pile into the white van, drive to London—it's almost ten-thirty.

I say goodbye—Poe scowling at me. "Have a nice *date,* Dia," he growls before slamming the door in my face. They're heading back to the island, so after dinner I'll hail a cab to take me back to Darkly Pier.

Minutes later, I'm wandering a constricted cobblestone alley in search of an address I'm sure I wrote down wrong—13 Gibman's Mistake. I'm also positive Choke Newington, if he even showed up in the first place, is no longer waiting for me. I call and text, but there's bad service and it goes to voicemail.

I can't find the restaurant. I go into a mobile phone shop for help. The cashier flags down a cabdriver eating a hot dog who explains in a thick Cockney accent that Gibman's Mistake is a mews that is an offshoot of Gibman's *Path,* a dead end off Gibman's *Way,* of course. Now even more confused, I make my way through a small black gnome-door at the end of what looks like a private driveway, more wizened vein than road, and down a steep set of stairs. I push open another door, this one red, and stumble into a hip restaurant.

It's pulsing with club music. The model hostess in the crop top doesn't even deign to give me a dirty look. I think it's either because she's so tall I don't make her peripheral vision or because I, in my jeans, frizzy hair, and strong brine stench, blend in with the umbrellas tossed by the door.

Choke is not here. Of course he's not.

"Dia!"

I turn to see Choke Newington far across the restaurant, climbing out of a wooden booth that appears to have been built in the form of an actual gold Japanese pagoda from the Edo period.

He is wearing a suit and tie, and he looks good. Not Poe Valois III good. But he has a debonair air of London about him now. His hair is long, his eyes knowing. He looks a little princely as his gaze drops to the brown stains on my legs that I got when I was either climbing the stone wall after Felix or splashed with some kind of teriyaki sauce as I ran through the pub kitchen.

Suddenly nervous, I make my way toward him across the blue lit-up floor. The tables are all in the form of *yubune,* I notice— traditional Japanese fishing boats—and seated everywhere around me are the most beautiful and polished people I have ever seen in my life. With every step I feel idiotic, dirty, and sweaty, and I know I need to leave immediately. But then, reaching Choke, the prospect of walking back through the restaurant a second time sends me scrambling into the pagoda booth. Except that's when Choke bends to kiss me on the cheek and bumps the top of my head, causing him to bite his lip and say "Ow," as my hair gets caught in the links of his wristwatch, which he then has to unfasten and pull off, handing the very expensive, hefty thing over as I try to free my hair.

When I finally sit down across from him, I realize he's mad.

"Sorry I'm so late. I couldn't get through on my cell."

He only glares at me.

"It's late," I manage. "Let's do this some other time."

When he still says nothing, I start to climb out, but he grabs my arm, pulling me back.

"I'm just going to come out and say it, point blank. What the hell is going on here, Dia?"

"We're meeting for dinner?"

Choke hunches forward, lowering his voice. "My mom went to Prologue Antiques when I couldn't get in touch with you. She asked your mom if she knew where you were staying, and your mom couldn't tell her. She eventually gave my mom the address of your *'residence'*"—he uses air quotes—"which my mom gave me. Which I visited two days ago and learned was completely bogus, unless you are Mermosa Louisa Caliente and you work as a massage therapist above a Turkish fortune-telling shop."

"You shouldn't be checking up on me."

"Well, I did. And you need to be checked up on. You're completely naive. You're a vulnerable minor without supervision in a foreign country. Where are you living? You can't even tell me. This is how bad things happen to good people."

"I don't have to tell you where I live. I don't *know* you—"

"Actually, you do. Since you were four. And thank God for that. Because without me, you'd be in a crate right now headed to Thailand."

"What is that supposed to mean?"

"I called the American Embassy about you."

"Ex*cuse* me?"

"There's a case number for you now. Paper trail. Oh, yes. I gave them your name—the names of those other kids, too. Poe. Everleigh? Are these people even real, or are they bots? Because they sure don't *sound* real—"

"You're here! Welcome to Shinrin-Yoku! May I bring you a cocktail this evening?"

A server has appeared. Her smile fades as she gathers what's happening at our table.

"I can come back—"

"Wait, no, I'm having the, uh . . ."

I grab the drink menu in front of me, forcing my eyes to focus on the "whimsical and extraordinary global sake concoctions" so I don't throw a vase of lotus flowers in Choke's face.

His condescending, arrogant, brazenly parental outrage is so maddening and over the top that I want to run out of here and never speak to him again—but not before I tell him off. Except I've never been able to tell off anyone, except the Barnabys in Prologue.

"The Ikigai, please. Thank you."

"I'll go to the State Department next. Unless you tell me what you're involved in. Right now."

"I don't have to do anything. You don't *know* me—"

"I do, as a matter of fact. In kindergarten, your mom packed you lunches with moldy SunWise sandwiches and brown celery sticks, which is why *I* always had my mom pack extra sushi for *you*. You're welcome."

For some reason, this, of all things, feels like a punch in the face. I can feel my cheeks burning. "Is that what you toast at the country club? How you and the other boys in plaid shorts are saving the world one poor girl at a time?"

"No. We talk about how regal you look when you wear your hair in a bun, and how interesting you might be if you ever let anyone talk to you. Which you don't, because you're too cool in your brown T. S. Eliot sweaters and tweed skirts that smell like World War Two."

He shouts this pretty loudly, so now people in all the surrounding boats are turning, eyeing us with faint concern.

"You are not my friend."

"Wrong again. I took three different Tube lines and a double-decker bus to track you down, *Mermosa*. That's a friend."

"It's none of your business what I'm doing here. But I'm not involved in some criminal cabal, if that's what you're hoping to uncover so you can write about it in an essay on your college application."

"Prove it." He sits back, crossing his arms.

"I'm working on a secret project."

"What project?"

"I can't say."

"Yeah, okay, that's enough of that. We're calling your mom right now. Or we're calling *my* mom."

He's on his phone, swiping to FAVORITES, where I see MOM and DAD are the first two numbers.

"Wait."

I grab his hand.

"I'm safe. I swear."

I'm lightheaded with anger, but then Choke is leaning forward, staring into my eyes, his fingers grazing the inside of my wrist. Suddenly, I feel alone with him, naked and unfastened, as if he's seeing everything I've ever dreamed about him, as if he is rooting around my head, seeing the Darkly factory and the island and Valkyrie and Poe.

"Tell me what is going on," he says.

"Ask the people you work for. Derringer Street Chambers? They're behind the whole thing."

He sits back with an irritated frown. "They're a bunch of toffs who refer to their wives and husbands as Diddums. And sure, there's a certain creepy glee when they bill clients eight hundred pounds an hour for a three-minute phone conversation. But other than that, weekends in the Cotswolds, the odd senior partner who's a lord, there's nothing sinister going on."

"Now who's the naive one?"

"One Ikigai."

With great fanfare, the server places a single martini glass in front of me. It's festooned with exotic fruit from Mount Fuji and filled to the trembling edge with a silvery pink liquid.

"Are you two ready to order, or do you need more time?"

"More time," says Choke.

That's when I have an idea.

I grab the drink and gulp about half of it down, Choke looking on with wide-eyed concern. The hot liquid fire drenches my heart and drips down to my toes, and as I lean forward, uncrossing my legs, I kick Choke in the shin.

"Ouch."

"I'll prove it," I say. "Let's get out of here."

I scramble out of the booth. Choke is on his feet, throwing a wad of pounds sterling on the table before running after me.

The front doors to Derringer Street Chambers are not locked. I follow Choke through the two sets of heavy doors, stopping at the reception desk.

Even though it's midnight, the security officer looks fresh and wide-awake as she considers us.

I now feel very tipsy.

I don't know why I decided, idiotically, to chug a cocktail when my only experience with alcohol has been trying some of the port Basil sometimes brings to Prologue in a small silver flask. "Now, *this* is assisted living," he says with a wink.

I do my best to stand beside Choke, looking bored, as he hands the woman his badge.

"Choke Newington, Membership 637? I came back for a brief that I forgot. I have to finish it for court tomorrow morning."

The woman scans the badge, eyeing me. "She'll stay here."

"Actually, can she come, too? I'll vouch for her."

She hands me a clipboard, where, suddenly scared and

unprepared, I sign my name Mermosa Howard. Then, Choke and I are slipping down the labyrinthine green hallways.

"What are we looking for? Democratic National Committee headquarters?"

"Nile Raiden's office."

"Partners are all top floor."

He points toward a staircase, twisting like a dark thought overhead. I start up and immediately trip—due to my sloshing head, which feels as if it has short-circuited, my thoughts afloat. Choke is right there to catch me, one arm on my back, the other around my waist, which even when I've regained my balance he still doesn't remove, like I'm some sort of crumbling octogenarian. I push his hands away, racing ahead. I don't have much time. That security officer at the reception desk is probably watching us—because Derringer Street's paranoia certainly must extend to cameras covering every square inch of this place. Or she's Googling my name.

"You're drunk, Dia."

"Shhh."

"Is that what you've been doing at this internship? Getting drunk every night? What else?"

I step into the hallway. It's the top floor, very dark. The darkness seems to conspire with the cocktail, blurring the edges of me and the edges of the law firm.

"If I wanted to find out about Louisiana's history with this place, where would I find it? Where would Nile Raiden hide evidence of the buried bodies?"

Choke laughs and beckons me in the other direction.

"The morgue's this way."

He leads me to the end of yet another hallway—two grand

mahogany doors haughtily closed underneath elaborate carved drapes of ivy. There is an elegant sign. NILE AITKEN RAIDEN.

I try the handles.

"Of course they're locked," I whisper.

And they don't sound like cheap little bolts that can be picked with a paper clip or credit card. I'm aware of Choke right beside me, judging me in the darkness.

"Show me your workspace," I whisper.

"Uh, at this stage in our nonfriendship, I'm not remotely comfortable with that."

"Seriously. Where do you sit? Where's your cubicle?"

"What makes you think I have a mere *cubicle*?"

Grinning, he steps across the hall a few doors down, fishing a key from his pocket. I step after him into a small office with mahogany shelving and a sprawling view of the park.

I should have known Choke Newington would come to London and land a dream office within two minutes.

I take a seat at his desk. "Log on to your computer."

"Aren't we going to talk first?"

"Do it."

Nodding with feigned shock, he leans over me to type passwords, hits RETURN, more passwords, my cheek brushing his arm. He smells different than he did the day I kissed him in the stairwell, more mature. It makes me wonder if he's using some new kind of British soap—the English are very into handcrafted soaps and lotions and cleanliness, I've noticed—which leads to the unfortunate mental image of Choke taking a hot shower every morning. Which leaves me so mortified and red-faced that it's a moment before I realize he has successfully logged on and is perched on the edge of the desk, staring down at me.

"You need a cup of coffee."

"Where can you search for history of court cases, like old clients, that kind of thing?"

He nods and bends over me again, opening some kind of file program, a search prompt.

I push his hand away to type "Louisiana Veda."

The program erupts with results. There are hundreds. They appear to be in some kind Derringer Street code, which Choke scrolls through and appears to understand.

"That's weird," he says.

"What?"

"Look up the names of most clients, you get a client number, which you can then take into the archive, searching for papers by subject matter. But this is different." He points to the end of the lines—all marked with *VV*.

vv3. vv14.

"What does the 'V' stand for?"

"Vault."

"But it's not a *real* vault."

"Actually it is."

He clicks open a floor plan of Derringer Street and scrolls to the final page. In the basement, there are two cavernous rooms, one marked *Y* and another *V*.

Choke points at the *Y*. "My boss, Lord Reed, needed an affidavit from here a week ago. Y Vault contains every tort case Derringer has tried against the British government. When I was down there, I passed this other room. V Vault. So if this section is all cases involving the British government, I wonder if this other might be—"

"Everything Darkly."

55

It's when Choke and I are hurrying down the echoing basement corridor through the absinthe-green light—after Choke unlocked his boss's office and removed the vault keys from a lockbox in the man's desk—that the effects of the cocktail start to wear off.

The subterranean coldness and our noisy footsteps on the concrete floor hit me in sharp detail. Suddenly, I understand the grave situation I've put us both in with no forethought and a devil-may-care attitude, which reminds me a little of my mom.

The anger on Nile Raiden's face the day he rescued us from Louisiana's manor will be nothing compared to what he will do when he finds out I was down here. He will dismiss me, faster than he wipes a speck of lint off his necktie.

Choke stops outside a black steel door.

"You should get out of here," I say.

He shoots me an amused look over his shoulder as he shoves in the key, the sound of giant bolts sliding back.

"Seriously. You shouldn't get fired because of me."

"It's a little late for that. It's my name on the entry sheet."

"You can still go. Tell them I stole your keys."

"After hypnotizing me and holding me hostage at gunpoint?"

Laughing, he pushes open the door and flicks on the overhead lights.

It's a massive room—filled with cylindrical silver steel cabinets. They look like an army of upright coffins. Each one has a number and name printed at the top.

VV1. MAXIMILIAN VALENTINE

VV5. LADY CLARE VALENTINE

VV9. BELLA DOWNLING

What is all of this?

I twist the handle on VV1, Maximilian Valentine, the door opening sideways, revealing carousels spinning with papers. They seem to be organized by date.

There is so much here. Letters, contracts, correspondence.

19 April 1983

The Steinlich Promise Center
Zurich, Switzerland

Thank you for the update on Patient 6-19B, Maximilian Valentine. Please continue his treatment according to the suggestions of applicable physicians. Your suggestion of a personal visit is untenable. However, Miss Gattie O'Cleary will be present. Payment will be remitted promptly. Please advise of the timing of his departure upon the completion of his care. We will

```
handle transportation to an agreeable living
facility.
```

```
Signed,

Wood Raiden

Senior Counsel
```

The name swims before my eyes. It's yet another thing Raiden failed to mention, how taking care of Darkly and preserving Louisiana Veda's name has long been a family affair.

"Wood Raiden?" I whisper. "What do you know about him?"

"Founder of Derringer Street," answers Choke, on the other side of the room.

"He is Nile's father?"

"*Was.* Long dead. You should see his portrait in the library. Looks like the love child of a vampire and a chunk of quartz."

I pull out another paper.

January 8, 1984

£50,000 to Exponential Accelerant LLC

"So many records of wire transfers," I say.

"Same thing over here," says Choke. "Thousands paid into tangles of anonymous LLCs into other LLCs. Germany. Singapore. Looks like Derringer Street has been spending a fortune paying off people on behalf of Louisiana for decades. She bought their silence."

I feel sharp irritation. "Not necessarily. This might be charity work she chose not to advertise."

"*Riiiight.* These people all had polio, I'm sure." Choke, sticking his head out from behind a filing cabinet, shoots me a doubtful look. "A better idea. Louisiana stole people's ideas and passed them off as her own. Face it. You don't really know anything about this woman."

His comment makes me think back to the ragged beaches of Bury St. Elmswood, Dove Gavenaught, Penny Malden, the library burned to the ground.

I clear my throat. "The desire to write off Louisiana Veda as a wily and deceptive con artist or a deep-conspiracy cartoon like the Wizard of Oz is yet another way detractors love to dismantle her legacy, because they're threatened by her. And they're jealous."

"Maybe these were people her games had injured, then. Lawsuits by personal injury lawyers. Broken necks after playing a Darkly?"

"No. She owned what happened with Rasputin. She didn't try to hide or make excuses."

Choke is yanking open another drawer. "Then why shell out millions if you have nothing to hide? Sorry, Dia, but if she was completely legit, she'd have gone to court. Truth shall set you free and all that."

I close the carousel on Maximilian Valentine and move deeper into the forest of steel cabinets. I stop in surprise at a familiar name.

VV13. BRITAIN'S ROYAL LOTTERY

I pull open the drawer.

Dear Dove,
Thank you for your proposal to purchase the Bavarian Bath House and Arabian Lounge. Unfortunately, your lottery win precludes such a commercial ownership.

Regretfully,
Peter Smith

I close the drawer, moving to the next cabinet, another name I know.

vv21. WOOD RAIDEN

I pull open the drawer. There are documents, contracts, more records of wire transfers.

£10,000,000 to Ventures LLC

The date on the wire is February 21, 1985. That was only four months before the fifteen-year anniversary party and Louisiana's suicide weeks later.

I pull out a faded typewritten letter, the letterhead swimming in front of my eyes.

Wood Raiden
25 Eaton Place
Belgravia, London

9 March 1980

Dear Detective Miles,

The next time you telephone telling me you have no idea where she is, expect that to be the noose around your fat neck. There is only one outcome here. My heart is found.

Wood

"Entire families have been paid off," Choke mutters. "The Valentines. The Downlings? Here's someone with an obviously fake name. Hackley Gallows? Sure, that sounds completely real. Oh, and here's someone's birth certificate."

I am barely listening.

My heart is found.

I don't know what any of this means. But something about the frank and fastidious documentation of this room, these people and their payments, feels very wrong. What also feels wrong is how Wood Raiden and Nile Raiden turn up whenever Louisiana's name appears.

There must be some logical explanation. I know it's not Louisiana Veda who was the evil one, the bad one, the cruel one. It was the people around her, plotting against her, trying to control her, use her, destroy her. And she's not here to speak up for herself, or fight for what she wanted or what was hers. She is silent, so absolutely gone. She can't say *Yes. No. This is not right at all. My words have been twisted, my image corrupted.*

I notice abruptly Choke has gone silent. The room feels empty—and eerily still. I close the drawer, darting between the filing cabinets.

vv41. 1980

vv98. MANSFIELD

Choke has vanished.

I turn, starting the other way. The cabinets seem to extend forever into the shadows.

"Dia?"

I whip around to see Choke in the doorway. He has an odd look on his face, his eyes devoid of light.

"Time to get out of here, I think," he says quietly.

I nod. Yet he doesn't move. Neither do I.

"Why did you want to have dinner with me?" I ask.

The question seems to startle him.

"Why are you checking up on me? Suddenly, out of nowhere, you're my friend? After years of ignoring me, and looking through me, and seeing nothing at all—"

"I never saw nothing."

"It's because of the internship. Close proximity to *her*. They put you up to this, didn't they? Derringer Street. Nile Raiden? They think I'm dangerous now, like all of these others here, with what I'm finding out. I now need to be controlled. What did they ask you to do? Take me out to dinner? Get me drunk? Then what?"

He only stares.

"Get out of my way."

"Hold on a minute—"

He tries to grab me as I start for the door, but I push him roughly away, so he stumbles, knocking into a cabinet. One of the doors drifts open, papers sliding to the floor.

He freezes. Then suddenly he takes a step, his massive black shadow climbing the wall.

"Dia! Wait!"

I kill the lights and slam the door behind me as I sprint out.

I run up the stairs, one flight, then another, blasting out into the
darkened hallway. I can hear Choke racing after me, so I slip
into an empty office, cramming myself under a desk to hide. I
see him barrel past. I wait a few seconds, then scramble out in the
opposite direction, my heart leaping in alarm as I dart past looming
corridors, shadowed offices. I can't think clearly—except that I have
to get out of here. I'm in danger. Because those raw secrets I just
rooted through down in the vault, dedicated to the careful manage-
ment of so many people in service to Darkly—while I don't know
why or what they are, I do know they're explosive.

This kind of knowledge cannot be returned to the package
with the receipt for a refund. It will ruin me, destroy me, if I'm not
smart, if I don't play the game brilliantly, staying six moves ahead.

But Choke Newington knows I know. He must have been
coached to play along, be charming, be her friend again, try to find
out what she knows, how far she will go.

He will report everything right back to Raiden.

She saw it all, I'm afraid, sir. She knows about the people you paid fortunes to in exchange for their obedience. Valentines. Downlings. She's going to find out why, sir.

I heave open the door, strolling out into the lobby, past the security officer behind the desk, who looks up with a prim smile as she hangs up the phone. Then I'm slipping outside, down the steps. Once I'm on the sidewalk, I break into a run, sprinting around the corner, passing one narrow street, then another. Reaching a deserted alley, I stop to catch my breath.

I have lost Choke. All of the running has cleared my head.

I consider calling Poe, wondering if he and the others might come get me. I don't want to be alone, not with this knowledge. I have to tell them what I saw. But then, no—my doubts about Franz, Cooper, and Everleigh—what they're hiding, who they are, that rogue Darkly employee dogging us, riffling through our things, attacking us, playing tricks—I cannot trust them either.

I turn off my phone. Paranoid? Probably. But it was supplied by Derringer Street. It's not exactly a stretch to imagine there's an active tracker on it, that somewhere some attorney isn't yawning as he monitors my little green dot on his computer.

She's standing under a lamppost at Hay's Mews, wondering what to do next, sir.

I wipe my face, shivering. I check over my shoulder to make sure I'm alone, then I take off once again, running around the next corner, emerging onto a busy road.

I step to the curb and hail a black cab.

"Twenty-Five Eaton Place. Belgravia."

It's the address I saw on the threatening letter from Wood Raiden.

It was written years ago. The man is dead. I have no idea who lives there now. It could very well be strangers. And yet if Nile

Raiden has grown up following in his father's footsteps, practicing the same vocation, working at the same firm for the same illustrious client, maybe he lives in the old family home.

When the cab pulls over, I stumble out onto a vertiginously long street. A crowd of white mansions stand shoulder to shoulder, imperiously ignoring me.

The windows of number 25 are dark. But I can make out elaborate curtains, shadows of art. I unlatch the iron gate, slip between the planters up the steps. Seeing the brass doorbell, the camera on the high-tech security intercom, I almost lose my nerve.

I press the button. There is a crack. Then a voice gasps, "What the devil?"

My instincts were right. It's Nile Raiden.

"We need to talk."

There's only silence. I know he is livid, wondering how I found his home address, probably cursing Choke, too: *The hometown heartthrob couldn't keep a handle on her? He let her get away?*

I wonder luridly if he's taking time to set up my murder. A gun with a silencer? A string of piano wire?

The lock clicks. I pull open the door, stepping into a white tiled foyer. Nile Raiden, wearing blue pajamas and yanking on a satin robe, is racing down the staircase.

With an infuriated wave, he strides right past me, beckoning me to follow him into a sitting room.

I move after him but remain in the doorway, watching him pour himself a glass of whisky.

Of course, I realize now what a foolhardy move this surprise visit is. I have no weapon, no insurance or trump card, nothing to defend myself or keep myself alive. No one knows that I'm here, not even Choke. What will Raiden do—kill me, then wait for the cleanup team?

We have another nuisance, he'll hiss into a burner phone.

No worries, sir. We're on our way.

Derringer Street Chambers will go into overdrive doing what they have always done—paying off, threatening, bricking over the ugly entrances and cementing the escape routes so it looks like they were never there. *Poor Arcadia insisted on driving the van. She went the wrong way down the motorway. Smashed into a lorry filled with chickens.*

Nile Raiden drains his drink, then pours another. When he looks up at me, it's with an acidic smile.

"Do take a seat, Miss Gannon. Don't fret. I'm not going to murder you. At least, not tonight."

Foreverless

Cabin 9

Cabin 8

Cabin 1

Welcome cocktails — 9:00
Presentation — 9:30
Dancing — 10:00

Torment Point
Guest Arrival
8:40 – 8:50

L Retrieval
omb 605
–10:10

Darkly Factory

Export Bay
10:15

Manufacturing
and Export Bay

57

I take a step inside, but do not sit. Raiden, clearly amused by my reluctance, throws himself into an armchair with a heavy sigh.

"I knew you'd be the problem," he mutters. "We never should have offered it to you. We should have gone with Natasha Murdov of Moscow, whose family owns the failing bread shop. Ever since you were suggested, I knew you'd be the maverick, the upstart, the flaw."

He shakes his head. "You're so close, Arcadia. A second round of Valkyrie? You could well make it to the third. You could find out who is behind this, where it's happening, and why. You could save lives, preserving Louisiana's name, becoming a powerful woman in the process. Someone young girls look up to. Instead, you're waking me up in the middle of the night to demand—*what* is it exactly you're looking for? The truth?"

He laughs acidly. "You are hardly a surprise tonight. I was notified hours ago that you were rooting around our offices and had managed to get into the basement." He chuckles. "So, what is it that you think you saw down there? I'd love to know the fantastical fairy tale your overactive imagination has concocted."

"I saw all of the people your firm has paid off."

"True."

"The fortunes you paid for silence."

"Also true."

"Including your own father. Wood."

He says nothing, lifting his chin to survey me closely. Yet I can see it takes effort to hide something—unease or distaste—which he disguises by draining his drink.

"You've silenced all of those people. Why?"

He frowns thoughtfully, interlacing his fingers. "You understand so little. You see someone beautiful and smiling in a photo against a backdrop of a beach—and oh, you envy that happy life there in the little square. You have no clue it's all an illusion. You young know nothing of the expanse of struggles and darkness, the Herculean effort it takes for someone—a woman like Louisiana, years ago—not to just scale the mountain but to remain there at the vertiginous pinnacle, where there is room for . . . only a handful? All men. To be legendary. The thing millions of girls tape to bedroom walls, you think that doesn't take obscene amounts of violence and compromise? Those who have the iron will and the insanity to go all the way to the top are faced with the most harrowing choices the higher they climb. And it isn't between right and wrong, good and evil. If only it were that simple. It's between wrong and criminal, unfortunate and utterly horrifying. To think otherwise is to believe in elves."

I do not move. I am aware that he is giving a performance, working hard to try and convince me of something. This is a courtroom. He's delivering his closing argument. He is going to try different tactics to defuse this situation, throw me off, to shame and manipulate, woo and befriend me. I need only to remain very still and hope that I can make out some fragile thread of truth, hidden in the lies that he's going to tell me.

"Louisiana was maddening." He sighs with theatrical exasperation. "She came from as dark a childhood as one can imagine."

"I know all about it," I say. "The library at Bury St. Elmswood. The books she stole before she torched the place. Dove and Penny and the phony lottery."

He is, much to my irritation, not even a little surprised.

"Say whatever you want about Louisiana," he continues matter-of-factly. "She knew who she was. That's why she made the arrangements."

He waves a hand in the air, a grim nod at me.

"There were three. Perhaps you already know that, too? Maximilian. Bella. And Kitten. Louisiana went to great care to find loving families for each of them. The process of selection was vigorous. Prospective fine English families were boiled down to the most stable, loving, imaginative, and happy. After a period of investigation—private detectives, round-the-clock surveillance—the selected family was approached. It was always Gattie who made the introduction. The loyal secretary. She had the sweet and unassuming presence. 'What a lovely family you have. May I pose a question?' The reaction was always the same. Shock first. Then dismay. Then curiosity, then eager acceptance of such a windfall. Louisiana did not wash her hands of her children. Quite the contrary. She was always there, keeping watch behind the scenes, sending Gattie to drop in, spy, adding this to their education, taking that away, as if it were all a terrifying new Darkly game."

He talks in an easy, congenial voice as if we are longtime friends. At first, I don't follow what he's telling me.

Then, it hits me: he's talking about Louisiana's children.

"In theory, it should have been a success. Every variable and potential outcome polished and scrutinized three times over. Yet all three ended in ruin. Louisiana paid the price dearly. Now Derringer Street does so, quite literally, on her behalf. And we will continue to do so, according to the wishes of her will."

I cannot breathe.

He's telling me that Louisiana had three children and gave them away in secret, hiding this truth from the world. There is something violent about this secret, so sad, that I can only stand there, unable to move or say a word.

"First came the son, Maximilian." Raiden slips to his feet, pouring himself a fresh drink. "A shy, sensitive boy. Conniving and vicious as a teenager. When he learned he was the child of Louisiana Veda, that's when the shakedown began."

He chuckles. "Little Bella was a handful from the start—heart problems, colic, in and out of hospital. She showed promise as a swimmer, then it was horses, then French cuisine, all of it slapdash and spoiled. She fell in with a London criminal gang. That's the last we heard of her."

He considers me with a sad smile, perching on the arm of the sofa. "And Kitten. We'll never know what would have become of her. She was my half sister. My father, Wood, fell for Louisiana in spite of every sordid thing he knew about her. It was he, after all, in the mud pit with her, cleaning up the bombed-out cities in her wake. Still, he found himself a victim of hers, much to his surprise. The child perished at three years old in a house fire, a month before my father even learned of her existence. He died not long after, a broken man."

Raiden is a liar. These things he's telling me are only a plot to make me hate Louisiana, to dismiss her as cruel, selfish, and heartless, so he can manipulate me.

That's what I want to believe.

But somehow, I know he's telling the truth.

He is also aware of the impact of this confession. Yet he doesn't stop. He is so smooth, so relentless, his words firing at me with clinical coldness, like a surgeon going into gruesome detail about the operation he's about to perform, explaining every gory detail, as if it's nothing more than directions to a bus stop. And I can't help but hang on his every word.

"Louisiana knew, given her background, she was not meant to be a mother. She was too driven. She would never slow down. In a misguided attempt to do the right thing, she placed them with perfect families—and unwittingly spawned two monsters."

He nods at the look on my face, shrugging. "The identities of the other fathers? We never knew. Still don't. Presidents? Movie stars? Nameless passersby who caught her eye? It was no one's business but her own. Louisiana answered to no one. She was an underground tomb with no door. My father and Derringer Street worked closely with her, but she remains to this day an enigma. She would go silent, vanish for months at a time. Was she holed up in her factory tower, concealing the fact that she was pregnant, poring night and day over the games? My father was of the belief that she actually traveled the world, ever the itinerant stranger. There would be great anxiety and fighting in the ramp-up to release, frenzied anticipation, the fear Darkly would not deliver, certainly not on time. Then, at the eleventh hour, Louisiana would come barreling into home plate like clockwork with a new addictive masterpiece.

Manufacturing organized, supplies intact. It always worked out for her. And the public ate it up."

"So, you knew her."

I don't know why I blurt this, of all things—something about the lazy familiarity he has when he says her name.

"She is part of my recollection as a child, yes. The icy draft that whips through a room, papers flying, candles blowing out. My mother loathed her for the riptide that she was, brutally pulling my father asunder, dominating his life. Even I hated her for a time."

"And now you work for her."

It's the first time I see his composure falter. I see surprise, then a flash of anger, though almost as swiftly it's replaced by a bemused smile.

"I suppose there is a doomed symmetry to it." He shrugs. "But why should I squander the opportunity to preserve such brilliance, ushering her work into the twenty-first century? The original games are as sought-after as the rare Klimt or Monet. An empire of mystery and creativity that deserves to live on. So what if the human being who created it turns out to be not as divine as the art?" He chuckles. "They never are."

I feel so foolish. I am aware that my picture of Louisiana—the one I stared at every day of my childhood—is now defaced and dismantled and lying on the ground. I wonder how I could have been so gullible to believe and even love someone I knew nothing about, to have that be the thing against which I judged the rest of the world.

"Where are they now?" I ask. "Maximilian and Bella."

"Deceased, we believe. Though we actively search the world for both of them, their trails have gone cold. Because the most powerful, surefire indicator of life—that of asking the Veda estate for a handout—has ceased entirely. The only explanation for that is that they're dead."

He turns to me, considering my face with careful focus. "So there you have it," he says. "The autopsy. Now, do you wish to go home empty-handed? Or will you finish what you started?"

I have no answer. I've never felt more like a child, frozen in the doorway, waiting for him to dismiss me, tell me there's nothing more and I am free to go. I do want to go home. I am reminded of my own threadbare family. I feel ashamed of the occasions I sat with Gigi at a restaurant and longingly observed another family in the booth behind us, jealous of their laughter, wishing I could go home with them. To have a mom who was brave, who could sit alone at a table, who wasn't worried about looking pretty, a mom who was confident and built things and didn't care what others thought of her.

"Finish the game, Arcadia. Do it for yourself. For Louisiana."

"I don't know what that name means anymore."

He scoffs. "I didn't take you for someone with a weak stomach. Go be happy and quiet in a farmhouse in Missouri. Or hike to the top of the world and walk with your severed heads on a spear. The radio songs you sing along to with the windows down? The money you dump into your savings account at the banks that stand so grandly at the end of the avenue? Every world power from here to China, the rulers danced with the unthinkable. Those names so pristine in the title chapters of your history books, all of those burnished oil portraits in the gold frames in the museums—don't you know those subjects, seconds before, were splattered in blood? That's what it takes to be mythical. To craft the immortal beauty, the timeless work of art. And they are masterpieces, her games. Say what you will about Louisiana, she was undeniable, she was a genius. No different from the monstrous Picasso, the cold and exploitive Warhol turning his camera on the dying and whispering 'Action!' The Vanderbilt counting his pile of gold as he sent impoverished workers into the tunnels with the dynamite to build his beloved railroad. She was an artist who lived and died for her art, ravaging the human being that barely held it all in place for thirty-six years. The human being was only a temporary rowboat for her. And so it is for all of us. Put art and commerce first—if you're a man, you're a pillar of society. If you're a woman, you're monstrous. This is it. This is what is real in our world. Keep your eyes open, Dia, or closed, it's your choice."

He falls silent. He looks triumphant but spent, the actor who just exited offstage after a marathon performance. I am aware of his stare, like a bayonet pressing into my neck. I can't help but brace myself, sensing he is not finished with me.

"Go where you're forbidden again, Arcadia Gannon," he says as he rises, striding past me with a wave of dismissal, "disobey my orders, I will send you home. You've run out of chances. Now, get out of my house."

58

Raiden has already called a black cab. It's waiting for me by the curb.

As I step outside, I turn back, wanting to say something to him, I'm not sure what. *Thanks for telling me the truth?*

But with a tight smile, he's already closing the door. He seems to know he did a first-rate job of bringing me into the fold, quashing my outrage, rendering me speechless and shaken with the brazen panorama he presented of the ugly truth.

I climb into the taxi. Within minutes, we are lurching down cobblestones and back alleys, past crowded Leicester Square and solemn roads stuffed with dark houses and cars. I wonder for one petrifying minute and another and another—if this is my final ride.

Now that I know what Louisiana did, it's not too far-fetched, is it, to imagine that Raiden would decide I need to be eliminated, strangled by this silent, morose driver, buried in a field somewhere?

But an hour later, we are bouncing through the gate at Darkly Pier.

I scramble out, the taxi taking off as I make my way toward the dock. The captain, doubtless alerted by Raiden of my ensuing arrival, is already at the helm of the *Elvira*.

I can tell she has been ordered by Raiden to stop talking to me, to ignore my questions—or else. She puts a blanket around me with a grim nod and steps behind the helm, steering us into the choppy waters.

It's when we're almost there, when I can see the island rising like an impenetrable black cloud out of the darkness, that her dutiful silence infuriates me so much that I move beside her, tossing off her blanket.

"I went to see Nile Raiden," I shout. "He told me everything that she did. Louisiana? Her three secret children? Did you know about them?"

The captain does not react, her gaze on the approaching pier.

Of course she knew.

"She had them and gave them away," I go on. "Sent them into a Darkly experiment, a twisted game of family musical chairs. She eavesdropped on them, spying from afar like she did at her factory, always hiding inside the walls."

I can see that nothing I'm shouting is news to the captain.

"Don't you have anything to say? At least make excuses for her, let her off the hook!"

"All of us get blood-splattered on the battlefield. The only question is, who do we save and who do we carry to safety on our backs?"

"As far as I can tell, Louisiana saved no one except herself."

"You're the one peering with one eye through a porthole, child."

The captain ducks away, out onto the stern, tossing the ropes over the mooring posts.

"What's that supposed to mean? Hello? Answer me."

She ignores me, tying the ropes.

I want to keep shouting, force her to face me. I am so angry, for reasons I can barely explain.

Maybe it's the captain's unending adoration of Louisiana, which does not falter no matter what calculated and selfish things the woman did. Maybe it's my disgust that Louisiana isn't who I thought she was, how the brilliant woman I have so long revered has so little resemblance to this manipulator who did dark things. Louisiana Veda—this woman I'm forcefully wheeling out of the shadows—it seems with every inch her face slips into the light, it would be better for all involved that I stop, return her to the darkness and the tall tales.

I'm also very tired. I step off the boat without another word, though I can feel the captain's eyes on my back as I race down the planks and up the steps. Halfway up, when I turn back, I see the *Elvira* is already gone, bobbing out of sight around the rocks.

Let her keep her precious, golden, fake memories of Madam.

The winding paths and gnarled trees and sculptures drowning in the overgrown grasses, the dry fountains and sagging roofs, the crumbling walls—it's probably my exhaustion and the meeting with Raiden, but the island seems to have sunk even deeper into the ground. The stone paths feel as lonely as the skeletal remains of an unseen creature no one ever discovered. I round the pond, approaching the fork, pausing to stare at the boys' cabin, the windows dark.

I have the sudden idea that I should wake Poe, tell him everything. He would find the pattern inside the truth. *It was a different time back then. Women were discounted. Motherhood was considered a weakness and a vulnerability. It still is. So she hid it. She did her best.*

But the insistent way the wind whips through the grass, plunging over the cliffs, it seems to be pushing me away.

I tiptoe inside my cabin, pulling on my pajamas. Cooper, Torin, and Everleigh are asleep. And even though the wind is rattling the old latches in the windows and battering the walls, making the shingles whistle, I am out before my head hits the pillow.

59

The six of them stare at me, incredulous.

It was with mad ferocity that I woke everyone at the crack of dawn. My eyes shot open, the strange events of last night jolting me awake, and I took off running, telling them to assemble in Cabin 1 for an emergency meeting.

"Kitten is her *child*?" says Everleigh. "Her secret child is buried in the tomb with her?"

I nod.

"Okay, yeah, it's twisted, what she did," says Cooper. "But it's also not *that* different from a million men in the olden days who left children at every port, washing their hands of all responsibility, leaving the children impoverished and the women who loved them in disgrace, while they conquered the world. At least Louisiana gave them to loving families. Even if the whole thing did backfire."

"It's so sad," says Torin.

For a moment, no one says anything else, all of us considering it. I am very much aware of Poe, sitting opposite me, at the other end of the table, tipping back his chair. His dark eyes are hollowed from a lack of sleep, his hair mussed. And though instantly I imagine him tossing and turning all night as he imagined me enveloped in the passionate arms of Choke Newington, it's only my wishful thinking, I know.

"We have a new set of suspects," he says. "The disaffected loser offspring. It could be one of them."

"Behind the release of Valkyrie?" says Mouse.

Poe nods. "Think about it. Take control of the very thing your absent, coldhearted parent loved and cherished. What she chose over you. Then destroy it."

"There are thirteen words in German for revenge," says Franz. "This is 'die Abrechnung.' A highly devastating, long-overdue payback."

"Raiden is pretty confident they're all dead," I say.

"That's what he chose to tell you," says Poe.

"I agree," says Cooper, crossing her arms. "One thing we can count on is that Raiden will always tell the story that serves Derringer Street. Dia cornered him. So he decided to let her in on this dirty little secret. He knew he had nothing to lose."

"We have to get back into Louisiana's house," says Everleigh. She eyes me with a nervous shrug. "Remember when I went up to Louisiana's bedroom? Before I heard the screaming?"

I nod.

"I never told you what I found up there."

Everyone waits for her to go on.

"I remembered what you said, how you found the trapdoors at the factory, so I looked for a way into the floors. I noticed the giant portrait in her bedroom was sealed tight against the wall. A little lever unlocked it, disguised as a fire poker by the mantel. The painting swung open, revealing a small door. Painted blue. Bolted closed. After Cooper was locked in the tomb, I went back up, trying to break in, wondering if the stranger could be hiding in there. I even thought I heard someone. But I could never open it. I didn't want Raiden to know I'd found anything, so I swung the painting back into place."

"A hidden blue door," says Poe with a thoughtful nod. "Definitely a few skeletons behind that one."

"Let's go find out," I say.

"But how can we ever go back there?" asks Torin.

60

The captain peers at us uncertainly from the doorway of her lighthouse.

We seem to have woken her from a deep sleep, and it's too early even for her scowls or grimaces. She's wearing a gray bathrobe and yellow pajamas, tufts of her electrocuted-looking silver hair standing on end.

"I'm forbidden from setting foot on the property, much less ferrying the likes of you there for a guided tour. Raiden's orders."

"But there's something in the house that might tell us who stole Valkyrie," I say.

I was worried our argument last night over Louisiana would cause her to slam the door in my face. But I'm relieved to see she doesn't appear to hold any of that against me. Still, she shakes her head.

"It's out of the question, I'm afraid. Raiden finds out, he'll banish me from this island faster than I can say 'By the black beard of Jeremiah.'"

"He won't know," says Poe.

"We swear to be in and out of the house in less than an hour," says Everleigh.

"And if we get caught, we'll tell Raiden we kidnapped you," says Franz.

The captain considers us with a grim stare. "When Madam died, I knew they'd still be coming for her, the dark forces always swirling around her. Now, they're here. Well, if it's time to form an advancing army"—she breaks into a wide grin, her eyes gleaming mischievously—"I will be driving the first tank. But we really must move. There's an epic storm rolling in. Meet me at the western pier."

She slams the door, leaving us eyeing each other in surprise.

We file down the steps twisting through the rocks. This is the raw side of the island, where the grasses are even more overgrown, broken boulders and brambles, the captain's black lighthouse lancing the sky.

Minutes later, we are aboard the *Elvira,* the captain at the helm in a heavy oilskin coat. It's choppy, and all of us grip the railings. I sit next to Poe, but within minutes, he moves deliberately away. He's now frowning at the sky, which has turned a morose gray.

It is a slow traverse. When the demolished dock comes into view, the waves are increasingly ferocious and the clouds are black. That's when the rain starts, a violent lashing, thunder roiling.

"I can't get any closer!" shouts the captain. "You'll have to swim!"

No sooner does she shout this than Poe is pulling off his shirt and diving in, surfacing seconds later on the beach. Mouse and Everleigh jump right after him, then Torin and Cooper.

"I'll motor back to the pier to wait out the storm! I'll return in one hour!"

I'm last to jump. The water slams my body, the cold making

me cry out. I kick toward the surface, but a strong current finds me, yanking me deeper into darkness. I keep kicking as hard as I can, but I only somersault backward. The sound of waves crashing on the rocks is retreating, and I start to panic. I have the sudden horrifying thought that this is the end, that I might be drowning.

That's when I feel a strong arm around my waist, another around my shoulders. Poe is sweeping me against him, hauling me roughly to the surface and depositing me unceremoniously on the sand.

"Thank you," I sputter, coughing.

He doesn't even look at me, only stares coldly at the ground as he vanishes into the underbrush.

Rain pummels me as I struggle to my feet. Though the sight of the captain motoring away into the darkness, leaving us to this haunted place, fills me with dread, I turn and hurry up the steps after them.

A minute later, I'm scaling the rusted fence, the others already swallowed by the shadows on the porch. I race to catch up through the grass, trying not to stare for too long at the house with its strange towers and flocks of stone birds, its all-seeing eyes of dark glass.

61

The front door swings open with a moan.

We step into the foyer. Everything looks exactly the way it did before, untouched. The clock stopped at 9:07. The mirror. The bowl of pound notes. The black gloves.

"It's this way."

Everleigh heads for the staircase, the others hurrying after her.

"I'll follow in a minute," I say. "I'm going to get the nine books. We need them for Valkyrie."

I slip through the portrait gallery into the library, shivering because I'm drenched and it's freezing in here, much colder than before. Yet I also notice a smell of ashes—something burning.

I see at once the room has been disturbed. The library books from Bury St. Elmswood still line the shelves, but one of the windows is wide open, the storm sending in wild gusts of rain.

I race to close it. Muddy footprints now track across the carpet.

That's when I notice the glass dome. It's totally empty.

The library books I saw before in the display are now gone.

Suddenly, I hear footsteps. Startled, I turn to see Poe barging in, on the verge of telling me off, by the furious look on his face. But then, he stops.

"What? What's the matter, Paradise?"

"The books. The nine I saw before. Someone took them." I'm running around the room, checking under the table and chairs, even though I know I'm not going to find them.

Poe walks to the glass dome, lifting it off the metal stand. "It must have been Raiden."

"Or that stranger playing tricks on us. The one who ransacked our things and locked Cooper in the tomb."

Poe heads for the fireplace and, grabbing iron tongs, digs through the ashes.

"Well, they weren't stolen. They were destroyed right here."

I step beside him. He is right. The books were burned—and recently, from the smell. There are a few pages left, the spine of a blue book.

"Someone doesn't want you to win the third round of Valkyrie," says Poe. He is fishing out the remains, carefully taking them back to the library table. "Which I understand. *I* don't want you to win the third round of Valkyrie."

"Why not?"

"I don't want you to be visited by an ethereal death spirit and taken away from me."

"Please. I'm not *with* you."

I sift a few more pages out of the ashes, and moving to the table beside Poe, lay them beside the others. These scraps do not have titles, the words faint.

"An outrage I intend to rectify."

"How do you plan to do that?"

When he doesn't answer, I turn to him.

"How do you think?" he whispers.

He grabs my wrist, yanking me against him—and he kisses me. Or do I kiss him? That's when the floor upends, the room falls away, and the rain and the wind hush to whispers.

This is what I wanted to do from the first moment I saw him, but swore on my life never to do. Still, nothing has prepared me for the dark warmth and perfection of it, how easily he takes me away from the coldness of this room, this empty house.

He is kissing my neck. When he pulls away, staring down at me with an intense look, it feels like I have to swim miles across a sea to even hear what he's saying.

"This internship will end. Maybe with a winner. Most likely with a wash. Raiden will get rid of us quickly. His teenage experiment a flop, he'll wish to cut his losses and move on. We won't be able to talk about what happened. You'll be wooed by that walking tennis racket. Actually, he's more of a putter for miniature golf."

I wrap my arms around his neck, giggle. "You're threatened by Choke."

"Promise never to forget me."

"Like someone named Poe with his own Darkly could be forgotten. Have you seen your face?"

He pulls off my arms, forcing me to look at him again. I see in surprise that he is serious.

"If I reach out to you one day, Dia, will you answer me? No matter what?"

"Sure."

"Swear on it."

"Well, it depends on what I've got going on with the golf putter. But yes, I swear."

We're kissing again, against the library table, pages slipping to the floor.

But then we both freeze.

Someone just screamed.

That's when I know it happened again.

We race out of the library. The screaming has stopped, but there are voices—not coming from upstairs, but outside. Poe and I sprint onto the porch, then follow the commotion around the side to the cobblestone courtyard, where Mouse is sitting on the ground, getting drenched by the rain, immobile. Torin and Everleigh crouch beside him.

"What happened?" Poe shouts.

"One of those gargoyles toppled off the roof and hit him," says Everleigh.

That's when I see one of the giant stone birds lies in smashed pieces a foot away.

"It slammed his shoulder," says Torin. "Barely missed his head."

Mouse appears to be in a state of shock. He stares up at the roof, blinking dully in the rain. I see Franz and Cooper are staring out of two windows on opposite sides of the third floor.

It's only when we've led Mouse out of the storm into the music room, where he sits shaking on the sofa, that he seems to be able to focus on our faces. Franz and Cooper come barreling in, out of breath.

"That was insane," says Cooper, wide-eyed. "I saw it all happen—"

"Wahnsinn," says Franz. "Pure insanity."

"She tried to kill me," Mouse whimpers.

"Who?" asks Poe.

"Louisiana."

"You saw her?" asks Everleigh.

Mouse nods.

"Tell us what happened," says Poe.

"I was out there in the courtyard, studying the roof so I could tell them if there was a window into the locked room, when there was a crack. The bird was moving on the gable. It came fast. I barely had time to duck before it crashed into my shoulder, sending me to the ground. When I looked up, I saw a tiny, hunched woman in a black hooded robe. She was there for less than a second. Then gone."

"Where was everyone when this happened?" asks Poe.

"I was alone in the courtyard. The others were all in the different rooms along the north side of the hallway."

"I was in a guest bedroom," says Torin. "Everleigh was in Louisiana's office."

"I was in Louisiana's bathroom," says Franz.

"I was in the reading room," says Cooper.

I swear I notice her exchange a knowing look with Franz.

"Did anyone else see this figure?" asks Poe.

"No," says Torin, "but I was leaning out the window and I heard someone race by right outside the hallway. A second before Mouse screamed."

"Where were you two?" asks Everleigh, frowning.

"We were in the library," says Poe with a mild smile.

I nod. "The favorite books of Louisiana, the same blood-soaked nine, were burned to nothing in the fireplace. Someone got rid of them."

"What about the secret room behind the blue door?" asks Poe.

"We still can't get in," says Torin. "It's like it's cemented shut."

"That's why I went outside to see about the window," says Mouse. "And there is one. A tiny porthole window in the roof."

"Our best bet is for one of us to bust in that way," says Everleigh. "They can see what's there and unlock the door for the rest of us from the inside."

We fall silent. I can't tell what the others are thinking, but from the looks on their faces, I wonder if it's hit them, too: even if it *is* Louisiana somehow, impossibly alive and hiding out here in exile from the world—or a dangerous loner squatting here, unbeknownst to Raiden—these possibilities actually pale in comparison to a chilling third possibility.

It was one of us.

Cooper, Franz, Everleigh, Torin—they were all in different rooms, without a view of the others. One could feasibly have noticed the sculpture was loose, climbed out onto the roof, and sent it toppling onto Mouse.

Whatever the truth, the danger is still in play. Especially because I have every intention of finding out what's behind the blue door.

"I'll do it," I say. "I'll climb onto the roof and break in the window."

"Too dangerous," says Poe. "I'll do it."

"You're too big, man," says Mouse. "It's tiny. Has to be Dia, Cooper, or Torin."

"I don't do heights," says Torin.

"I have poor spatial awareness and claustrophobia," says Cooper.

Mouse is trying to move his right shoulder—Everleigh folding a blanket around him—as the rest of us head upstairs.

Poe is careful not to look too long at me, though I notice a small, knowing smile on his face as he helps me around the broken glass of Louisiana's bedroom.

"Be careful, Paradise," he whispers as I climb out the shattered window.

"And do not worry, I'll be on the lookout for a murderous Louisiana ghost," says Franz.

The roof's old slate tiles are slippery from the rain still falling, and it's steep and windy, but I manage to make my way to the porthole. I shade my eyes to peer inside. I can't see a thing. The glass is black. It appears to have been painted. I smash it with the peacock bookend I tucked down my jeans, and though it's tight, I manage to cram my way inside without cutting myself.

"I'm in," I shout, crashing onto a wood floor.

"Wunderbar!" says Franz from the other side of the door.

I move to my feet, and when I see what surrounds me, I'm so stunned that I can't move.

I know immediately that this room has nothing to do with the children—Maximilian, Bella, and Kitten.

No, there's a giant hand-drawn map of Darkly Island on the wall, arrows and times written in faded black pen.

Darkly Anniversary Party is printed along the top. *15 June 1985.* Under this map is a small desk, layered in dust. I notice a black card propped under a reading lamp.

It's the actual invitation to the Darkly anniversary party.

With scares, scars, and a surprise unveiling of Darkly's most terrifying game yet.

15 June 1985. 8 o'clock sharp.

"Everything okay, Paradise?" Poe calls out.

"Can you open the door?" shouts Cooper. "What do you see?"

"Hold on," I manage. "Just getting my bearings."

What is this map? I move toward it, tracing my finger along the black arrows. They begin at Torment Point.

Guest Arrival 8:40–8:50.

Welcome Cocktails 9:00.

It's a minute-by-minute schedule for the party.

My first thought is that Louisiana dedicated this room to trying to figure out who stole Valkyrie.

But then I read *L Retrieval Tomb 605 10:10. L* for Louisiana?

From there, the arrows move to the Export Bay and into the water, following the rocks around the island to the western pier under the captain's lighthouse.

Elvira 10:23. Here from the boat, the final arrow points due west, away from the pier and off the map entirely, as if heading out into the open sea.

That's when I realize something I never considered before.

This was her escape plan. Louisiana Veda was planning to leave that night.

It was she who stole Valkyrie.

"Dia?" shouts Poe.

"Hello?" says Cooper. "Are you going to open the door?"

"She's helping herself to a free Darkly," says Franz.

"I'm coming!"

Lightheaded, I step to the little wood door, slide the old bolt, whisk it open—only to stare at a gray brick wall.

"It's completely bricked over. It must be on the other side of your door."

"Oh, God. Seriously?"

"What's in there?" asks Poe.

I don't know why I decide to lie. Maybe it's because I don't trust any of them. I feel skittish, jumping at every growl of thunder and the rain slashing the roof.

"It's mostly cleaned out. There are some scraps. Nothing about her children."

My deceit makes me on edge. I lurch around the room, wondering what to take. I need something to show them. Not the map. No, I don't want someone to see it who shouldn't, for it to get into the wrong hands. I grab the most benign things I can find—a stack of cocktail napkins printed with the red number 281, a few sheets of Darkly stationery. I shove them in my pockets and scramble back out onto the roof.

Poe is at the bedroom window to help me back inside. Mouse and Everleigh have joined the group.

"Okay," says Mouse. "What did you really see?"

They crowd around me, inspecting the napkins and stationery.

"There was nothing else. Clearly Derringer Street already cleaned it out."

I'm careful to keep my expression of utter disappointment so no one has the slightest inkling of the truth: *Louisiana meticulously planned to escape her life. Isn't that what I just saw?*

Franz points out, looking at his watch, that the captain should be back within minutes to pick us up. So we all start down the staircase.

Yet I hold back—something catches my eye on the landing.

A black corner of fabric sticking out of an urn positioned along the wall by the window.

I don't know what compels me to stick my hand inside, but immediately I feel sopping wet satin. I pull it out. It's a soaked black hooded robe. It smells of rain, salt water, and seaweed. There's even sand on the sleeve.

Only the seven of us swam in the ocean tonight.

That's when I am absolutely certain: one of them is working for Valkyrie.

"She's bloodthirsty! Murderous!"

The captain shouts this with mad glee as she hauls us, waterlogged and shivering, onto the deck of the *Elvira,* bucking and pitching in the storm. "No use wrestlin' this harpy! We'll retreat to the mainland until the vixen tires herself out!"

For the first time since we met her, the captain looks like she's actually exerting herself as she grips the wheel, maneuvering the groaning boat away from the rocks—where it looked like we were seconds from being pulverized. As the motor screeches and lightning flashes, the others flee into the hull, Franz looking particularly queasy. I don't follow. I stay with the captain.

"In case you need help," I tell her.

The captain grins, tossing me an extra oilskin coat. "Hang on to your head!"

Of course, the true reason is that in the close quarters of the hull, it's possible the others will see it on my face: I am lying about what I saw.

By the time we make it to the mainland, the storm has picked up. We clamber off the boat, fleeing into the boathouse. It's sparsely furnished with an old couch and TV, and a wicker basket that contains a single Darkly.

It's The Red Hounds of Garsington, the one about the haunted English manor house. Cooper and Franz start to set it up on the table, Franz flipping through the beat-up, faded gaming manual, which looks as if it has traveled around the world twice. Everleigh goes upstairs to the bedrooms in search of towels. Torin and Mouse turn on the TV, watching a show called *The Dagger Archives* with bug-eyed zombie exhaustion.

And Poe—every time our eyes meet, I'm jolted with electricity. From the soft smile on his face, I know he's thinking about what happened between us in the library. But he, too, seems absorbed in the unspoken anxiety of the situation.

I sense he is thinking the same thing I am: *one of us is a liar.*

He must know who it is.

And though I'm tempted to pull him aside, confess about the hooded robe and what I really saw in that room—and kiss him again, I certainly wouldn't mind that—instead, I sit with Cooper and Franz, staring dazedly at the cracked old game board featuring the manor house and a maze of garden pathways.

" 'The objective of the game is to trap all seven of the bloodthirsty red hounds and return them to their cages in the underground shed, whereupon you must set it on fire in order to win the game. In order to get them into their cages, you must trace their histories, for they are each ghosts of the seven strange families that inhabited the mansion over the course of three hundred years. Follow the murderous truth of their history from one doomed generation to the next, collect the evidence, drive with it to the newspaper's office.' "

Cooper is emptying the velvet satchel on the table, counting out the small red painted wolfhounds. "Looks like we're missing three dogs. Franz, you want to be the blind grandmother or the widowed gardener?"

I am barely listening. Questions burn through my head.

Louisiana stole Valkyrie. If she was truly leaving that night, leaving it all behind, of course she would need to take the game— her incendiary confession and autobiography. If she left it at the factory, it could fall into the wrong hands.

But where did the arrow on her map that night end? She was planning to run away. To where? For how long? Forever? Was she fleeing something? Someone? Or did she want to start over, disappear, kill off Louisiana Veda, leaving her inside out on the floor as if she were nothing but a costume she had grown tired of wearing?

We spend the rest of the day rooting around the kitchen and watching TV. Poe wanders upstairs to take a nap, passing out with his arm slung over his eyes. Everleigh makes tea. All of us are polite, but watchful. I catch Mouse staring at me. And I swear I see Everleigh smiling with strange poise as she stares out the window, then just as quickly wonder if my paranoia is making me see things.

There are no accusations. No one says it outright: *Who is working against us?* But when there's a deafening thud, and everyone, even Poe, jolts to their feet, racing upstairs to see who or what made the noise—only to find a tree branch crashed onto the skylight— from the brazen looks of suspicion, it's clear we are all on edge.

And we don't trust each other.

It's midnight by the time the storm relents. The captain—now with a healthy flush on her cheeks—waves from the dock.

"How did you make out? Anyone need a hair dryer?"

"That must be grizzled-captain humor," says Franz.

It's when we are motoring back to the island that I have an idea. A trap. There isn't much time.

We're minutes away from the pier when I duck down into the hull with the others, hunched under the blankets.

"I've been thinking about what I saw in that hidden room," I say. "There wasn't much left. But I did see a blueprint of the factory. On the page for Imagination and Expansion, I noticed the rows of locked chambers, or tombs, as Louisiana called them. But there wasn't just one locked space per room. There were two. There was the obvious compartment in the corridor, but also a second one in the floor, accessible in the cabinet under the sink."

I nod at their skeptical stares. "Think about it. There are two original prototypes of every Darkly. There must be a second copy of Valkyrie. It's in the floor of Tomb 605 in the cabinet under the sink. That's what I saw on the blueprint. It's possible the investigators had no idea about the factory plan, and right now there is a second copy of Valkyrie just sitting there. Buried. We get our hands on that? We will have the gaming manual and a complete view of the board and the wheel. Everything we need to win Valkyrie."

"You're only telling us this now?" asks Everleigh.

"I didn't understand what I was seeing."

"And you didn't think to *confiscate* this blueprint?" says Franz. "So we could all inspect it?"

"It was huge. I couldn't very well stick it in my pockets. I also wasn't thinking. I was really scared after what happened to Mouse."

Poe is considering me with a pointed look. He knows I'm lying.

"It's too dark to go back to the factory now," I say. "We'll go get it first thing in the morning."

I am aware of how flimsy this sounds. But thankfully everyone is too soaked and freezing to disagree or ask questions. We trudge back to the cabins.

Poe and I are the last ones, and as we approach the fork in the path, he grabs my hand and, pulling me closer, kisses my palm.

"Sweet dreams, Paradise," he whispers.

Then he jogs down the path without another word.

I doubt my plan will work.

Still, I only pretend to go to bed, climbing into my bunk with a noisy yawn. As soon as I hear Cooper, Torin, and Everleigh's breathing go heavy, I tiptoe out of bed, pulling on my jacket and sneakers. Then I'm outside, sprinting down the winding paths to the factory. It's still drizzling, leaving the island in blurred green focus. I scale the chain-link fence and slip in through the front steel doors, ducking under Ophelia.

I totally get you, girl, I think as I glance up at the upside-down form, hanging from a chain by her ankle. *I feel the same way.*

I check behind me. There is no one here.

Not yet. The traitor has not arrived *yet.*

I'm probably crazy. This is harebrained and weird.

I race up the stairs, trying my best to be fast and silent, all the way up the demolished steps to Louisiana's office. It looks even emptier in the dark. I fling open the trapdoor and start down the ladder, stealing into the blue-lit walls, as I did that first day.

It takes forever to find Tomb 605 on the fourth floor, Imagination and Expansion.

The door is open, and the room is empty, apart from a table, the cabinets and sink. Though there is a red rope strung up in the doorway, this little room looks like all the others.

I step to the porthole with a clear view of the hallway—and I wait.

How long? I sit on the floor, feeling the plush rubber padding, trying to calm myself, feel at ease with the blue-iced claustrophobic darkness. Maybe he—*she?*—will not even show. Maybe I'm wrong. Maybe I didn't think this through correctly. I didn't lay enough bait.

But wouldn't the traitor take the risk to come here? Eager to get here first, so they could remove the game, and all chances of my winning, just as they did when they torched Louisiana's favorite nine books.

I hear footsteps. I scramble to my feet. They're light. A girl. Cooper? She's taking care to be quiet.

A giggle. Heavy footsteps. Whispering.

There is more than one person coming.

I hear the door at the end of the hallway creak. Silence. Then it thuds closed.

And when I see who it is, all I can think is *No, no, it can't be.*

I understand all over again where I'm standing, hidden inside the walls. It's where Louisiana stood watching the secrets unfold, and the lies.

No wonder she built it this way.

Here she watched, and here her heart broke—how many times?

65

It's Poe.

He walks in front of me, Torin right behind him. They stop inches away, the acoustics so clear I can hear his ragged breathing and her throaty laugh. She wraps her arms around him, hugging him, pressing herself languidly into his back. He turns and kisses her slowly, messily, then he steps inside the tomb.

"Cabinet under the sink?"

"That's what she said."

"Oddly specific. I don't know how much longer we can stay ahead of her. Paradise is due to win the whole goddamn thing, and then where will I be?"

"She's not that smart."

"Oh, and next time, my dear? Try not to murder anybody?"

Torin bites her lip, cringing. "Sorry. That scared me, too. He stepped right under it after I pushed it."

Poe is opening the cabinets under the sink, inspecting the wood. He produces a pocketknife to cut into it, prying a beam loose. He does this for another minute, then abruptly he stands.

I know at once he understands what I did.

He heads to the wall, inches away from where I'm watching.

He is smiling. He knows I'm here.

"Paradise?" he whispers.

I stumble back, my heart in my throat as I race down the ladder, blast into the lobby. I sprint outside, across the island. I don't want to believe it. *No, not Poe.* I shake Franz and Mouse awake, Everleigh and Cooper.

"Come with me. Right now. Hurry."

"What's happening?"

They blearily follow me back to the factory. As we barge into the lobby, Poe and Torin are descending the staircase.

"It's time for a little honesty," I say coldly. "Something we've never quite had before. Poe and Torin have been working against us."

Torin scowls. "What are you talking about, Dia?"

"Don't bother lying," Poe snaps. "She was inside the wall. She saw everything."

"Can someone please explain what is going on?" asks Franz.

Poe jogs down and sits on the final step. "All of us have been lying to each other about a great many things. But I've been lying the most. She called me the first time when I was with you at the airport, Dia."

"Who?"

"Louisiana. Her voice recording. She knows something I did. *Do.* I'm a liar and a cheat. I've cheated on every test I've ever taken."

He pauses, letting his confession sink in. There's no trace of shame or embarrassment on his face. In fact, it has the tinge of a boast.

"Yes. It's ugly, but it's the truth. It's more exciting for me to design a method of invisible deception than to take any actual test in the light of day. On the eve of Chavannes, I entered the house of the director of testing and stole the test from his office—all six thousand questions. Private school exams, a maze in Venice—there are many, many instances. Louisiana knows all about it, how I'm a swindler and a thief. She threatened to expose me, to my school, to the police, to my father, who would promptly cut me out of his will, of course—unless I made sure none of us advanced through Valkyrie."

He nods at Torin. "She had nothing to do with it. She only came upon me at the factory, singlehandedly feeding myself to the Darkly machine. I had to tell her. If I was attacked, none of you would suspect me."

I can feel his gaze lingering on me. *I'm sorry,* he seems to whisper.

I ignore this, turning to Torin. "You locked Cooper inside the tomb, shouting my name. And you tossed the gargoyle onto Mouse."

She starts to cry. "I'm so sorry. I didn't mean to hurt anyone. Poe and I loosened it the night we came back to burn the books. We had to destroy them. They were too crucial a piece of Valkyrie."

"And you rifled through our things in the cabins, stealing things—to mess with us?"

"No, in fact," says Poe.

Torin shakes her head. "Yeah, that wasn't us. We don't know who it was."

Everyone looks mystified.

I point at Cooper and Franz.

"What about you two? I saw you together, your friendship is much deeper than you ever let on."

They exchange knowing glances.

"Ja, okay," Franz says. "We met in Heathrow Airport baggage claim. We decided to team up and do our own detective work, because we were freaked out by this situation. We always thought this was some twisted Darkly experiment."

"You two were planning something. 'Still on for tonight?'"

They seem puzzled. Then Cooper widens her eyes. "Oh, she must mean when we planned to steal the key from Poe's neck because we wanted to take a look at Eighteen Lost Icelandic Sailors, hoping it might help us play Valkyrie. Only he never takes off the key. Franz and I were leaning over him for like an hour, trying to unlock it, and we were unsuccessful, so . . ." She nods sheepishly at Poe. "You snore really loudly."

I turn to Everleigh.

"And you? Your scared-little-girl act. You pretend to know nothing about Louisiana. But you know *everything* about her."

She nods, a guilty look as she stares at the floor. "My stepsister was the one who won. Everleigh. I'm her younger sister, Eva. I decided Derringer Street doesn't know what I look like or what she looks like. So when she died in a car accident, two weeks before she was supposed to arrive here, I took her place. I dyed my hair blond like hers. My parents think I'm spending the summer at La Sorbonne."

Everyone is astonished. No one moves. We stare at each other, a strange raw stillness in the room.

There's no reason why I should believe them, but somehow, I do. That's when the door bangs open behind us and the captain stumbles in.

"I am so sorry."

Raiden enters behind her, followed by his two goons.

"The seven of you broke into Louisiana's personal residence, a Darkly property specifically off-limits," he says. "You are in violation of the terms of our agreement. You will each be transported to the airport, where you will be deposited back in your lives. Return to the cabins. Pack up your things. This internship is hereby defunct."

"No," I say.

He turns in furious astonishment, glaring. "Excuse me?"

"This isn't finished."

"It is for you, Miss Gannon." He motions to the men. "Get her out of here."

I realize my phone is ringing.

Everyone goes still.

I pull out the phone, staring down at the name.

UNKNOWN.

SKY IS THE LIMIT FOR YOUNG ART STUDENT

Tatler 1971

A young woman has reinvented the board game market.
JEREMIAH POLK sits down with the innovator behind OPHELIA—
crafted in abandoned classrooms at night, manufacturing in an abandoned paper plant,
selling a million copies. Now, she answers, What's next?

When I first meet Louisiana Veda, the living mystery behind the mystery company Darkly, I am struck by how young she is. With a scrubbed face, she greets me at the door of her London hotel room in bare feet. She scarcely looks older than 18. "I haven't had time to buy a house," she says with a sigh. "I was living in the stairwells of the Royal College of Art when the idea hit me for a scary board game about Ophelia. She always struck me as the best character in *Hamlet*. What if she ran away from Elsinore? And if they did lock her away in the tower of a madhouse—how would she use her intelligence and wit to get out?"

It's a question that appears to have fascinated a great many people, considering how customers line up by word of mouth at midnight in pastures, unmarked warehouses, and abandoned lots across Britain, where a Darkly truck, often driven by Louisiana herself, pulls up to sell the games, some going for as much as £200, fights even breaking out. Now, the

66

"*Bring her to me now!*" Raiden bellows.

The men are shouting. Poe and the other interns scatter somewhere behind me, chaos breaking out as I race across the lobby to the elevators and stare into the cavernous darkness below, my phone still ringing. It's thick with shadows, but I can still make out the silvered limbs of the tree. I crouch, then leap down onto the branch. It cracks under my weight, sending me plummeting with a scream.

I slam into a cushioned examining table, falling backward into a chalkboard.

"Stop running, Dia. There's nowhere to hide."

I scramble to my feet, catching a fleeting glimpse of Raiden staring down at me, livid, as I dart out the defunct elevator doors.

I am sprinting down a long, dank hallway. Electrical wires hang from the low ceiling.

"Hello?" I say, answering the phone.

"Dia, will you play Valkyrie with me tonight?"

Louisiana sounds so close, so real.

"Yes. Of course."

I pick up my pace, madly running my hand along the wall. I have to find the opening to the trapdoor, to get inside the walls where I can hide, be safe like Louisiana, wander where the witch lies. It has to be here somewhere.

"Go to the Black Lamb in London. Be there in one hour, and if you make it this time, I'll come for you. I'll take you away from everything. From all your pain and heartbreak. I'll be there for you. Forever."

"Are you real? Are you alive? Where are you? Louisiana, if you're being imprisoned, say something, some kind of code, and I'll come find you—"

The line goes dead.

There's no break in the wall, no elegant black scripted *D,* only dozens of little doors on either side, black and red, black and red.

What did the directory say about the basement? Incubator? Orphanage?

No obvious pattern. Two black. One red. Four black. Six red. The opaque glass windows on all have been shattered, revealing cramped, white-tiled laboratories within, mottled with mildew, filled with junk. On the outside, I realize there are small signs on the walls, yellowed index cards with faded type.

BEACH DAY.

BUTTERFLY.

CONSTANTINOPLE.

Maybe down here the ideas for new Darkly games were hatched and cared for—developed or abandoned. The wanted and hopeful painted with black doors, the unwanted painted red? Precious and prized, discarded and discounted.

Suddenly, I hear a crash. Footsteps echo behind me and ahead—Raiden's goons barreling down the stairs to try and cut me off. I wheel around, trying the doors.

INSIDIOUS.

INVERTEBRUM MYSTERIUM.

Locked. Everything is locked, the windows too high and small to climb through.

MERMAID.

This one opens. I lurch in, tripping on debris—wood beams, sketchpads. A large tank spans the back wall, half filled with putrid black water, a ladder hanging off the side.

I can hear Raiden in the hall. "Check the laboratories."

"I heard her. She's in one of these."

"Dia? There's no need to run! We can talk this over."

He's trying to sound reasonable now, to be calm. I start up the ladder, throw my legs over. I ease into the water. A deep breath, trying not to gag, I'm totally submerged, my feet knocking the slick. I reach out, feeling slimy walls. How long can I hide here? I'm too afraid to open my eyes. I wait and wait. Only when my lungs are going to explode do I let myself drift up, break the surface, trying not to make a sound.

I see in horror that Raiden is here—feet away, his back to me, opening cabinets, slamming them closed. He steps to the tank. My heart stops. I'm sure he's noticed me, even through the mildewed glass. But he turns on his heel, slips out.

I listen to his retreating footsteps and pull myself out. I scramble down the ladder, puddles of water trailing across the floor.

Where is the way into the walls? I move along the counters. That's when I notice the ghostly shadow of the *D*. I hurry over to it and press against the wall. It cracks.

I slip into the murky blue darkness of the corridor inside.

The layout has to be the same, doesn't it? As I creep along, I can hear the men talking in one of the laboratories.

"We're going to have to round them up."

"They can't get far."

"You'd be surprised."

"I won't have what happened last time," Raiden growls. "Understand?"

"Yes, sir. There won't be any problem."

Last time? What last time?

There's no time to think about it. I start up the ladder, fumbling on the rungs. After about twelve feet, I reach the next corridor. This one spans the lobby of the Darkly factory. I stare out one of the portholes. The expanse is deserted.

Where did everyone go?

I keep going, feeling my way along the wall. This corridor stretches into the Darkly Manufacturing and Export Bay. I see the sign.

I am reminded of the escape route Louisiana drew on the map. What was the path?

Export Bay to the ocean, hiding among the rocks, swimming to the western pier.

I take off, aware of whispering all around me. There is shouting, chattering. It's everything spoken all over the factory, picked up by microphones, piped in here beside me.

"Let's go back—"

"It's this way—"

"We have to find her—"

I race on. Within minutes, I'm inside the walls of the manufacturing hall.

"We've got a team at Darkly Pier—"

They have a team there already? That means I have no way to get to the Black Lamb. No hope of playing Valkyrie.

I've reached the Export Bay. It's a vast opening, big enough for a giant vessel to dock here and load the games, to take them around the world. Black shipping containers are stacked thirty, forty feet high. DARKLY, they read. A distance ahead, double steel doors have been closed to shelter the dock from the ocean. But seawater still laps at the ramp mottled with barnacles.

I fumble to find the exit, stumbling out of the wall behind a crate, *D* emblazoned on the wall. I move to the water and wade in, swimming a few yards, then turn back at the sound of footsteps. Shadows are rising over the shipping containers. Flashlights sweep the aisles. I take a deep breath and dive under, kicking toward the steel doors. They appear to be only a few feet deep.

Ocean waves pummel me as I break the surface on the other side. I hold on to the ledge, the bolts covered with seaweed, gripping it so I'm not thrown out to sea, and I follow it to the rocks along the shore.

Above me on the cliff towers the black lighthouse where the captain resides, the pale white circling light blinking like a beacon. And far ahead, beyond the rocks, the western pier juts into the whitecaps. The *Elvira* is docked there.

I only need to make it there without drowning. I can make it. Did Louisiana think the same thing that night? Did she see she was so close to freedom?

If I can get to the boat, I can get to the mainland, flag down a stranger, beg for a ride—

I start swimming, pummeled by the waves. One of Raiden's goons is scouring the pathway atop the cliffs, the beam of his flashlight sweeping the rocks. I kick my way to a spot where the rock overhangs the water, waiting. I swim, pushed under again and again. When I climb the ladder and step aboard the *Elvira,* I'm so cold I can hardly make my fingers work to untie the ropes.

"Stop!"

I turn to see the captain scowling at me.

"You're not going anywhere in my boat."

She breaks into a wide grin, winking me.

"Not without me at the helm."

She strides aboard, digging in the hull, tossing me a set of fresh coveralls and a blanket.

"Let's go. We don't have much time."

I ask the captain to drive me to a hidden spot on the mainland where I can try to find a ride, though I am already almost out of time.

Gripping the wheel, the captain stands staunch as a war monument against the onslaught of the sea. The rain is gone, but the waves are violent. The little boat pitches and lurches, motor yowling. The captain urges me to go inside, to change my clothes.

But something is bothering me.

"You saw me from the lighthouse," I shout. "The only spot on the island, other than Louisiana's office, where you can see everything. You saw her that night, didn't you?"

The captain is startled. Yet her gaze remains fixed straight ahead.

"The night of the anniversary party. You saw Louisiana trying to leave on the boat with the game. She wasn't planning to ever come back, was she?"

"It was all my fault. I should have let her go."

The captain starts to cry, her voice scarcely audible over the lashing sea.

"The manual is an autobiography of every horror she ever suffered, every joy and every lie. It was the truth of who she was. She was going to take the boat to the middle of the ocean and leave Valkyrie at the bottom of the sea. To leave it here would destroy the kingdom she had built. She would not return. She had created Louisiana Veda from nothing. She started as a feeble sketch on the page, then carefully filled in the color, the shadows, the light. Now, she wanted to start a new sketch. Someone ordinary. She had been planning her exit for years. It was always the reason for the party. I argued with her. I told her such a life, sitting still, wasn't possible for someone like her. She was monumental. I told her she was being rash, short-sighted, that to flee what she had created was giving up, letting evil win over good."

"You mean Wood Raiden? He was trying to destroy her because she had never told him about their child, giving the baby away?"

"Wood. Anderson. Hector. Jack. Bill. The men were interchangeable parts. I was adamant. I did not take no for an answer. The world needed her. Better to face the mess, no matter how bad, than to run. Such cowardice was not in Madam's makeup. She would regret it. 'Don't go, don't leave us yet.' I suppose I was being selfish, afraid to be without her. Also afraid of what she might do alone in the ocean. I thought after she dropped Valkyrie in, she might make the rash decision to follow it. She was sad then. I told her *I'd* destroy the game. She needn't worry. I, her most loyal servant. Gattie let her down. But I wasn't going to. I'd smuggle the game as far as I could out into the middle of the ocean and toss it in.

"I shoved Madam onto the dock, game under my arm, and I took off. I locked it in the safe in the hull. I didn't have much time. I traveled for eight hours into the middle of the Atlantic, nothing around but seagulls, sharks, and sky. I readied the trunk filled with cinder blocks where Valkyrie was to be buried for eternity in the darkness of the ocean floor. But when I unlocked the safe—never in my life have I had such a shock."

She presses a fist over her mouth. "It was gone. A ghost had robbed me. Nothing else could explain it. It was like looking in the mirror and seeing my eyes were gone. It could only have been an act of magic, for never in those eight hours did I leave the boat unattended. I passed no port, no dock, no boat. No other living soul was with me. Had a spirit carried it away? Had I been hit in the head and woken without my memory? The *Elvira* is tiny. There is no space for a stowaway.

"I had to return and tell Madam what happened. I saw the life drain from her face, and the little hope that she had left blew out like a little match. Madam was dead three weeks later."

The captain jerks upright, gripping the wheel and shouting a maritime war cry. A monster wave sends the boat flying high into the air, then slamming the ocean. I am tossed to the ground, hitting the sides. Then the captain hauls me to my feet.

"You must find out who is behind this. For her sake."

I can only stare as she shoves a set of keys into my hand. Then she is back behind the wheel, spinning it hard so the boat banks on a wave.

"Climb the hill, over the fence, into the woods. You'll see a black barn. That's her garage. The Red Hornet is still working. I've made sure of it. Louisiana would want you to go."

I realize that the captain has driven the *Elvira* to Louisiana's house. I can see the remnants of the lost dock along the beach.

The captain is strapping a life jacket to me. Her eyes hold a spark of light.

"Well, go on, then. Jump."

68

I sprint up the hill, sliding in the mud. My mind is still screaming about everything the captain just told me.

I climb the fence and throw myself on the other side.

The house sits far in front of me, expectant somehow, then sullen as I turn and start running away, leaving it behind. *Don't leave me,* it seems to whisper. *Not again.* I keep looking over my shoulder. It wasn't that long ago that I believed someone was living here in secret, someone who might be Louisiana, before I found out it was Poe and Torin.

But the feeling remains—the hope that Louisiana is somewhere here.

Not dead.

I race into the forest, down a path. Within a few yards, I spot it—the barn, a rusted padlock on the door. It takes me a minute to find the right key. Then I'm staring at a fleet of ancient cars crowded like forgotten horses in a corral—a black 1980s Porsche, a green army truck, a silver Jaguar roadster.

Red Hornet? I move to the red Alfa Romeo convertible. The key is in the ignition. It doesn't start at first, only whines, but then the engine roars. I take off down the driveway, open the gate, and speed down the road.

The blindfold is removed from my head.

I am staring at the game board of Valkyrie.

It floats on the bright-green felt gaming table in an anxious sea of darkness.

My little black pawn, I see, has again barely advanced, only another inch along the top of the board. It barely entered the library at all.

And now, tonight, I have one more chance.

Blinded by the spotlight, I can't see much. So I lurch out of the wheelchair and lean right over the board—which, from the gasps and whispers, they didn't expect. I can tell at once this is the original game, meticulously painted, carved by Louisiana. I can also see in some places discoloration of the paint, rotting wood, splintered corners. The pawn is nearest to the square marked RADIO TO MARS.

What does it mean?

He said there was a method to it all. That's what Felix insisted George said. *A design that unlocks the entire thing.*

"No—"

"Get her back!"

I catch sight of the other ghostly words—DEAD KING, CLOUDS, TIMBUKTU—as hands grip my shoulders, pushing me back.

They don't want me to get too close, see too much. Why? Will something on there give them away? Will I see the design that George saw, the pattern that unlocks Valkyrie?

The wood spinner is placed before me. I grip the brass winding key, cranking it. The solemn face floats out of the smoke, blinking at me before retreating, vanishing, the wheels slowing.

It is a child, I realize. It's May.

The wheel spins and spins, then stops.

SECRET SOCIETY. DARK.

Secret Society. What book will I be inside? It would be the small orange one, wouldn't it, with the bowler hat? *Secrets of the World's Most Dangerous Cabals, Conspiracies, and Conjures.*

They are bringing the heavy gray velvet bag to me.

The loot.

And there it is, I see, leaning forward as I dig my hand in: there's a location for it along the bottom of the board.

I pull out the first thing I grab. Because the details of this round of Valkyrie don't matter—not when I have fifteen minutes to crawl beyond the borders of the game and find out, once and for all, who is behind this, who was the ghost on the boat, who stole the game from the captain's safe.

I peer down at the small bronze figurine in my palm.

It's a moth, a thick body, heavy wings.

The mallet raps twice.

"Find the moth in the dark at the secret society."

An old man intones this with a strange croak, his voice giving out.

The game board is floating away from me again, lost in the shadows. I am dumped violently forward, dropping fast through the hole, crashing into the old canvas cart.

And I'm off—clattering wheels, sprinting footsteps. I take a deep breath to steady my mind, prepare myself, tell myself again that all I have to do is make it beyond the boundaries of the game and run, run, run for my life. I cannot fail.

And yet, through it all, I can hear a cacophony of voices.

Fifteen minutes— He said there was a method— Let those stories keep her safe in the dark— My May was clever like that— They never harmed her—

As we clatter through the warehouse, I can't see a thing, not even a doorway. The driver of the cart is breathing hard, moving fast. Just as the cart tips, a door creaks open. I land hard on the floor—a slam, a hiss of bolts.

It's the same brick hallway, a single black door at the end. I run blindly toward it—*14 minutes, 49 seconds*—shoving it open.

Secret Society.

I step into a dark, wood-paneled room, door whisking closed, locks sliding into place behind me. A crowd of twenty, thirty people whisper in small, nervous groups. The only light is from the fire in the fireplace. All of the people, both men and women, wear tuxedos and identical cat masks. They are leopard masks, I see, elaborate but made out of paper, velvet ribbons holding them in place. A violin player—also wearing the mask—plays a mournful tune.

High on the wall over the mantel is the pale-blue digital counter. *13 minutes, 9 seconds.*

This scene I recognize. It was inside *Secrets of the World's Most Dangerous Cabals*, a chapter called "The Leopard Society."

I take off along the wall, keeping to the periphery. It's so dark no one seems to notice me.

I appear to be the only Valkyrie player here. I can see a large rectangular table at the center of the room and a single, arched row of empty wood chairs facing the fireplace.

I scan the faces, the masks, looking for some sign of the witch or her cart.

But she doesn't appear to have arrived—yet.

I have reached a wall of windows, half covered with heavy blue velvet curtains. I duck behind them, inspecting the windows. They are old-fashioned, and the latches are glued shut, the panes opaque with black paint.

I feel my way past one window, keeping behind the curtains, then another, running my hand along the floor. No trapdoor.

Slipping out from the curtains, I stumble into a potted palm tree.

It's plastic and fairly tall—reaching all the way up to the paneled ceiling.

I crouch behind it, feeling the floor.

Nothing.

Staring out, I see by the door where I entered there is a glass phone booth. On the opposite wall, directly across from me, stands a life-sized skeleton wearing a leopard mask.

She'd fiddle with my skeleton in Human Anatomy. Steal from Lost and Found.

I've seen these things before. What did Felix say again about George?

He had noticed certain items are present in every setting.

I step out from the palm tree as the violin abruptly stops. I make a beeline for the phone booth.

"If you could please take your seats. The ceremony is about to begin." It's the same anxious redheaded man who tore my ticket at the Fox sisters and prayed at the deathbed. He wears a leopard mask—and points right at me. "Miss? Yes, you there! If you could please take your seat!"

I ignore him, ducking into the inky darkness of the phone booth.

There is a black candlestick telephone—from 1920 or 1925?—and, on a ledge, a small notepad and black pencil. I shove both into the pocket of my tunic, unhook the receiver, and hold it to my ear, marveling for a surreal second at the sound of the crackling dial tone.

What am I supposed to do? Who do I call?

The red-haired man looms in the doorway. "If you do not take a seat at once, miss, you will be barred from the proceedings."

I am sure he's going to grab me. Instead, he thrusts a leopard mask in my face.

I pull it on, knotting the ribbon at the back of my head, and exit the booth, following the man as he beckons me—careful to make sure I don't dart away—to take a seat in the remaining chair. I am aware of all of those leopard masks turned to me, staring, expectant.

11 minutes, 12 seconds.

A masked woman stands in front of the fire. "Today we meet. Tomorrow we rise. *E caeca turba deum graditur.*"

The crowd repeats in unison: *"E caeca turba deum graditur."*

At that moment, I hear the door creak. Turning, I see with a shiver that the witch has arrived.

She wears a black dress and leopard mask, but this time there is no cart. She carries a large wood tray secured by a heavy strap around her shoulders. She's dressed like one of those ornamental cigarette girls from speakeasys and gentlemen's lounges in old black-and-white movies. Her tray is heavy with a selection of the same bottles and jars as before.

The nine books have to be somewhere on that tray.

"Now, we commence the nominations."

The redheaded man is distributing flat white stones and markers. I take mine, wondering what to do. Then, watching the two women on either side of me carefully writing—*My husband, Roger, My sister Victoria*—I scribble *My brother John* on my stone and place it in the red velvet bag the man holds in front of me.

He moves with it to the fireplace and drops the stones into a cauldron I now see is suspended over the fire. Then he closes the top and cranks a knob so the cauldron rotates, the rocks bouncing and clattering within.

"*E caeca turba deum graditur,*" he chants.

9 minutes, 8 seconds.

I crane my neck to see where the witch has wandered off to— *Wander where the witch lies*—the words dancing in my head like a jingle, a chorus. A man at the end of the row is buying a pack of cigarettes from her, and she bends over, letting him browse the bottles and potions she's selling. Abruptly, I leap to my feet, darting behind my chair, moving right behind the witch.

Sure enough, I can see, lining the bottom of her tray, the colored covers of all nine books, the orange one under a jar in the corner.

And I don't hesitate. I reach over her shoulder and grab the orange book. Bottles fly as the witch wheels around with a shriek. She tries to grab me, tray spilling, but I shove her to the floor. I dart behind the velvet curtains, the crowd shouting and whispering as I fumble my way along the wall, then out by the palm.

I catch a fleeting glimpse of the red-haired man helping the witch to her feet as I sprint back into the telephone booth and close the door. I jam the metal hook into the hole, so it's locked.

I open the book. There's so little time. I don't even know what I'm looking for.

Secrets of the World's Most Dangerous Cabals, Conspiracies, and Conjures.

Table of Contents. Chapter 4. Leopard Society. I madly flip to the correct page.

The Leopard Society, a murderous group of the anonymous rich. Every year at an undisclosed location, the wealthiest people of the world convene—not to celebrate their good fortune or even to design the future, but to commit three murders. Nominations are inscribed on moonstones placed into a cauldron over a fire. Three stones are drawn by fire poker, dooming the three chosen names to assassination within a year. The group is careful to protect their members' anonymity at all costs. In fact, in 1949, at its secret chalet meeting in France, there was an incident when someone losing his temper tore off the masks of three members. He was beaten to death on the spot.

What am I meant to do?

A leopard face peers in at me through the window. He's trying to open the door, latch rattling. A second leopard face appears.

They're coming for me. The latch won't hold much longer.

I stare out, past the masks floating toward me. They're banging on the glass.

That's when I see it. A cardboard box wedged under a table by the mantle. It is directly behind the table, and a straight line from me in the telephone booth.

These critical pieces are laid out in a neat geometric pattern in this room—

And then it hits me.

Only his photography. Geometry. And violin.

The design. It was right there, under our noses, in George's room.

The dozens of shapes drawn on the graph paper that Mouse pulled from a drawer—the 4 he drew over and over.

He has a thing for four.

It wasn't about the number. No, that was the pathway he thought could unlock Valkyrie.

5 minutes, 12 seconds.

I feel a sudden lightness as I open the latch. As the leopards swarm, reaching for me, I pull their masks off, one after the next. They scream, hiding their faces in their hands.

I elbow them off and race to the cardboard box. *The lost and found,* Felix called it.

Sure enough, it contains things from the gray bag of loot: a doll, clock, test tube, bowler hat, and a small corked wire cage, a live black moth fluttering inside. *They are there to help you. Like a secret weapon.*

I grab the cage, wheeling around, trying to visualize my path.

If this is the Valkyrie game board, I'm at the bottom center. *Loot.* Directly in front of me is the table marking the middle of the room. *Beast Bed.* Beyond that is the phone booth. *Radio to Mars.* A few feet at a diagonal on the left stands a gramophone. *Space Rocket.* And continuing the line from the record player on the wall is the skeleton. *Dead King.*

After that is *Clouds.* What did Penny say? *Electrician found the girl living in my ceiling like a rat.* I must have to climb up into the ceiling, the clouds, to form the crossbar of the 4. Then it's straight down to *Timbuktu,* the palm tree. The end.

A perfect 4. The pathway May took through the library—how she survived the night.

I don't know if it will work. I'll be sprinting toward the witch, who now stands at *Beast Bed,* returning bottles to her tray.

But there's no time now. I have nothing to lose.

I take off, darting past the witch, dodge around the chair into the telephone booth, yanking the notebook from my pocket, slamming the door.

I flip the pages. I see there is a number—907—scribbled on the last page. I grab the receiver and dial.

Instantly a phone starts to ring at the table. *Beast Bed.*

So I went there at night to watch, Penny told us. *Slept there.*

"Hello?" the witch answers. "Hello?"

I heave open the door and run to the gramophone, a few feet away.

Locked me in the listening booth.

I lift the needle and set it on the record. Music begins to play—the strident chords of "Ride of the Valkyries." I dart away, running to the skeleton.

The red-haired man is waiting. He grabs me, strangling me with an open mouth. I open the moth cage, wrenching it toward his face, moth fluttering into his eyes. He lets go immediately, startled. I lurch behind the skeleton, where I see there's a ladder at the back of the stand. I climb up, punching the panels of the ceiling. They give way easily and I scramble through.

I stand, staring in surprise at the narrow walkway in glowing green paint. I follow it straight to the wall, and when I scramble onto my stomach and lift the panel, I am gazing directly down at the potted palm tree.

Timbuktu.

I am lightheaded. Because I realize the solution to Valkyrie is here. To make it to South America—or Timbuktu, as little May must have called it. *A real jungle for the children to run around.*

This is the truth behind the Darkly motto, *Wander where the witch lies.*

May's way out—her means of escape—was buried inside the plants. To wander where the witch lies was to find an unlikely pathway out of hell, a chance for good, for creation, a better life.

And she did kill me in the end. Took away my retirement. Gone from the birds-of-paradise.

They say she was in with the South Parade Gang.

Hiding in the ceiling, May must have witnessed where Penny buried her stolen fortune—inside the pots of the plants.

She stole the money, and rode away on her bike, and became Louisiana.

37 seconds.

I drop through the ceiling, losing my balance, stumbling. The crowd descends, swarming, all of them. But as soon as I start to dig through the dirt in the planter, they stop—almost by magic, as if they've been given strict orders not to touch me. I keep digging, faster and faster, dirt flying as they assemble in a silent circle around me. I feel the corner of something at the very bottom. It's black wood.

7 seconds.

6 seconds.

A box of money? Of Darkly secrets?

Bright lights drench the room. The record abruptly cuts out. Every one of the figures—the red-haired man, the witch, all of them—stand around me, motionless.

I realize I have won. I solved the game. And now the Valkyrie will come for me.

I need only to dig it up, this black box, and then—

I can feel the corner with my fingers.

Instead, I grab the chair beside me, lurch to the window, and smash it as hard as I can through the glass.

I scramble out into a dim alcove, identical to the one from before—filthy tiles, racks stuffed with tuxedos, a box of leopard masks. I race to the door, throw it open and run out.

"Hey! Stop her!" I can hear them coming.

Which way? This hallway looks the same: grim green light, torn notebook papers taped to the doors.

Maria Tallchief. The Greys.

I reach the end of the hallway and round the corner. I pass Whispers Beyond the Grave. I stare ahead, heart pounding, hearing that faint techno music again, trying to orient myself. I already went this way, and there was no way out.

Abruptly, the door opens to Whispers.

"—not paying me enough."

"At least you're not wheeling around a library cart like a goddamn Seeing Eye dog."

The three Fox sisters step into the hallway in front of me.

They stare at me in surprise, and I take off again, in the other direction. I pull off the tunic as I tear around the corner.

"What the hell—"

"Why the fuck is a *pawn* wandering down here?"

"Call security—"

I dart past Secret Society, where the crowd is streaming out.

"Hey!"

"She's right there—"

I round the corner into another corridor, reaching two double black doors, pulsing music within. I pull one open and slip inside.

It's a vast basement, long tables where a dozen people sit hunched over laptops, typing, whispering grimly into earbuds, shelves of hard drives. A massive flat-screen covers the wall with a map of England spangled with blue dots. Beside that on a table are blueprints, sketches and maps, what looks like plans for an amusement park, the paper yellowed and torn.

The original plans for Valkyrie?

"Who are you?"

A bearded man glares at me. I take off, running around the table, seizing one of the laptops at the end, yanking it from the tangle of cords. As I start to climb the shelves on the wall, boxes filled with missing-persons flyers crash to the floor. There is shouting, black-masked figures racing in, alarm wailing. I reach the windowsill and use the laptop to smash the glass. I hit it once, twice. It shatters. I swing my leg up and roll out.

I'm in dense forest, fallen branches. I take off running, still gripping the laptop. This is the evidence. This is the hope. I can hear people shouting through the night, a screeching alarm. I venture a look back. The warehouse where Valkyrie is played is even bigger than I thought—a towering brick structure.

Headlights slash the trees, motors roaring to life.

They're coming for me.

Within minutes, I can see something far ahead, beyond the trees—an open field. I sprint for it, emerging onto a driveway, a mansion rising on the hill.

I stop dead in shock.

Because I know this place. I've been here. The mottled centuries-old columns, the commanding facade of fifty windows staring me down.

It's Manderson Gate. The home of George Grenfell.

I whip around, seeing far at the end of the driveway—the gate. I could sprint there, try to scale the fence along the road, beg a passing car for help before the black vans catch up—

Instead, I turn and start running for the mansion. When I look back, I see a crowd of black-clad figures fanning out behind me, radios screeching. A line of vans are tearing up the drive.

I stumble up the steps, heave open the door, and run inside, coming face to face with—

Penelope Grenfell.

She is striding across the foyer in a silver satin robe, an enraged look—alerted by her security team at Valkyrie, no doubt.

Emergency. Player number 407 has escaped.

Penelope carries an old hunting rifle. It looks like one of the 1940s Winchesters in Basil's Armory section, which means it will have a slow response and nearsighted aim. All I have to do is keep moving, never standing still for long.

"What did you do to your son?" I ask. "Where's George?"

She is loading the cartridge, aiming for my head.

"Put it down," she orders quietly.

I slowly set the laptop on the entry table and slip to the other side, careful to keep the orchid in the porcelain urn between us.

"He knew it was you behind Valkyrie," I say. "Bella—is that your real name?"

"George got a little too loud. That appears to be your problem, too."

"I know how you did it. I know how you stole Valkyrie."

I am lightheaded. What did Raiden say about her that night at his house?

Little Bella was a handful from the start—heart problems, colic, in and out of hospital. She showed promise as a swimmer, then it was horses, then it was French cuisine.

In a misguided attempt to do the right thing, she placed them with perfect families—and unwittingly spawned two monsters.

"You were at the party. You were the server from the shelter. You followed Louisiana out of the Export Bay to the *Elvira*. You overheard the argument, and when you saw that the captain was taking the game, you tied yourself to the side of the boat. It must have been hours that you held on in the water."

Penelope grins, her eyes flashing. "I planned to throw her overboard. But I didn't need to. She unlocked the safe as she prepared the trunk of cinder blocks. It was sitting right there like a ham sandwich, my mother's masterpiece, Valkyrie. And the two-thousand-page manual, my poor mother's confession, her harrowing life story, her dreams and desires, her journey of self-sacrifice that made her a legend."

She laughs. "I wrapped the game in trash bags and returned to my hiding spot. You should have heard the captain's howls of confusion to find it gone. It was when she was back on the island, half-deranged with despair, and headed to the factory to deliver the news to her master—that the game had flown away as if a Valkyrie had taken it—that was when I swam ashore. I nearly drowned. But the prospect of owning my mother's true story was enough to keep me going. I landed at her house, where she'd never invited me, mind you. I was too dirty, too damaged, too crazy. I changed my clothes, and, stealing a saltshaker, I left with the hinge on which her beloved empire hung—her insidious masterpiece, Valkyrie. I owned her from that moment on. She was mine."

I can hear the vans pulling up, footsteps rushing up the steps.

"But why are you releasing Valkyrie now? To destroy her?"

She only smiles as she releases the safety and takes aim.

Boom!

I duck as a shot blasts the vase, porcelain exploding. I sprint for the staircase. Penelope is right behind me.

Boom!

A shot cracks the banister. I hear the front door slam, black-masked figures racing in.

"Stop!"

Boom!

A shot hits the chandelier, crystals raining. I shield my face and keep running, up and up, passing the first landing, the second. The key is to keep moving and the gun will miss.

"My mother was poison. Dropped me off when I was a day old with strangers."

"She thought she was doing the right thing," I say. "She didn't think she was fit to take care of anything—"

Boom!

The shot hisses inches from my head, hitting a gilt portrait, wood cracking.

"They looked like the perfect family. But they were criminals. They made me one."

Boom!

I've reached the top. I barrel down the hall, duck into a dark sitting room. I grab a bronze sculpture of a fox off a table and scramble behind a cabinet, crouching, holding my breath.

"My mother has no right to such glory. All of that grandstanding? The way people love her and worship her is unfair. She didn't deserve it. The ugly truth will come out now—"

Boom!

A shot hits the cabinet, inches away. I roll to my feet, sprint past Penelope to the window, shatter the glass with the sculpture, throwing myself out.

Boom!

I am screaming, tumbling down the pitched roof, unable to stop my momentum as I fly over the edge. I reach out—and manage to grab hold of the gutter.

"Dia!"

I venture a look down. A host of police cars far below, blue lights. A crowd. Poe is shouting. Franz and Cooper, Everleigh, Torin, Mouse—they are all here. Nile Raiden is here, too. Police officers are streaming into the house, radios crackling.

"Dia! I'm coming! Do not let go!"

Someone else is bellowing this. It takes me a second to place the voice.

Choke Newington.

A blaring megaphone cuts through the night. "Penelope Grenfell, lower the gun and put your hands in the air, or we will use force—"

"I did it to bring her back."

Penelope Grenfell whispers it, her voice eerily childlike as she looms over me.

"It's the only way. To destroy the thing she loved most. Only that will bring her out of hiding. Not me. Not any of us. Only Darkly."

"Louisiana is never coming back," I say. "She's dead."

Penelope laughs shrilly. "You really think she's dead?"

Boom!

A shot blasts Penelope in the chest. The rifle drops as she somersaults past me in an explosion of blood, and slams the driveway below.

After that, all sound cuts out.

I'm losing my grip. I shout, but I hear nothing. I can see Choke yelling my name, climbing toward me along the roof, reaching my hand.

But my fingers are slipping.

I am aware of nothing but Louisiana's dead daughter staring up at me with a mad grin, the world crumbling in silver slow motion as I fall toward her.

DARKLY

From the desk of Louisiana Veda

30 December 1984

Gattie,

Where are you? Did you start the fire? Are you a murderer? The smile you gave me for the past twenty years--you, my confidante, friend, my family--scaring away the monsters when they came for me in the night, as they always do--who is behind it?

They say 12 Hollywick is too incinerated to recover much. Not even the teeth of the victims. But some bones were found. They pieced a few together--jaws, fingers, knees--and found a discrepancy. They are going back to make sure, days before the city razes the lot. But there is the suggestion that one child is unaccounted for in the rubble. One was missing. One escaped.

So, I ask, was it you? Did you take her? Please get word to me, however anonymously. I must know if she is still alive. Two children are lost to me. I cannot lose another.

I am not like others. Most of my life, I've found being a woman is a lethal camouflage. I was born and raised in the dark and in the dark swims my head. I've wanted what men wanted, and like most of them, I do not look back. But even my most dreadful secrets were attempts to save people from the fatal blade that is me. I knew Max and Bella and Kitten would be better off with happy mothers making spaghetti and meatballs and Friday-night Charades in the living room, laughter and church and Bing Crosby, dancing until midnight to "White Christmas."

I have loved as best I could. That includes trusting you, which means your unexplained vanishing on the eve of my child's death is a blow from which I will never recover.

I only ask why.

Louisiana

I am staring at a circular game board intricately carved out of pale white oak.

It's a tower. The simple black pawn progresses down a twisted black staircase marked with traps, ladders, and prison cells housing mysterious shadows. Captives? Ghosts? There are arched and barred windows filled with moonlight and a view of gray sea. The legendary Darkly scroll has been carved across the top. *Ophelia.* The lettering looks Victorian, windswept and drowsy. There is a deck of cards in a black box, an elaborate *O* carved on the front, a blood-red velvet bag filled with crude wood charms, including a walking cane, a hammer, a tulip, a skull.

"Nothing quite prepares you," marvels my attorney, Mr. Harneth.

He leans toward the game, his bushy white eyebrows kneading together.

"I've heard the rumors. Bewitching, certainly. Very much alive. But between you and me, I'd prefer a simple Picasso."

"It's perfect," I say, nodding at Nile Raiden across the conference table.

I rise from my chair, closing the lid on the handmade Darkly box, snapping the latches into place.

Raiden stands. "Congratulations, Miss Gannon. A job well done. You are now the exclusive owner of an authentic Darkly, one of two original prototypes. You own all associated trademarks, patents, and copyrights for Darkly One, commercially known as Ophelia. On behalf of Derringer Street Chambers, we wish you the very best."

I shake his hand, sensing from his hesitation that he means to add something. *Sorry for that bit back at the factory when I screamed like a fiend and chased you through the dark.*

I am still lightheaded with disbelief—at how quickly it all came together. The monstrous truth behind Valkyrie flew out of the tumultuous, inky sea—so wild and yet so efficiently netted, slain, and disposed of by Derringer Street and the police, it makes my head spin, how fast the internship is now retreating into the past.

I don't want it to be over. Not yet. I want to stay on the island a little longer, wandering those windswept paths with the other interns, my friends.

These past few weeks, as attorneys hammered out my ownership agreement for Ophelia, Darkly One, I did not see Nile Raiden. I have not had the chance to ask him questions, clear the air, even thank him for saving my life—because it was Nile Raiden who, spotting me dangling from the roof, sprang into action, shouting to the police officers, asking if they had an inflatable jumping cushion. When none was found, the fire truck still minutes away, he produced a parachute from one of the SWAT trucks and, holding it with Poe and the other interns, managed to break my fall. They had stolen the white van from Darkly Pier, driving to the spot where the captain told them I was headed. They tailed a black van down a dirt service road, which led onto the back property of Manderson Gate. Raiden had a tracking device on the Darkly van, and so he had also shown up, still intent on hauling everyone to the airport, putting an end to his misguided experiment.

They had all ended up where I was, where Penelope Grenfell, born Bella—unbeknownst to her husband, who spent weeknights in London—executed the gaming ring that was Valkyrie, with the assistance of her old criminal gang, which included a group of high-level hackers. This is how we believe they got our school photos, and infiltrated Poe's laptop, where they found evidence of his cheating.

George Grenfell was found to be alive and well on a private island owned by his mother in Greece. He had been quite the handful there, by all accounts, complaining to the men holding him captive that with little hot water, no girls, goats and roosters waking him up at four o'clock every morning, the place was the opposite of Valhalla. He had assumed they were holding him for ransom.

He is home now, apparently. And though I asked to meet him, my request was politely declined by "all persons involved." Eighteen people have been arrested so far. Though no one is talking, we've been officially told the extras in Valkyrie were illegal immigrants, threatened with deportation, imprisonment, or worse if they did not play along. If they did survive the night, they were returned to their families with a windfall of one thousand pounds and the promise of a job.

My lawyers demanded I have an opportunity to inspect Valkyrie in the light of day.

It is the least Derringer Street can do, they contended, considering that it was because of me the game was recovered successfully, from the warehouse at Manderson Gate, before it was destroyed—as it was surely going to be.

We asked for ten minutes with the game—fully supervised.

Our request was denied. "Possession of the rights to an original Darkly of her choosing—excluding the defunct and terminated Darkly Twenty-Nine—is payment enough for Ms. Gannon's services," was the curt reply.

So I'll never again have the chance to inspect Valkyrie, to find out if my fitful understanding of it was correct—that it was built to be both a trial and a journey through fire, the nightmare of Louisiana's childhood. I'll never read the two-thousand-page gaming manual—Louisiana's autobiography and origin story, if her daughter is to be believed—detailing how to play and win, maybe even recounting the tales of those nine beloved books, how they kept her alive in the dark. I'll never know what those extensive blueprints were that I saw on the tables. Were they Louisiana's original plans to build the game in the real world, a nightmare theme park, a terrifying Darkly fun house?

I can only believe her original intention for Valkyrie was good, that she saw the game as a way to test young people, show them that they are all much stronger than they know, that they can survive the unimaginable and fly on to paradise like the Valkyrie. They can take anything that comes at them, good and bad, and still build the life that they long for, like she did. A means of triumph, so they are never afraid of the dark or the monsters inside it again.

She must have realized the game would never work. Had she gone too far?

I'll never know.

And yet another question remains—why did Penelope do it? Why did she put her glamorous life on the line to partake in this secret she had been hiding? Derringer Street said it was for the power, to destroy the legacy of her mother. They reluctantly informed us that Met Police had found out from confiscated laptops that over three thousand kids across the UK were waiting to play. Calls were still coming in. I told them what Bella said, that she was convinced what she was doing would summon her mother out of hiding, forcing her to come back to save what she had loved most, her empire. Derringer Street had scoffed at the suggestion that Louisiana was still alive.

"A great many ludicrous rumors, innuendos, and conspiracies surround the life and the death of Ms. Veda," Derringer said. "If we were to address any or all of them, the blaze already surrounding her could very well consume her entirely."

And as for Choke Newington appearing when he did at Manderson Gate—it turned out that something had spooked him inside the vault back at Derringer Street that night, something he did not have the stomach to tell me when I confronted him at the door.

He saw me in a filing cabinet. My photo.

I was exiting Prologue.

And it wasn't just me in there. There were other people, too. Choke hardly had time to root through a handful of surveillance photos, birth and death certificates, dental records, maps—no names he recognized, no face he knew but mine—taking note of the vault number, VV393, and the odd code written there, X3X4, before he sensed we were in danger.

Of course, I misread his unease, running away from him. When Choke couldn't find me, he called his parents, who phoned the US Embassy and Met Police. They put a tail on Raiden, who led them to Manderson Gate, where Choke showed up with a special ops unit.

But the filing cabinet. X3X4. What exactly did he see in there?

My lawyers submitted a request to inspect the vault, or there would be no deal. The reply was that a basic security screening had indeed been executed in preparation for the internship. After much back-and-forth, when a physical inspection was finally agreed to, mere days ago, the vault was searched. Every cabinet was found to be locked, the names I had seen before, like Valentine and Downling, all removed. We were told that the files were "proprietary and confidential information and trade secrets that are the sole and exclusive property of Darkly in perpetuity."

VV393—whatever it was—was not there.

There is no VV393, we were informed.

But Choke knows what he saw.

So, what was it—surveillance of hundreds of thousands of applicants for the internship, to make sure the choices Raiden made were sound? Kids just smart enough to get into Valkyrie, just lost enough to be controlled?

I think back to that night when I swore I heard someone in the shop with me.

Was it one of Raiden's faceless goons, taking note of a few more details, stuff to use for blackmail or intimidation? But the timing doesn't quite work. Because that night was months before I knew I had won, before I'd even submitted my application.

So, why would I have been watched? Unless the noise was just the prowling Barnabys, after all?

Another odd detail: the day after my fall, when I approached the detectives itemizing the warehouse where Valkyrie was played, combing it for evidence, I asked to see the black box I had dug up when I won Valkyrie. But they could find no such thing. They found the planters and palm trees, and a bunch of torn-up paper leopard masks, but no black box. Sorry.

Someone was lying. Or they had stolen my prize. Did an employee of Valkyrie manage to escape with it in the tumult? Or was it Derringer Street, swiftly confiscating one more thing that could potentially reveal too much?

Now, I am aware of Nile Raiden considering me thoughtfully.

"It has been an adventure, Miss Gannon. I hope you enjoy your good fortune."

I open my mouth to say thank you, and it's funny—I actually mean it. But he's already gone, striding briskly out in a blink of gray pinstripes, leaving his army of young associates rising smoothly to their feet to shake our hands.

When we are alone, Mr. Harneth heaves a sigh of relief, stuffing the two-inch-thick contracts into my briefcase and sliding it toward me.

"Like negotiating the Treaty of Versailles with Stalin," he mutters. "But we did well. There's still much to do, of course. As of thirty seconds ago, you're a young woman of enviable means. Which means you need a will. Estate planning. Tax attorneys. Security. I'll send a draft this afternoon and a few choice names. Derringer Street will be contacting you periodically with requests—every Joe Scrugg hoping to license images of Ophelia to sell beach towels, energy drinks, the next Bitcoin. And every time there's a sale of an original at auction, you must be contacted, right of first refusal."

"What about the trust?"

"Set up for your six friends. Yes, all in place. They don't yet know. First windfall payment in six months through Britain's Royal Lottery, as requested. They will be paid annually from the interest, about a million pounds apiece. Of course, I must reiterate, for what—the thousandth time, Miss Gannon? The unusual nature of this so-called confidentiality clause. Again, you realize no entity can bind you to silence or censor you in any way, in order to conceal acts of intimidation or illegal conduct?"

I meet his gaze. Of course, Mr. Harneth senses there is a great deal to the story that I never told him.

"I understand," I say.

He sighs. "Then it stands. You're never to speak of her, or return to the island, or even contact Derringer Street ever again. You're putting it all behind you, which, from the bits and pieces I've heard of this affair, is a healthy thing."

Holding open the door, he winks at me. I grab the briefcase and the handle of the Darkly—I'm surprised by its weight—and I slip out.

"So I'm free to go home."

"You're free to go to the moon, Miss Gannon."

It was something I insisted on. Derringer Street would pay for us to stay at a hotel while the internship was terminated, the reward negotiated and paid. We were all banned from returning to the island. Nile Raiden was adamant about that. There had been, he'd said, "severe damage to various Darkly properties and grounds as a result of our flagrant disregard for the legacy of Darkly and our personal safety." Louisiana's private estate and her factory, given their age and "immeasurable worth within the Darkly empire, required professional engineers and contractors for refurbishment." But they had reluctantly agreed to my provision that they would not immediately send us home.

They also let us see the captain a final time. I had to be sure she wasn't being punished for helping us, that she still had her spot on the island forever. We met her at Darkly Pier, some nameless Derringer Street goon looking on as we all hugged her and said goodbye. I thanked her for trusting me. And though she clearly did not like farewells or maudlin outpourings of sentiment, and she was eager to get back aboard the *Elvira,* muttering about the stone wall that needed mending and the host of contractors about to descend, I could see well enough that she was safe and even pleased with the outcome.

And when I hugged her for the fifth time, the others loading into the van, she whispered in my ear, "You be sure to come and visit one day. Promise, my dear."

Only in my dreams, I wanted to say.

And so these past few weeks, all of us have been together, hashing over the experience, ever aware that time is running out, that we are going our separate ways, returning to our old lives, and the events of the summer and the strange truth behind the release of the stolen Valkyrie would be packed securely away, like a secret in an attic in an old ghost story no one will ever remember.

While I was mad at Poe and Torin for their deception, I forgive them. Those minutes of passion, or whatever it was, when we were alone together in the library are a memory I have chosen to forget.

Poe promised us there would be no more cheating when he returned home, that getting caught was ushering in a new dawn of honesty, and that even if it might be a little boring to follow the rules, he would use his brainpower to build something monumental. I choose to believe him. I hate what they did, of course. But after everything I learned about Louisiana, I now understand the dark hope for something—a dream—fighting so hard to keep it alive, afloat, without too much mud or blood splattered on it, even as the walls cave in and the ceiling gives way. And though I had once believed I was in love with Poe, I have decided it was only the fog of the island. Now, far away from that mystical place, I see everything clearly.

We pack up our hotel rooms and suitcases, making our way

out of the lobby into the black cab Derringer Street has sent to take us to the airport. Mouse is heading back to Nigeria, where he is going to take a job at a detective agency. Cooper is off to Washington, DC, where she will help rescue the family funeral home from foreclosure. Franz is flying back to Berlin, where he plans to send his mother to rehab. Torin is back to Dublin to hire a private detective to find her birth mom. And Everleigh, or Eva—I still have trouble calling her by her real name—is back to Iceland to mourn her sister.

I'll be back in Eminence, where I suspect I'll be manning the register at Prologue within an hour of landing.

"Well, that's that," says Mouse with a wistful sigh as the black cab coasts through the traffic of Piccadilly Circus.

Poe looks at Eva and frowns. "What's the matter?"

She looks pale. "Are we really all going to meet secretly every year in Paris at Christmas? Because I have a feeling our plans are going to fall by the wayside when we get swept up in the reality of university and jobs."

"Exams and parents," adds Torin.

"Love," says Poe, turning from the window to look deliberately at me.

"Of course we're going to meet," says Franz. "And it must be Paris. London is too close to Derringer Street, ja? And the Raidens. I'll be happy never to be on the same continent as *that* family dynasty again. Anyway, what else are we going to do—pretend we're like everyone else now?"

"Yeah, we're pretty much cursed with the weight of too much knowledge," says Mouse.

"Anyone else feel it was all a little too sudden?" says Eva, shivering. "Bella dead and George home, the reward paid to Dia. And now we're being summarily tossed, like a bunch of extra plastic forks and napkins at the bottom of a fast-food bag."

"Steal back to the island," says Franz. "I'm sure the captain would love a first mate."

Eva sighs, turning to the window. "Maybe."

"Nein, it's the ferocious tide of time," says Franz. "It is our plight, as humans, all of us tossed along in the current, the same direction—we can't stop it. We are veterans, shell-shocked, and now we must limp home after our war."

"But we can't even *talk* about it," says Mouse. "How will we healthily process this? Does our code of silence extend to mental health professionals?"

"Didn't you read the contract you signed?" asks Poe, arching an eyebrow. "That was clause five point two."

"We'll have to get together every year to talk about it," says Cooper. "For our own sanity. Banned from ever breathing a word about Louisiana Veda or little May Gavenaught."

"The horror library at Bury St. Elmswood—" adds Torin.

"—the librarian demon-woman from hell," says Cooper.

"Those horrible things forged Louisiana Veda," says Poe. "Raw talent plus a dash of sadistic childhood trauma equals the greatest artists who ever lived."

"And the poor mother still thinking no one ever saw little May again—are we ever going to tell her the truth?" asks Torin.

"No," I say.

Eva wipes away a tear. "All of it will be like a house fire blazing forever in our hearts. We'll *have* to get together once a year to put it out. For the rest of our lives. Closing the windows so it's contained and getting out the fire extinguishers until the smoke clears and every ember is gone, at least until the next year, so the whole building doesn't come crashing down."

We laugh, nodding in agreement, linking arms. But I admit there is something flimsy about our plans. I can see what Eva means. The undertow of life moves in a direction no one can anticipate. It's so much easier to look forward at the unmarred gold horizon than behind you at the rubble. This taxi ride might be the last time we are ever all together. I hate to think this, but it's possible.

"I *still* don't know why Dia's going home," says Torin, scowling at me. "I mean, if I were you, I'd be buying a castle in Scotland right now."

I t's hours later. I'm joining the line waiting to board a plane bound for New York City.

"Paradise!"

I turn to see Poe sprinting through the concourse. He's got his Darkly masterpiece, 18 Lost Icelandic Sailors, handcuffed to his wrist. He stops in front of me, out of breath, without a word, his eyes traveling all over my face and even down to my feet.

"What?" I ask.

He smiles, squinting at my face as if reading fascinating words in a book. "Oh, yes, I see it now. You're going to forgive me. For lying to you. For Torin. Which is over, by the way."

"I already did forgive you, Poe."

He holds up a hand. "I hereby vow to make it up to you. One day, I will be there. And you'll see. It's me."

"Excuse me?"

"You will choose me, Paradise. You cannot fight fate."

I can only laugh. Sometimes the arrogance of boys is so big

that's all you can do. He takes my hand, opening the palm, and drops a chain into it.

"Until we find our lock."

It's the ingenious key worn around his neck, the one that unlocks his Darkly game.

"I'll see you in four months, Arcadia Gannon! *Ave, imperatrix, morituri te salutant!*"

I have no idea what it means, but with strange glee, he's running away, lost in the crowd, more than a few women and even some men staring after him, wondering who he is.

"Ticket?"

I'm last to board. The agent scans my pass, eyeing the Darkly case.

"Would you like a gate-check ticket for your carry-on?"

"No, thank you."

74

I take out Ophelia on the plane.

The old woman beside me blinks at it with a pleased smile.
The five-year-old across the aisle comes over and tries to grab the
red velvet bag before being stopped by her mother. The businessman sitting in front of me, returning from the bathroom, does a
double take. He can't help but approach.

"Is that one of those Louisiana masterpieces?"

"Yes."

"Pretty cool," he says with a laugh. "Such a work made by a nut.
Funny how crazy can spawn such magnificence."

"She wasn't crazy."

He eyes me with an irritated frown. *So she's one of those no-fun
girl-power types,* he must be thinking. He retreats to his seat.

I only smile as I turn to the window. How well everyone believes they know her. To her mother, she was a little girl to keep
safe. To the librarian Penny Malden, she was an endless problem.
To the captain, she was a savior. To Nile Raiden, she is a trou-
blesome fountain in a monumental landmark, from which riches

endlessly spring—along with constant leaks that must be tended and mended, broken pieces that must be put right before the whole thing explodes. To the world, she is a genius, a fraud, a groundbreaker, an inspiration, an out-of-date kook, a legend.

And to me?

For so long she was something I revered, someone I wanted to be like, someone so strong and illustrious she made the real people in my life look feeble, drab and unfinished. But now, I see she was a real person—who made many harrowing mistakes. But she tried her best. And presented with the edge and the open space, she took the running leap, the one everyone else is too afraid to take, and she jumped. For that, I still love her and always will.

I realize the businessman, peering at me over his seat now, has asked me a question.

"What?"

"Right now. Name your price. You'll have the cash in your account before we land."

"It's not for sale," I say.

75

"Forty–love! Match point!"

In his tennis whites and deep tan, bouncing the ball three times as he prepares to serve for the match, Choke Newington looks like an advertisement for high-end leather goods made in France. He slams the ball onto the court—not nearly as hard as he actually can. I swing, hoping to summon a decent fore-hand. I do make contact, but the ball sails high, clearing the net—and the fencing around the tennis courts *and* the heads of Choke's parents, his older sister, and her fiancé, who are standing under the pink-and-green umbrellas. The ball bounces garishly on the roof of the pro shop before being swallowed by a cluster of golf carts behind the GLADSTONE-HILL GOLF AND TENNIS CLUB sign.

"Game. Set. Match."

Choke throws down his racket, pumping the air with faux Grand Slam elation, and jumps over the net, wrapping his arms around me.

"You really need to work on your return, Dia."

"Add that to volleys, backhand, lob, and serve."

"I'll check my schedule, but I'm free to work on your game, like, all senior year. And probably forever after."

"Oh, Arcadia!" His mom is beaming at us. "Are you joining us for lunch?"

"I'd love to, Mrs. Newington. But I'm working at the shop this afternoon."

I catch her shooting a knowing look at Mr. Newington, who raises his eyebrows. Choke and I, waving goodbye, start up the hill.

After the harrowing events of the summer, the Newingtons have been left with an even more unfortunate view of Gigi Gannon's parenting—especially after they called my mother with news that I had fallen off a British mansion roof, was shaken and bruised but otherwise fine. Gigi had breathed a sigh of relief, then launched into a tale about the estate sale she once attended in Cornwall, where she found a pair of solid gold Italian candlesticks—a steal for only fifty pounds.

Choke opens the door to his convertible, helping me in. As we speed away from the club, I glance over at his handsome profile, feeling incredulous all over again.

Because yes, it worked out. Despite the deceptions and betrayals, everyone came through in the end. And the end was everything— we saved poor George, unmasked the culprit, I now owned the rights to an authentic Darkly.

But I can't help wondering how big a part Choke played in this.

When Nile Raiden chose me to be an intern, he did not anticipate Choke, who had loved me since the pre-K mud kitchen. That love, long dormant, was reignited in the stairwell. Still, he'd found me impossible to approach. *Remote as an uncontacted tribe who worships some kind of monkey god,* as he put it. But then, when his parents suggested he find work at a law firm, it was during the whole Veda

Seven circus. He found himself wondering about London and breaking up with Hailee. He wrangled an internship at Derringer through his parents' connections, in the hope of seeing me over the summer. *I had in mind fish-and-chips at a pub. Maybe a game of pool, where I might try to kiss you again,* he said. *Not an underground legal conspiracy of quicksand floors and dangerous motives—but I'll take what I can get.*

He had sounded all of those alarms—giving the whole thing a glaring spotlight out of Raiden's control. Sure, maybe Derringer Street was always going to follow through on what they'd promised. But they had no choice except to be the good guys in the end, backed into a corner, knowing what we knew.

As we pull up in front of Prologue, I spy three silhouettes in the window, peering over the antique bicycles and picnic baskets on display. They've surely been waiting for me for hours—Gigi, Basil, and Agatha—though as soon as they see Choke's convertible, they vanish.

"Pick you up at eight, Mermosa? For a casual lobster dinner at the Newington compound? Which won't be casual at all, by the way, because there's a state senator coming."

I laugh. "Sure."

We are about to kiss, but Choke settles for a quick peck on my cheek, because the three silhouettes have appeared again. He waves cheerfully at them—prompting them all to scatter out of sight.

AGATHA O'CLEARY

Secretary to Miss Louisiana Veda

9 February 1985

My dearest Louisiana,

So, you know. I have done what I swore I would never do. I have left you. It breaks my heart, but I cannot remain at your side in the darkness that surrounds you.

Here, I stop. Here, I walk my way back to the light--however long it takes me.

It was a fluke--my decision to leave the island early and take Kitten to walk the Christmas lights on Regent Street. I had been in the habit of visiting her without telling you. I loved the child's angelic nature and bright laugh. I was petrified that your plan--leaving her with perfect strangers again--however well we thought we knew them, however much money we dumped on their doorsteps, however often we dictated and dropped in and engineered, pretending this time the experiment would work--I knew she would meet the same doomed fate as her poor siblings.

Kitten and I returned that evening to a fleet of fire trucks. Flames leapt through the roof. Neighbors sobbed about the little girls trapped inside--unaware that one stood right beside me, safe and sound. And in that split second I made a decision. I saw this fork in the road as her only chance, and my chance, a hope for a new beginning, in a world away from you.

You will never find us. Neither will Wood. One day, perhaps we will come back. But I have stood by your side, doing your bidding with a smile and sympathy, for too long. I have seen the destruction, obsession, and dark cravings of power in your heart. I will hold your secrets no longer.

Please know that I love you. You were never like the others. I pray one day you face the monsters and slay them, so one night you leave the doors open and your windows unlocked, so the breeze wanders in with the crickets and the moths and moonlight. I wish that very elusive bird to land on your windowsill at last--peace.

Walk toward the light, my child.

Yours forever,

Gattie

Gattie

76

Prologue Antiques did not change while I was away—not as much as I'd hoped, at least.

The Barnabys had kittens—but only four.

And their fragile cries, their flying leaps out from under the Venetian art deco credenza, the neck rest on the Eames lounge chair, the early twentieth-century pedestal table with dolphin feet, have actually been great for business.

Customers spend so much time fussing over the kittens—helping Gigi rescue one from the top of the eight-foot porcelain display with dust balls the size of grapefruits—they linger in the shop. They end up buying a third Victorian hatbox, the Slim Aarons *Poolside,* the rare six-foot bronze sculpture of a heron in Ming dynasty style.

Basil and Agatha sport the same hopeful expressions as before, though as they drift around the shop with whispers of some torn conversation from a decade ago, I notice their movements seem a little slower. They recruited another employee from assisted living to fill in while I was gone, but like some brand-new tropical fish introduced to an old fish tank, he only worked a day at Prologue before vanishing.

The only real difference is Gigi. Her newfound knowledge of shar-pei dogs, her penchant for wearing hacking jackets, and her hair slicked into a no-nonsense bun is confusing—until I learn Mr. Asquith has been "coming to call." He takes her to the senior buffet at a Thai fusion restaurant in Kansas City, after that to the symphony. He is thinking of investing in the antiques business.

"Old things never go out of style" and "When we scale Prologue" are the latest phrases Gigi has been flinging with great gusto into conversations with random customers. And though I want to tell her she's crazy, those sentences are oxymorons, I only smile—maybe because I'm in love, maybe because, after everything I learned about Louisiana, I understand the fantasies, lies, and dreams, however outrageous, that keep people hiking the steep hill of life each day.

Of course, I meant to tell them—about the island, my friends, Valkyrie.

Yes, I've agreed to a lifetime of secrecy. Mr. Harneth and my entire legal team warned me of the dangers of speaking even to innocuous relatives. But confessing to Basil and Agatha is like whispering into a cave on a deserted island. And Gigi has a reputation for stretching the truth. Even if she *did* boast to every customer waiting for coffee at the Grind that her daughter now owns an original Darkly and knows all of Louisiana's deep dark secrets— secrets the world would kill to know—no one would believe her.

"Did you visit Buckingham Palace?" Basil asked. "Any glimpse of His Majesty on the old balcony?"

I tried telling them the truth more than a few times. Every time I chickened out.

Because wouldn't they be deeply upset? Wouldn't they be bothered by all I'd faced while they'd remained so far away, so perfectly oblivious? The truth would be a devastating blow to all three of them. There's a strong possibility it would send Agatha and Basil straight from assisted living into skilled nursing.

So I say nothing. There will be a right time one day, but not yet.

What I do know is how much they missed me, how pleased and relieved they are that I'm home.

Now, as I pull open the door to Prologue and step inside, they're hunched around the cash register, pretending to be busy.

"Oh, hi, babe."

"She's sometimes . . . ," starts Agatha.

"Why, it's the tennis ace!" shouts Basil, clapping his hands. "How was the match?"

"I lost."

"So very happy . . ."

"Choke is your young gentleman's name? Things have changed since my era of Jack and Charles."

"His real name is Herbert," says Gigi.

I slip my racket and bags behind the register. "How's the sale going? Any increased traffic from the ad?"

"His parents are big-time lawyers with a capital *B*. I love the way she does her hair. So chic. What's her first name?"

"Katherine. You met her when I was in preschool, Mom."

"I did?"

"Choke's picking me up for dinner, so how up to date is inventory?"

My mom sighs theatrically. "We're losing her, aren't we, Basil? To clambakes on the Cape, and golden retrievers named Sully, and sailboats."

"She's going to start wearing her hair in a bob and reading *Franny and Zooey*," says Basil.

I check my watch. "We have five hours, fifty-seven minutes and counting."

"I don't know. Maybe clean out that storage room by the boiler? I didn't get down there yet."

Normally, I would refuse. But in this case, I actually want to be away from their moony stares, even if it is among the cobwebs in the hollowed darkness of the basement. So I leave them whispering—"Is *that* an actual tennis sweater?"—and take off downstairs.

I have to surf through stacks of boxes to get past the boiler. I pull open the storage room door and yank the string to the bare bulb.

It's dank and empty—except for a pile of garbage bags.

I'm tempted to just carry it all up to the dumpster and be done with it. But knowing my mom, how she might have inadvertently stored a Sèvres vase down here, mistaking it for something sold by Joan Rivers on QVC, I move to the pile and rip open a bag.

Inside are piles of old baby clothes, an embroidered cushion that reads ANGEL, flannel blankets, one with an embroidered *K*. The next bag is filled with old newspapers, *Tatler*, a stained scrapbook stuffed with Polaroids. A little girl in red—*Bella 1976*, someone wrote. A mother and child on a beach—*May 1953*. Beneath this is a stack of letters bound with rubber bands. The envelopes are addressed to Miss Gattie O'Cleary, Agatha O'Cleary, Agatha Sweeney.

It takes me a second to understand it's Agatha—*my* Agatha. O'Cleary must have been her maiden name. She must have stored some personal items down here years ago, when she moved into assisted living.

I open the letter on top.

```
Gattie,
Where are you? Did you start the fire?
```

I read the letter, something familiar about the story. Then I see the name at the bottom.

Louisiana

Chills crawl up my arms.

Her name is alive, trembling on the page.

I open the next letter, my hands shaking, breath in my throat.

```
My dearest Louisiana,
So, you know. I have done what I swore I would
never do. I have left you.
```

I read the letter. It was never sent. I grab the bag and tear back upstairs.

"Mom!"

I barrel toward the three of them, throwing the bag at their feet, a map and letters flying.

I stare at Agatha.

"You? You're Gattie? Her secretary? Her shadow?"

Agatha holds her mouth open, her blue eyes wide behind her glasses. "I . . . Who . . ."

"You kidnapped my mom as a child? Took her away? Hid her here all these years? *Tell me what you did!*"

Basil gasps. "What the devil has gotten into you, shouting at her like this?"

"You . . . you . . ."

"How do you know this woman, Mom?"

"Agatha?" Gigi blinks. "You know. She worked with your grand-mother here in the shop—"

"How did they meet?"

"Somewhere in town? The park. She came up to Mama and Papa and said they . . . looked like a nice family."

I point at her. "You're Kitten. Kitten is your real name, Mom. It's why they were watching us. Have you noticed strange cars? People loitering?"

I'm pacing and shouting, my thoughts lethal shards from the exploding windows in my head.

The filing cabinet.

VV393. The code written there. X3X4.

Heirs three and four? Successors three and four? Problems three and four. Eliminations three and four.

My mom. Me.

Though we actively search the world for both of them, their trails have gone cold.

If they were searching for Maximilian and Bella, they were looking for Kitten. Louisiana suspected she was still alive, so Der-ringer certainly knows. There must have been hundreds of people to weed through, year after year, to review and rule out as potential heirs. How many more could come out of the woodwork, lay claim to the billion-dollar throne, topple all of those carefully laid plans?

Choke saw a photo of me in the filing cabinet. But other kids were in there, too, birth and death certificates. Who were they? Was it all of us? Was that why we were chosen?

Seven interns. Seven potential descendants to be vetted.

My mother—a woman of uncertain origin and repute—was a cabaret dancer.

I'm adopted. *But my biological mom used an alias. I've never been able to find her.*

Our toothbrushes were all moved to different sinks.

Someone went through my makeup.

I can't find my comb.

Derringer used the crisis of Valkyrie to bring us together, kill two birds with one stone. They fished us out of the sea, keeping us captive on the island, where we could be watched while DNA tests were performed on the items taken from the cabins. Then they threw us back. We signed the contracts. Bound to a lifetime of silence. Chapter ended, book closed, placed high on the shelf in the locked library.

"I signed it all away," I whisper. "When I took Ophelia, I gave her up."

"Who?"

"I'm her granddaughter."

"What is she saying, Gigi?" asks Basil.

"Now it's all gone. I'm too late—"

"Arcadia Gannon, if you do not calm down, I will march you straight to the VA Hospital and order a mental health evaluation—"

"I gave her away—they made sure of it. Oh my God."

"Kitten. You know? Agatha called me that when I was . . ." My mom's voice trails off as if she's holding a heavy object in her hand that is magically disintegrating into sand.

Suddenly, everything is still. They are all turned to me, expectant, as if I know how this story ends.

And maybe I do. Maybe this is the beginning of my story.

That's when I notice the shop window. Old bicycles, banana seats, a circus unicycle.

I run over, scrambling into the display. I climb around the painted mountain backdrop. It tips over and crashes to the floor.

"Dia?"

I shove the tables, silverware spilling, and grab the only bike with air in the tires.

"What are you doing?"

I elbow open the shop door, stumbling outside with the bike, the rusted bell on the handlebars trilling uncertainly. I pull it off the curb and climb on.

"Dia? Dia, come back!"

When I reach the line of cars waiting for the light, I stop, looking back through my tears. My mother stands on the curb with Agatha, who is shading her eyes. Gigi must be calling after me, but I can't hear her. Basil is waving, a pleased smile. He seems to understand. He seems to hear me whisper "I love you."

Fly on, child, he says. *As high and far as you wish.*

The light is green. I take off, pedaling past the Wendy's, the used car lot, bouncing over the railroad tracks.

That's when I understand. Whatever they did, Derringer Street—whatever they know or don't know—it doesn't matter anymore.

Because it's all right here in front of me, inside the noise and glare, the hot wind burning my eyes. Everything to build, everything to love. There is no limit to my hope or my path. I don't need to hold on to anything to steady myself—no railing to keep me from flying over the edge, no net. I will fall, and I'll keep riding. Everything I do will be essential and good and bold—if only I can remember to keep my eyes open and my heart brave, ready for what comes.

This is my world. It's my time. It will be gone one day. I'll be forgotten.

Or maybe, just maybe, my name, like Louisiana's, will be something people whisper for a brief spell, my faded picture held up to the light, deciding something in a second that has little to do with who I was. There is only what we make today, what we leave behind, the people we cherish—sand castles all of it, but so beautiful.

I ride on, not looking back, grabbing my life with both hands, holding on and on—just as it was for her that day.

And so it will be for me.

ACKNOWLEDGMENTS

So many incredible talents contributed to this book. First and foremost, I would like to thank my editor, mentor, and dear friend, Beverly Horowitz. To work with you has been a master class, and your insight, humor, enthusiasm, and gut instincts are forever an inspiration.

To my dream team, Binky Urban and Hillary Jacobson—thank you for your tireless faith in me and for shepherding this book along from its infancy. Thank you to my foreign rights agent, Sarah Mitchell, and my film team, Josie Freedman and Berni Vann, for your care and vision.

To my stellar publishers at Delacorte Press, Barbara Marcus and Wendy Loggia, you are superhero champions of all books, writers, and readers. It's a gift to work with you.

A million thank-yous to the amazing Rebecca Gudelis, who so gracefully juggled so many balls when it came to the details of this book, never letting one drop and making it all look easy.

Thank you to the genius Casey Moses for creating such a glorious work of art for the cover (and diving right in with my Easter eggs), and to Megan Shortt for making the lost archives of Darkly come alive in the interiors and illustrations. Thank you to Tamar Schwartz for somehow making it all happen on time and so seamlessly.

Thank you to Colleen Fellingham and Lisa Leventer for

scouring my every word, date, location, and fact. Thank you to the head of production, Tim Terhune, for magically turning all of the above into an actual book.

Thank you to the PRH sales team for so passionately passing *Darkly* into so many hands: Joe English, Jackie Izzo, Brenda Conway, Emily Bruce; to the entire field rep sales team: Becky Green, Amanda Auch, Christina Jeffries, Carol Monteiro, Rita King, Mark Santella, Madalyn Dolan, and Enid Chaban; and to the education reps, Linda Sinisi and Caroline Riordan.

Thank you to the amazing Joshua Redlich, Svengali of publicity and Louisiana's brilliant champion. Thank you to the marketing team for your ingenuity and creativity: John Adamo, Shannon Pender, Kelly McGauley, Jenn Inzetta, Natalie Capogrossi, and Michael Caiati.

Thank you to my family—I could not do this job without you. Thank you to my powerful girls, Winter, Avalon, and Raine—you teach me more about what is possible than I can ever reciprocate. Thank you to my mom, Anne, still my first reader and so enthusiastically forgoing sleep, food, and conversation to read my books in one sitting. Thank you to the love of my life, my muse, David— your heart, humor, critical eye, and eternal support keep me going (while laughing). You will always have the keys to the garden.

Most of all, I want to thank my readers. I am so grateful for the way you have stuck by my side for so many years with such passion and loyalty. You are my inspiration every morning when I get to work. My wish is that you, too, find your bicycles.

INTERIOR ART CREDITS

Letter, page 14: Paper image by inhabitant_b/stock.adobe.com, texture used under license from Shutterstock.com. Text copyright © 2024 by Marisha Pessl.

Invitation, page 33: Black paper with distressed overlay by Артём Ковяеин /stock.adobe.com. Text copyright © 2024 by Marisha Pessl.

Factory image, page 34: https://commons.wikimedia.org/wiki/File:Iconographic _Encyclopedia_of_Science,_Literature_and_Art_540.jpg#metadata, paper texture used under license from Shutterstock.com. Handwritten text copyright © 2024 by Marisha Pessl.

Typewritten letter on letterhead, page 52: Paper image by Pakhnyushchyy /stock.adobe.com, paper edges by Anelina/stock.adobe.com, vintage banner drawing by Ardiyan/stock.adobe.com, paper texture used under license from Shutterstock.com. Text copyright © 2024 by Marisha Pessl.

Newspaper clipping, page 58: Newspaper image by Stillfx/stock.adobe.com, paper texture and house photo used under license from Shutterstock.com. Text copyright © 2024 by Marisha Pessl.

Newspaper clipping, page 86: Newspaper image by scol22/stock.adobe.com, paper texture and photograph of woman used under license from Shutterstock .com. Text copyright © 2024 by Marisha Pessl.

Contraption illustration, page 118: Architectural drawing artwork by Jinna Shin copyright © 2024 by Penguin Random House LLC. Vintage paper image by RPL-Studio/stock.adobe.com, paper texture used under license from Shutterstock.com.

Photo, page 130: Photograph of child by Martinan/stock.adobe.com, instant photo border by Photobeps/stock.adobe.com, distressed vintage photo texture by Unleashed Design/stock.adobe.com, paper texture used under license from Shutterstock.com.

Photo, page 151: Photograph of woman and child by sutulastock/stock.adobe .com, instant photo border with texture by donatas1205/stock.adobe .com, additional instant photo border edge texture used under license from Shutterstock.com.

ABOUT THE AUTHOR

MARISHA PESSL is the *New York Times* bestselling author of *Night Film* and *Special Topics in Calamity Physics,* as well as the young adult novel *Neverworld Wake.* She lives with her husband and three daughters in New York.

MARISHAPESSL.COM

FIVE FRIENDS.
ONLY ONE CAN SURVIVE.
NOW CHOOSE.

"YOU WON'T BE ABLE TO STOP READING." —*REFINERY29*

NEVERWORLD WAKE

MARISHA PESSL

NEW YORK TIMES BESTSELLING AUTHOR OF *DARKLY* AND *NIGHT FILM*

After narrowly avoiding a car crash during a night out, Beatrice and her friends find themselves at Wincroft, the mansion where they're staying. There's a terrible storm, and then . . . a stranger appears. He calls himself the Keeper. And he reveals a chilling choice: One of them can live, and the rest will die. Unanimous agreement is required.

As time bends and loops, Beatrice and her friends relive the same day repeatedly. Each replay brings new twists and fears. To escape, they must vote—but how do you decide who lives and who dies?